BABYCAKES

BABYCAKES

Armistead Maupin

1817

HARPER & ROW, PUBLISHERS, New York

Cambridge, Philadelphia, San Francisco, London

Mexico City, São Paulo, Singapore, Sydney

This work was published in somewhat different form in the *San Francisco Chronicle*.

Grateful acknowledgment is made for permission to reprint:

Lyrics from *Sail Away*, by Noel Coward. Copyright © 1950 by Chappell & Co., Ltd. Copyright renewed, Chappell & Co., Inc., publisher in U.S.A. International copyright secured. All rights reserved. Used by permission.

FIRST EDITION

Designer: C. Linda Dingler

Library of Congress Cataloging in Publication Data

Maupin, Armistead.
  Babycakes.

   I. Title.
PS3563.A878B3 1984   813'.54   83-48368
ISBN 0-06-015262-1   84 85 86 87 88 10 9 8 7 6 5 4 3 2 1
ISBN 0-06-091099-2 (pbk.)   84 85 86 87 88 10 9 8 7 6 5 4 3 2 1

For Christopher Isherwood and Don Bachardy
and in loving memory of
Daniel Katz
1956–1982
and
once again
for Steve Beery

Memo to Lord Jamie Neidpath

Easley House may bear a marked resemblance to
Stanway House, but Lord Teddy Roughton is nothing like you. You and I know that. Now the others
do. Cheers.

A.M.

When you feel your song is orchestrated wrong,
Why should you prolong
Your stay?
When the wind and the weather blow your dreams sky-high,
Sail away—sail away—sail away!

—Noel Coward

BABYCAKES

One

She was fifty-seven years old when she saw San Francisco for the first time. As her limousine pulled away from the concrete labyrinth of the airport, she peered out the window at the driving rain and issued a small sigh over the general beastliness of the weather.

"I know," said Philip, reading her mind, "but they expect it to clear today."

She returned his faint smile, then searched in her handbag for a tissue. Since leaving the Reagans' ranch she'd felt a mild case of the sniffles coming on, and she was dashed if she'd let it get the best of her.

The motorcade veered onto a larger highway—a "freeway," she supposed—and soon they were plunging headlong into the rain past lurid motels and posters of nightmare proportions. To her left loomed a treeless hillside, so unnaturally green that it might have been Irish. There were words on it, rendered in white stones: SOUTH SAN FRANCISCO—THE INDUSTRIAL CITY.

Philip saw the face she made and leaned forward to study the curious hieroglyphic.

"Odd," he murmured.

"Mmm," she replied.

She could only hope that they had not yet arrived in the city proper. This tatty commercial district could well be the equivalent of Ruislip or Wapping or one of those horrid little suburbs in the vicinity of Gatwick Airport. She mustn't imagine the worst just yet.

Her original plan had been to arrive in San Francisco on board the *Britannia*—an operation that would have entailed the pleasant prospect of sailing under the Golden Gate Bridge. The sea had become quite treacherous, however, by the time she reached Los Angeles, and the same storms that had brought six California rivers to flood level would almost certainly have played havoc with her undependable tummy.

So she had settled on this somewhat less than majestic entrance via aeroplane and automobile. She would spend the night in a local hotel, then reinstate herself on the *Britannia* when it arrived in the harbor the following day. Since she was almost sixteen hours ahead of schedule, this evening's time was completely unclaimed, and the very thought of such gratuitous leisure sent surprising little shivers of anticipation down her spine.

Where would she dine tonight? The hotel, perhaps? Or someone's home?

1

The question of *whose* home was a sticky one at best, since she had already received feverish invitations from several local hostesses, including—and here she shuddered a bit—that dreadful petrol woman with all the hair.

She dismissed the issue of dinner for the moment and once more turned her attention to the passing scene. The rain seemed to have slacked a tiny bit, and here and there in the slate-gray skies a few dainty patches of blue had begun to make themselves known. Then the city materialized out of nowhere—a jumble of upended biscuit boxes that reminded her vaguely of Sydney.

"Look!" crowed Philip.

He was pointing to a dazzling rainbow that hovered like a crown above the city.

"How perfectly splendid," she murmured.

"Indeed. Their protocol people are more thorough than I thought."

Feeling giddier by the minute, she giggled at his little joke. It seemed appropriate to commemorate the moment by a cheery wave to the citizenry, but public assembly was quite impossible along this major artery, so she ignored the impulse and set about the task of repairing her lipstick.

The rain had diminished to a drizzle by the time the motorcade descended from the highway into a region of low-lying warehouses and scruffy cafés. At the first intersection, the limousine slowed dramatically and Philip signaled her with a nod of his head.

"Over there, darling. Your first well-wishers."

She turned her head slightly and waved at several dozen people assembled on the street corner. They waved back vigorously, holding aloft a black leather banner on which the words GOD SAVE THE QUEEN had been imprinted in silver rivets. It was not until she heard them cheer that she realized they were all men.

Philip smirked sleepily.

"What?" she asked.

"Poofs," he said.

"Where?"

"*There*, darling. With the banner."

She glanced back at them and saw that they were standing outside a building called the Arena. "Don't be silly," she replied. "They're sportsmen of some sort."

Two

To commemorate the coming of Elizabeth II, the Marina Safeway had run specials all week on English muffins, Imperial margarine and Royal Crown Cola. The Flag Store on Polk Street had reported a rush on Union Jacks, while no less than three bars in the Castro had set about the task of organizing "Betty Windsor" look-alike contests.

All this and more had been painstakingly documented by Mary Ann Singleton—and a thousand reporters like her—in the grueling days that preceded the royal visit. Mary Ann's own quest for queenly minutiae had led her from tearooms on Maiden Lane to Irish bars in North Beach to storefront bakeries in the Avenues where rosy-cheeked Chicanas made steak-and-kidney pies for "Olde English" restaurants.

It was little wonder that Her Majesty's actual arrival had come as both a profound relief and a disappointing anticlimax. Tormented by the incessant rain, Mary Ann and her cameraman had waited for almost an hour outside the St. Francis, only to discover (after the fact) that the royal limousine had ducked discreetly into the hotel's underground parking garage.

Mary Ann salvaged the story as best she could, telecasting a live report from the entrance to the garage, then dragged herself home to 28 Barbary Lane, where she kicked off her shoes, lit a joint and phoned her husband at work.

They made a date to see *Gandhi* later that night.

She was warming up a leftover pot roast when the phone rang.

"'Lo," she muttered, through a mouthful of cold roast.

"Mary Ann?" It was the crisp, patrician voice of DeDe Halcyon Day.

"Hi," said Mary Ann. "Don't mind me. I'm eating myself into oblivion."

DeDe laughed. "I saw your newscast on *Bay Window*."

"Great," said Mary Ann ruefully. "Pretty insightful, huh? I figure it's all over but the Emmy."

"Now, now. You did just fine."

"Right."

"And we all loved your hat. It was *much* prettier than the mayor's. Even Mother said so."

Mary Ann made a face for no one's benefit but her own. That goddamn hat

3

was the first hat she had worn in years, and she had bought it specifically for the royal visit. "I'm glad you enjoyed it," she said blandly. "I thought it might have been a bit much for a parking garage."

"Look," said DeDe, "why aren't you down here? I thought for sure you would be."

"Down where? Hillsborough?"

DeDe uttered an exasperated little sigh. "Trader Vic's, of course."

Most rich people are annoying, Mary Ann decided, not because they are different but because they pretend not to notice the difference. "DeDe," she said as calmly as possible, "Trader Vic's is not exactly a hangout of mine."

"Well, O.K., but . . . don't you want to see her?"

"See *who?*"

"The Queen, you ninny."

"The Queen is at Trader Vic's?" This was making no sense whatsoever.

"Wait a minute," said DeDe. "You didn't *know?*"

"DeDe, for God's sake! Is she there?"

"Not yet. But she's on her way. I thought for certain the station would've told you. . . ."

"Are you sure?"

"Somebody's sure. The streets are crawling with cops, and the Captain's Cabin looks like opening night at the opera. Look, Vita Keating told Mother, and Vita heard it from Denise Hale, so it must be the truth."

Mary Ann's disbelief lingered like an anesthetic. "I didn't think the Queen ever went to restaurants."

"She doesn't," DeDe laughed. "Vita says this is her first time in seventeen years!"

"God," said Mary Ann.

"Anyway," DeDe added, "we've got a ringside seat. I'm here with Mother and D'or and the kids, and we'd love for you to join us. You and Brian, that is."

"He's at work," replied Mary Ann, "but I'd love to come."

"Good."

"Are there other reporters, DeDe? Do you see any television people?"

"Nope. If you haul ass, she's all yours."

Mary Ann let out a whoop. "You're an angel, DeDe! I'll be there as soon as I can grab a cab!"

Seconds after hanging up, she phoned the station and alerted the news director. He was understandably skeptical, but assured her that a crew would be dispatched immediately. Then she called a cab, fixed her face, strapped her shoes back on, and scrawled a hasty note to Brian.

She was striding through the leafy canyon of Barbary Lane when she realized what she had forgotten. "Shit," she muttered, hesitating only slightly before running back home to get her hat.

4

As she climbed from the cab at the entrance to Cosmo Place, she marveled anew at the enduring mystique of Trader Vic's. When all was said and done, this oh-so-fashionable Polynesian restaurant was really only a Quonset hut squatting in an alleyway on the edge of the Tenderloin. People who wouldn't be caught dead amidst the Bali Hai camp of the Tonga Room on Nob Hill would murder their grandmothers for the privilege of basking in the same decor at Trader Vic's.

The *maître d'* seemed particularly formidable tonight, but she placated him with the magic words—"Mrs. Halcyon is expecting me"—and made her way to the banquettes near the bar, the holy of holies they called the Captain's Cabin. DeDe caught her eye with a sly Elizabethan wave.

Striding to the table, Mary Ann slipped into the chair they had saved for her. "I hope you went ahead and ordered," she said.

"Just drinks," answered DeDe. "Is this a zoo or what?"

Mary Ann looked around at the neighboring tables. "Uh . . . who exactly is here?"

"Everybody," shrugged DeDe. "Isn't that right, Mother?"

Mrs. Halcyon detected the irreverence in her daughter's voice and chose to ignore it. "I'm delighted you could join us, Mary Ann. You know D'orothea, of course . . . and the children. Edgar, don't pick your nose, dear. Gangie has told you that a thousand times."

The six-year-old's lip plumped petulantly. His delicate Eurasian features, like those of his twin sister, seemed entirely appropriate in a room full of quasi Orientalia. "Why can't we go to Chuck E. Cheese?" he asked.

"Because," his grandmother explained sweetly, "the Queen isn't eating at Chuck E. Cheese."

D'orothea rolled her eyes ever so slightly. "It was her first choice, actually, but they wouldn't take a reservation for a party of sixty."

Mary Ann let out a giggle, then squelched it when she saw the look on Mrs. Halcyon's face. "I would think," said the matriarch, casting oblique daggers at her daughter's lover, "that a little decorum might be in order for all of us."

D'orothea's eyes ducked penitently, but contempt flickered at the corner of her mouth. She realigned a fork, waiting for the moment to pass.

"So," said Mary Ann, a little too brightly, "what time does she get here?"

"Any minute," DeDe replied. "They're putting her in the Trafalgar Room. That's upstairs and it's got its own entrance, so I guess they'll sneak her in the back way and . . ."

"I have to piss." Little Anna was tugging at DeDe's arm.

"Anna, didn't I tell you to take care of that before we left home?"

"*And*," added Mrs. Halcyon, with a look of genuine horror, "little girls don't use such words."

Anna looked puzzled. "What words?"

"Piss," said her brother.

"Edgar!" The matriarch gaped at her grandson, then spun around to demand reparation from her daughter. "For heaven's sake, DeDe . . . tell them. This isn't my job."

"Oh, Mother, this is hardly . . ."

"Tell them."

"The French say piss," D'orothea put in. "What about *pissoir?*"

"D'or." DeDe discredited her lover's contribution with a glacial glance before turning to her children. "Look, guys . . . I thought we settled on pee."

"Oh, my God," groaned the matriarch.

Mary Ann and D'orothea exchanged clandestine grins.

"Mother, if you don't mind . . ."

"What happened to tinkle, DeDe? I taught you to say tinkle."

"She still does," said D'or.

Another glare from DeDe. Mary Ann looked down at the tablecloth, suddenly afraid that D'or would try to enlist her as a confederate.

"Come along," said Mrs. Halcyon, rising. "Gangie will take you to the little girls' room."

"Me too," piped Edgar.

"All right . . . you too." She took their tiny hands in her chubby, bejeweled ones and toddled off into the rattan-lined darkness.

D'orothea let out a histrionic groan.

"Don't start," said DeDe.

"She's getting worse. I wouldn't have thought it possible, but she is actually getting worse." She turned and addressed her next remarks to Mary Ann, shaking a rigid forefinger in the direction of the restrooms. "That woman lives with her dyke daughter and her dyke daughter-in-law and her two half-Chinese grandchildren by the goddamn delivery boy at Jiffy's . . ."

"D'or . . ."

". . . and she *still* acts like this is the goddamn nineteenth century and she's . . . goddamn Queen Victoria. Grab that waiter, Mary Ann. I want another Mai Tai."

Mary Ann flailed for the waiter, but he wheeled out of sight into the kitchen. When she confronted the couple again, they were looking directly into each other's eyes, as if she weren't there at all.

"Am I right?" asked D'orothea.

DeDe hesitated. "Partially, maybe."

"Partially, hell. The woman is regressing."

"All right . . . O.K., but it's just her way of coping."

"Oh. Right. Is that how you explain her behavior out there in the street?"

"What behavior?"

"Oh, please. The woman is obsessed with meeting the Queen."

"Stop calling her 'the woman.' And she isn't obsessed; she's just . . . interested."

"Sure. Uh-huh. Interested enough to hurdle that barricade."

DeDe rolled her eyes. "She didn't hurdle any barricade."

D'orothea snorted. "It wasn't for lack of trying. I thought she was going to deck that secret service man!"

The air had cleared somewhat by the time Mrs. Halcyon returned with the children. Mary Ann submitted to polite chitchat for a minute or two, then pushed her chair back and smiled apologetically at the matriarch. "This has been a real treat, but I think I'd better wait out front for the crew. They'll never get past the *maître d'* and I'm not sure if . . ."

"Oh, do stay, dear. Just for one drink."

DeDe gave Mary Ann a significant look. "I think Mother wants to tell you about the time she met the Queen."

"Oh," said Mary Ann, turning to the matriarch. "You've met her before?" Her fingers fussed nervously with the back of her hat. Being polite to her elders had been her downfall more times than she cared to count.

"She's perfectly charming," gushed Mrs. Halcyon. "We had a nice long chat in the garden at Buckingham Palace. I felt as if we were old friends."

"When was this?" asked Mary Ann.

"Back in the sixties," said DeDe. "Daddy used to handle the BOAC account."

"Ah." Mary Ann rose, still gazing solicitously at Mrs. Halcyon. "I guess you'll be seeing her later, then. At the state dinner or something."

Wrong. The matriarch's face became an Apache death mask. Aflame with embarrassment, Mary Ann sought DeDe's eyes for guidance. "The problem," explained DeDe, "is Nancy Reagan."

Mary Ann nodded, understanding nothing.

D'orothea's lip twisted wryly. "At least, we all have the same problem."

DeDe ignored the remark. "Mother and Mrs. Reagan have never been the best of buddies. Mother thinks she may have been . . . blackballed from the state dinner."

"*Thinks?*" snapped Mrs. Halcyon.

"Whatever," said DeDe, handling Mary Ann's mortification with a sympathetic wink. "You'd better scoot, hadn't you? C'mon, I'll walk you to the door." She rose, making it easier for Mary Ann to do so.

"Good luck," said the matriarch. "Look pretty, now."

"Thanks," she replied. "Bye, D'orothea."

"Bye, hon. See you soon, O.K.?" *Away from the old biddy,* she meant.

"Where is she going?" Edgar asked his grandmother.

"To be on TV, darling. Anna, precious, don't scratch yourself there."

"Why?"

"Never mind. It isn't ladylike."

"The kids are looking great," Mary Ann said. "I can't believe how big they're getting."

"Yeah . . . Look, I'm sorry about all that squabbling."

"Hey."

"D'or hates these scenes. She's O.K. when it's just Mother, but when Mother's with her friends . . ." She shook her head with weary resignation. "D'or calls them the Upper Crustaceans. There's a lot of the old radical left in her still."

Maybe so, thought Mary Ann, but it was becoming increasingly difficult to remember that the woman in the Zandra Rhodes gown with the understated smudge of purple in her hair had once toiled alongside DeDe in the jungles of Guyana. DeDe's own transition from postdebutante to urban guerrilla to Junior League matron was equally rife with contradiction, and sometimes Mary Ann felt that the embarrassment both women suffered over the monstrous inconsistencies in their lives was the glue that held their marriage together.

DeDe smiled gently at her own dilemma. "I didn't *plan* on having a family like this, you know?"

Mary Ann smiled back at her. "I certainly do."

"Anna called Edgar a faggot the other day. Can you believe that?"

"God. Where did she pick *that* up?"

DeDe shrugged. "The Montessori School, I guess. Hell, I don't know. . . . Sometimes I think I haven't got a handle on things anymore. I don't know what to tell *myself* about the world, much less my children." She paused and looked at Mary Ann. "I thought we might be swapping notes on that by now."

"On what?"

"Kids. I thought you and Brian were planning . . . God, listen to me. I sound like Mother."

"That's all right."

"You just mentioned . . . the last time I saw you . . ."

"Right."

"But I guess . . . the career makes it kind of difficult to . . ." She let the thought trail off, apparently shamed into silence by the realization that they sounded like a couple of housewives pounding a mall in Sacramento. "Tell me to shut up, O.K.?"

They had reached the door, much to Mary Ann's relief. She gave DeDe a hasty peck on the cheek. "I'm glad you're interested," she said. "It's just that . . . things are kind of on hold for the time being."

"I hear you," said DeDe.

Did she? wondered Mary Ann. Had she guessed at the truth?

The rain was clattering angrily on the canopy above the restaurant's entrance. "Are those your people?" asked DeDe, indicating Mary Ann's camera crew.

"That's them." They looked wet and grouchy. She didn't relish the thought of making them wetter and grouchier. "Thanks for the tip," she told DeDe.

"That's O.K.," her friend replied. "I owed you one."

Three

Brian Hawkins found his wife's note when he got home from work, and he went up to the house on the roof to await her appearance on television. The tiny penthouse had been his bachelor pad in the old days, but now it functioned as a TV-room-cum-retreat for all the residents of 28 Barbary Lane. Nevertheless, he still seemed to use it more than anyone.

He worried about that sometimes. He wondered if he qualified as a full-fledged TV junkie, a chronic escapist who needed the tube to fill a void he was no longer capable of filling himself. When Mary Ann wasn't home, he could almost always be found in his video aerie, lost in the soothing ether of the Quasar.

"Brian, dear?"

Mrs. Madrigal's voice startled him, since her footsteps on the stairway had been drowned out by Supertramp singing "It's Raining Again" on MTV. "Oh, hi," he said, turning to grin at her. She was wearing a pale green kimono and her hair hovered above her angular face like random wisps of smoke.

Pursing her lips, she studied the television, where a man in his underwear was threading his way through a forest of open umbrellas. "How very appropriate," she said.

"Really," he replied.

"I was looking for Mary Ann," the landlady explained.

It was a simple statement of fact, but it made him feel even more extraneous. "You'll have to wait in line," he said, turning back to the set.

Mrs. Madrigal said nothing.

He was instantly sorry for his pettiness. "She's got a hot date with the Queen," he added.

"Oh . . . another one, eh?"

"Yeah."

She glided across the room and sat down next to him on the sofa. "Shouldn't we be watching her channel?" Her huge Wedgwood eyes forgave him for his irritation.

He shook his head. "She won't be on for another five minutes."

"I see." She let her gaze wander out the window until it fixed on the intermittent blink of the beacon on Alcatraz. He had seen her do that so many times, as if it were a point of reference, the source of her energy. Turning back to him, she shook his knee playfully. "It's a bitch, isn't it?"

"What?"

"Being a media widower."

He came up with a smile for her. "It isn't that. I'm proud of her."

"Of course."

"I had just . . . counted on being with her tonight. That's all."

"I know the feeling," she said.

This time he was the one who looked out the window. A small pond had formed on a neighboring rooftop and its surface was being pitted by yet another downpour. It wasn't night yet, but it was definitely dark. "Do you have a joint?" he asked.

She cocked her head and mugged at him—a reaction that said, "Silly question." Then she foraged in the sleeve of her kimono until she located the familiar tortoiseshell case. He selected a joint, lit it, and offered it back to her. She shook her head, saying, "Hang on to it."

He did so, without a word, for almost a minute, while Michael Jackson minced down a make-believe street protesting that "the kid is not my son." It wasn't all that hard to believe him, Brian decided.

"The thing is," he said at last, "I was going to talk to her about something."

"Ah."

"I was going to buy her dinner at Ciao and take her to *Gandhi* and talk to her about Topic A one more time."

She was silent, so he glanced at her to see if she knew what he meant. She did. She knew and she was pleased. It made him feel a lot better. If nothing else, he would always have Mrs. Madrigal on his side.

"You can still do that," she said finally.

"I don't know . . ."

"What do you mean?"

"I mean . . . it scares the hell out of me. I'm not sure it's a good idea to make her say no one more time. This time . . . it might sound like she means it."

"But if you don't at least talk to her . . ."

"Look, what good would it do? When would she find the *time,* for God's sake? Tonight is so fucking typical, you know. Our private life has to take a back seat to every dumbass little news story that comes down the pike."

The landlady smiled faintly. "I'm not sure Her Majesty would appreciate that description of her sojourn."

"O.K. Maybe not tonight. The Queen is excusable. . . ."

"I should think."

"But she's done this half a dozen times this month. This is *always* the way it is."

"Well, her career is terribly . . ."

"Don't I show respect for her career? Don't I? That can be her career, and the baby can be mine. That makes a helluva lot of sense to me!"

His voice must have been more strident than he had intended. She stroked him with her eyes, telling him to calm down. "Dear," she murmured, "I'm the last person who needs convincing."

"Sorry," he said. "I guess I'm practicing on you."

"That's all right."

"It's not like we have that much time. She's thirty-two and I'm thirty-eight."

"Ancient," said the landlady.

"It is for making babies. It's shit-or-get-off-the-pot time."

Mrs. Madrigal winced, then arranged a fold in her kimono sleeve. "Your metaphors need work, dear. Tell me, when exactly did you last talk to her about this?"

He thought for a moment. "Three months ago, maybe. And six months before that."

"And?"

"She keeps saying we should wait."

"For what?"

"You tell me. For her to become an anchor, maybe? That makes a lot of sense. How many pregnant anchors have you seen?"

"There must have been some."

"She doesn't want to," he said. "That's the bottom line. That's the truth behind the excuses."

"You don't know that," said the landlady.

"I know her."

Mrs. Madrigal peered out at the Alcatraz beacon again. "Don't be too sure about that," she said.

That threw him. When he looked for clues in her face, her brow seemed to be furrowed in thought. "Has she talked to you?" he asked. "Has she said something about . . . the baby thing?"

"No," she answered hastily. "She would never do that."

He remembered the time and reached for the remote control. At the slightest touch of his finger, Mary Ann's face appeared on the screen, only slightly larger than life. She was standing in an alleyway behind Trader Vic's, smiling incongruously in a deep blue sea of cops.

"My goodness," beamed Mrs. Madrigal. "Doesn't she look just splendid?"

She looked better than that. A rush of pure affection swept over him. He smiled at the set for a few proud moments, then turned back to his landlady. "Tell me the truth," he said.

"All right."

"Does she look like a woman who wants to have a baby?"

Mrs. Madrigal's forehead wrinkled again. She spent a long time scrutinizing Mary Ann's face. "Well," she began, tapping a forefinger against her lips, "that hat is deceptive."

Four

Michael Tolliver had spent rush hour in the Castro, the time of day when the young men who worked in banks came home to the young men who worked in bars. He watched from a window seat at the Twin Peaks as they spilled from the mouth of the Muni Metro, stopping only long enough to raise the barrels of their collapsible umbrellas and fire at the advancing rain. Their faces had the haggard, disoriented cast of prisoners who had somehow tunneled to freedom.

He polished off his Calistoga and left the bar, then forked out three dollars to a man selling collapsible umbrellas on the corner. He had lost his last one, and the one before that had sprung a spoke, but three dollars was nothing and he embraced the idea of their expendability. There was no point in getting attached to an umbrella.

Deciding on a pizza at the Sausage Factory, he set off down Castro Street past the movie house and the croissant/cookie/card shops. As he crossed Eighteenth Street, a derelict lurched into the intersection and shouted "Go back to Japan" to a stylish black woman driving a Mitsubishi. Michael caught her eye and smiled. She rewarded him with an amiable shrug, a commonplace form of social telepathy which seemed to say: "Looks like we lost another one." There were days, he realized, when that was all the humanity you could expect—that wry, forgiving glance between survivors.

The Sausage Factory was so warm and cozy that he scuttled his better judgment and ordered half a liter of the house red. What began as a mild flirtation with memory had degenerated into maudlin self-pity by the time the alcohol took hold. Seeking distraction, he studied the funk-littered walls, only to fix upon a faded Pabst Blue Ribbon sign which read: DON'T JUST SIT THERE—NAG YOUR HUSBAND. When the waiter arrived with his pizza, his face was already lacquered with tears.

"Uh . . . are you O.K., hon?"

Michael mopped up quickly with his napkin and received his dinner. "Sure. I'm fine. This looks great."

The waiter wouldn't buy it. He stood there for a moment with his arms folded, then pulled up a chair and sat down across from Michael. "If you're fine, I'm Joan Collins."

Michael smiled at him. He couldn't help thinking of a waitress he had known years ago in Orlando. She, too, had called him "hon" without ever knowing his name. This man had a black leather vest, and keys clipped to his Levi's, but he reached out to strangers in exactly the same way. "One of those days?" he asked.

"One of those days," said Michael.

The waiter shook his head slowly. "And here we are on the wrong side of town, while Betty is having dinner at Trader Vic's."

Michael skipped a beat. "Bette *Davis?*"

The waiter laughed. "I *wish.* Betty the Second, hon. The Queen."

"Oh."

"They gave her a fortune cookie . . . *and she didn't know what it was.* Can you stand it?"

Michael chuckled. "You don't by any chance know what the fortune was?"

"Uh . . ." The waiter wrote in the air with his finger. " 'You . . . will . . . come . . . into . . . a . . . great . . . deal . . . of . . . money.' "

"Sure."

The waiter held his hands up. "Swear to God. Nancy Reagan got the same thing in hers."

Michael took another sip of his wine. "Where did you get this?" This guy was awfully nice, but his dish seemed suspect.

"On the TV in the kitchen. Mary Ann Singleton has been covering it all night."

"No kidding?" *Good for her,* he thought, *good for her.* "She's an old friend of mine." It would tickle her to know he had bragged about that.

"Well, you tell her she's all right." The waiter extended his hand. "I'm Michael, by the way."

Michael shook his hand. "Same here."

"Michael?"

"Yep."

The waiter rolled his eyes. "Sometimes I think that half the fags in the world are named Michael. Where did they ever get this Bruce shit?" He rose suddenly, remembering his professionalism. "Well, you take care, hon. Maybe I'll see you around. You don't work in the neighborhood, do you?"

Michael shook his head. "Not usually. I did this afternoon."

"Where?"

"Across the street. At the switchboard."

"Yeah? My friend Max worked there for a while. He said it was exhausting."

"It is," said Michael.

"This one guy called every other afternoon, while his wife was at her Dan-cercise class. He usually wanted Max to be . . . you know . . . a butch trucker type. Max said it took him *ages* to come, and he said the same thing over and over again. 'Yeah, that's right, flop those big balls in my face.' Now, how the hell you can flop your balls in some guy's face over the *telephone* . . ."

"Wrong place," said Michael, feeling a faint smile work its way out.

The waiter blinked at him. "Dial-a-Load?"

Michael shook his head. "The AIDS hotline."

"Oh." The waiter's fingers crept up his chest to his mouth. "Oh, God. I am such a dipshit."

"No you're not."

"There's this phone sex place upstairs from that new savings and loan, and I thought . . . God, I'm embarrassed."

"Don't be," said Michael. "I think it's funny."

The other Michael's face registered gratitude, then confusion, then something akin to discomfort. Michael knew what he was wondering. "I don't have it," he added. "I'm just a volunteer who answers the phones."

A long silence followed. When the waiter finally spoke, his voice was much more subdued. "My ex-lover's lover died of it last month."

An expression of sympathy seemed somehow inappropriate, so Michael merely nodded.

"It really scares me," said the waiter. "I've given up Folsom Street completely. I only go to sweater bars now."

Michael would have told him that disease was no respecter of cashmere, but his nerves were too shot for another counseling session. He had already spent five hours talking to people who had been rejected by their lovers, evicted by their landlords, and refused admission to local hospitals. Just for tonight, he wanted to forget.

Five

It was almost midnight when Mary Ann got home. A winter full of rain had left a moss-green scum on the wooden stairway to Barbary Lane, so she climbed it cautiously, holding fast to the rail until she felt the reassuring squish of eucalyptus leaves under her feet. She noticed that Michael's lights were still on when she reached the lych-gate at Number 28. For some reason, that worried her, activating an instinct that might roughly be described as maternal.

She hesitated on the second-floor landing, then rapped on his door. He appeared moments later, looking rumpled and a little discombobulated. "Oh, hi," he said, raking his hair with his fingers.

"I hope you weren't asleep."

"No. Just lying down. C'mon in."

She stepped into the room. "Did you catch my little coup, by any chance?"

He shook his head. "I heard about it afterwards, though. The Castro was all abuzz with it."

"Really?" The upward inflection of her voice was a little too girlish and eager, but she was hungry for reinforcement. Her secret fear was that her performance had been clumsy and sophomoric. "What exactly were they saying?"

He smiled at her sleepily. "What exactly would you like them to say?"

"Mouse!" After seven years of friendship, she still couldn't tell when he was kidding.

"Relax, Babycakes. My waiter was raving about you." He withdrew from her slightly and gave her a once-over. "I'm surprised he didn't mention the hat, though."

That stopped her cold. "What's wrong with the hat?"

"Nothing." He stayed poker-faced, teasing her.

"Mouse . . ."

"It's a perfectly nice hat."

"Mouse, if every queen in the city was laughing at this hat, I will *die*. Are you reading me? I will crawl under the nearest rock and die."

He gave up the game. "It looks fabulous. *You* look fabulous. C'mon . . . sit down and tell me about it."

"I can't. I just thought I'd stop by . . . and say hi."

He regarded her for a moment, then leaned forward and pecked her on the lips. "Hi."

"Are you O.K.?" she asked.

He made a little circle in the air with his forefinger, giving her a rueful smile.

"Me too," she said.

"It's the rain, I guess."

"I guess." It had never been the rain, and they both knew it. The rain was just easier to talk about. "Well . . ." She nodded toward the door. "Brian must think I've dropped off the face of the earth."

"Hang on," said Michael. "I've got something for him." He ducked into the kitchen, returning seconds later with a pair of roller skates. "They're ten-and-a-halfs," he said. "Isn't that what Brian wears?"

She stared at the skates, feeling the pain begin to surface again.

"I found them under the sink," Michael explained, avoiding her eyes. "I gave them to Jon two Christmases ago, and I completely forgot where he kept them. Hey . . . not now, O.K.?"

She fought back the tears, to no avail. "I'm sorry, Mouse. It's not fair to you, but . . . sometimes, you know, it just creeps up without any . . . Christ!" She wiped her eyes with two angry sweeps of her hand. "When the hell is it gonna stop?"

Michael stood there, hugging the skates to his chest, his features contorted horribly by grief.

"Oh, Mouse, I'm so sorry. I'm such a turkey."

Unable to speak, he nodded his forgiveness as the tears coursed down his cheeks. She took the skates from him and set them down, scooping him into her arms and stroking his hair. "I know, Mouse . . . I know, baby. It'll get better. You'll see."

She had a hard time believing that herself. Jon had been dead for over three months, but she suffered the loss more acutely now than ever before. To gain distance on the tragedy was to grasp, for the first time, the terrible enormity of it.

Michael pulled away from her. "So . . . how about some cocoa, media star?"

"Great," she said.

She sat at his kitchen table while he made it. Still pinned to the refrigerator door by a magnetized seashell was the snapshot she had taken of Jon and Michael at a pumpkin patch in Half Moon Bay. Averting her gaze, she commanded herself not to cry again. She had done quite enough damage for one night.

When the cocoa was ready, Michael removed a blue Fiesta cup from the shelf and placed it on a gray saucer. Frowning slightly, he studied the pairing for a moment, then substituted a rose-colored saucer for the gray one. Mary Ann observed the ritual and smiled at his eccentricity.

Michael caught her reaction. "These things are important," he said.

"I know." She smiled.

He chose a yellow cup for himself and set it on the gray saucer before joining her at the table. "I'm glad you came by," he said.

"Thanks," she replied. "So am I."

While they sipped their cocoa, she told him about DeDe and Mrs. Halcyon, about her rebellious crew and the rude police, about the few brief moments she had actually laid eyes on the Queen. The monarch had seemed so unreal, she explained, unreal and yet totally familiar. Like the cartoon image of Snow White, walking amidst ordinary human beings.

She stayed long enough to make him laugh out loud several times, then said good night to him. When she reached her own apartment, Brian wasn't there, so she left the skates in the living room and climbed the stairs to the house on the roof. There, as usual, she found her husband asleep in the flickering light of MTV. She knelt by the sofa and laid her hand gently on his chest. "Hey," she whispered. "Who's it gonna be? Me or Pat Benatar?"

He stirred, rubbing his eyes with the knuckles of his forefinger.

"Well?" she prodded.

"I'm thinking."

She smoothed his chest hair, following the lines of its natural swirls. "I'm sorry I broke our date."

He smiled drowsily at her. "Hey."

"Did you see me?" she asked.

He nodded. "Mrs. Madrigal and I watched."

She waited for his reaction.

"You were terrific," he said at last.

"You're not just saying that?"

He raised himself slightly on his elbows and rubbed his eyes again. "I'm never just saying that."

"Well . . . the fortune cookie stuff was pretty fabulous, if I do say so myself. Of course . . ." She was silenced when he reached out and pulled her onto the sofa next to him.

"Shut up," he said.

"Gladly," she replied.

She kissed him long and hard, almost ferociously, in direct proportion to the intensity of her workday. The more public her life became, the more acutely she relished such moments of unequivocal privacy. Within seconds, Brian's hands had found the hem of her tweed skirt and pulled it up over her hips. Lifting her gently under the arms, he propped her up against a nubby cotton bolster and began kissing her knees. She felt faintly ridiculous.

"Let's go downstairs," she whispered.

He looked up from his single-minded mission. "Why?"

"Well . . . so I can get out of this hat, for one thing."

A boyish leer transformed his face. "Keep it on, O.K.?" His head went down again, and his sandpapery cheek scraped against her pantyhose as he moved his tongue up the inside of her thighs. "What is this?" she asked. "Your Evita fantasy?"

He laughed, enveloping her in a wave of warm breath, then yanked off her pantyhose in a single, efficient movement. She laced her fingers through his chestnut curls and pulled his face into her groin, warmth into warmth, wetness into wetness. Moaning softly, she arched her neck and fell back into the embrace of the sofa. At a time like this, she decided, ridiculous was the last thing that mattered.

They were back at the apartment when she finally took off the hat. "The skates are from Mouse," she said. She tried to sound matter-of-fact about it.

"What skates?" He was sitting on the edge of the bed in his boxer shorts.

"In the living room." She avoided his eyes by pretending to arrange the hat in its box.

He rose and left the room. He was gone so long that she stopped brushing her hair and went to look for him. He was seated in the wingback armchair, staring into space. The skates were at his feet. He glanced briefly in her direction. "They're Jon's, right?"

She nodded, but moved no closer.

He shook his head slowly, a thin smile on his face. "Jesus God," he said quietly. He brushed a piece of imaginary lint off the arm of the chair. "Is Michael doing O.K.?" he asked.

"O.K.," she replied.

Brian cast his eyes down at the skates. "He thinks of everything, doesn't he?"

"Uh-huh." She moved to the chair and sat on the floor between his knees. He stroked her hair methodically, saying nothing for almost a minute.

Finally, he said: "I almost lost my job today."

"*What?*"

"It's O.K. I didn't. I smoothed things out."

"What happened?"

"Oh . . . I punched out this guy."

"Brian." She tried not to sound too judgmental, but this had happened before.

"It's O.K.," he said. "It wasn't a customer or anything. It was just that new waiter. Jerry."

"I don't know him."

"Yeah, you do. The one with the Jordache Look."

"Oh, yeah."

"He shot off his mouth all day about one goddamn thing or another. Then he saw me eat a french fry off a plate that had just been bused and he said, 'Shit, man, you've played hell now.' I asked him what the fuck he meant by that and he said, 'That was a faggot's plate, dumbass—your days are numbered.' "

"Great."

"So I pasted him."

She wrenched her head around and stared at him. "Do you really think that was necessary?"

He answered with a shrug. "I got a big kick out of it."

"Brian . . . they told you if it happened again . . ."

"I know, I know."

She kept quiet. These half-assed little John Wayne scenes were simply a reflection of his frustration with an unchallenging job. If she didn't tread carefully, he would use her disapproval as an excuse to remind her that fatherhood was the only job that really mattered to him.

"Did you ever read *Nineteen Eighty-Four?*" he asked.

The question made her wary. "Years ago. Why?"

"Remember the guy in it?"

"Vaguely."

"Do you know what I remember about him the most?"

She shifted uncomfortably. "I don't know. They put rats on his face. What?"

"He was forty," he answered.

"And?"

"I was sixteen when I read it, and I remember thinking how *old* the guy was, and I realized that *I* would be forty in nineteen eighty-four, and I couldn't imagine what it would be like to be that far gone. Well . . . nineteen eighty-four is almost here."

She studied his expression for a moment, then took the hand lying on his knee and kissed it. "I thought we agreed that one menopause in the family was enough."

He hesitated, then laughed. "O.K., all right . . . fair enough."

She sensed that the crisis had passed. He seemed to know that this wasn't the time to broach the subject, and she was more than grateful for the reprieve.

Six

When Michael went down to breakfast, Mrs. Madrigal's kitchen smelled of coffee brewing and bacon frying. The rain that streaked the long casement windows above her sink only served to heighten the conspiracy of coziness that ensnared even the most casual of visitors. He sat down at the landlady's little white enamel table and sniffed the air.

"That coffee is heaven," he said.

"It's Arabian Mocha," she replied. "It's the sinsemilla of coffees." She tore off a length of paper towel and began laying the bacon out to drain.

He chuckled, but only because he understood exactly what she meant. If he was a true pothead—and sometimes he thought that he was—this fey sixty-year-old with the flyaway hair and the old kimonos was the fiend who had led him down the garden path. He could have done a lot worse.

She joined him at the table, bringing two mugs of coffee with her. "Mary Ann was up awfully early."

"She's in Silicon Valley," he said. "Mr. Packard is showing the Queen around."

"Mr. Packard?"

"The computer man. Our former deputy secretary of defense."

"Ah. No wonder I forgot."

He smiled at her, then picked up his mug and blew off its halo of steam. "He's giving the Queen a computer."

She made a quizzical face. "What does the Queen want with a computer?"

19

He shrugged. "It's got something to do with breeding horses."

"My word."

"I know. I can't picture it either."

She smiled, then sipped her coffee for a while before asking: "You haven't heard from Mona, have you?"

It was an old wound, but it throbbed like a new one. "I've stopped being concerned with that."

"Now, now."

"There's no point in it. She's cut us off. There hasn't been so much as a postcard, Mrs. Madrigal. I haven't talked to her for at least . . . a year and a half."

"Maybe she thinks we're cross with her."

"C'mon. She knows where we are. It's just happened, that's all. People drift apart. If she wanted to hear from us, she'd list her phone number or something."

"I know what you're thinking," she said.

"What?"

"Only a silly old fool would fret over a daughter who's pushing forty."

"No I'm not. I'm thinking what a silly old fool your forty-year-old daughter is."

"But, dear . . . what if something's really the matter?"

"Well," said Michael. "You've heard from her more recently than I have."

"Eight months ago." The landlady frowned. "No return address. She said she was doing O.K. in 'a little private printing concern,' whatever that means. It's not like her to be so vague."

"Oh, yeah?"

"Well . . . not in *that* way, dear."

When Mona had moved to Seattle at the turn of the decade, Michael had all but begged her not to go. Mona had been adamant, however; Seattle was the city of the eighties. "Go ahead," he had jeered. "You like Quaaludes . . . you'll *love* Seattle." Apparently, he had been right; Mona had never returned.

Mrs. Madrigal saw how much it still bothered him. "Go easy on her, Michael. She might be in some sort of trouble."

That would hardly be news. He couldn't remember a time when his former roommate hadn't been on the verge of some dark calamity or another. "I told you," he said calmly. "I don't think about that much these days."

"If we had a way of telling her about Jon . . ."

"But we don't. And I doubt if we ever will. She's made it pretty clear that she . . ."

"She loved Jon, Michael. I mean . . . they squabbled a bit, perhaps, but she loved him just as much as any of us. You mustn't doubt that . . . ever." She rose and began cracking eggs into a bowl. They both knew that nothing was to be gained by pursuing the subject. All the wishing in the world wouldn't make a difference. When Mona had fled to the north, she had put more than the city behind her. Starting from scratch was the only emotional skill she had ever mastered.

Mrs. Madrigal seemed to share his thoughts. "I hope she has someone," she murmured. "Anyone."

There was nothing he could add. With Mona, it could well be anyone.

He tried not to think about her on the way to work, concentrating instead on the dripping wound in the roof of his VW convertible. A knife-wielding stereo thief had put it there three weeks earlier, and the bandage he had fashioned from a shower curtain required constant readjustment against the rain. It was no wonder the car had begun to smell like a rank terrarium; he had actually discovered a small stand of grass sprouting in the mildewed carpet behind the back seat.

By the time he reached God's Green Earth, the downpour was much worse, so he gave the plastic patch a final fluffing before making a mad dash to the nursery office. Ned was already there, leaning back in his chair, cradling his bald pate in his big, hairy hands. "That hole is a bitch, huh?"

"The worst." He shook off the water like a drenched dog. "The car is forming its own ecosystem." He peered uneasily out the window, beyond which the primroses had dissolved into an impressionistic blur. "Jesus. We'd better get a tarp or something."

"What for?" Ned remained in repose.

"Those bedding plants. They're getting beat all to hell."

His partner smiled stoically. "Have you checked the books lately? There isn't exactly a major demand for primroses."

He was right, of course. The rain had played hell with business. "Just the same, don't you think . . . ?"

"Fuck it," said Ned. "Let's hang it up."

"What?"

"Let's close for a month. It won't hurt us. It can't be any worse than this."

Michael sat down, staring at him. "And do what?"

"Well . . . how about a trip to Death Valley?"

"Right."

"I'm serious."

"Ned . . . *Death Valley?*"

"Have you ever been there? It's a fucking paradise. We could get six or eight guys, camp out, do some mushrooms. The wildflowers will be incredible after this rain."

He was less than thrilled. "How about during?"

"We'll have tents, pussy. C'mon . . . just for a weekend."

Michael could never have explained his panic at the prospect of unlimited leisure. He needed a routine right now, a predictable rut. The last thing he wanted was time to think.

Ned tried another approach. "I won't try to fix you up. It'll just be a group of guys."

He couldn't help smiling. Ned was always trying to fix him up. "Thanks anyway. You go ahead. I'll hold down the fort. I'll be glad to. Really."

21

Ned regarded him for a moment, then sprang to his feet and began rearranging the seed packets in the revolving rack. It struck Michael as a defensive gesture. "Are you pissed?" he asked.

"Nope."

"It just isn't there right now, Ned."

His partner stopped fiddling. "If you ask me . . . a good jack-off buddy would do you a world of good."

"Ned . . ."

"O.K. All right. Forget it. I've done my Dolly Levi for the day."

"Good."

"I'm going, though. If you want to stay here and watch the roots rot, that's O.K. by me."

"Fine."

They had little to say to each other for the next hour as they busied themselves with minor maintenance chores, things that didn't get done when customers were there. After Ned had finished stacking pallets in the shed, he stepped into the office again and confronted Michael at the desk. "I wanted your company, you know. I didn't do it to be nice."

"I know." He looked up and smiled.

Ned tousled his hair, then reached for his flight jacket. "I'll be at home, if you change your mind. Go home, at least. There's no point in hanging around here."

He did go home eventually, and he spent the rest of the afternoon sorting laundry and cleaning his refrigerator. He was searching for another project when Mrs. Madrigal phoned just before five o'clock.

"Are you free for dinner, I hope?"

"So far," he said.

"Marvelous. I've found a festive new place for Mexican food. I want us all to go. We haven't had a family outing in ages."

He accepted, wondering if this adventure was being organized specifically for his benefit. His friends were awfully solicitous these days and he often felt enormous pressure to be visibly happy in their presence. The reborn joy they sought in his eyes was something he would never be able to fake.

Mrs. Madrigal's Mexican discovery turned out to be a cavernous room at the end of an alleyway near the Moscone Center. For reasons that no one could explain, it was called the Cadillac Bar. Its kitschy Lupe Velez ambience met with everyone's approval, and they guzzled margaritas like conventioneers on a three-day binge in Acapulco.

Maybe it was the liquor, but something about Mary Ann's demeanor seemed curiously artificial to Michael. She hung on Brian's arm throughout much of the meal, laughing a little too loudly at his jokes, gazing rapturously into his eyes, looking more like the Little Woman than Michael had ever seen her look. When her gaze met Michael's for a split second, she seemed to sense his puzzlement. "This place is great," she said far too breezily. "We should all be sworn to secrecy."

"Too late," he replied, parrying her diversionary tactic with one of his own. "Look who just walked in."

Both Mary Ann and Brian jerked their heads toward the door.

"Not *now!*" he whispered.

Mary Ann mugged at him. "You said to look."

"It's Theresa Cross," he muttered, "with one of those fags from Atari."

"Jesus," said Brian. "Bix Cross's widow?"

"You got it."

"She's on all his album covers," said Brian.

"*Parts* of her," amended Mary Ann.

Brian leered. "Right."

A cloud of confusion passed over Mrs. Madrigal's face. "Her husband was a singer?"

"You know," said Michael. "The rock star."

"Ah."

"She wrote *My Life with Bix,*" Mary Ann added. "She lives in Hillsborough near the Halcyons."

The landlady's eyes widened. "Well, my dears, she appears to be coming this way."

Michael assessed the leggy figure striding toward their table. There were probably no twigs lodged within the dark recesses of her hair, but the careful disarray of her hoyden-in-the-haystack hairdo was clearly meant to suggest that there might be. That and her red Plasticine fingernails were all he could absorb before the rock widow had descended on them in a sickly-sweet aura of Ivoire. "You!" she all but shouted. "You I want to talk to."

The crimson talon was pointing at Mary Ann.

Clearing her throat, Mary Ann said: "Yes?"

"You are the best," crowed Theresa Cross. "The best, the best, the best!"

Mary Ann reddened noticeably. "Thank you very much."

"I watch you all the time. You're Mary Jane Singleton."

"Mary Ann."

Mrs. Cross couldn't be bothered. "That hat was the best. The best, the best, the best. Who are these cute people? Why don't you introduce us?"

"Uh . . . sure. This is my husband, Brian . . . and my friends Michael Tolliver and Anna Madrigal."

The rock widow nodded three times without a word, apparently regarding her own name as a matter of public knowledge. Then she turned her gypsy gaze back to Mary Ann. "You're coming to my auction, aren't you?"

So *that* was it, thought Michael. Mrs. Cross could smell media across a crowded room.

Mary Ann was thrown off balance, as intended. "Your . . . ? I'm afraid I don't . . ."

"Oh, no!" The rock widow showed the whites of her eyes, simulating exasperation. "Don't tell me my ditzy secretary didn't send you an invitation!"

Mary Ann shrugged. "I guess not."

"Well . . . consider yourself invited. I'm having an auction out at my house this weekend. Some of Bix's memorabilia. Gold records. The shirts he wore on his last tour. Lots of stuff. Fun stuff."

"Great," said Mary Ann.

"Oh . . . and his favorite Harley . . . and his barbells." The moving finger pointed in Brian's direction. "This one looks like he works out a little. Why don't you bring him along?"

Mary Ann shot a quick glance at "this one," then turned back to her assailant. "I'm not sure if we have plans that day, but if . . ."

"*W* is coming for sure, and the *Hollywood Reporter* has *promised* me they'll be there. Even Dr. Noguchi is coming . . . which strikes me as the very least he could do, since he was the one who broke the story when Bix . . . you know . . . bit the big one."

Michael listened with a mixture of fascination and revulsion. It was this kind of candid banter that had earned Theresa Cross a rung of her very own on San Francisco's social ladder. She might be a little common at times, but she was anything but boring. Besides, her husband's death (from a heroin overdose at the Tropicana Motel in Hollywood) had left her a very rich woman.

Whenever local hostesses needed an "extra woman"—as they often did in San Francisco—Theresa Cross could be counted on to do her part. Largely because of her public image, Michael had once referred to her in Jon's presence as "the fag hag of the bourgeoisie." Jon's reaction had been typically (and maddeningly) cautious: "Maybe so . . . but she's the closest thing we have to Bianca Jagger."

Unnerved by Theresa's "frankness," Mary Ann was still fumbling for words. "This place is really charming, isn't it?"

The rock widow made a face. "It was *much* more fun last week." Radar-like, her eyes scanned the room until they came to rest on a diminutive figure standing at the entrance. Everyone seemed to recognize her at the same time.

"Holy shit," Brian muttered. "It's Bambi Kanetaka."

"Gotta run," said Theresa, already inching toward her new quarry. "I'll see you at the auction."

"Fine," came Mary Ann's feeble reply.

Now two tables away, the rock widow yelled: "Ten percent goes to charity."

"Right," said Michael, unable to resist, "and ninety percent goes up her nose."

"Mouse . . . she'll hear you."

He snorted. "She's not hearing squat." He pointed toward the entrance alcove, where Mrs. Cross was already giving her pitch to Bambi Kanetaka.

Mary Ann's unfulfilled ambition burned behind her eyes like a small brushfire. "Well," she said dully, "I guess an anchorperson takes precedence over a reporter."

There was a long, pregnant silence, which Mrs. Madrigal punctuated by reaching for the check. "Not at our house, dear. Shall we pick up some gelato on the way home?"

When bedtime finally came, Michael slept fitfully, pestered by the alcohol and unfinished business. If Jon had been there, Michael might have woken him to say that Theresa Cross was an asshole, that he had always done fine without even *one* Bianca Jagger, that the nervous pursuit of chic was a weakness unworthy of a doctor of medicine.

He lurched out of bed and felt his way to the telephone. In the light of the streetlight on Barbary Lane, he punched out Ned's number. His partner answered on the second ring.

"It's me," said Michael.

"Hey, kiddo."

"Is it too late to change my mind?"

"About what?"

"You know . . . Death Valley."

"Hell, no. That's great. How about this weekend?"

"Perfect," said Michael.

Seven

While rain pelted the press platform at Pier 50, Mary Ann huddled under her cameraman's umbrella and scarfed down a breakfast of Cheerios and milk. "Where did *this* come from?" she asked, meaning the cereal.

"The local protocol people," answered her co-worker. "It's a joke."

She shot him a rueful look. "I'll say." She had long ago wearied of chasing this pleasant but lackluster Englishwoman through the rain. They could have done a helluva lot better than cold cereal.

25

Her cameraman smiled indulgently. "A *real* joke, Mary Ann. The Queen is leaving, see? We're saying Cheerio to the Queen, get it?" Her reaction must have registered immediately, for he chuckled sardonically and added: "Doesn't help a goddamn bit, does it?"

Mary Ann set the bowl down and glanced across at the *Britannia*. A band on deck was playing "The Anniversary Waltz"—an obvious reference to the Reagans, who had celebrated their thirty-first on board the night before. Soon they would emerge from the royal yacht, along with the Queen and the Prince, to board limousines bound for the airport.

While the *Britannia* sailed to Seattle, the Queen and her consort would fly to Yosemite to continue their vacation. The President would jet to Klamath Falls, Oregon, to make a speech about the decline of logging, and his bride would catch yet another plane to Los Angeles, where she was slated to appear in a special episode of *Diff'rent Strokes* concerning drug abuse among children.

Normally, such a hodgepodge of absurdities would have provoked at least a brief cynical monologue from Mary Ann, but she was far too absorbed in her own dilemma to wax witty about the Reagans. Instead, she set her jaw grimly and waited in silence for the final ritual of this inane tribal extravaganza.

The rain let up a little. A kilted band trooped bravely along the pier. Fireworks exploded in the pale gray skies, while a blond woman in limp marabou feathers argued audibly with the guard at the entrance to the press platform.

"But I *am* with the press," she pleaded. "I just don't have my . . . uh . . . card with me today."

The guard was unyielding. "Look, lady. You got your job, I got mine."

Mary Ann went to the edge of the platform and shouted down at the sentry. "She's with me," she lied. "I'll take responsibility for it."

Elated, the wet-feathered blonde beamed up at her savior and yelled: "Mary Ann! Thank goodness!"

Mary Ann replied in a monotone, already embarrassed. "Hi, Prue."

It was a sad sight, really, this ersatz socialite looking like Big Bird in a monsoon. Prue Giroux had apparently come unglued since losing her job as social columnist for *Western Gentry* magazine. Her life had been built around parties—"events," she had called them—but the invitations and press passes had dried up months before.

Among the people who thought of themselves as social in San Francisco, no one was more expendable than an ex-columnist—except maybe the ex-wife of a columnist. Prue was obviously feeling the pinch.

Fluffing her feathers, she wobbled up the steps in spike heels. "You are so sweet to do this," she said, speaking much more quietly this time. "Isn't this just the most thrilling thing?"

"Mmm," Mary Ann replied, not wanting to burst her bubble. Prue's naiveté was the only thing about her that invited respect.

26

"Look!" Prue exclaimed. "Just in time!"

Wearing a white hat and a beige coat, the Queen approached the gangplank on the arm of the President. As Mary Ann signaled her cameraman, thunderous applause swept across the pier and Prue Giroux sighed noisily. "Oh, Mary Ann, look how *beautiful* she is! She is truly beautiful!"

Mary Ann didn't answer, engrossing herself in the technicalities of her job. The entire spectacle took less than fifteen minutes. When it was over, she slipped away from Prue and the crew and downed a stiff drink at Olive Oil's, a waterfront bar adjoining the pier. She sat at the bar, beneath a row of signal flags, and watched the *Britannia* as it steamed toward the Golden Gate.

The man on the stool next to her hoisted his glass in the direction of the ship. "Good riddance, old girl."

Mary Ann laughed. "I'll say. Except the old girl isn't out there. She's flying to Yosemite."

Her barmate polished off his drink, then teased her with warm brown eyes. "I meant the ship." He had an English accent, she realized.

"You must be with the press," she said.

"Must I?" He was being playful again. Was he trying to pick her up?

"Well, the accent made me think . . . Oh, never mind."

The man laughed, extending his hand. "I'm Simon Bardill."

She gave him a businesslike handshake. "I'm Mary Ann Singleton." Her first real assessment of the Englishman made her realize how much he looked like Brian. He had the same chestnut curls, the same expressive eyes (though brown, not hazel), the same little tuft of fur sprouting beneath the hollow at the base of his neck.

True, his face was somewhat more angular—more foxlike than bearlike—but even a disinterested observer would notice the resemblance. There was an age difference, of course, since this man appeared to be in his late twenties.

He sensed her distraction immediately. "Uh . . . I haven't lost you, have I?"

She smiled apologetically. "For a moment, maybe. You look a lot like . . . somebody I know." To say "my husband" would have sounded far too intimate. Even so, the remark still came off like a pickup line, so she added hastily: "You must be from around here."

"Nope," he replied. "From there." He pointed a long, elegant finger at the departing ship.

She sensed that he enjoyed the mystery he was weaving. "You . . . uh . . . you're taking leave or something?"

He shook the ice in his glass. "Of my senses, perhaps." He peered out the rain-varnished windows of the saloon, fixing his gaze on the royal yacht, now a diminishing smudge of dark blue on the gray canvas of the bay. "There's a distinct possibility of that."

She blinked at him. "O.K. *Now* you've lost me."

Again, he rattled his ice. "It's simple, really. I jumped ship."

Her mind raced frantically toward an undesignated deadline. Had she stumbled across the only *real* story in this whole media circus?

"You know the expression?" he asked.

"Yes . . . of course. You're a crew member or what?"

"Oh, no no no. An *officer*." He signaled the bartender by raising his empty glass. "May I?" he asked Mary Ann, nodding toward her glass.

"Oh . . . I'm fine." Was it too late to catch up with her crew? "Look, I'm sorry to be so thick about this, but . . . you were supposed to be sailing on the *Britannia* and . . . you just decided not to?"

"Precisely."

"You . . . defected?"

He laughed heartily. "From Mrs. Thatcher to Mr. Reagan?" He thought for a moment, stroking his well-defined jaw. "You're on the right track, mind you. I suppose one *could* say that I have defected. Yes . . . yes . . ."

He seemed to reflect on the concept, as if intrigued by it, until the bartender arrived with his drink. Hoisting it in her direction, he said: "To the new Simon Bardill and the lovely lady who shares his dark secret."

She lifted her empty glass. "I'm honored . . . what is it? *Lieutenant* Bardill?"

"Very clever. You even pronounced lieutenant correctly."

She bowed demurely, feeling curiously regal in his presence. "But you're not supposed to take ice in your drink, are you?"

His brow furrowed. "When were you last in England?"

"Never, I'm afraid."

"There's no need to be afraid." He smiled. "We keep ice on the bar now. *They* keep ice on the bar now."

"I see."

"A great deal has changed. A *great* deal." He gazed at the bay again, as if to assure himself that the last trace of England had vanished. It had.

"And to think," he said, turning back to her again, "I was going to be the last of the Snotty Yachties."

She smiled, eager to show him she recognized the nickname for the *Britannia*'s crew. "Aren't they going to miss you?"

"Oh . . . terribly, I'd imagine. I'm a likable fellow, don't you think?"

"I meant professionally. What's going to happen when you don't show up at . . . wherever you're supposed to show up?"

"I'm a radio officer," he answered, "and it's already happened . . . whatever *it* is. I expect they've found another twit with breeding to take my place. Have you ever seen the city from Point Bonita?"

She missed a beat, noticeably, before she managed to reply: "Many times."

"Isn't it marvelous?" He intoned it so earnestly that she realized he had not been issuing an invitation but asking a simple question.

"Beautiful," she replied.

"You should never let people see San Francisco from Point Bonita if they're seeing it for the first time." He took a sudden swig of his Scotch, setting the glass down with deliberate grandeur. "They could very well run amok."

She smiled skeptically at this too-cute explanation. "So you did it for the scenery, huh?"

"In a manner of speaking."

"Would you mind telling that to a camera?"

He regarded her for a moment, then shook his head with a weary chuckle. "I should have known."

"I mean, it's really a fantastic . . . ."

"What station do you work for?"

His tone somehow suggested betrayal. She resented that. They were just two people talking in a bar. "You don't have to, if you don't want to," she said.

The lieutenant ran his forefinger around the rim of his glass. "Do you want a story or do you want a friend?"

She answered without hesitation. "A friend."

He winked at her. "Excellent choice."

She knew that already. A friend just might relent and agree to a story after all. A friend who could trust her to present him in the best possible light. She explained her reasoning to Brian as they opened their Lean Cuisines that evening.

"He might be calling," she added.

"Calling? You gave him our number?"

She nodded. "I doubt if he will, though."

"But he might?"

"He might. He doesn't know a *soul*, Brian. I told him to call if he needed help with anything."

He nodded slowly. "Sort of a . . . Welcome Wagon gesture."

She glanced across at him, then blew on the surface of her steaming dinner. "You're not jealous. Don't pretend to be jealous, Brian."

"Who's pretending?"

"He'll be a nice new friend for both of us. He worked on the royal yacht, for God's sake. He's bound to be interesting, if nothing else."

He plunged a fork into his dinner. "So what's the name of our interesting new friend?"

"Simon," she answered grumpily. "Simon Bardill."

"What does he look like?"

"Gorgeous. Well, sort of gorgeous. He looks a lot like you, as a matter of fact."

Brian stroked his chin. "Why do I find that disquieting?"

She rolled her eyes in retort. "What in God's name would I do with a younger, English version of you?"

"The mind fairly boggles," he replied.

Eight

As dawn crept over Death Valley, Michael stirred in his sleeping bag and catalogued the sounds of the desert: the twitter of tiny birds, the frantic scampering of kangaroo rats, the soothing rustle of the wind in the mesquite trees . . .

"Oh, no! The vinaigrette leaked!"

. . . the voice of Scotty, their chef for this expedition, taking stock of his inventory in preparation for breakfast. His plight provoked a burst of laughter from Ned's tent, followed by more of the same from the sandy bluff where Roger and Gary had slept under the stars.

"What's so fucking funny?" yelled Scotty.

Ned answered: "That's the nelliest thing that's ever been said in Death Valley."

"If you want butch," the chef snapped, "try the third RV on the right—they're eating Spam and powdered eggs. Us nellie numbers will be having eggs benedict, thank you."

General cheers all around.

A tent was unzipped, probably Douglas and Paul's. Boots crunched against gravel, then came Paul's voice, froggy with sleep. "Does anybody know the way to the bathroom?"

More laughter from Ned. "You didn't really believe that, did you?"

"Listen, dickhead, you told me there was running water."

Roger came to the rescue. "All the way down the road, on the right-hand side."

"Where's my shaving kit?" asked Paul.

"Behind the ice chest," said Douglas.

Turtle-like, Michael inched out of his sleeping bag, found the air decidedly nippy, and popped back in again. There was no point in being rash about this. His absence from the banter had not yet been observed. He could still grab some sleep.

Wrong. Scotty's smiling face was now framed in the window of his tent. "Good morning, bright eyes."

Michael emerged part of the way and gave him a sleepy salute.

"Are you heading for the bathroom?" the chef asked.

"Eventually."

"Good. Find me some *garni*, would you?"

"Uh . . . *garni?*"

"For the grapefruit," explained Scotty. "There's lots of nice stuff along the road."

"Right."

"Just something pretty. It doesn't have to be edible, of course."

"Of course."

Garni in Death Valley. There was bound to be a message there somewhere—about life and irony and the gay sensibility—but it eluded him completely as he stood at a sink in the middle of nowhere and brushed his teeth next to a fat man in Bermuda shorts and flip-flops.

On the way back to the campsite, he left the path long enough to find something suitably decorative—a lacy, pale-green weed that didn't appear to shed—then decided on an alternate return route. He felt strangely exhilarated by the brisk, blue morning, and he wanted to enjoy the sensation in solitude.

They had pitched their tents along the edge of a dry creekbed at the northern end of the Mesquite Springs campground, where a kindly quirk of geography kept the neighboring RVs out of sight behind a rocky rise. As a consequence, he had trouble finding the campsite until he spotted the sand-colored gables of the Big Tent—a free-form communal space Ned had built with bamboo poles and tarps from the nursery.

Breakfast was a success. Scotty's eggs benedict were a triumph, and Michael's *garni* received a polite round of applause. When the table had been cleared, Douglas and Paul began heating water for dishwashing, while Roger and Gary repaired to their corner to divide the mushrooms into seven equal portions. After each had downed his share, Ned proposed a hike into the Last Chance Mountains. "I have something to show you," he told Michael in private. "Something special."

Scotty stayed behind to fix lunch while everybody else followed Ned into the hills, stopping sporadically to exclaim over a flowering cactus or an exotic rock formation. (Douglas was positive he had seen hieroglyphics at one point, but his unimaginative lover assured him it was "just the mushrooms.")

They came to a windy plateau scattered with smooth black rocks that had split into geometric shapes. At the edge of the plateau, a six-foot stone obelisk rose—a man-made structure which struck Michael as considerably less precise than the landscape it inhabited.

Douglas stood and stared at the stack of rocks. "It's very Carlos Castaneda," he murmured.

"It's very phallic," said Gary.

"Well, don't just stand there." Ned grinned. "Worship it."

"Nah," said Gary, shaking his head. "It isn't big enough."

Their laughter must have traveled for miles. Ned began walking again, leading the way.

Michael caught up with him. "Was that it?"

"What?"

"The thing you wanted to show me?"

Ned shook his head with a cryptic smile.

They had yet another slope to climb, this one with a staggering view of the valley. Reddish stones arranged along the crest seemed to be fragments of a giant circle. "It used to be a peace symbol," Ned explained. "Remember those?"

As they scurried down the slope, Michael said: "That wasn't it, I guess?"

"Nope," answered Ned.

The terrain leveled out again, and they proceeded uncomfortably close to a crumbly precipice. The mushrooms were singing noisily in Michael's head, intensifying the experience. And distances were confusing in a land where the tiniest pebble resembled the mightiest mountain.

Suddenly, Ned sprinted ahead of the group, stopping near the edge of the drop-off. Michael was the first to catch up with him. "What the hell are you doing?"

"Look!" His partner laughed. He was crouching now, pointing to the valley floor beneath them where five brightly colored tents squatted like hotels on a Monopoly board. Behind them, shiny as a Dinky toy, was Ned's red pickup. They had circled back to the ridge above the campsite.

"Well?" asked Ned.

Michael peered down at the tiny tribal settlement and smiled. He didn't need to ask if this was Ned's surprise; he *knew* what Ned was saying: Look at us down there! Aren't we magnificent? Haven't we accomplished something? See what we mean to each other? It was a grand gesture on Michael's behalf, and he was deeply touched.

Ned cupped his hands and shouted hello to a Lilliputian figure standing by the campfire. It was Scotty, no doubt, already making preparations for lunch. He searched for the source of Ned's voice, then waved extravagantly. Ned and Michael both waved back.

After lunch, the group became fragmented again. Some withdrew for siestas and sex; others enjoyed the gentle downdrift of the mushrooms by wandering alone in the desert. Michael remained behind in the Big Tent, a solitary sultan engrossed in the silence. By nightfall, it seemed he had lived there forever.

He rose and walked toward the hills, following the pale ribbon of the creekbed through the mesquite trees. It was much cooler now, and fresh young stars had begun to appear in the deep purple sky. After a while, he sat down next to a cactus that was actually casting a shadow in the moonlight. A breeze caressed him.

Time passed.

He got up and headed back to camp, almost mesmerized by the amber luminescence of the Big Tent, the faint heartlike pulse of its walls, the gentle laughter from within. As he was about to enter, one of the canvas tarps trapped the rising wind like a spinnaker on a galleon, then ripped free from its restraints. Several people groaned in unison.

"Can I help?" he hollered.

"Michael?" It was Roger's voice.

"Yeah. Want me to make repairs?"

"Fabulous. It's over here. This back part just flapped open again."

"Where?" His hands fumbled in the shadows until he found the hole. "Here?"

"Bingo," said Gary.

Bringing the errant canvas under control, he laced the twine through the eyelets and pulled it tight. Then he made his way back to the front of the tent and lifted the flap.

They had dispensed with the Coleman lantern, having learned the night before that it didn't have a dimmer switch. Paul's inspired alternative was a heavy-duty flashlight in a brown paper bag, which was presently casting a golden Rembrandt glow on the six men sprawled across the Oriental rug Gary had received from his wife in their divorce settlement.

Gary sat against the ice chest, Roger's head resting in his lap. Douglas and Paul, the other pair of lovers, were idly rummaging through a pile of cassette tapes in the far corner of the tent. Ned was giving the hard-working Scotty a foot massage with Vaseline Intensive Care Lotion.

It was a charming tableau, sweet-spirited and oddly old-fashioned, like a turn-of-the-century photograph of a college football team, shoulder to shoulder, hand to thigh, lost in the first blush of male bonding.

"Thanks," said Gary, as Michael entered.

"No sweat," he answered.

Ned looked up from his labors on Scotty's feet. "You got some sun, bubba."

"Did I?" He pressed a finger to his biceps. "I think it's the lighting."

"No," Gary assured him. "It looks real good."

"Thanks." He entered and stretched out on the empty spot next to Ned and Scotty.

Scotty grinned at him blissfully. "There's some trail mix and cheese, if you're still hungry."

"No way," he replied.

After a brief exchange of eye signals, Roger and Gary rose, dusting off the seats of their pants. "Well, guys," said Roger, "it's been a long day. . . ."

"Uh-oh," piped Scotty. "We just lost the newlyweds."

Roger's embarrassment was heartrending. With a sudden stab of pain, Michael remembered the early days when he and Jon had been equally awkward about this maneuver. "Give 'em a break," said Ned, laughing. "They don't have a tent. They have to have privacy sometime."

"And they've been working like Trojans," added Douglas.

The departing Gary shot a look of amiable menace in Douglas's direction. "I'll get you for that."

"For what?" asked Scotty, after the lovers had left.

Douglas smiled. "Gary brought rubbers."

Three people said *"What?"* at the same time.

Douglas shrugged. "They don't call it a crisis for nothin'."

"Well, I know, but . . ." Douglas was almost sputtering. "Forget that. I'm willing to do my bit . . . but *c'mon.*"

Ned unleashed one of his mysterious grins. "I think they're kinda fun myself."

"Why?" asked Douglas. "Because they make you think of straight boys?"

"Marines," said Paul, embellishing on his lover's theme.

"I don't fantasize about straight men," Ned said flatly. "I've never sucked a cock that wasn't gay."

"So what's so great about them?" asked Scotty, his left foot still nestled in Ned's hands.

"Cocks?" asked Ned.

"Rubbers," grinned Scotty.

"Well . . ." Ned's nut-brown brow furrowed. "They're sorta like underwear."

"Calvin Klein Condoms," said Paul.

Everyone laughed.

"Why are they like underwear?" asked Scotty.

"Well . . . didn't you ever ask a guy to put his Jockey shorts back on just because it looked hot?"

"Yeah, sure, but . . ."

"And all there was between you and that incredible cock was this thin little piece of white cotton. So . . . that's kinda what rubbers are like. They get in the way, keep you from having everything at once. That can be the hottest thing of all."

Scotty rolled his eyes. "They are *balloons,* Ned. Face it. They will always be balloons. They are ridiculous things, and they are meant for *breeders.*"

More laughter.

"I remember," offered Douglas, "when the rubber machine always said 'For Prevention of Disease Only.'"

Paul looked at his lover. "They still do, dummy."

"But they always scratched out the 'Disease' part and wrote in 'Babies.' Now straight people don't even use them anymore."

"Yes they do."

"No they don't. They use the pill, or they get vasectomies or something."

While Douglas and Paul continued with this halfhearted quarrel, Michael signaled Ned, to indicate he was leaving. He slipped under the flap and made a beeline for his tent, avoiding even the slightest glance at the rise where Roger and Gary were encamped. He was almost there when a voice called out to him.

"Is that you, Michael?" It was Gary.

"Uh-huh."

"Come on over," said Roger.

He picked his way through the darkness until he found the path leading up to the rise. Only the moon lit the faces of the lovers, snuggled together under a zipped-open sleeping bag. "See"—grinned Roger—"we didn't run off to fuck."

"It must be the mushrooms," said Gary. "We've been telling ghost stories. It's really nice up here. Why don't you get your sleeping bag and join us?"

He looked back at the dark dome of his two-man tent, sitting empty under the stars. "I think I'll take you up on that," he said.

They fell asleep, the three of them, after Gary had told the one about the man with the hook.

Michael dreamed he was once again on the ridge above the campsite, only this time it was Jon who knelt beside him. "Look," Jon whispered, "look who's down there." Mona emerged from one of the tents, so tiny she was almost unrecognizable. Michael waved and waved, but she never saw him, never stopped once as she walked into the desert and disappeared.

Nine

Seattle had once struck Mona as an ideal retirement spot for old hippies. Its weather was moderate, if wet, its political climate was libertarian, and a surprisingly large number of its citizens still looked upon macrame with a kindly eye. In the time it had taken Jane Fonda to get around to exhibiting her body again, almost nothing had changed in Seattle.

Almost nothing. The lesbians who had baked nine-grain bread in the sixties and seventies now earned their livings at copy centers across the city. Mona was one of those lesbians, though she was every bit as puzzled as the next woman by this bizarre reshuffling of career goals. "Maybe," she told a friend once, in a moment of rare playfulness, "it's to prove we can reproduce without the intervention of a man."

Mona lived on Queen Anne Hill in a seven-story brick apartment house the color of dried blood. She worked four blocks away at the Kwik-Kopy copy center, a high-technocracy in varying shades of gray. Neither place did very much for her soul, but when was the last time she had worried about *that?*

"Cheer up, Mo. It can't be as bad as that." It was Serra, her co-worker at the neighboring copier. Serra, the perky young punk.

"Oh, yeah?"

Serra looked down at the huge manuscript she was collating. "It can't be as bad as this."

"What is it?" she asked.

" 'A Time for Wimmin,' " answered Serra.

She made a face. "How is it spelled?"

"How do you think?" said Serra. "Maybe we should call the *Guinness Book.* If my hunch is right, this could be the longest dyke potboiler in the history of the world."

"Any sex?"

"Not so far," said Serra, "but a helluva lot of nurturing."

"Yawn."

"Really," said Serra. "What have you got there?"

"Much worse," she replied. "That queen from the Ritz Café is having a thirtieth-birthday party."

"An invitation?"

"A Xerox collage, no less. Featuring a lovely photo of his dick and some old stills from *I Love Lucy.* He's made me do it over twice."

"Of course," said Serra.

"The dick is too orange and Lucy's hair is too green. Or maybe it's the other way around. Who gives a shit, huh? Is this art or what?"

Serra laughed, but her face registered concern. "You need a day off, Mo."

She looked down at her work again. "I need a lobotomy."

"No, Mo. I mean it." Serra left her machine and moved to Mona's side. "You're pushing too hard. Ease up on yourself. Holly can spare you for a day or two."

"Maybe so," she retorted. "But Dr. Sheldon can't."

"Who?"

"Dr. Barry R. Sheldon," she explained. "A periodontist on Capitol Hill who's on the verge of repossessing my gums." She offered Serra a helpless smile. "As we speak, young lady."

Serra's sympathy seemed mixed with embarrassment. "Oh . . . well, if you need a loan or something . . ."

"That's nice." She squeezed Serra's hand. "It's a little more serious than that."

"Oh."

"I could use a little more overtime, as a matter of fact."

"I just thought . . . I thought you could use a change."

"You got that right," said Mona. "Your machine is jamming."

"Shit," muttered Serra, sprinting back to her post.

When noon came, Serra insisted on treating Mona to lunch at the Ritz Café, a perfect backdrop for Serra's squeaky-clean Kristy McNichol bob. They both ordered Pernod Stingers, and Serra raised hers in an earnest toast to Mona's recovery.

"Things will get better," she said flatly. "I really believe that."

"That's because you're twenty-three," Mona replied.

"Are things so different at thirty-seven?"

"Thirty-eight," said Mona. "And they're not a bit different. Just harder to take."

"I don't know about that," said Serra.

Mona made a face at her. "Tell me that again in fifteen years. It's O.K. to Xerox dicks when you're twenty-three. It's not O.K. at thirty-eight. Trust me. I wouldn't lie to you."

For a moment, Serra seemed lost in thought.

"What is it?" asked Mona.

"Nothing. Nothing yet."

"Now wait a minute . . ."

"It's just an idea."

"C'mon," said Mona. "Out with it."

"I can't. Not until I see if it's possible." She took a sip of her drink, then set it down suddenly. "Oh, God!"

"*What?*" asked Mona.

"Guess who our waiter is?"

The waiter recognized Mona instantly. "Oh, hi! The invitations look fabulous!"

She gave him a thin smile. "I'm glad you like them."

After lunch, they received a rush order for five hundred fliers announcing a "British Brunch" in honor of the *Britannia*'s recent arrival in Seattle. Mona glowered at the layout—Queen Elizabeth saying, "I just love a good banger"—then looked up and glowered at the customer.

"Would somebody please tell me why every homo in Seattle is so obsessed with this woman?"

The customer drew back as if he'd been slapped. "What are you? The editorial board?"

She glanced impatiently at the clock. "I suppose you want this today?"

The man let his irritation show. She really didn't blame him; she had always been detached enough to know when she was being a bitch. "Look," he said, "tomorrow will be just fine. And I've had a bad day too . . . so slack off, will you?"

"Maybe I can help?" It was Serra, intervening as sweetly as possible.

Mona felt herself reddening. "It's no problem. I'll just fill out the . . ."

37

"Go home, Mo." Serra squeezed her forearm gently. "I can manage."

"Are you sure?" She felt like a real ogre.

"You deserve it," said Serra. "Go on. Scoot."

So Mona got the hell out, stopping briefly on the way home to write a bad check for tuna fish and detergent at the S & M Market. Once upon a time—three years ago, to be exact—she had gotten a big laugh out of the S & M Market. She had promised herself she would take Mouse there if he ever came to Seattle.

But Mouse had never come, and the irony inherent in the name of her corner grocery had faded like her California tan. They had drifted apart gradually, and she wasn't sure whose fault that was. Now the thought of a reunion was embarrassing at best, terrifying at worst.

Still, she couldn't help wondering if Mouse was doing O.K., if he had found someone to hug him occasionally, if he would still call her Babycakes the next time they met. She had thought of phoning him three or four times, while on Percodan from her periodontist, but she didn't want his sympathy for her dud of a life.

When she reached her apartment, her neighbor Mrs. Guttenberg accosted her in the lobby. "Oh, thank God, Mona! Thank God!" The old lady was a wreck.

"What is it?" asked Mona.

"It's old Pete, poor thing. He's in the alley out back."

"You mean he's . . . ?"

"Some fool kid ran over him. I couldn't find a soul to help me, Mona. I've got a blanket over him, but I don't think . . . The poor old thing . . . he never deserved this."

Mona rushed into the alley, where the dog lay immobile in a light drizzle. Only his head stuck out from under the blanket. A rheumy eye looked up at Mona and blinked. She knelt and laid her hand carefully against his graying muzzle. He made a faint noise in the back of his throat.

She looked up at Mrs. Guttenberg. "He doesn't belong to anyone, does he?"

The old lady shook her head, fingertips pressed to her throat. "All of us feed him. He's lived here for ten years at least . . . twelve. Mona . . . he's got to be put out of his misery."

Mona nodded.

"Could you drive him to the SPCA? It's just a few blocks."

"I don't have a car, Mrs. Guttenberg."

"You could push him."

Mona stood up. "Push him?"

"In that shopping cart I take to the S & M."

So that was what they did. Using the blanket to hoist him, Mona laid Pete in Mrs. Guttenberg's shopping cart and pushed him six blocks to the SPCA. An attendant there told her there was no hope for the dog. "It won't take long," he said. "Do you want to take him back with you?"

38

Mona shook her head. "He isn't mine. I don't know where I'd . . . no . . . no, thank you."

"There's a surrender fee of ten dollars."

A surrender fee. Of all the things they could have called it.

"Fine," she said, feeling the tears start to rise.

Five minutes later, when the deed was done, she wrote another bad check and pushed the empty cart home in the rain. Mrs. Guttenberg met her at the door, babbling her gratitude as she fumbled in her change purse for "something for your trouble."

"That's O.K.," she said, trudging toward the elevator.

During her slow, clanking ascent, she thought suddenly of the maxim Mouse had called Mona's Law: *You can have a hot lover, a hot job and a hot apartment, but you can't have all three at the same time.*

She and Mouse had laughed about this a lot, never dreaming that one day, two out of three would be regarded as something akin to a miracle.

The lover part didn't bother her much anymore. By living alone she could maintain certain illusions about people that helped her to like them more—sometimes even to love them more. Or was that just her rationale for being such a crummy roommate?

The apartment part went straight to the pit of her stomach when she reached the fourth floor and opened the door of the drab little chamber she had learned to call home. There was something profoundly tragic—no, not tragic, just pathetic—about a thirty-eight-year-old woman who still built bookshelves out of bricks and planks.

She was on the verge of reevaluating the job part, when the telephone rang. "Yeah?"

"May I speak to Mona Ramsey, please?" It was a woman's voice, unrecognizable.

"Uh . . . I'm not sure she's here. Who's calling, please?"

"Dr. Sheldon's bookkeeper."

Mona tried to sound breezy. "I see. May I take your number?"

"She's not there, then?"

"'Fraid not." Less breeze this time, more authority. This bill hound wasn't giving up without a fight.

"I tried to reach her at her place of business, and they said she had gone home sick today. This *is* her residence, isn't it?"

"Well, yes, but . . . Miss Ramsey has left for a while."

"I thought she was sick."

"No," Mona answered. "In mourning."

"Oh . . ."

"Her best friend died this afternoon." That sounded a little too conventional, so she added: "He was executed."

"My God."

"She took it kinda hard," she said, getting into it. "She was a witness."

This was almost overkill, but it worked like a charm. The caller audibly gulped for air. "Well . . . I guess . . . I'll call her when . . . Just say I called, will you?"

"Sure will," said Mona. "Have a nice day."

She set the receiver down delicately, then yanked the phone jack out of the wall. If periodontists had any link with organized crime, she was in deep, deep trouble.

She made herself a cup of Red Zinger tea and withdrew to the bedroom, where she searched the mirror for even the tiniest clue to her identity. In an effort to be charitable, Serra had once told her that she looked "a lot like Tuesday Weld." Mona had replied: "I look a lot like Tuesday Weld on a Friday." Today, the wisecrack was all too applicable.

Her "character lines" made her begin to wonder if there was such a thing as too much character. What's more, the frizzy red hair had stopped looking anarchistic years ago. (Even Streisand had finally abandoned the rusty-Brillo-pad look.) Was it time to relent, to throw in the towel and become a lipstick lesbian?

Some of the most political dykes in town had already converted, tossing out their Levi's and Birkenstocks in favor of poodle skirts and heels. It was no longer a question of butch vs. femme, liberation vs. oppression. Clothes did not unmake the woman; clothes were just clothes.

The prospect of a total makeover was strangely thrilling, but she needed a second opinion. She went straight to the phone, plugged it back in, and dialed Mouse's home number, suddenly delighted to have such an off-the-wall excuse to break the silence between them. But Mouse wasn't at home.

Where was he, then? The nursery? Another call produced the same result. It was Saturday, for God's sake! Why would the nursery be closed on a Saturday? What the hell was going on?

The door buzzer squawked at her from the other room. She got up and went to the ancient, paint-encrusted intercom. "Yeah?"

"Is this Mona Ramsey?"

A moment's hesitation. "Who wants to know?"

"A friend of Serra Fox. She said I might find you here. I tried ringing you from . . ."

"Just a minute." Mona dashed to the window and peeped down at an elegantly dressed brunette waiting in the entrance alcove. She certainly *looked* like a friend of Serra's. The lipstick lesbians were everywhere.

Mona addressed the intercom again. "This isn't about money, is it?"

The woman tittered discreetly. "Not in the way you might think. I shan't take a great deal of your time, Miss Ramsey." She spoke with an English accent.

Mona counted to ten and buzzed her up.

Ten

Brian was surprised to find himself thinking of Mona Ramsey when he and Mary Ann arrived at Theresa Cross's auction in Hillsborough. During the course of their half-assed little affair in 1977, he and Mona had shared a passion for three things: the movies *Harold and Maude* and *King of Hearts,* and Bix Cross's *Denim Gradations* album.

Mona's favorite song from that album had been "Quick on My Feet." Brian had found "Turn Away" more to his taste, and here, gleaming at his fingertips, was the platinum record heralding its success.

"Look at *this,*" whispered Mary Ann, as they moved along the trophy-laden tables in the late rock star's screening room. "She's even raided the liquor cabinet." She lifted a half-empty bottle of Southern Comfort.

Brian read the tag on it. "Yeah, but he drank out of that with Janis Joplin."

"Big deal," murmured his wife. "Who cares?"

Was she spoiling for a fight? He cared a great deal, and she knew it. "It's history," he said at last. "For *some* people, anyway."

She made a little grunting noise and kept moving. "How about this?" she asked, indicating a broken toaster. "Is this history?"

The playful look in her eyes kept him from getting angry. "You'd sure as hell think so if this were Karen Carpenter's estate sale."

Her eyes became hooded. "That was *low,* Brian."

He chuckled, pleased with himself.

"And I wasn't *that* big a fan."

He shrugged. "You bought her albums."

She groaned as she examined a box of plastic forks. "I bought *an* album, Brian. Stop being so hipper-than-thou."

The debate was cut short by the arrival of their hostess. She swept into the room wearing a black angora sweater over black Spandex slacks. Mary Ann nudged Brian. "Mourning garb," she whispered.

"Hi, people!" The rock widow strode toward them.

"Hi," echoed Mary Ann, practically chirping. For all her private bad-mouthing, his wife was intimidated by Theresa Cross. Brian could always tell that by the tone of her voice, and it always brought him closer to her.

"Is your crew here yet?" asked Theresa.

"Any minute," Mary Ann assured her. "They must have had a little trouble finding the . . ."

"Did you see the Harley?" Now the rock widow was talking to him, having dispensed with media matters.

"Sure did," he replied.

"Isn't it the *best?*"

Mary Ann's cameraman appeared in the doorway. "There he is," she said.

"Fabulous," exclaimed Theresa. "It won't take long, I hope. *Twenty/Twenty* is coming at noon."

"Half an hour," Mary Ann replied. "At the very most. I just need to talk to him about the stuff I want." She turned to Brian. "Will you be all right for a while?"

"I'll take care of him," said Theresa.

"Great," said Mary Ann, backing off.

Theresa turned to him. "C'mon. I'll give you the grand tour."

She led him out of the screening room through padded gray flannel corridors trimmed in chrome. "Were you a big fan of my husband's?"

"The biggest," he answered.

She shot a wicked glance in his direction. "I hope that's not false advertising."

By the time he had figured out her meaning, she had brought him to a halt in front of double doors, also flannel-covered. "I'll show you something you won't see on *Twenty/Twenty.*" She flung open the doors to reveal an Olympic-size bedroom lined with lighted Lucite boxes. Showcased in the boxes were dozens of pickaninny dolls—"coon art" from the thirties and forties. Cookie jars shaped like black mammies, Uncle Tom ashtrays, Aunt Jemima posters.

"This is amazing," he said.

The rock widow shrugged it off. "Bix was always just a little bit sorry he wasn't born black. That's not what I wanted to show you, though." She moved to a huge chest of drawers near the bed. "*This* is." With a flourish, she yanked open one of the drawers.

He was dumbfounded. "Uh . . . underwear?"

"*Panties,* silly."

He shifted uneasily. What the fuck was he supposed to say?

"From his *fans,*" explained Theresa, removing one of them from a labeled Baggie. "This one, for instance, is from the Avalon Ballroom, nineteen sixty-seven."

His laughter was nervous and sounded that way. "You mean they threw these on stage?"

She winked at him. "You're a quick one."

"And he saved them?"

"Every goddamn one!" She ran a crimson nail across the panties, like a secretary explaining her filing system. "We've got your Be-In panties from Golden Gate Park. Remember that? George Harrison was there. An-n-nd . . . your basic Fillmore panties, nineteen sixty-six. That was a good year, wasn't it?"

He laughed, liking her for the first time. At least, she had a sense of humor. "These ought to be in the auction," he grinned.

"No way, José. These are *mine*."

"You mean . . . ?"

"You better believe it! I wear every goddamn one of them!"

This time he roared.

"I look pretty fucking wonderful in them too!"

He had already pictured as much.

"C'mon," she said. "You're starting to sweat. Let's get you back to the wife."

Eleven

Two days later, Mary Ann found herself on Union Square, shooting a promo for Save the Cable Cars. Since the cable cars were out of commission during their renovation, she was using the one that sat on blocks beside the Hyatt, a melancholy relic whose embarrassment she could almost sense, like the head of a moose on a barroom wall.

She delivered her spiel in a very tight shot, while dangling recklessly from the side of the stationary car. To add to her humiliation, a small crowd gathered to witness the ordeal, applauding her good takes and laughing at the fluffs.

When she was done, a pregnant woman stepped forward. Her condition, though easily discernible to the average idiot, was confirmed by a yellow maternity smock bearing the word BABY and an arrow indicating the direction the baby would have to go in order to get out.

"Mary Ann?"

"Connie?"

Connie Bradshaw squealed the way she had always squealed, the way she had squealed fifteen years before in Cleveland, when she had been head majorette at Central High and Mary Ann had been a mildly celebrated member of the National

Forensic League. Some things never change, it seemed, including Connie's inability to make it through life without things written on her clothes.

A clumsy embrace followed. Then Connie stood back and looked her former roommate up and down. "You are such a *star!*" she beamed.

"Not really," said Mary Ann, meaning it more than she wanted to.

"I saw you with the Queen! If that's not a star, what is?"

Mary Ann laughed feebly, then pointed to the arrow on Connie's belly. "When did this happen?"

Connie pushed a tiny button, consulting her digital watch. "Uh . . . seven months and . . . twenty-four days ago. Give or take a few." She giggled at the thought of it. "Her name is Shawna, by the way."

"You already know it's a girl?"

Connie giggled again. "You know me. I hate suspense. If there's a chance to peek, I'll do it." She laid her hands lightly on the Shawna-to-be. "Pretty neat, huh?"

"Pretty neat." Mary Ann nodded, wondering when she had last used the phrase. "God, it's so easy to lose track of things. I didn't even know you were married."

"I'm not," came the breezy reply.

"Oh."

"See?" Connie held up ten ringless fingers. "Magic."

For the first time in fifteen years, Mary Ann felt slightly more middle-class than Connie.

"I got tired of waiting around," Connie explained. "I mean . . . hey, I'm almost thirty-three. What good is a bun in the oven, if the oven is broken? You know what I mean?"

"Mmm," answered Mary Ann.

"I mean . . . Jees . . . I want a baby a lot more than I want a husband, so I said to hell with it and stopped taking the pill. You can have a husband any ol' time. There's a time limit on babies." She paused and studied Mary Ann with a look of earnest concern. "Am I freaking you out, hon?"

Mary Ann laughed as jauntily as possible. "Are you kidding?"

"Good. Anyway, the father is either Phil, this software executive who took me to the Us Festival last year, or Darryl, this really super accountant from Fresno." She shrugged, having made her point. "I mean . . . it's not like they weren't both great guys."

In some ways, it made a lot of sense. Leave it to Connie to name the baby before she had named the father. "You look just great," Mary Ann said. "It really becomes you."

"Thanks." Connie beamed. "You and Brian got married, didn't you?"

The question came out of left field, but Mary Ann wasn't really surprised.

According to Brian, he and Connie had slept together once back in '76. Later that year he had brought her to Mrs. Madrigal's Christmas party. Nothing had ever come of it. To hear Brian tell it, the interlude had meant a lot more to Connie than it had to him.

Mary Ann nodded. "Two years ago this summer."

"That's great," said Connie. "He's a neat guy."

"Thanks. I think so too."

"But no babies, huh?"

Mary Ann shook her head. "Not yet."

"Your career, huh?"

In a matter of seconds, Mary Ann weighed her options. It was time to talk about this to *someone*, and Connie suddenly struck her as a logical candidate. She was decent, practical and completely detached from the tight little family unit at 28 Barbary Lane.

"We need to catch up," said Mary Ann. "Why don't I buy you a cup of coffee?"

"Super!"

So they walked across the square to Neiman-Marcus, where Connie elaborated on the joys of impending motherhood. "It's like . . . it's like this friend you've never met. I know it sounds dumb, but sometimes I just sit and talk to Shawna when I'm home alone. And you know . . . sometimes she even thumps back."

Mary Ann set her cup down. "That doesn't sound dumb at all."

"I don't know why it took me so long to do it," said Connie. "It's the best thing that ever happened to me. I kid you not."

"Are you on maternity leave or what?"

Connie looked puzzled.

"Aren't you still with United?" asked Mary Ann.

"Oh." Connie let out a little laugh. "You *are* behind the times, hon. I quit that five or six years ago. The glamor was gone, if you know what I mean."

Mary Ann nodded.

"In my day, we were *stews*," Connie continued. "Now they have flight attendants. It's just not the same thing."

"Yeah. I guess that's true."

"I saved some money, though, so I have my own little house in West Portal. I manage a card shop there. You should come by sometime. I'll give you a press discount or something." She smiled wanly at Mary Ann, suspecting that it would never happen. "You must be superbusy, though."

"I'd love to come," said Mary Ann.

"There might even be a story in it. It's a cute place."

"Mmm."

Connie reached across the table and took Mary Ann's hand. It was a sisterly gesture, reminiscent of the days when Mary Ann had camped out on Connie's sofa in the Marina, crying her eyes out over rotten times at Dance Your Ass Off. Connie had been her only refuge, a benevolent link between Cleveland and her family at Barbary Lane.

"What's the matter, hon?"

Mary Ann hesitated, then said: "I wish I knew."

"About what?"

"Well . . . Brian wants a baby very much."

Connie nodded. "And you don't, huh?"

"No. I want one. Maybe not as much as Brian does . . . but I want one."

"And?"

"Well . . . I stopped taking the pill eight months ago."

Connie's mouth opened slightly.

"Nothing's happened, Connie. Zilch."

Connie cocked her head, showing sympathy. "And Brian is freaked, huh?"

"No. He doesn't know about it. I haven't told him."

Connie screwed up her face in thought. "I don't get it. You didn't tell him when you went off the pill?"

"I wanted it to be a *surprise,* Connie. Like in the movies. I wanted to see the look on his face when I told him I was pregnant."

"Like in the old days," said Connie. "That's sweet."

"Now I have to see the look on his face when I tell him I'm not."

"Bummer," said Connie.

"The thing is . . . it means so *much* to him." She chose her words carefully. "I think he's proud of me and my career—I *know* he is—but his self-respect has suffered a lot. He sees himself as the waiter who's married to the TV star. I mean, he's warm and kind and loving . . . and incredibly sexy, and that's always been enough for me . . ."

"But not for him," Connie added.

"Apparently not. This baby is a major obsession. I guess it's . . . something *he* could do, you know? A mark he could leave on the world. His own flesh and blood."

Her confidante nodded.

"Only it *can't* be, Connie. It can never be."

"You mean . . . ?"

Mary Ann nodded. "I've seen a doctor. It isn't me."

"And you're sure he's the one who's . . ."

"Positive."

"Connie's brow furrowed. "But if they haven't tested his sperm yet . . ."

"Connie . . . they have."

"What?"

46

"They tested it at St. Sebastian's about a month ago. His sperm count is practically nonexistent. It just won't cut it."

"Wait a minute. I thought you said you hadn't told him."

She might have known it would come to this. "I did, Connie. But it's possible to have his sperm tested without . . . Oh, c'mon, Connie . . . think about it."

Connie thought about it, then said: "Jees. That must've been a bitch."

Mary Ann looked at her nails, saying nothing.

"How on earth did you . . . ?"

"Connie, please . . . don't ask, O.K.?" The last thing she needed was to rehash the horrors of that trying day: the mad dash to the bathroom, where she'd hidden the jar, the feeble excuse she'd made to get out of the house before breakfast, the Chinese funeral that almost kept her from making it on time . . .

"He isn't wearing jockey-style shorts, is he?"

"What?"

"I read that in 'Dear Abby.' Sometimes they can cause sterility."

"No . . . it isn't that." She wondered momentarily if Brian had worn jockey-style shorts when Connie had slept with him.

They both fell silent for a moment. Mary Ann knew what Connie was thinking, so she beat her to the punch. "Time to face the music, huh?"

Connie looked up from her cup with a game little smile. "Seems that way to me, hon."

Mary Ann suddenly felt silly. "I should have told him weeks ago. I just thought there might be some way I could spare him the . . . hell, I don't know. If I tell him what I did . . . you know . . . with the sperm and all . . ."

"Don't tell him that."

"But I can't make him go through it again. He'll insist on that, I'm sure."

"You could tell him *you're* sterile."

Mary Ann rejected the idea with a frown. That would jeopardize their relationship even more than the current bag of worms. It was better to stick with the whole truth . . . or wait for a miracle.

When she arrived home that night, she found Brian in the house on the roof, watching *Three's Company* in his KAFKA baseball cap. She had hated that stupid cap ever since Brian had read about it on a matchbook cover and mailed away for it, but tonight was hardly the time to tell him so.

"I brought us some Eye of the Swan," she said, holding up the bottle.

He peered at her over the back of the sofa. "Oh . . . hi. Great. What's the occasion?"

"No occasion."

"Fair enough."

She moved to the window. "The rain has stopped. See? There's even some blue over there. Shit!"

"What?"

"I forgot to bring glasses."

"No sweat."

"I'll run down and . . ."

"Mary Ann . . ." He caught her free hand. "Just relax, O.K.? We're fine. We can pass the bottle."

"It won't take a minute . . ."

"No one's watching, Mary Ann. This isn't a segment on *Bay Window*."

Thank God for small favors, she thought.

He tugged her back to the sofa. She set the bottle down and settled in with him, giving him a long kiss. Then she pulled back and looked into his long-lashed hazel eyes. "Do you realize how lucky we are?"

He regarded her for a moment, then said: "I do."

She picked up the bottle, took a swig from it, and handed it to him. He took a similar swig and gave the bottle back to her. "Why are we counting our blessings?" he asked.

She placed the bottle on the floor beneath their feet. "What do you mean?"

"I don't know . . . you always talk about how lucky we are right before you drop one of your bombs."

"No I don't."

"O.K., you don't." He gave her his I'm-not-looking-for-a-fight smile.

"I just . . . well, as a matter of fact, I did want to talk to you about something."

He folded his arms across his chest. "Great. Shoot."

"Well, I thought it would be nice if we hyphenated our names."

"Huh?"

"You know . . . if I became Mary Ann Singleton-Hawkins."

Brian studied her. "Is this a gag?"

"No. I told you before I *feel* like Mrs. Hawkins. Keeping my own name was never a big deal."

"It was to the station," said Brian.

"O.K. So if I become Mary Ann Singleton-Hawkins, they'll still have their precious name recognition factor and . . . you know . . . it'll be more like I'm married."

He sat there slack-mouthed.

"Besides," she added, "I think the name's really pretty. It's distinctive."

Brian frowned. "Making me . . . what?"

"What do you mean?"

"I mean . . . what do I tell the guys at work? That I've just become Brian Singleton-Hawkins?"

That stopped her cold. "Oh . . . well . . . yeah, I see what you mean."

"What in the world are you . . . ?"

"Forget it, Brian. I didn't think it out. It was a stupid idea." She smiled sheepishly. "Gimme that bottle, handsome."

He did so. She took another swig. He reached out and touched the side of her head. "You know the name business doesn't bother me. I told you that a long time ago."

"I know."

He laid his arm across her shoulder. "Christ, I'm a modern sonofabitch."

The phone rang downstairs.

"I'd better get that," she said, grateful for the reprieve. She clattered down the narrow wooden stairway and caught the call after the fourth ring, gasping "Hello."

"Miss Singleton?"

"Yes."

"Simon Bardill here."

"Simon! How are you? Is everything going O.K.?"

"By and large. I'm in a bit of a scrape as far as accommodations are concerned."

"Oh . . ."

"Do you think I might solicit your advice at some point? At your convenience, of course."

"Of course! Hold on a sec, O.K.?"

She dashed back upstairs and confronted Brian. "It's that Englishman from the *Britannia*. I thought I might invite him to dinner tomorrow night . . . if you'd like to meet him, that is."

Brian's hesitation was almost imperceptible. "Fine," he said.

Twelve

He had already pictured the Englishman as a sort of latter-day Laurence Harvey, a spoiled aristocrat with pretentious airs and esoteric tastes. He couldn't have been more surprised when Simon Bardill ambled over to his record collection and perused the cover of *Denim Gradations*.

"A bloody shame," he said.

Brian was caught off guard. "What? Oh . . . his death, you mean?"

"Mmm. Free-basing, wasn't he?"

Brian shook his head. "Smack. According to the coroner."

"Ah."

"You . . . uh . . . you're a fan of Bix Cross?"

The lieutenant smiled dimly. "More of a freak than a fan. I played nothing else in my rooms at Cambridge." He held out the album so Brian could see it. "The lovely breasts belong to his wife, I understand."

Brian smiled back. "You understand correctly. I met the lady this weekend."

"Indeed?" If an arching eyebrow was any indication, the lieutenant was clearly impressed. "Katrina, isn't it? No, Camilla . . . something exotic."

"Theresa," Brian told him.

The lieutenant rolled the name across his tongue. "Theresa . . . Theresa." He turned and gave Brian a knowing, man-to-man look. "Is her face as delicious as the rest of her?"

"Better," said Brian. That was somewhat of an exaggeration, but he enjoyed being an expert on Theresa Cross.

The lieutenant breathed a sigh of relief. "Thank God!"

"Why?"

"Well, one doesn't enjoy seeing one's fantasies dashed on the rocks."

"Yeah." Brian nodded. "I guess that's true."

The lieutenant looked down at the album again. "I banged the bishop over *this* one more times than I care to count."

Brian didn't get it. "I think you'd better run that by me again."

The lieutenant chuckled. "You know." He made a jerking-off gesture with his fist.

Brian grinned. *"Banging the bishop?"*

"Right."

"Where did that come from?"

The lieutenant thought for a moment. "I haven't the foggiest."

They shared a brief laugh. The lieutenant returned the album to its place on the shelf. Brian decided to take advantage of the silence. "So," he said, "why aren't you in chains by now?"

The lieutenant seemed little disconcerted by his direct approach. "I think you've been reading too much Melville. The modern navy isn't nearly as stringent as you might think."

"Yeah, but . . . you jumped ship, didn't you?"

"More or less."

"Well, isn't that a court-martial offense?"

"Sometimes," answered the lieutenant. "It can vary, though, depending on the individual."

Brian looked him squarely in the eye. "You mean you have friends in high places?"

The lieutenant seemed tremendously uncomfortable. He was about to say something, when Mary Ann bounded into the room, letting him off the hook. "Well," she said, "I'm afraid she's not home yet." She glanced apologetically at their guest. "This is so disappointing. It's such wonderful stuff. She named it after the Queen Mother and everything."

The lieutenant looked puzzled.

Brian translated for him: "Our landlady names her pot plants after women she admires."

"I see."

Mary Ann turned to Brian. "I checked Michael's too. He isn't back from Death Valley yet. I could look for roaches in the ashtray in the car."

"Too late," he answered. "I did that last week. We'll just have to face your chicken straight."

She gave him an evil eye before addressing the lieutenant. "I can get you some wine."

"Lovely," he said.

Mary Ann disappeared into the kitchen. The lieutenant sidled to the window, turning his back to Brian. "That beacon must be Alcatraz," he said. He obviously had no intention of picking up where they'd left off.

"That's it," said Brian.

"They don't still keep prisoners, do they?"

"No. It's empty. Has been for a long time."

"I see. Lovely view from here."

"Yeah," said Brian. "It's not bad."

Mary Ann sailed into the room with the wine stuff on a tray. "Have you ever had Eye of the Swan?"

The lieutenant turned around. "No . . . I can't say that I have."

"It's a white Pinot noir. Very dry." She set the tray down on the coffee table, then knelt in front of it and began pouring.

"Glasses and everything," murmured Brian.

She handed him a glass, ignoring the remark.

"So," she chirped, giving the lieutenant a glass. "You've been having trouble finding a place to stay?"

"Not exactly," he replied. "I took a room at the Holiday Inn on Fisherman's Wharf."

Brian and Mary Ann groaned in unison.

The lieutenant chuckled. "Yes, it is, rather. I was hoping for something with a little more character. I don't fancy breaking that little paper seal every day."

"What seal?" asked Mary Ann.

"You know . . . on the toilet."

"Oh." She laughed a little nervously, Brian thought. "How long do you plan on staying?"

"Oh . . . about a month. I plan on returning to London several days after Easter."

Mary Ann frowned. "That makes renting a little difficult."

"Actually," said the lieutenant, "I was rather hoping for a swap."

"A swap?"

"My place in London in exchange for someone's place here. Could such a thing be arranged?"

Mary Ann was already deep in thought.

"It's a tatty little flat," added the lieutenant, "but it's in a colorful neighborhood and . . . well, it might be an adventure for someone."

Mary Ann looked at Brian with dancing eyes. "Are you thinking what I'm thinking?" she asked.

Thirteen

Ned's red pickup and its seven weary passengers had survived sandstorms in Furnace Creek, snowstorms in South Lake Tahoe, and a blowout near Drytown by the time their ten-hour trans-California odyssey had ended.

Michael climbed from the truckbed, hoisted his bedroll to his shoulder, and trudged up the stairway to Barbary Lane, stopping long enough on the landing to wave goodbye to his campmates.

Ned answered with a toot of the horn. "Go to bed," he yelled. Like a master mechanic who could diagnose an engine problem simply by listening, he knew that Michael's emotional resistance was down.

Michael gave him a thumbs-up sign and followed the eucalyptus trees into the dark city canyon of the lane. He whistled during this last leg of the journey, warding off demons he was still unable to name.

Back at the apartment, he dumped his gear on the bedroom floor and drew a hot bath. He soaked for half an hour, already feeling the loss of his brothers, the dissolution of that safe little enclave they had shared in the desert.

After the bath, he put on the blue flannel pajamas he had bought the week before in Chinatown, then sat down at his desk and began composing a letter to his parents.

The warming sound of Brian's laughter drifted through the window as a new moon peeked from behind the clouds. Then came another man's laughter, less hearty than Brian's but just as sincere. Michael set his pen down and listened to enough dialogue to determine that the visitor was British, then returned to the task at hand.

Boris, the neighborhood cat, slunk along the window ledge, cruising for attention. When he spotted Michael, he stopped in his tracks, shimmied under the sill, and announced his arrival with a noise that sounded like a rusty hinge. Michael swung his chair away from the desk and prepared his lap for the inevitable. Boris kept his distance, though, rattling his tail like a saber as he loped about the room.

"O.K.," said Michael. "Be that way."

Boris creaked back at him.

"How old are you, anyway?"

Another creak.

"A hundred and forty-two? Not bad."

The tabby circled the room twice, then gazed up expectantly at the only human he could find.

"He's not here," said Michael. "There's nobody to spoil you rotten now."

Boris voiced his confusion.

"I know," said Michael, "but I'm fresh out of Tender Vittles. That wasn't my job, kiddo."

There were footsteps outside the door. Boris jerked his head, then shot out the window.

"Mouse?" It was Mary Ann.

"It's open," he said.

She slipped into the room, closing the door behind her. "I heard talking. I hope I didn't . . ."

"It was just Boris."

"Oh."

"I mean . . . I was talking to Boris."

She smiled. "Right."

"Sit down," he said.

She perched on the edge of the sofa. "We have this really delightful Englishman upstairs."

He nodded. "So I hear."

"Oh . . . we haven't been too . . . ?"

"No," he assured her. "It sounds nice."

"He's from the *Britannia*. He used to be a radio officer for the Queen."

"Used to be?"

"Well . . . it's a long story. The thing is . . . he needs a furnished apartment for a month, and he wants to swap with somebody from here. He's got a cute flat in Nottingham Gate . . . or something like that. Anyway, it's just sitting there waiting for somebody to come live in it."

"And?"

"Well . . . doesn't that sound perfect?"

"For me, you mean?"

"Sure! I'm sure Ned wouldn't mind if . . ."

"We're closed for a month," he said.

"So there you go! It *is* perfect. It's a ready-made vacation."

He said nothing, letting the idea sink in.

"Think of it, Mouse! England! God, I can hardly stand it."

"Yeah, but . . . it still takes money."

"For what? You can live as cheaply there as you can here."

"You're forgetting about air fare," he said.

Her shoulders drooped suddenly. "I thought you'd be *excited.*"

She looked so crestfallen that he got up and went to the sofa, kissing the top of her head. "I appreciate the thought. I really do."

She looked up with a wan smile. "Can you join us for a glass of wine?"

"Thanks," he answered, tugging at the lapels of his pajamas. "I was just about to crash and burn."

She rose and headed for the door. "Was Death Valley fun?"

"It was . . . peaceful," he said.

"Good. I'm glad."

"Night-night," he said.

He made himself some hot milk, then went to bed, sleeping soundly until noon the next day. After finishing his letter to his parents, he drove to the Castro and ate a late breakfast at the communal table at Welcome Home. When the rain began to let up a little, he wandered through the neighborhood, feeling strangely like a tourist on Mars.

Across the street, a man emerged from the Hibernia Bank.

His heart caught in his throat.

The man seemed to hesitate, turning left and right, revealing enough of his profile to banish the flimsy illusion.

Blond hair and chinos and a blue button-down shirt. How long would he live before those things stopped meaning Jon?

He crossed the intersection and walked along Eighteenth Street. In the days before the epidemic, the house next door to the Jaguar Store had been called the Check 'n Cruise. People had gone there to check their less-than-butch outer garments (not to mention their Gump's and Wilkes Bashford bags) prior to prowling the streets of the ghetto.

The Check 'n Cruise was gone now, and in its place had blossomed the Castro Country Club, a reading room and juice bar for men who wanted company without the alcohol and attitude of the bars. He sometimes repaired there after his stint at the AIDS switchboard.

Today, as he entered, an animated game of Scrabble was in progress. At the bar, two men in business suits were arguing about Joan Sutherland, while another couple rehashed the Forty-Niners' victory at the Super Bowl.

He found a seat away from the conversation and immersed himself in the latest issue of the *Advocate*. An ad for a jewelry company caught his eye:

It was too much. He growled and threw the magazine on the floor, attracting the attention of the Forty-Niners fans. He gave them a sheepish grin and left without further explanation, heading straight for his car.

When he got back to Barbary Lane, sunlight was streaming into the courtyard for the first time in weeks. Wisps of steam, like so many friendly ghosts, hovered above the courtyard as he passed through the lych-gate. He stopped long enough to savor the sweet, wet, ferny smell tingling in his nostrils.

A figure rose from behind a low hedge, startling him.

"Oh . . . Mrs. Madrigal."

The landlady wiped her hands on her paisley smock. "Isn't it a grand day?"

"It's about time," said Michael.

"Now, now," she scolded. "We knew it was coming. It was just a question of when." She looked about her on the ground. "Have you seen my trowel, dear?"

He scanned the area, then shook his head. "What are you planting?"

"Baby tears," she answered. "Why aren't you going to London?"

"Hey." She had pounced without warning.

"Never mind. I guess I'm being selfish. Still . . . it would have given me *such* vicarious thrills." She fussed delicately with a strand of hair at her temple. "Oh, well. Can't be helped."

These days, Mrs. Madrigal almost never tried to pull off her helpless-old-lady routine. Michael couldn't help smiling at the effort. "I hope Mary Ann also told you it was a question of finances?"

"She did."

"So?"

"I'm not as gullible as she is." The landlady found her trowel and slipped it into the pocket of her smock. Then she removed a pale yellow parchment envelope and handed it to Michael. "So I'm hereby eliminating it as an excuse. You'll just have to come up with another one."

He opened the envelope and removed a check for a thousand dollars. "Mrs. Madrigal . . . this is awfully sweet, but . . ."

"It isn't a bit sweet. It's a cold-blooded investment. I'm commissioning you to go to London and come back with some happy stories for us." She paused, but her great blue eyes remained fixed on him. "We need that from you, Michael."

There was nothing he could say.

"But money's not the reason, is it? Not really." She sat down on the bench at the end of the courtyard and patted the place next to her. "You haven't finished settling up with Jon yet."

Typically, she had lured him onto the appropriate set. He sat down less than ten feet away from the brass plaque that marked the spot where Jon's ashes had been buried. "I'm not sure I ever will," he said.

"You must," she replied. "What more do you want him to know?"

"What do you mean?"

"I mean . . . if we had him back with us right now . . . what would be your unfinished business?"

He thought for a while. "I'd ask him what he did with the keys to the tool chest."

Mrs. Madrigal smiled. "What else?"

"I'd tell him he was a jerk for needing to hang around with pissy queens."

"Go on."

"I'd tell him I'm sorry it took me so long to figure out what he meant to me. And I wish we'd taken that trip to Maui when he suggested it."

"Fine."

"And . . . I wore his good blazer while he was in the hospital and somebody burned a hole in the sleeve and I never told him about it . . . and I love him very much."

"He knows that already," said the landlady.

"I'd tell him again, then."

Mrs. Madrigal slapped her knees jauntily. "Does that about wrap it up?"

"More or less."

"Good. I'll take care of it."

He blinked at her, uncomprehending.

"He'll get your message, dear. I talk to him at least twice a week." She patted the bench again. "Right here." She leaned over and kissed him softly on the cheek. "Go to London, Michael. You're not going to lose him this time. He's a part of you forever."

He clung to her, tears streaming down his face.

"Listen to me, child." Now she was whispering directly into his ear. "I want you to run along the Thames in the moonlight . . . take off all your clothes and jump into the fountain at Trafalgar Square. I want you to . . . have a wild affair with a guard at Buckingham Palace."

He laughed, still holding tight to her.

"Will you take the old lady's money?" she asked.

All he could manage was a nod.

"Good. *Good.* Now run upstairs and tell Mary Ann to make all the arrangements."

He had reached the front door when she shouted her final instruction: "The toolbox keys are on a hook in the basement."

Fourteen

On the eve of Michael's departure, Mary Ann found herself on a vigil at the San Francisco Zoo, awaiting the birth of a polar bear. She and her crew had camped out for seven hours beside the concrete iceberg which Blubber, the expectant mother, was compelled to call home. As the eighth hour approached, so did a smiling Connie Bradshaw, hunched over from her own pregnancy like some noble beast of burden.

"Hi! They told me at the station I could find you here."

This was just what she needed. The Ghost of Cleveland Past. "Yeah," she said dully. "If it keeps up like this, it may be a permanent assignment."

Connie peered through the bars at Blubber's lair. "Where is she?"

"Back there." She pointed. "In her den. She's not real fond of the cameras."

"I guess not, poor thing. Who would be?"

Mary Ann shrugged. "Those women on the PBS specials seem to love it."

"Yuck." Connie mugged. "Screaming and yelling and sweating . . . then waving at the baby with that dippy expression on their face. Only people are that dumb."

"I'm sure Blubber agrees with you, but she hasn't got much of a choice. There are hearts to be warmed out there in the naked city."

Connie gazed wistfully at the iceberg, then turned back to Mary Ann. "Can you take a break and have a Diet Coke with me?"

Mary Ann hesitated.

"It won't take long," added Connie. "O.K.?"

"Sure," she replied, her curiosity getting the best of her. "Just for a little while, though. Blubber's looking close."

She told her cameraman where she would be, then joined Connie under a Cinzano umbrella near the snack bar. Her old high school chum had rearranged her face into a mask of sisterly concern. "I'll get right to the point, hon. Have you broken the news to Brian yet?"

Mary Ann was beginning to feel badgered. "No," she said flatly. "I haven't."

"Super." Connie beamed. "So far so good."

Mary Ann clenched her teeth. What the hell was so far so good about that?

"I've been really thinking about this," Connie added, "and I've got this terrific idea."

Ever since the time she had taken Mary Ann to singles night at the Marina Safeway, Connie and her terrific ideas had been nothing but trouble. "I don't know," said Mary Ann. "If it's about getting pregnant, I'd just as soon . . ."

"Don't you even wanna *hear* it?" Connie was crushed.

"Well . . . I appreciate your concern . . ."

"Hear me out, O.K.? Then I'll shut up. It's not as weird as you might think."

Mary Ann doubted that, but she murmured a reluctant O.K. and fortified herself with a sip of Diet Coke.

Connie seemed enormously relieved. "Remember my little brother Wally?"

Why was it that people from home always expected you to recall minutiae from fifteen years ago, things that weren't even that important at the time? "'Fraid not," she said.

"Yes you do."

"Connie . . . Cleveland was a long time ago."

"Yeah, but Wally used to deliver your paper. He delivered most of the papers on that side of Ridgemont."

The light dawned, however dim. A dorky kid with Dumbo ears and a bad habit of mangling the petunias with his Schwinn. "Yeah," she said. "Sure. Of course."

"Well, Wally's at UC med school now."

Mary Ann whistled. "Jesus."

"I know," Connie agreed. "Does that make you feel old or *what?* He's kind of a hunk too, if I do say so myself."

That was almost too much to imagine, but she let it go. She had a creepy feeling she already knew where this conversation was going to lead her. All she could do was pray that the polar bear would go into labor and rescue her from the embarrassment.

"Anyway, Wally and some of his friends make donations from time to time to this sperm bank in Oakland."

Right on the button.

"They're not exactly donations," Connie continued, "since they get paid for it. Not much. Just a little . . . you know . . . extra cash."

"Mad money."

"Right."

"Besides," Mary Ann deadpanned, "they're lying around the dorm all night with nothing to do . . ."

Connie's face fell. "O.K. I'm sorry. Forget it. I shouldn't have brought it up."

She should never have used irony on Connie Bradshaw. "Hey," she said, as gently as possible, "I appreciate the thought. I really do. It's just not for me, that's all. The people at St. Sebastian's suggested it, but . . . well . . ."

"I thought it would be so perfect," Connie lamented.

"I know."

"They have these three cold-storage vats at the sperm bank—one for known donors, one for unknowns, and an extra one in case the freezer craps out. Wally's stuff goes into the 'unknown' vat, but I thought maybe we could get his number or something . . . or get him moved into the 'known' vat . . . so you'd know what you were getting."

"It was a sweet thought. Really." Not so sweet was the vision looming hideously in her brain: a turkey baster brimming with the semen of her former paperboy.

"Plus," added Connie, still plugging away, "it seems like the perfect solution if you want to get pregnant and you don't want Brian to know that he's not the father. There wouldn't be any strings attached as far as Wally is concerned, and . . . well, everything would work out for everybody."

And the blessed event would be Connie's niece or nephew. It was touching to think that Connie might regard this arrangement—consciously or unconsciously— as a means of cementing a friendship that had never quite worked out. It was downright heartbreaking, in fact.

"Connie . . . I'd go to Wally in a second, if I thought I could handle artificial insemination."

"It's not all that complicated, you know. They send you to this fertility awareness class and teach you how to measure your dooflop, and you just *do* it. I mean, sperm is sperm, you know?"

"I know, Connie. It also comes with an attractive applicator."

"What?"

"Don't you see? I know it's easy. I know *lots* of people do it. I can see your point entirely. It's the artificial part that stops me cold." She lowered her voice to a vehement whisper. "I can't help it, Connie. I want to be fucked first."

Connie's jaw went slack. "You want Wally to *fuck* you?"

"*No!*" She proclaimed it so forcefully that a Chinese woman at the next table looked up from her chili dog. Modulating her voice, she added: "I meant that in a general sense. I want the baby to grow out of an act of love. Or . . . affection, at least. You can blame my mother for that. That's what she taught me, and that's what I'm stuck with."

"This is amazing," said Connie.

"What?"

"Well . . . I've seen you on TV. You look so *hip.*"

59

"Connie . . . it's *me*, Mary Ann. Remember? Vice-president of the Future Homemakers of America?"

"Yeah, but you've changed a lot."

"Not that much," said Mary Ann. "Believe me."

"Mary Ann! She's doin' it!" It was her cameraman, bearer of glad tidings. She sprang to her feet. "That's my cue."

Two minutes later, the wet cub plopped onto the concrete floor without so much as a tiny grunt from his mother.

"Animals have it so easy," said Connie, watching from the sidelines.

Mary Ann spent the rest of the afternoon editing footage at the station. As she headed home at twilight, the security guard in the lobby handed her a manila envelope. "A lady said to give you this."

"What kind of a lady?"

"A pregnant lady."

"Great."

She didn't open it until she had reached the Le Car, parked in an alleyway off Van Ness. Inside the envelope were two brochures with a note attached:

Mary Ann—Don't get mad, O.K.? I'm leaving you these cuz I thought they might explain things better than I did. Just between you and I, Wally was a little ticked when he found out I didn't give you some literature first. Let's get together real soon. Luff ya. Connie.

She couldn't decide what annoyed her more—Connie's chronic breeziness (a style she had picked up years before from inscribing *dozens* of Central High yearbooks) or the realization that Brian's sterility was now a topic of major concern to the entire Bradshaw family.

She began to read:

We believe that women have the right to control our own reproduction and in doing so, determine if, when and how to achieve pregnancy. Donor insemination is a process of introducing semen into the vaginal canal or cervix with a device for the purpose of fertilizing an egg and achieving pregnancy. Fresh or thawed-out frozen semen can be used.

Its safety and effectiveness have been well established. Currently in the U.S., 15–20,000 children a year are conceived by insemination. Since WWII, well over 300,000 children have been born as a result of this method, and since 1776, when the technique of freezing sperm was developed, over a million children have been . . .

Shuddering, she put down the brochure. Frozen sperm during the Revolutionary War? Where had *that* happened? Valley Forge? Brian had been right about one thing, at least; 1984 was almost here. Something had gone haywire if science had advanced to the point that babies could be made without sexual intimacy.

No. She couldn't do it.

If this was the future, she wasn't ready for it.

She would tell Brian the truth. They would go somewhere for the weekend. She would be gentle and loving and he would accept it. Maybe not at first, but eventually. He would *have* to accept it; there was no other way.

It was dark by the time she got home. As she fumbled for her key in the entrance alcove, she spotted yet another manila envelope, propped on the ledge above the buzzers. She was ready to scream when she realized it was addressed to Mouse. Taking it with her, she went upstairs and knocked on Mouse's door.

"Come in."

He was leaning over his sofa, arranging clothes in a suitcase. "Hi, Babycakes."

"Hi. Somebody left this at the front door." She laid the envelope on a chair.

He glanced at it, still packing. "Must be Ned's bon voyage package. He said he was dropping something by."

"Ah."

"Sit down," he said. "Talk to me."

She sat down, noticing another suitcase on the floor. "You're taking an awful lot for a month, aren't you?"

"Just this bag," he answered.

"What about that one?" She pointed to the suitcase on the floor.

"Oh." He grinned. "That's Simon's. He left it here a little while ago. He's having dinner down at Washington Square."

"I see."

He gave her an impish sideways glance. "Why didn't you tell me what a hunk he is?"

She shrugged, commanding herself not to blush. "You didn't ask."

"I was expecting one of those horse-faced dudes with big ears and crooked teeth. This guy looks like a skinnier version of Brian."

"You think so?"

"Now, don't tell me you didn't notice that."

"No," she replied. "Not really."

"Well, look again, woman."

"Are those jeans new?" she asked.

"These?" He held up the pair he was packing. "I got them today."

"They look black."

"They *are* black. All the rage. See?" He pretended to model them. "The Widow Fielding Goes to London."

She giggled. "You are the worst."

"Well . . . I figure they haven't got them there yet. I might be able to barter with them in an emergency."

"Sell your pants, you mean?"

"Sure." He folded the Levi's and placed them in the suitcase. "I remember when American kids used to pay their way across Europe that way."

"*Ages* ago, Mouse."

"Well . . ."

"When were you last in London?"

"Uh . . . late sixties."

"Late?"

"Nineteen sixty-seven."

"Right," she said. "And they called it Swinging London."

"O.K."

"And Twiggy was around."

He pretended to be shocked. "Twiggy is *still* around, and don't you forget it!"

"How old were you?"

"Sixteen," he replied. "It was sixteen years ago, and I was sixteen. Half my life ago." He turned and smiled at her. "I came out there, too."

"You *did?* You never told me that."

"Well . . . had my first sex, anyway."

"Whatever," she said.

"Does Brian get along well with Simon?" he asked.

"Wait a minute. I thought we were talking about London."

He patted a side pocket of the suitcase. "I already have my instructions."

"What?"

"Simon left a small tome about the operation of his apartment."

"Have you looked at it yet?" she asked.

"Nope. Don't want to. I want it to be a complete surprise."

That made sense to her.

"Well?" he asked. "Do they?"

"What?"

"Get along well together."

"Mouse . . . what is this?"

"Nothing," he shrugged. "I'm just curious."

She hesitated. "I don't know. They seem to like each other. They both have the hots for Theresa Cross."

Michael made a face. "Brian told you that?"

"He doesn't have to. I know how he is. He's got a sleazy streak in him a mile wide."

He grinned at some private movie. "Yeah . . . that figures. Any man who would make you wear leg warmers during sex . . ."

"Mouse . . ."

His languid grin remained.

"I should never have told you that. I knew you'd throw it back at me. Besides . . . he doesn't make me do it. I do it of my own accord."

He nodded solemnly. "I admire a woman who takes responsibility for her own sleaziness."

"That's the *last* juicy tidbit you get from me."

"Juicy tidbit? You told me it was a transcendental experience. You said it made you feel like one of the girls from *Fame.*"

She stomped into his kitchen. "I'm pouring myself some wine."

"Help yourself," he hollered back. "Pour me some, too."

She stood there for a moment in the light of his refrigerator, enjoying the afterglow of his teasing. She had loved this sentimental, funny, adorable man longer than she had loved Brian even, and it warmed her heart to realize they were getting back to normal again. Returning with two glasses of wine, she handed one to him and asked: "Aren't you going to open your package?"

He looked confused.

"The one from Ned," she added, pointing to it. She couldn't stand it when people didn't open things *immediately*.

"Oh." He set his wine down and reached for the envelope, tearing off the end. "And the winner *is* . . ." He peered down into it, then pulled out a note written on a card with a naked fireman on the front. " 'Don't do anything I wouldn't do. I'll miss you. Your buddy, Ned.' "

"That's sweet," she said.

He nodded, with a little smile.

"That's not all, is it?"

Another nod.

"Mouse . . . there's something in there."

"There is, huh?"

"I felt it moving around." She took the envelope from him and shook it over the sofa. Five foil-wrapped rubbers fell out. "Oops," she said.

Mouse just grinned at her. He didn't look particularly upset. "It's Ned's way of saying . . . you know . . . be careful and have a good time." He scooped them up in both hands. "Here . . . from me to you."

"What?" She was sure she was scarlet.

"C'mon. Take 'em. I'm celibate. You guys can use them more than I can."

"Uh . . . Mouse. Thanks just the same, O.K.?"

He looked at her for a moment, then dropped the rubbers back into the envelope. "Hooked on the pill, huh?"

She picked up her wine and downed it.

He sipped his slowly, peering at her over the rim. "Do I still get that ride to the airport?"

"Sure. You bet. What time?"

"Well . . . I guess we should leave no later than three-thirty. Just to be sure."

"Great." She pecked him on the cheek. "See you then."

When she got back to her own apartment, she found Brian washing the breakfast dishes. She leaned into his back and kissed his neck. "Mouse is so excited," she said.

"I don't blame him," he replied.

"Maybe we should do the same."

He dried his hands on a towel and turned around. "Go to London?"

She smiled at him. "Get out of town, at least."

"All right. Our savings account should get us as far as, say, Oakland."

She touched the tip of his nose. "*Exactly* what I had in mind."

"*Oakland?*"

"Sure. A weekend for two at the Claremont. All expenses paid."

"How come?"

She looked as cavalier as possible. "No reason."

"No. I meant: how come all expenses are paid?"

"Oh. I did a feature on them last month. It's a freebie."

"Not bad."

"I know. Jacuzzi, sauna . . . baking by the pool. Nothing to pack but swimming suits and something for the dining room."

"And leg warmers."

"And leg warmers," she echoed. "*Sold!* To the gentleman with the hard-on."

Fifteen

When she returned from the airport the next day, she found Simon sitting on the bench in the courtyard. He gave her a jaunty little wave as she passed through the lych-gate. "You look like you belong there," she said.

He smiled at her. "It certainly feels that way."

"Well . . ." She made a graceless gesture in the general direction of Daly City. "Mouse is off in the wild blue yonder." It sounded as lame as the gesture must have looked.

Simon pointed to the brass plaque in the garden. "Is this his lover?"

She nodded.

"His ashes?"

Another nod.

He shook his head slowly. "No wonder he wanted to get away."

She couldn't bear to think about Jon just now. "Simon . . . let me know if I can . . . you know . . . help with anything."

"Thank you," he said. "You've been a great help already."

"Well, hey . . . no problem . . ." She was *backing* toward the door, she realized, like some awkward teenager.

"Do you have a moment?" he asked, leaning toward her slightly.

"Sure."

"Wonderful. Come sit, then."

She joined him on the bench. "You're lucky," she said. "You're getting some of our sunshine. The poor Queen missed it completely."

He gave her a lazy smile. "I'm sure this irony isn't lost on Her Majesty."

She laughed uneasily. What did he mean by *that*? That the Queen had personal knowledge of his escapade? That she was envious of irresponsibility? "Is the Queen a nice person?" she asked.

A deep chuckle. "The Queen is a lovely person."

"Have you ever actually talked to her?"

"Oh . . . four or five times at the most."

"She doesn't seem to smile very much."

He shrugged. "Smiling is her job. When smiling is one's job, one is very circumspect about the way one doles it out. Otherwise, it means nothing."

"That's very well put," she said.

Another half-lidded smile. "It's our regulation answer."

"Do you have to be . . . like . . . a lord or something to be an officer on the *Britannia*?"

"Not at all."

"Are you, though?"

His laughter was hearty but not malicious. "You Americans just jump right in there, don't you?"

She was enough of a Californian to resent being called an American. "Well, I think it's only natural to wonder if . . ." Her search for the right words proved futile. She *was* pumping him, and it showed.

Simon leaped gallantly into the silence. "The only titled member of my immediate family is my aunt, my mother's sister, a grotty old duchess by marriage who wears waders and messes about in boats."

"The Queen does that," she put in.

"Not with *this* duchess, I assure you."

She laughed without knowing exactly why. "And your mother and father?"

"They're both dead," he replied evenly.

"Oh, I'm . . ."

"My mother was an actress in the West End. My father was a barrister who moved from Leeds to London after he met my mother. What about yours?"

She was thrown for an instant. "Oh . . . well, my father runs an electrical shop, and my mother is a housewife. They live in Cleveland." She reminded herself of a contestant on *Family Feud*.

"Cleveland . . . Indiana, is it?"

"Ohio."

He nodded. "They must be very proud of you."

"I guess they are," she said. "They don't see me on TV, of course, since I'm . . . you know . . . local. But I send them copies of *TV Guide* when I'm in it. That sort of thing. Your parents must've been young when they died."

"Mmm. Very. I was still at Cambridge." He anticipated her next question, looking faintly amused by her curiosity. "It was an automobile accident. On the M-One. Do you know the M-One?"

"A highway, right?"

"Right."

"Was your mother a good actress?"

He seemed to like that question. "As a matter of fact, I've wondered about that lately. I thought she was marvelous at the time. She was funny. And very beautiful."

"That makes sense," she said.

He passed over the ambiguous compliment. "When I was fourteen, she introduced me to Diana Rigg backstage at the Haymarket. I thought that was the loveliest thing any mother could do for her son."

"I can see how you would," she smiled.

A long silence followed, during which she remembered the joint in her purse. "I almost forgot," she told Simon. "You haven't sampled the Queen Mother yet."

"I beg your pardon?"

She giggled, holding up the joint. "Mrs. Madrigal's primo homegrown."

"Ah."

She lit the joint, took a toke, and handed it to him. "I rolled a couple for the trip to the airport. Mouse was feeling no pain when he took off."

He didn't respond, holding the smoke in his lungs.

She watched him, tickled by his dignity during the performance of this near-ridiculous ritual.

"Very tasty," he said at last.

"Mmm. Isn't it?"

"Do you still want that story?"

For a moment, she thought he was accusing her of weakening his resistance with dope. Then she realized the question was in earnest. "Do you mean . . . ?"

"The one about me. 'Queen's Officer Jumps Ship in Frisco.' "

She smiled. "I think I'd handle it a little more tastefully than that."

He handed the joint back to her. "Do you want to?"

She hesitated. "Simon, I meant it when I said I wouldn't do anything if . . ."

"I know that. You've been perfectly honorable." He retrieved the joint

66

and took another toke off it. "I've given this some thought, Mary Ann. Frankly . . . I don't see what harm it would do. If you're still game, that is."

She said nothing, wondering about his motives.

"Is it what you want?" he asked quietly.

She nodded. "Yes."

He smiled. "Then it's what *I* want."

"Simon . . ."

"I reserve the right to edit content, of course. I don't want to embarrass anyone."

"Of course not."

Another smile, a little warmer than the last. "Wonderful. It's settled, then?"

"You bet."

He returned the joint. "When shall we start?"

Brian materialized under the lych-gate, panting heavily in shorts and a tank top. Simon wasn't facing the gate, but he detected the change in her expression and turned around. "Oh . . . hello there."

"'Lo," said Brian, running in place.

"We're trying out the new weed," she offered cheerfully.

"I see." He was shaking out his arms now, like a marionette in a high wind.

"Do you run regularly?" asked Simon.

"Fair amount," Brian answered. He wasn't wasting an ounce of energy on friendliness.

"You must show me where you do it," said Simon. "I've been frightfully remiss in my own regimen."

"Sure thing," said Brian, loping past them into the house.

Simon turned to her with a rueful little smile.

"It isn't you," she said.

"I hope not."

"He's been . . . I don't know . . . not himself lately."

"Mmm."

The joint had gone out, so she lit it again and offered it to Simon. He shook his head. She took a short drag and extinguished it. "So . . . you're a runner, huh?"

He nodded. "Second generation."

"Really?"

"My father and I both ran at Cambridge."

"How *Chariots of Fire*," she said.

He laughed. "We weren't quite that competitive. It was mostly to keep fit. Ill health was considered very poor form in the Bardill family."

"Was?"

"Well." His eyes were twinkling again. "There's not that much left of the family, is there?"

67

Sixteen

The rain seemed to follow Michael to London. It clattered like spilled gravel against the great vaulting roof of Victoria Station as he grabbed his suitcase and scrambled toward the first available black cab. His driver, a sixtyish man the color of corned beef, touched the bill of his cap.

"Where to, mate?"

"Uh . . . Nottingham Gate."

"Eh?"

"Nottingham Gate." He said it with more authority this time.

"Sorry, mate. No such place. Now, there's a Notting *Hill* Gate. . . ."

"The address is Forty-four Colville Crescent."

The driver nodded. "That's Notting Hill Gate."

"Great," said Michael, sinking down into burnished leather. "Thank God for that."

The flight had been a living nightmare. Despite the effects of the Queen Mother dope and the ministrations of a chummy gay flight attendant, he had been completely unable to sleep. When he arrived at Gatwick Airport, cotton-mouthed and cranky, he was detained for almost two hours while customs officials ransacked the luggage of three hundred African nationals who had landed at the same time.

After losing another hour as he waited to change money, he had boarded a packed London-bound shuttle train, where he shared a litter-strewn compartment with a brassy couple from Texarkana who insisted on talking about the Forty-Niners, despite his fearless display of indifference to the subject.

His driver glanced toward the back seat. "A Yank, eh?"

"Uh . . . right."

"See what we done to them Argies?"

RGs? A soccer team, maybe? "Oh, yeah . . . that was somethin'."

A wheezy chuckle. "And we did it without the help of your bloody President."

It wasn't sports, then. It was politics.

"Mind you, you Yanks always come in late on the big wars. You come in late, or you don't come at all. Nothin' personal."

The light dawned. The Falklands war. The Argies were Argentines. Americans didn't call them that, because Americans had never cared. You had to start killing people before you took the trouble to give them nicknames. Japs, Krauts,

Commies, Gooks . . . Argies. He had no intention of prolonging the war by arguing with this man. "I like your battle hymn," he said.

"Eh?" The driver looked at him as if he were crazy.

" 'Don't Cry for Me, Argentina.' Isn't that what the troops sang, or something?"

The driver grunted, apparently convinced that Michael *was* crazy. What did a bloody *song* have to do with anything? He stopped talking altogether, and Michael breathed a secret sigh of relief as the cab sped past the pale green blur of Hyde Park.

He had been away from this city for sixteen years, the longest time he'd been away from any spot on earth. He had lost his innocence here—or, more accurately, found it—at a time when mod was in flower and the streets were swarming with legions of white-lipped, black-lashed "birds." He had met a corduroy-clad bricklayer on Hampstead Heath and gone home with him and learned in an instant just how simple and comforting and beautiful real life could actually be.

The bricklayer had resembled a younger, leaner Oliver Reed, and Michael could recall every detail of that distant afternoon: the statue of David next to his bed, the brown sugar crystals he used in his coffee, the physique magazines he left lying around where anyone could see them, the silken feel of his hairless scrotum. Your first stranger, it seemed, is the one you remember for the rest of your life.

Where was he now? How old would he be? Forty-five? Fifty?

The cab veered left at Marble Arch, a landmark he recognized, then they appeared to follow the Bayswater Road along the edge of a large public garden. Which one? He couldn't remember. He was punch-drunk with fatigue and depressed by the rain, so he seized upon passing English icons to bolster his morale:

A shiny red mailbox.

A zebra crossing like the one on the *Abbey Road* album.

A pub sign banging in the wind.

The game became tougher when the cab moved into a region of plastic Pizza Huts and tawdry ethnic restaurants. It wasn't an unpleasant district, really, just surprisingly un-English—more akin to the Haight-Ashbury than anything he had experienced during his earlier visit.

Then the landscape became residential again. He caught glimpses of tree-lined streets and oversized Victorian row houses with crumbling plaster facades. Black children romped in the rain beside a yellow brick wall on which someone had spray-painted: STUFF THE ROYAL WEDDING.

He spotted a street sign that said COLVILLE. "Isn't this it?" he asked the driver.

"That's Colville Terrace, mate. You want the Crescent. It's just up the way a bit."

Three minutes later, the cab came to a stop. Michael peered out the window with mounting dread. "Is this it?" he asked.

The driver looked peeved. "You wanted Number Forty-four, didn't you?"

"Right."

"Then that's it, mate."

Michael checked the meter (a modern digital one that looked odd in the classic cab) and handed the driver a five-pound note with instructions to keep the change. He was overtipping, but he wanted to prove that a man who knew nothing about wars and streets could be generous just the same.

The driver thanked him and drove off.

Michael stood on the street and gaped at Simon's house. Its plaster facade, apparently a victim of dry rot, was riddled with huge leprous scabs which had fallen away completely in places to expose the nineteenth-century brick beneath. For some reason, this disfigurement went straight to the pit of his stomach, like bone glimpsed through a bloodless wound.

He dismissed a flickering hope that there might really be a Nottingham Gate and headed past overturned garbage cans (dust bins, the English insisted on calling them) to the front door of the three-story building. His dread became palpable when he found the name BARDILL printed on a card by the door buzzers.

He set his suitcase by the door, found the designated key, and wiggled it into the lock. A dark corridor confronted him. He located the light switch—a circular push thing—on a water-stained wall papered with purple roses. The door to Simon's ground-floor flat was at the end of the corridor on the right. By the time he had found the right key and slipped it into an obstinate lock, he was engulfed in darkness so complete that he thought for a moment he'd gone blind.

The light switch. Of course. It was on a timer. He recalled this sensible oddity of British engineering from his last visit. It had charmed him at the time, like electric towel warmers and teakettles that shut off automatically as soon as they whistled.

He turned the knob and pushed against the door with his shoulder, causing light to spill into the corridor from Simon's flat. A vile odor, like the halitosis of an old dog, rolled over him in waves. He held his breath and lunged for the nearest window, cracking it enough to let in a gush of rain-scented air.

As Simon had promised, the living room had fourteen-foot ceilings, which did lend it a certain aura of seedy elegance. *Tatty* was the word he had used, and that was a fair enough description for the lumpy, junkshop furniture grouped around the room's nonfunctioning fireplace. The pale green walls were dotted with tin engravings from Victorian times, the only visible concession to interior decoration. Simon's stereo and a stack of records completed the grim tableau.

Michael followed a narrow hallway in search of the bedroom. Once there, he dropped his suitcase and sank numbly to the edge of the bed, ordering himself not to jump to conclusions. He was bone tired from the ten-hour flight, so his mounting despair could well be a function of fatigue, not to mention the airlines Danish that flopped about in his stomach like a dying rodent.

It was noon now, he supposed. What he needed was a hot bath and a good sleep. When he awoke, the old wonderment would be back again, bringing with it his invaluable capacity for finding quaintness in hardship. What had he expected, anyway? Some sanitized, Disney-like version of English charm?

Yes, he decided, when he saw the bathroom. He had expected something along the lines of the cozy town house in *101 Dalmatians*. Something with roses in the garden and mellow paneling and—*yes*, goddamnit—towel warmers in the bathroom. What he found instead was a cramped room smelling of stale pee and painted to simulate blue sky and clouds. Like the ceiling of an organic bakery in Berkeley.

The tub had legs, which scored a few points for quaintness, but the hot water ran out as soon as it reached the top of his knees. He lay there immobile, racked with disillusionment, and chastised himself for ever agreeing to swap apartments with a heterosexual he didn't know.

Moments later, he collapsed into bed, but he didn't fall asleep for at least an hour. As he finally drifted off, he had a vague impression of rain pounding on the packed earth of his "garden" and another, more rhythmic sound. Was it . . . drums?

It was dark when he awoke. He stumbled about in search of a light switch, then went into the kitchen to take stock of the stuff he would need. There was no food, of course—except for some moldy noodles and a can of herring—and eating utensils were in sparse supply.

For starters, he would buy some cereal and milk, some bread and peanut butter. But that would be tomorrow. Tonight, he would find a neighborhood pub that served Scotch eggs and Cornish pasties and get just as shit-faced as the situation required.

Returning to the bedroom, he decided to make things official by unpacking his suitcase. He was almost done when he remembered the note from Simon stashed in the side pocket. He sat down on the bed and read it:

Michael—

I thought you might be able to use a few words of advice about the many enigmas of 44 Colville Crescent: The hot water (or lack thereof) is a bit of a nuisance, I'm afraid. You'll find the tank in the nook between the lav and the kitchen, should you have any serious problems with it. (Truly serious problems should be referred to Mr. Nigel Pearl, a plumber in Shepherd's Bush. His number is posted on the door of the fridge.)

The automatic turn-off whatsit on the stereo does not turn off automatically. The central heating has been shut off for the season; I doubt you'll need it. There's an extra duvet in the bottom drawer of the cupboard in the bedroom. The bed, as you must have noticed by now, is propped up at one corner by my vast collection of *Tatlers*, which is quite the best place for them to be.

For basic foodstuffs, I recommend Europa Foods in Notting Hill Gate. For toiletries, try Boots the Chemist (a "drug store" in your quaint colonial parlance). For real drugs, try one of the black gentlemen in All Saints Road, but do not, under any circumstances, go there at night. Their grass is no match for Humboldt County's finest, but it does the job nicely if you lace it with hashish.

The gas cooker in the kitchen shouldn't present any problems. Trash is kept under the sink-basin, as is furniture polish, buckets, dustpan, etc. There is also a stopcock for the water. If there is ever any kind of flood, just turn that off (clockwise) and the water supply is blocked.

The launderette (service-wash) and dry cleaners are round the corner at the junction of Westbourne Grove and Ledbury Road. The Electric Cinema in Portobello Road has good old movies, if you like things like *Glen or Glenda* (my personal favorite) and Jessie Matthews retrospectives.

A certain Miss Treves (Nanny Treves to me) will be popping in from time to time to keep an eye on things. Please introduce yourself and tell her you are a friend of mine. When she asks you about my ship-jumping caper (and she will, I assure you), feel free to tell her what you know and say I'll be home just after Easter. I'll give her the gory details in a letter. Miss Treves is a manicurist now, but she was my nanny for many years. She's fretted over me ever since I got away from her in the British Museum (I was six), so she's likely to be a bit distraught. That's all you need to know about her except the obvious, which I'm sure you'll handle with your usual grace and gallantry. London is yours.

Simon

The note, rendered on flimsy blue paper in a spidery handwriting, gave Michael the soothing sensation of another human presence in the apartment with him. He could almost hear Simon's voice as he read it. When you came right down to it, the place wasn't *that* awful, he decided. All he really needed was a base camp from which to explore the city.

But what was the "obvious" thing he was soon to discover about Simon's former nanny?

And what the hell was a duvet?

To answer the simpler question, he checked the contents of the bottom drawer of the bedroom cupboard. There he found a threadbare quilt, faded from many washings. He held it against his cheek for a moment, like a housewife in a fabric softener commercial, feeling a rush of inexplicable tenderness toward this common household item. So what if the heat didn't work? He had his duvet to keep him warm.

He finished his unpacking, took inventory of his strange new money, and headed out into the night. It was roughly nine o'clock. The rain had stopped, but the fruit stalls in Portobello Road—empty and skeletal—were still beaded with moisture. As he left Colville Crescent and entered Colville Terrace, a corner pub beckoned him with yellow lights and the voice of Boy George.

Inside, he ordered a cider, the alcoholic English variety that had served him so well as a teenager in Hampstead. The other patrons were decidedly working-class. Two pudding-faced men in tweed caps argued jovially at the bar, while a stately Rastafarian in dreadlocks nursed a dark ale at a table near the video games.

His cider was gone in a flash, so he ordered a second one to wash down a couple of Scotch eggs. By the time he had quaffed his third, he was winking playfully at a plump woman who sat across from him under a gilt-lettered mirror. She was well past forty and her makeup had been applied with a trowel, but there was something almost valiant about her cheerfulness as she drank alone, jiggling her large calves to the beat of "Abracadabra." She reminded him of one of those jolly barflies from *Andy Capp*.

He paid up at the bar and ordered an ale to be sent to the lady's table. Then, brimming with goodwill, he gave one last wink to his brave sister and stumbled out into the street to make his peace with London.

Seventeen

The lunchtime mob at Perry's had been even rowdier than usual, but Brian managed to cope with it by reminding himself that his weekend getaway to Oakland was less than four hours away. He was returning an order for a picky diner ("Surely you don't call that rare?") when Jerry of the Jordache Look sidled up to him with a greasy smirk on his face.

"Your wife is at my station, Hawkins."

"Make sure the goddamn thing is bleeding," Brian told the cook.

"You hear me, Hawkins?"

"I heard you. Tell her I'll be out in a minute." He checked two plates to see if they matched his orders, then shouted over his shoulder at the departing Jerry. "Tell her I'm up to my ass in customers."

"Don't worry," Jerry yelled back. "She's up to her ass in Englishmen."

He was still fuming over the remark when he stopped by Mary Ann's table ten minutes later. As reported, Simon was with her. She was autographing a menu for a fat woman at the next table, so she didn't notice him until Simon signaled her by clearing his throat.

"Oh, hi. Is this a bad time?"

"Busy," he replied. "I really can't talk."

"No problem." She gave him her secret Be Cool smile. "I just wanted Simon to see the place."

He addressed the lieutenant. "So what do you think?"

"It's . . . very jolly."

He nodded. "Like a Japanese subway."

Mary Ann and the lieutenant both laughed, but not much. She looked strangely ill-at-ease, and he was beginning to think she had every reason to be. What the fuck was she doing, anyway, bringing this guy here?

He turned to her. "Are we still on for tonight?"

"Of course."

"My wife breaks dates," he told Simon.

"Now wait just a damn minute!" she piped.

"There's always a good reason, of course. Earthquakes, queens, polar bears . . ."

"Excuse me . . ." The fat woman was back, this time tugging on Simon's arm. "I got so excited I completely forgot to get your autograph too."

Simon looked grossly uncomfortable. "Really, madam, that's awfully kind of you, but I don't see what possible . . ."

"Oh, *please*. . . . My daughter will be livid if I don't bring her some proof that I met you!"

The lieutenant cast an apologetic glance at Mary Ann, then scrawled his name hastily across the menu. His face was bright red.

"Oh, thank you." The woman's upper lip was sweating as she added in a stage whisper: "My daughter is just gaga over men with hairy chests." Giggling to herself, she waddled back to her seat.

Simon shook his head slowly.

"The price of exposure," said Mary Ann.

"What does she have?" Brian couldn't help asking. "X-ray vision?"

Mary Ann laughed uneasily. "I did a little profile on Simon that aired this morning."

"Ghastly," mugged the lieutenant.

"With your shirt off?" asked Brian.

"Well . . ."

"Just for a jogging segment," Mary Ann explained. "We needed footage for a voice-over."

Brian became her echo. "Footage for a voice-over. That makes sense. Well . . ." He backed away from the table. "I think they need me in the Back Forty."

Moments later, as he'd expected, she cornered him in the kitchen. "O.K. Why are you bent out of shape?"

He stepped out of the way of another waiter. "It'll have to wait. This is our busiest time."

"I did a little profile on the guy," she whispered. "Why should that freak you out?"

"It didn't freak me out. It . . . surprised me, that's all. You said he didn't want to be on TV."

She shrugged. "So I talked him into it."

"Right. And made him a beefcake star in the bargain."

"Oh, *c'mon*, Brian." She ducked as Jerry sped by with a tray. "What if I did? Hey . . . I did that story on the Tom Selleck look-alike contest and you didn't say a word."

He leaned forward and answered in an angry whisper. "The goddamn Tom Selleck look-alike wasn't living in our fucking house!"

She shook her head. "I can't believe you're threatened by this."

Her sanctimoniously modern tone annoyed the hell out of him. "I'd just like to know why you came *here* to celebrate your big media coup."

"Brian . . ."

"Just . . . go. It's no big deal."

"Brian, listen to me. I brought him here because I want you guys to be friends. I want the three of us to be friends. I just thought it would be fun if . . ."

"O.K., O.K."

She gave him a cautious smile, sensing the passage of his anger. "My timing was rotten, I guess. I'm sorry about that. Want me to pick up your laundry?"

He shook his head.

"I'll be home packing, if you need me." She kissed him on the cheek and walked out of the kitchen. When he returned to the front room three minutes later, she and Simon had already gone.

Back in the kitchen, Jerry was waiting for him. "Your wife's friend is a big tipper."

"He's my friend too," he answered.

"Really?" Jerry's lip curled.

"Yes, *really*, asshole."

Jerry nodded slowly. "Well . . . it's convenient, at least."

"What the hell do you mean by that?"

A surly shrug. "Look, man . . . I only know what I saw."

"Meaning?"

"Well . . . the guy bears a certain resemblance to you, that's all."

"So?"

"So . . . nothing." He walked away muttering the rest of it. "If the lady wants a matched set, it's none of my . . ."

He was cut short when Brian grabbed him by his collar, spun him around and rammed him against the wall.

"Watch it," said Jerry. "You know what Perry said. Do that in here and you're out on your ass."

Brian hesitated. "A very good point."

He secured a firmer hold on Jerry's collar, dragged him into the restaurant, and let fly with a right hook that sent his tormentor hurtling backward into a table

75

full of empty plastic hamburger baskets. The table overturned, dumping Jerry on the floor. Customers scattered. A woman screamed. The fat lady with the autographed menu stood slack-mouthed at the cash register. Brian strode up to her, took the menu from her hands, signed his name with the ballpoint in his pocket, returned the menu, and walked out the door without looking back.

He didn't break stride until he had reached the top of Russian Hill, six or seven blocks away. His heart was pounding like crazy as he stopped for a moment outside Swensen's Ice Cream and considered his next move. He decided to maintain a normal pace for the last block or so. If his boss had already called, it would only increase his humiliation to arrive home out of breath.

When he got there, ten minutes later, Mary Ann was preoccupied with their escape to the Claremont. She was on her hands and knees in the bathroom, combing the cabinet under the sink for last year's Coppertone.

"I'm sure we can buy some there," he said.

"I know, but this was my number and everything."

"They'll have your number."

She stood up, brushing off her hands. "Aren't you off work early?"

He faked her with a smile. "They took mercy on me. I told them we needed to beat the Friday traffic."

"Perfect. Let's do it." She walked briskly into the bedroom; he followed. "You won't believe it," she said, "but I crammed us both into one suitcase."

"Great." He edged closer to the telephone, ready to grab it.

"I packed your sunglasses with the green lenses. I wasn't sure if those were . . ."

"They'll do fine," he said.

"Well, if you want the others . . ."

He hoisted the suitcase. "I want to go."

They had very little conversation until the Le Car reached the East Bay. "You know," said Mary Ann, keeping her eyes on the freeway, "I think Simon was hurt by your abruptness this afternoon."

He hesitated before answering. "Then . . . I'll apologize to him."

"Will you?" She glanced at him hopefully.

He nodded. "The minute we get back."

"Well . . . whenever. He likes you a lot, Brian."

"Good. I've got nothing against him."

She reached over and rubbed his thigh. "Good."

Minutes later, the Claremont materialized on the green hillside above them. "Isn't it wonderful?" gushed Mary Ann. "It turns seventy this year."

"It's a little too white," he replied.

"Well . . . tough titty."

"You know what I mean." He grinned. "It looks like a sanatorium in Switzerland. Sanitarium. Which is it?"

76

"Huh?"

"C'mon. One is for crazy people; the other is for face-lifts and stuff."

She shook her head. "They both mean the same thing."

"Nah."

She looked out the window. "Just drive," she said.

When they reached the hotel, they left the Le Car with the doorman and went straight to their room. It was sunny and spacious and overlooked the tennis courts. They smoked a joint and changed into their swimming suits, saying almost nothing for five minutes. Then they headed down to the Jacuzzi adjoining the swimming pool, where the sunshine and the dope and the jet of warm water pulsing at his back lulled him into the gentlest of reveries. The catastrophe at the restaurant seemed like a bad dream.

Mary Ann submerged herself completely, then rose like a naiad and gazed up at the old hotel. "Pink," she said finally. "No, *peach*."

He thought he had missed something. "What?"

"The color they should paint it."

He looked up at the hotel before turning to smile at her.

She returned the smile, then grazed his calf with the side of her foot.

"You know what?" he said.

"What?"

"I don't like anybody as much as I like you."

She skipped a beat before replying. "Then why don't you tell me the truth?"

The look on her face said it all. "You got a call?" he asked.

She nodded.

"From Perry?"

Another nod.

"Did he can me?"

"Brian . . . you broke the guy's jaw. They could just as easily have had you arrested."

He thought about that but said nothing.

"They took him to St. Sebastian's. They had to wire his jaw."

He nodded.

"What was it this time?" she said.

He had no intention of adding jealousy to his list of cardinal sins. "It doesn't matter," he said.

"Swell. Terrific."

"Look . . . he made another crack about a gay customer. He told an AIDS joke. I didn't mean to hit him that hard. He'd been spoiling for it all day. . . ."

"Why didn't you tell me about it?"

He shrugged. "I was going to. I didn't want to fuck up our weekend before it started."

She stood there blinking at him.

He still wasn't sure, so he asked again: "They canned me, huh?"

"Yes."

"I'm sorry you had to be there to catch the flak."

"He was nice about it," she said.

A small boy and his father, both brilliantly redheaded, trotted past his field of vision on their way to the locker rooms. The boy tripped on the laces of his Keds, and the father stopped to tie them for him. The tableau cut Brian to the quick, underscoring everything that was missing from his life.

"Earth to Brian, earth to Brian." Mary Ann coaxed him back into the here and now with a bemused smile.

"I'm sorry," he said. "What can I tell you?"

"I don't want you to be sorry. I want you to tell me the truth. Jesus, Brian . . . if we can't talk to each other, who can we talk to?"

"You're right." He nodded, feeling the weight of his guilt begin to lift.

"It's not just you," she said.

"What do you mean?"

"Well . . . I'm just as bad about that sometimes."

"About what?" he asked.

"You know . . . telling the whole truth. I gloss over things because I'm afraid of . . . damaging what we have . . . because I don't want to lose you."

He had never known her to lie, and he was touched by this unlikely confession. She wasn't explaining her own motivation so much as letting him know that she understood his. He cupped his hand against her wet cheek and smiled at her. She stuck her tongue out at him, ducked under the water, and goosed him. The crisis had passed.

He noticed that Mary Ann drank a little more wine than usual at dinner, but he matched her glass for glass. By the time their raspberries and cream had arrived, they were both just a couple of silly grins hovering in the candlelight. A gut instinct told him this was the moment to open Topic A again.

"I hated that job, you know."

She reached over and stroked the hair on the back of his hand. "I know."

"Sooner or later I would've quit anyway, and this way . . . wasn't half bad."

She waited awhile before saying anything. "I'm kinda sorry I missed it, actually. It didn't look dumb, did it?"

He shook his head.

"Heroic?"

He tilted his hand from side to side to indicate something in between. She laughed. "And now," he said softly, "I have all this time on my hands."

Her smile became a photograph of a smile. She knew exactly what he was saying.

"You said to tell the truth," he said.

She nodded. Her smile had disappeared.

"The way I see it, John Lennon was a househusband, and he did all right . . . and I bet he spent a lot more time with that kid than Yoko ever did. . . ."

"Brian . . ."

"I'm not saying you wouldn't love the kid or anything. I just mean you wouldn't have to be as involved with it as I would be. Hell, women bore the brunt of that for centuries. There's no reason we can't make it work the other way around. Don't you see? Wouldn't it be great to have this little person around who's . . . a mixture of you and me?"

Her face was unreadable as she pushed back her chair and dropped her napkin on the table. Was she pissed? Did she think he had gotten himself fired to force her into this position? "What about our raspberries?" he asked.

"I'm not hungry," she replied.

"Are you . . . upset?"

"No." She cast her eyes at the neighboring tables. "I brought us here to tell you something, but I don't want to do it here."

"O.K. Fine." He got up. "What about the check?"

"It's on the tab," she said.

They went back to their room, where she brushed her teeth and told him to put on his windbreaker.

"Where are we going?" he asked.

"You'll see," she said.

After slipping into one of his old Pendleton shirts, she produced a large brass key and opened the door leading to the suite above theirs in the tower. They passed through this space, climbing still another stairway in the semidarkness.

She flung open the last door with a flourish. They had reached a tiny, open-air observation deck at the summit of the tower. Before them stretched the entire Bay Area from San Mateo to Marin, ten thousand electric constellations glimmering beneath a purple sky.

She moved to the edge of the parapet. "This should do nicely."

He joined her. "For what?"

"Just be quiet now. You'll screw up the ritual." She unbuttoned the pocket of the Pendleton and removed a pink plastic case roughly the size of a compact. She held it up like a sacred talisman. "Farewell, little Ortho-Novums. Mama doesn't want you anymore."

In a flash, he realized what she was doing. "Jesus, you dizzy . . ."

"Shh . . ." Her arm swung forward in an arc, launching the pills into the night, a tiny pink spaceship bound for the stars. She cupped her hands around her mouth and shouted: "Did you see that, God? *Do you read me?*"

He threw back his head and roared with joy.

"You approve?" She was smiling into the wind, looking more beautiful than he had ever seen her.

"I don't deserve you," he said.

"The hell you don't." She took his hand and pulled him toward the stairway. "C'mon, turkey, let's go make babies."

Eighteen

Michael had always regarded jet lag as an affectation of the rich, but his first three days in London changed his mind about that forever. He awoke without fail at the magic hour of three o'clock—sometimes in the morning, sometimes in the afternoon. His disorientation was heightened by the fact that he found himself in a house where the telephone never rang and the drums never stopped.

The drums were actually next door, but their basic rhythms were easily audible at dawn, when he invariably lay in four inches of lukewarm water and watched the cold, gray light of another rainy day creep across the bogus blue sky of his bathroom ceiling.

In search of a routine, he touched base with his launderette, his post office, his nearest market. Then he trekked into other parts of town to check out familiar haunts from bygone times: a rowdy pub in Wapping called the Prospect of Whitby (more touristy than he had remembered), Carnaby Street (once mod and cheesy, now punk and cheesy), the charming old cemetery in Highgate where Karl Marx was buried (still charming, still buried).

When the skies cleared on the third afternoon, he ambled through Kensington and Chelsea to the river, then followed the Embankment to Cleopatra's Needle. As a sixteen-year-old, he had been intrigued by the Egyptian obelisk because the bronze lions flanking it—when viewed from a certain angle—had strongly suggested erect cocks. True, almost everything had suggested that when he was sixteen.

He left the river, mildly disenchanted by his reunion with the lions, and threaded his way through the streets in the general direction of Trafalgar Square. For reasons of economy, or so he told himself, he ate lunch at a McDonald's near the Charing Cross tube station, feeling wretchedly American about it until the man in front of him ordered "a strawbry shike to tike away."

Arriving in Piccadilly Circus, he bought a copy of *Gay News* and perused it amidst a crowd of German backpackers assembled at the foot of the Eros statue. Judging from the classified ads, gay Englishmen were perpetually searching for attractive "uncles" (daddies) with "stashes" (mustaches), who were "non-scene" (never in bars) and "non-camp" (butch). A surprisingly large number of advertisers made a point of saying that they owned homes and cars. On the women's news front, a group of North London lesbians was organizing a Saturday jog to the tomb of Radclyffe Hall, and everyone was looking forward to Sappho Disco Night at the Goat in Boots, Drummond Street.

Back at Colville Crescent, he did his best to rid the bathroom of its stench by anointing the ratty carpet with a concentrated room deodorant he had found at Boots the Chemist. (In some ways, English drugstores were the most unsettling institutions of all. The boxes and bottles looked pretty much like the ones in the States, but the names had been changed to protect God-knows-whom. Was Anadin the same thing as Anacin? Did it matter?) He shook the little amber bottle vigorously, releasing a few drops of the pungent liquid. It merged instantly with the pee smell, eliminating nothing. He flung the bottle into the wastebasket and stormed into the bedroom, where he searched his suitcase for the last of the joints Mrs. Madrigal had rolled for him.

He was on the verge of lighting it when a rude noise startled him. It took him several seconds to realize that he had just heard his door buzzer for the first time. Returning the joint to its hiding place, he left the apartment, walked down the dark corridor and opened the front door.

The woman who stood before him was about sixty. Her hair was gray and framed her face nicely with Imogene Coca bangs. She wore a brown tweed suit and sensible brown shoes. And that, as Simon had put it, was everything but the obvious. She was also no taller than the doorknob.

"Oh," she said in a startled chipmunk voice. "I saw the lights. I thought it best to ring first."

He sought to reassure her. "You must be Miss Treves. I'm a friend of Simon's, Michael Tolliver."

"Oh . . . an American."

He laughed nervously. "Right. We swapped apartments, in fact. Simon's in San Francisco."

She grunted. "I know all about the naughty lad."

"He's fine," he said. "He asked me to give you his love and tell you he's coming back right after Easter."

This news provoked another grunt.

"He just sort of . . . fell in love with San Francisco."

"That's what he told you, did he?"

"Well . . . more or less. Look, I'm not very settled in, but . . . can I offer you a cup of coffee? Or tea?"

She thought for a moment, then nodded. "Don't mind if I do."

"Good."

She led the way back to the living room and took a seat—her feet dangling just above the floor—in a low-slung chintz armchair. The slightly underscaled proportions of the chair seemed to suggest it had been provided specifically for her use.

Miss Treves brushed a fleck of dust off the armrest, then arranged her hands demurely in her lap. "Simon didn't tell me you were coming," she said. "Otherwise I might have tidied up a bit."

"I don't mind," he replied. "It's fine."

She looked around the room disgustedly. "'Tisn't a bit. It's perfectly vile." She shook her head slowly. "And he's supposed to be the gentleman."

Her indignation made him feel much better. He had begun to wonder if he was being too prissy about the apartment, too American in his demands. This second opinion, considering its source, reinforced his earliest suspicions about Simon's basic slovenliness.

He remembered the tea he had offered her. "Oh . . . excuse me. I'll put the kettle on for us." He spun around to make his exit, crashing ingloriously into a shadeless floor lamp. He steadied the wobbling pole with one hand, while Miss Treves tittered behind his back.

"Now there, love. You'll get used to it."

She meant her size, apparently. He turned and smiled at her to show that he was a Californian and knew his way around human differences. "What do you take in your tea?" he asked.

"Milk, please . . . and a tiny bit of sugar."

"I'm afraid I don't have sugar."

"Yes you do. On the shelf to the right of the cooker. I keep it there for myself when I stop by."

In the kitchen he ran hot water into the teakettle, removed a milk bottle from the refrigerator, and located Miss Treves's private cache of sugar. Sugar *crystals*, actually, like the stuff he had shared with his first sex partner, the non-scene, non-camp bricklayer from Hampstead Heath.

When he returned to the living room, he handed Miss Treves her tea and sat down on the end of the sofa closest to her. "So . . . Simon tells me he ran away from you once in the British Museum." It was a weak opener, but it was all he had.

She took a cautious sip of her tea. "He has a nasty habit of doing that, doesn't he?"

He assumed that was a rhetorical question. "He says you were a wonderful nanny."

She looked into her teacup, trying to hide her pleasure. "We made a sight, the two of us."

He started to say "I can imagine," but decided against it. "And now you're a manicurist, huh?"

"That I am." She nodded.

"Do you have a shop?"

"No. Just regular customers. I visit them in their homes. A select clientele." She cast a reproving glance at his hands. "You could use a bit of help yourself, love."

Embarrassed, he looked down at his jagged nails. "It's a new bad habit, I'm afraid. I had flawless nails for thirty years." He decided to change the subject. "How did you know that Simon had . . . left the royal yacht?"

She sighed. "Oh, love . . . The *Mirror* went daft over it. You didn't read it? It was just a few days ago."

"No . . . actually, I didn't."

"They made it sound as if he'd slapped the Queen."

He made an effort to look duly concerned. "It was nothing like that," he said. "He just got tired of the navy."

"Balls," said Miss Treves.

"Uh . . . what?" He wasn't sure he had heard her correctly.

"The navy is one thing, love. The *Britannia* is quite another. It's a terrible disgrace."

"How did the press find out about it?"

She growled indignantly. "Some bally woman on the telly."

"In San Francisco?"

She nodded. "Then the *Mirror* did their own snooping about and found his address. Printed it, if you please."

He thought about that for a moment. "Is Simon's family . . . upset about it?"

Miss Treves chuckled. "You're lookin' at it, love."

"Oh . . ."

"His mum and dad came to a tragic end when Simon was still at Cambridge."

"Oh . . . I didn't know that."

Her hands fidgeted in her lap. "Simon doesn't like to talk about it. A dreadful wreck."

He nodded.

"Don't mention it to him, will you? The poor lad has spent eight years getting over it."

"Who wouldn't?" said Michael. He had already begun to forgive Simon for the apartment and to regard this miniature nanny as a kind of guardian angel in tweeds. "He's so lucky to have had you," he added.

Her small pink rosebud of a mouth made a smile that was just for him. "Simon always has such lovely friends."

Nineteen

Mary Ann had left for the Peninsula to do a human interest story on the closing of an auto plant, so Brian sought tangible ways to celebrate his first official day as a househusband at 28 Barbary Lane: He trimmed the ivy on all the windowsills. He scoured the crud off the grout in the shower stall, then organized the cleansers and sponges under the kitchen sink. Slithering under the bed, he went after dust balls with the single-minded frenzy of a terrier routing a gopher from its lair.

He was working for three now. Every sweep of the dustcloth, every squirt of Fantastik, every mouse turd he banished from the pantry, made the house just that much safer for The Kid.

The Kid.

He capitalized it in his mind, paying superstitious homage to the seed which, even as he swabbed the toilet, could already be sprouting in Mary Ann's womb. The Kid was everything now. That incredible, microscopic little bugger had turned his life around and given him a reason to get up in the morning. And that was nothing short of a miracle.

He took a break and made himself a ham sandwich, eating it in the little house on the roof while a rust-red tanker slid silently across the great blue expanse of the bay. Above the terra-cotta tile of the Art Institute, a rainbow-striped kite flickered in the wind.

There was so much to show a child in this city, so many commonplace glories to be seen again through the eyes of The Kid. The windmill in Golden Gate Park. Chinatown in the fog. The waves that come crashing over the seawall at Fort Point. In his mind's eye, they were frolicking on a generic beach, he and this little piece of himself, this bright and lovable boy-or-girl who called him . . . what?

Daddy?

Dad?

Papa?

Papa wasn't bad, really. It had a kindly, old-world ring to it—stern but loving. Was it too stern? He didn't want to come off as autocratic. The Kid was a *person*, after all. The Kid must never fear him. Corporal punishment was out of the question.

He returned to the apartment, dropped his plate into the sink, then decided to scour the sink. As he worked, he could hear Mrs. Madrigal going about her gardening chores down below in the courtyard. She was humming a fractured version of "I Concentrate on You."

He was dying to tell her about The Kid, but he squelched the urge. For reasons he couldn't exactly pinpoint, he felt the news should come from Mary Ann. Besides, it would be more fun to wait until they had some indication that Mary Ann was pregnant.

He wanted to show Simon that there were no hard feelings, so he went downstairs and invited the lieutenant to go running with him. Later, as they huffed and puffed past deserted docks toward the Bay Bridge, he was impressed by Simon's endurance. He told him as much.

"We're a good match," was the gracious reply.

"Not only that," Brian continued, "but you seem to do O.K. in other departments too."

"How's that?"

Brian cast a brotherly leer at the lieutenant. "I saw her when she left this morning."

"Ah."

"Ah is right. Where did you find her?"

"Oh . . . a little *boite* called the Balboa Café. Do you know it?"

"Used to," he replied. "It's been a while. Was she good?"

"Mmm. Up to a point."

Brian laughed.

"No pun intended, sir."

"Right."

"She was a little too . . . uh . . . shall we say enthusiastic?"

"Gotcha," said Brian. "She bit your nipples."

The lieutenant was clearly dumbfounded. "Well, yes . . . as a matter of fact, she did."

"That's big with her," said Brian.

"You know her, I take it?"

"Used to. Before I was married. Jennifer Rabinowitz, right?"

"Right."

"Quite a lady."

"She's made the rounds, then?"

Brian chuckled. "She's the head shark in the Bermuda Triangle."

"Sorry?"

"That's what they call it," he explained. "The neighborhood where the Balboa Café is."

"I see."

The lieutenant seemed a little nonplussed, so Brian tried to buck him up. "I mean . . . it's not like she's the town whore or anything. She doesn't sack out with just everybody."

"Gratifying," said Simon.

They stopped running when they reached the bridge, then walked inland from the Embarcadero and sat at the base of the Villaincourt Fountain. A small Vietnamese child approached them, bearing a net bag. Brian waved him away.

"What was that about?" asked Simon.

"He wanted to sell us garlic."

"Why garlic?"

"Beats me. They get it in Gilroy and sell it on the streets here. Dozens of little Artful Dodgers hustling the white men who invaded their parents' country. Poetic, huh?"

"I should say."

"You're a great running partner," said Brian.

"Thank you, sir. So are you."

He shook the lieutenant's knee heartily. He liked this guy a lot, and not just because Jennifer Rabinowitz had made them equals. "You're looking at one happy sonofabitch," he said.

"Why is that?"

"Well . . . Mary Ann and I have decided to have a baby. I mean, she's not pregnant yet, but we're working on it."

"That's wonderful," said Simon.

"Yeah . . . it sure as hell is."

They sat there in silence, lulled by the splash of the fountain.

"Don't tell her I told you," said Brian.

"Of course not."

"I don't want her to feel like there's . . . you know . . . pressure on her."

"I understand."

"What will be, will be . . . you know?"

"Mmm."

"By the way, you're more than welcome to use the TV room whenever you feel like it."

"Thank you. Uh . . . where is it?"

"On the roof. All the way up the stairs. Everybody in the house uses it."

"Marvelous."

"I'll show you how to work the VCR. You might have some fun with that. I've got *Debbie Does Dallas*."

"Sorry?"

"It's a porn movie."

"Ah."

"I haven't played it very much . . . only when Mary Ann goes on assignment or something. Then I put that baby on and . . . wrestle with the ol' cyclops."

A slow smile spread across Simon's face. "You mean bang the bishop?"

"You catch on fast." Brian grinned.

Twenty

Michael's teenage sojourn in London had been spent with a family in Hampstead who housed him through a student program sponsored by the English-Speaking Union. Mr. and Mrs. Mainwaring had been childless, and they'd fussed over him as if he'd been their own, taking him to plays in the West End, plying him with shortbread at teatime, stocking the pantry with his favorite brand of thick-cut English marmalade.

He'd lost touch with them years before, so he couldn't help wondering if they were still watching their beloved telly in that snug little house off New End Square. Even if they weren't, the thought of seeing Hampstead again was wonderfully exhilarating. There was nothing quite like going back to an old neighborhood.

Leaving Simon's house, he wound his way through the vegetables and bric-a-brac of Portobello Road until he reached the ragtag commercial center of Notting Hill Gate. The familiar circle-bar brand of the London Underground beckoned him to a hole in the sidewalk, where he pumped coins into a ticket machine that listed Hampstead as a destination.

An escalator carried him still deeper, to the platform of the Central Line, from which he caught an eastbound train to Tottenham Court Road. Disembarking, he strode as knowingly as possible to the platform of the Northern Line, where a once-dormant signal in the back of his brain advised him that the Edgware train, *not* the High Barnet, would take him to Hampstead.

He loved the particulars of all this: The classic simplicity of the Underground map, with its geometric patterns and varicolored arteries. The warm, stale winds that whipped through the cream-and-green-tile pedestrian tunnels. The passengers—from skinheads to pinstripers—all wearing the same mask of bored and dignified disdain.

When the train stopped at Hampstead, his next route was indicated by a sign saying WAY OUT, a nobler phrase by far than the bland American EXIT. Since Hampstead was London's most elevated neighborhood, the lift to the street was London's deepest, a groaning Art Nouveau monster with a recorded voice so muted and decrepit ("Stand clear of the gate," it said) that it might have been a resident ghost. He remembered that voice, in fact, and it gave him his first shiver of déjà vu.

The streets of the borough were mercifully unchanged, despite the encroachment of fast-food parlors and chrome-and-mauve salons specializing in "hair design." He strolled along the redbrick high street until he came upon the hulking redbrick hospital that stood by the street leading to New End Square.

Four minutes later, he was hesitating in front of the house that had been his home for three months in 1967. The chintz curtains that had once shielded the living room from the gaze of passersby had been replaced by Levolors. Did a gay person live there now? Had the Mainwarings retired to some characterless "estate home" in the suburbs? Could he deal with the changes, whatever they were? Did he really want to know?

He really didn't. Returning to the high street, he ate lunch in one of the new American-style hamburger joints, a "café" decorated with neon cacti and old Coca-Cola signs. Once upon a time, he recalled, Wimpy bars had served the only hamburgers in London, but they had hardly qualified.

He downed several ciders at an old haunt in Flask Walk, then considered his options for the afternoon. He could stroll over to the Spaniards Inn and down one or two more. He could look for the house where the inventor of the Christmas card had lived. He could wander down to the Vale of Health and sit by the pond where Shelley had sailed his paper boats.

Or he could look for the bricklayer.

Another cider settled the issue. Shelley and the inventor of the Christmas card were no match for the memory of a hairless scrotum. He breezed out of the pub and ambled along the pale green crest of the city toward Jack Straw's Castle and the Spaniards Road.

The heath was much as he had remembered it—rolling reaches of lawn bordered by dark clumps of urban forest. There seemed to be more litter now (which was true of London in general), but the two-hundred-acre park was still rife with the stuff of mystery. On his last visit, the sound of the wind in its thick foliage had instantly evoked an eerie scene from *Blow-Up,* a movie which meant London to Michael in the way that *Vertigo* meant San Francisco.

He entered the heath from the Spaniards Road, following a broad trail through the trees. When he reached Hampstead Ponds, he stopped for a while and watched a trio of children romping along the water's edge. Their mother, a freckled redhead in a green sweater and slacks, smiled at him wearily as if to thank him for the tribute he had paid her offspring. He smiled back and skipped a stone on the water, just to get a rise out of the kids.

It was here, he remembered, that a road led down to the south end of the heath and the street where the bricklayer had lived. *The street where he lived.* He laughed out loud at his gay rewrite, then began humming the tune from *My Fair Lady.*

The street was called South End Road. He remembered it because it intersected with Keats Grove, the street where the poet had lived, and Keats had been one of the things they had discussed after sex, along with Paul McCartney, motorcycles and world peace.

He found the place almost immediately, recognizing the nightingales in the Edwardian stained glass above the door. This was no time to think, he decided. He threw caution to the winds and rang the bell of the ground-floor flat. An old man in a cardigan came to the door.

"This is kind of unusual," Michael began, "but a friend of mine lived here a long time ago, and I was wondering if he still does."

The old man squinted at him for a moment, then said: "What was his name?"

"Well . . . that's the unusual part. I don't remember. He was a bricklayer . . . a big, strapping fellow. He must be about fifty now." *Come to think of it, I believe he did have a hairless scrotum.*

The current occupant shook his head thoughtfully. "How long ago was this?"

"Sixteen years. Nineteen sixty-seven."

A raspy chuckle. "He must be long gone. The wife and me have been here longer than the other tenants, but that's just eight years. Sixteen years! No wonder you've forgotten his name!"

Michael thanked him and left, accepting the futility of the quest. It didn't really matter. What would he have said, anyway, had he found his savior? *You don't know me, but thanks for being there first?*

The sun was quite warm now and cottony clouds were scudding across the sky, so he crossed the heath again and headed for the wooded mound that locals knew as Boadicea's tomb. No one really believed that the ancient queen was actually buried under the hillock, but the name endured nonetheless. He had gone there once at midnight, upon reading in *The Times* that the Order of Bards, Ovates and Druids would gather at the site for their Midsummer's Night ritual. The intrigue had vanished like ectoplasm when he saw for himself that the "Druids" were bank clerks in bedsheets and grandmothers in harlequin glasses.

As another chunk of the past slipped away from him, he sat down on the grass and tilted his face to the sun. Fifty yards below him, a large black sedan crossed the heath slowly, then came to a stop. A woman got out—blond hair, white blouse, gray skirt stopping at midcalf—a striking figure against the endless green of the landscape. She turned in every direction, apparently searching for someone.

He observed her idly for a moment, then sprang to his feet, his mind ablaze with conflicting images.

"Mona!" he shouted.

The woman's head jerked around to find the source of his voice.

"It's me, Mona! Mouse!"

The woman froze, then spun on her heel and climbed back into the sedan. It sped out of sight into the trees.

Twenty-one

The deluge of publicity that hit Simon after the broadcast made Mary Ann begin to wonder if it had been too much for him. He *seemed* to be all right, but he was a funny bird in many ways, and she could rarely tell what was really on his mind. The last thing she wanted was to alienate him.

When the weekend came, she waited until the time was right (Brian had gone to the laundromat) and invited the Englishman to join her on her shopping rounds in North Beach. Half an hour later, all she had to show for it was a pint carton of Molinari's pickled mushrooms.

"This is your *weekly* shopping?" Simon asked. They were walking up Columbus toward Washington Square.

She laughed, abandoning the pretense altogether. "I just needed an excuse to get out of the house. I've been feeling . . . cooped up lately."

"Shall we walk somewhere?" he asked.

"I'd love to," she replied.

"Where? You're the local, madam."

She smiled. She liked it when he called her madam. "I know just the place," she said.

She walked him up Union Street to the top of Telegraph Hill, then down Montgomery to its junction with the Filbert Steps. "The penthouse directly above us," she explained, "is the one that Lauren Bacall had in *Dark Passage.*"

He craned his muscular, patrician neck. "Really?"

"The one where Bogart has the plastic surgery that makes him look like Bogart. Remember?"

"Of course," he replied.

"My friend DeDe used to live there."

"Ah. Do I know about her?"

"The one who escaped from Guyana."

"Right."

She led him halfway down the wooden stairway, then brushed off a plank and sat down.

"This is not unlike Barbary Lane," he remarked, joining her.

She nodded. "There are places like this all over the city. This is technically a city street."

"The garden is magnificent."

"The city doesn't do that," she told him. "A precious old lady did that—this used to be a garbage dump. She was a stunt woman in Hollywood years ago, and then she moved up here and started planting this. Everybody just calls it Grace's Garden. She died just before Christmas. Her ashes are under that statue down there."

He looked faintly amused. "You're a veritable font of local color."

"I did a story on her," she explained.

"I see." He was teasing her ever so subtly. "Do you do stories on everyone you know?"

She hesitated, wondering about his motives again. "Has it been too much?" she finally asked him.

The smile he offered seemed genuine enough. "Not at all."

"I hope not."

"I'm *astounded* there's been such a reaction. But it hasn't been unpleasant."

"Good."

"As long as you don't let any other journalists know where I am."

"Don't worry," she replied. "I want you all to myself."

He smiled again and bent a branch so that a large blossom touched the tip of his nose.

"They don't smell," she said.

He released the branch, catapulting the blossom toward the sky.

"It's called a fried egg plant," she added, "because it looks like . . ."

"Don't tell me, now. Let me guess."

She laughed.

"A bowling ball? No? A loaf of bread, perhaps?"

She shook his knee. "Stop teasing."

A silence followed. She felt awkward about her hand on his knee, so she removed it.

"Who lives in these houses?" Simon asked.

She was glad to take refuge in her role as tour guide. "Well . . . they're squatter shacks . . ."

"Really? I thought that was peculiar to England."

"Oh, no," she answered. "Are you kidding? During the gold rush . . ."

He cut her off with a brittle laugh. "We're in different centuries, I think. I meant *now*."

Thoroughly confused, she retraced her steps. "You . . . have squatters now?"

He nodded. "London is crawling with them."

"You mean . . . people just claim land?"

"Houses, actually. Flats. The hippies started it, back when the city allowed empty council flats to fall into disrepair. They moved in, fixed them up a bit . . . claimed them for their own."

"Well," she commented, "that sounds fair enough."

"Mmm," he replied, "unless you're the chap who goes on holiday and comes home to a family of Pakistanis . . . or what-have-you."

"Has that happened?"

"Oh, yes."

"They just move in? Take over the furniture and everything?"

He nodded. "To evict them, one must prove forceable entry. That's bloody difficult sometimes. There can be months of mucking about before they're booted out. It's a complicated issue, mind you."

"I can imagine."

"There are squatters in my building," he added. "They took over the vacant flat above me."

"You didn't see them do this?"

He shook his head. "I was on the royal honeymoon at the time."

"What are they like?"

"The Prince and Princess?"

She smiled. "The squatters."

"Oh . . . a middle-aged chap and his son. The father drinks too much. They're aboriginals. Half-castes, actually."

She had vague visions of grass-skirted natives with bones through their noses dancing around in circles, but she dismissed the subject in deference to a far more fascinating one. "O.K. Now you can tell me about the royal honeymoon."

The smile he sent back was tinged with diplomacy. "I thought we covered that in the interview."

"That was the official stuff," she said. "Now I want the dirt."

He pulled the blossom into sniffing range again. "Off the record?"

"Of course."

"Off the record, there is no dirt."

"C'mon."

"My job was working with the radios. I saw very little of the honeymooners."

"Is she pretty?"

"Very."

"Beautiful?"

"You're on the right track." He smiled.

"Would she know you if she saw you on the street?"

He nodded. "I took her out once."

"You . . . *dated* her?"

"I escorted her to a David Bowie concert. Her flatmate knew a friend of mine. The four of us went. It was years ago . . . when she was only a lady."

She giggled. "You *double-dated* with Lady Di."

"So far"—he grinned—"there have been no medals for that."

"Was she really a virgin when she married him?"

He shrugged. "Insofar as I had anything to do with it."

She looked him in the eye. "Did you try?"

His lip flickered. "You don't give up easily, do you?"

"Well," she replied, "it's not like it's a big deal or anything. People do these things. Times have changed. Everybody does everything and nobody cares."

"And discretion," he added with a gentle smile, "is the last act of gallantry."

It was all she could do to keep from showing her relief. He had passed with flying colors. She conceded her defeat with a demure smile. "Never kiss and tell, huh?"

He shook his head. "I like kissing too much."

The screeching which prevented her next remark was so sudden and shrill that it took her a moment to realize what it was.

"Good Lord!" murmured Simon. That beautiful neck was once again arched toward the heavens.

"They're parrots," she said. "Wild ones."

"They're remarkable! I had no idea they were indigenous."

"They aren't. Not exactly. Some of them were in cages originally. The others are descended from ones that were in cages. They just sort of . . . found each other."

He turned and smiled at her. "That's a nice story."

"Yes," she replied. "Isn't it?"

Twenty-two

Five hours after his hallucination on the heath, Michael languished in a shallow tub back at Colville Crescent. It had been that dream, he decided at last—that Death Valley dream in which Mona had ignored his cries from the bluff. Something about that hillside on the heath, something about the blond woman's stance or the angle from which he had watched her, had conjured up that dream again and caused him to lose touch with reality.

The woman hadn't *looked* like Mona, certainly. Not with that hair. And those clothes. Or even the way she carried herself. If anything, he had reacted to her aura—a concept so embarrassingly Californian that he vowed never to express it to anyone. This elegant stranger had simply touched a nerve somewhere, triggering his anxiety about a friendship which had all but collapsed.

He was determined not to think about that. He put on his black Levi's and his white button-down shirt and headed into Notting Hill Gate, where he ate a curry dinner at a cramped Indian restaurant. Afterwards, he cashed a traveler's check at the local *Bureau de Change*, picked up a *Private Eye* at his newsstand, and returned to the house. Miss Treves, all three feet whatever of her, was crossing the front yard as he arrived.

"Oh, *there* you are, love."

"Hi!" It was pleasant to notice how much she felt like a friend. "I was just out having dinner."

"Having a marvelous time, are you?"

"Of course," he lied.

"Good. I brought my case. You don't mind, do you?" She held up a green leather satchel, roughly the size and shape of a shoe box.

He didn't get it. "I'm sorry . . . mind what?"

Her free hand, tiny and pudgy as a baby's, grabbed one of his. "These horrors. Something must be done about them. We can't have a friend of Simon's looking such a fright." She cocked her head and winked at him. "It won't take long."

He was both embarrassed and touched. "That's really nice, but . . ."

"I shan't charge you. You haven't plans for the evening, have you?"

He had toyed with the idea of exploring the gay bars in Earl's Court, but that hardly seemed an appropriate answer under the circumstances. "No," he replied, "not for the next few hours."

"Lovely," she chirped, turning smartly to lead the way into the house. Once inside, she opened her manicure kit and removed a newspaper clipping, tattered from many unfoldings. "This is a load of rubbish, but I thought you might like to see it." The headline said: ROYAL RADIOMAN ON FRISCO PLEASURE BINGE.

He scanned the piece quickly. Simon came off sounding like a thorough hedonist, a bratty aristocrat squandering the family fortune on nameless excesses in the "fruit-and-nut capital" of the western hemisphere. He returned the document with a discrediting smile. "You're right. It's a load of rubbish."

Miss Treves grunted as she poured a soapy liquid into a little bowl. He immediately thought of Madge the Manicurist on TV and wondered if he'd be soaking in dishwashing liquid. The whole scenario struck him as supremely funny.

She took one of his hands and placed it in the bowl. "Did you notice they printed this address?"

"Uh-huh," he said.

She said nothing.

"Should that be . . . a problem?"

"I don't know, love." She poked through her kit, searching for something. "You haven't noticed anyone snooping about, have you?"

What on earth was she getting at? "Uh . . . no. Not that I've noticed. You mean like . . . burglars or something?"

"No. Just . . . general snooping about."

"No. Not a thing."

"Good."

"Look, I'd appreciate it if . . ."

"It's nothing, love. I'm sure it's nothing." She began jabbing away at his cuticles. "When they print your bally address, it makes me nervous, that's all."

The manicure proved to be a reassuringly intimate experience. To sit there passively while this vinegary little woman repaired his nails gave him a sense of being noticed for the first time since his arrival in London. "Have you done this long?" he asked eventually.

"Oh . . . about fifteen years, I suppose."

"And before that you were Simon's nanny?"

"Mmm."

"Did you do nanny work for other families?"

"No. Just the Bardills. Let's have the other hand, love."

He obeyed as she repositioned the stool. "Did you always want to be a nanny?" he asked. As soon as he had spoken, he wondered if the question was too personal. He had never stopped to think about what career opportunities were open to a midget.

"Oh, no!" she answered immediately. "I wanted to be in show business. I *was* in show business."

"You mean like a . . . ?" A circus was what came to mind, but he knew better than to finish the sentence.

"A musical revue," she said. "A traveling show. A bit of song and dance. Readings from Shakespeare. That sort of thing."

"How fascinating," he exclaimed, captivated by the thought of a miniature Lady Macbeth. "Why did you give it up?"

She heaved a sigh. "They gave *us* up, love. The audience. The telly killed us, I always said. Who wanted Bunny Benbow when they could have *Coronation Street* for nothing?"

"Bunny Benbow? That was the name?"

"The Bunny Benbow Revue." She giggled like one of the mice in *Cinderella*. "Silly, isn't it? It sounds so old-fashioned now."

"I wish I'd seen it," he said.

"Simon's mum and dad took me in after we folded. Their friends thought they were daft, but it well and truly saved my life. I owe them a great deal, a great deal." She finished filing a jagged nail and looked up at him. "What about you, love? How do you put bread on the table?"

"I'm a nurseryman," he told her.

"How lovely." She stopped her work for a moment and stared misty-eyed into space. "Simon's mum had a splendid garden at our country place in Sussex. Hollyhocks. Roses. The dearest little violets . . ."

He noticed that her lip was trembling slightly.

She sighed finally. "Time marches on."

"Yes," he replied.

When she had gone, half an hour later, his spirits had improved considerably, so he decided to follow through with his original plan and check out the gay bars in Earl's Court. The tube brought him within a block of Harpoon Louie's, a windowless bar which flew a Union Jack in an apparent effort to show that poofters could be patriots too.

Inside, the place was self-consciously American: blond wood, industrial shades on the lights, Warhol prints. Perhaps in deference to the current occupant of Kensington Palace, the tape machine was playing Paul Anka's "Diana." The barmaid, in fact, looked like a chubbier version of the Princess of Wales.

The crowd was decidedly clonish—tank-topped, Adidas-shod, every bit as inclined toward attitude as a standard Saturday night mob on Castro Street. They smoked more, it seemed, and their teeth and bodies weren't as pretty, but Disco Madness (circa 1978) was alive and well in Earl's Court.

Finding a seat at a banquette against the wall, he nursed a gin and tonic and observed the scene for several minutes. Then he read a story about Sylvester in a newspaper called *Capital Gay* ("The Free One") and wandered into the back garden, where the smoke and noise were less oppressive.

He left as a clock was striking ten somewhere and walked several blocks past high-windowed brick buildings to a gay pub called the Coleherne. These were the leather boys, apparently. He ordered another gin and tonic and stood at the bulletin board reading announcements about Gay Tory meetings and "jumble sales" to benefit deaf lesbians.

When he returned to the horseshoe-shaped bar, the man across from him smiled broadly. He was a kid really, not more than eighteen or nineteen, and his skin was the same shade as the dark ale he was drinking. His hair was the startling part—soft brown ringlets that glinted with gold under the light, floating above his mischievous eyes like . . . well, like the froth on his ale. In his white shirt and bow tie and sleeveless argyle sweater he came as welcome relief from the white men in black leather who surrounded him.

Michael smiled back. His admirer kissed the tip of his forefinger and wagged it at him. Michael lifted his glass as a thank you. The kid hopped off his barstool and made his way through the sullen throng to Michael's side of the bar.

"I fancy your jeans," he said. "I noticed them when you came in."

Michael glanced down at the black Levi's. "Thanks," he said. "I'm breaking them in."

"You dye them yourself?"

"No . . . no, they come that way."

"Really?"

The upward lilt of his voice was almost Dickensian, and Michael enjoyed being reminded that a man who sounded like that could look like this. Up close, his full lips and broad nose seemed distinctly African, but his unlikely hair (lighter than Michael's own, he noted) remained a mystery.

"Mine's just the regular sort." The kid hooked his thumbs proudly in the pockets of his 501's. They seemed somewhat out of sync with the rest of his getup, but he looked pretty good in them just the same.

"You don't see many of those," Michael remarked. "Not around here."

"Twenty pounds in Fulham Road. Worth every penny, if you ask me. You fancy this place, do you?"

"It's . . . fine," was all he could manage. The room looked like a pub, at least. Just the same, there was something almost poignant about pasty-faced Britishers trying to pull off a butch biker routine. They were simply the wrong breed for it. He was reminded of an English tourist who had all but lived in the back room at The Boot Camp, but had never uttered a single word. That man had come to grips with the truth: Phrases like "Suck that big, fat cock" and "Yeah, you want it, don't you?" sounded just plain asinine when muttered with an Oxonian accent.

The kid gave the room a disparaging once-over. "They look like the dog's lunch to me."

Michael laughed. "I don't know what that means, but it doesn't sound good."

"It's not, mate, it's not. What part of the States are you from?"

"San Francisco."

"Well . . ." The kid rocked on his heels. "Poofters out the arse, eh?"

Michael smiled. "I guess you could say that."

"The Queen went there, didn't she?"

"Right."

"Rained like bloody hell."

"Still is," Michael said, "as far as I know. Just like here."

Still rocking on his heels, the kid gave him a half-lidded smile. "So . . . what say we have a go?"

"Uh . . . what?"

"Have a *go*, mate." He banged his pale palms together to show what he meant.

Michael chuckled. "Oh."

"What say?"

"Thanks, but . . . I'm off the stuff for a while."

"Don't fancy wogs, eh?"

His directness seemed designed to throw Michael off balance. "Not at all. I just haven't been very horny lately."

"Well, what are you doin' here, then?"

"Good question. Seeing the sights, I guess."

"O.K., then . . . I'm one of 'em. My name's Wilfred." He extended his hand as an enormous grin spread across his face like a sunrise.

Michael shook hands with him. "I'm Michael."

For the next half hour, they remained side by side at the bar, but spoke very little. Meanwhile, the legions of would-be leatherettes grew shriller and smokier as rain sluiced noisily through the gutters outside the door.

"You didn't bring a brolly, did you, mate?"

"Nope. Like a dummy."

"C'mon, then. I did."

It sounded like another invitation to "have a go," so Michael took the easy way out. "Thanks. I think I'll just hang out for a little while longer."

"You'll be sorry," said Wilfred.

"Why?"

"Look at the time, mate."

A clock advertising Dane Crisps said ten forty-five.

"It's almost closing time," Wilfred pointed out. "It isn't a pretty sight."

"What do you mean?"

"They turn the lights up. If you think these blokes look grotty now, just you wait till eleven o'clock!"

Michael laughed. "A surefire way to empty the place."

"They know what they're doing." The kid grinned. "In straight pubs they turn the lights *down* at closing time. Who says we're just the same, eh? C'mon, now . . . what's your next stop?"

"The tube station. I'm going home."

"Super. So am I." He took Michael's arm and steered him through the crowd to the door, then opened his umbrella. "Here, c'mon . . . get under here, mate."

Since Michael was at least four inches taller than his escort, he held the umbrella while Wilfred acted as navigator and guide, his right hand snugly planted in the right rear pocket of Michael's 501's.

"Princess Diana lived down the way a bit . . . back when she was a teacher. Think of that, eh? Passing all these leather blokes on her way to the bleedin' kindergarten. Here! Mind the lorry!"

Michael jumped back onto the curb as a huge truck rumbled past, only inches away.

The whites of Wilfred's eyes flashed under the umbrella like a pair of headlights. "One more like that, mate, and we're married for all eternity." He pointed to white lettering on the street. "See? 'Look Right,' it says. We even paint it there for you bleedin' Americans."

They strode briskly past a newsstand, then a garish ethnic restaurant— Arabic, maybe—with the menu painted on plywood and a huge chunk of symmetrical mystery meat, floodlit by pink bulbs, spinning like a top on a vertical spit.

"Druggies eat there," said Wilfred. "It's open late. Do you have a lover back in the States?"

Michael laughed. "Nice segue."

"Nice what?"

"Nothing. Bad joke. No, I don't have a lover."

"Why not?"

He hesitated. "I used to have a lover. It didn't work out."

"A delicate subject, eh?"

"Yeah."

"I'd like to have a lover, I think, but I don't think I'm going to meet one at the Coleherne."

"I know what you mean," said Michael.

They rode the tube in virtual silence, as tradition seemed to demand, Wilfred's blue-denimed knee pressed against Michael's black one.

"What's your stop?" asked Michael.

"Same as yours, mate. Notting Hill Gate."

Michael was floored.

The kid grinned. "You've never even noticed me, have you?"

"I'm sorry. I don't know what . . ."

"I live upstairs from you, mate. Good ol' Forty-four Colville Crescent."

The final proof came when they reached the house and Wilfred produced a key that opened the front door. He flipped the timer switch before turning to peck Michael lightly on the lips. "G'night, mate. Thanks for walking me home."

Then he sprinted up the stairs to the second floor.

Twenty-three

Like other things about her, Mary Ann's menstrual cycle was so regular that Mussolini might have included it on his train schedules. When the world was going to hell in a handbasket and chaos ruled the day, she could always count on the prompt arrival of her period—or, as her mother had once explained it, "the bloody tears of a disappointed uterus."

Her uterus had been unusually disappointed today, which meant that her midmonth pains were due in another fourteen days, give or take a day or so. According to her doctor at St. Sebastian's (and several authors she had seen on

Donahue), those pains—*mittelschmerz* was the silly technical term—were the surest indication of ovulation.

While some women apparently showed no outward signs of ovulation other than uncomfortable periods, Mary Ann had all the evidence she needed, thank you. Flipping through her *New Yorker* appointment book, she counted fourteen days ahead and found herself landing squarely on Sunday, April 3—Easter Day.

Eggs at Easter. Cute.

Brian never asked her about her *mittelschmerz*, apparently preferring to trust romantically in what he called "the good ol' hunt and peck method of making babies." The term had always annoyed her (why were men so *proud* of their obliviousness?), but she was suddenly grateful for his blind traditionalism.

She closed the appointment book and leaned back in her chair, suddenly thinking of Mouse. She had explained her *mittelschmerz* to him once, partially as a way of explaining her bitchy flare-ups, and he had never let her hear the end of it. ("Uh-oh," he would say, catching her with a frown on her face, "you're not having your *ethelmertz*, are you?") She giggled at the thought of that, and blew him a kiss across the world.

The rest of her day was horrendous. She argued for at least an hour with a director who wanted to score her baby bear footage with cutesy-pie Disney music. Then Bambi Kanetaka insisted on ditching Mary Ann's Wildflowers of Alcatraz story to make room for a sleazy feature on sex surrogates in Marin.

When she got home at eight o'clock, Brian was bustling around in his denim apron while an aromatic beef stew waited on the stove. He pecked her on the cheek, then saw the fatigue in her face. "A ball-buster, huh?"

"Yep."

"Well . . . this should cheer you up. We got an intriguing invitation today."

"Yeah? Who from?"

"Theresa Cross. She wants us to come hang out for a weekend. Use the pool, kick back . . . Who knows? Maybe even make a baby or two." Seeing her expression change, he added: "Hey, I know she's not one of your favorite people, but . . . well, it's kind of a nice gesture, isn't it?"

"Yeah," she conceded. "It is."

He looked relieved. "She's having some of her rock-and-roll friends."

"Great. When does she want us?"

"Easter weekend."

Of course, she thought.

"What's the matter?" he asked.

"Well . . . I can't, that's all."

"Why not?"

"I just . . . well, I have to work."

"On *what?*" he asked feistily. "It's Easter, for God's sake."

"I know, but . . . I promised to do the Easter feature for them . . . the sunrise service at Mount Davidson, that sort of stuff. I know it's a bummer, Brian. I meant to tell you earlier. Father Paddy is doing the sunrise service, and they want me to . . . you know . . . cover it for *Bay Window.*"

He hung a scowl on his face. "Jesus," he muttered.

"I'm sorry," she replied softly, avoiding the Jesus jokes.

"*Easter*, for God's sake. Where do they get off telling you you have to . . ."

"Brian, it's my job."

"I know it's your job." His forehead was forming ugly little trenches, a sure danger sign. "Don't start with that it's-my-job crap. I know what your responsibilities are. And your priorities, for that matter. I'm just disappointed. All right? I have a right to that, don't I?"

"Of course."

"Forget I asked," he said in a calmer tone. "I'll tell Theresa we can't make it."

It jarred her to hear him call the rock widow by her first name—as if they were old buddies—but what else was he supposed to call her? Certainly not Mrs. Cross. "Don't do that," she said. "I think you should go."

He blinked at her.

"I *want* you to go," she added.

"I don't know . . ."

"Look, one of us should find out what it's like. Who's gonna be there, anyway?"

"Well . . . Grace Slick, for starters."

"Wow."

He eyed her suspiciously. "Since when did you say wow to Grace Slick?"

"That's not fair," she sulked. "I like Grace Slick."

"You do not like Grace Slick. You've never liked Grace Slick. Come off it."

"Well . . . I meant the wow for you. It was a vicarious wow. Oh, for God's sake, Brian, go to your rock-and-roll party. It's tailor-made for you. You'll be pissed at me forever if you don't go."

His eyes became doglike. "I wanted somebody to laugh at it with."

It was one of those moments of uncomplicated connection that made up for all the grueling compromises of marriage. She nuzzled his neck for a moment, then said: "We'll laugh about it later. I promise."

He drew away from her to add a missing detail. "She's asked her guests for overnight. I mean, like . . . the whole weekend."

She shrugged. Under the circumstances, she could hardly get huffy. "Fine. Great."

"Do you mean that?" he asked earnestly. "Or are you just being modern?"

"If she touches you . . ." She chewed her forefinger, pretending to ruminate. "I'll tear her tits off."

He laughed, then snapped his fingers. "I've got a great idea!"

"What?" He was making her nervous.

"I'll take Simon along with me."

"I don't know, Brian." She weighed several arguments and settled on one. "That's a little rude."

"Why?"

"Well . . . she invited the two of us. She doesn't even know Simon and . . . well, since it's our first real invitation, it might be a little pushy to drag along a perfect stranger . . . especially one who's kind of a groupie and all."

"That's what I thought would be perfect," he said. "He's crazy about her . . . and unattached."

"Yeah, but she's probably got a surplus of men as it is."

"Straight men?"

"Well . . . whatever. Don't fix them up, Brian."

"Why not?"

"Because . . . she's too much of a vulture."

He laughed. "I think Simon can take care of himself."

"Don't be so sure," she said, leaning against him again. "Have you forgiven me yet?"

"I'm working on it."

"Good. There's something else we can work on, too."

"What?"

"Save Palm Sunday for me, will you?"

"Why?"

"Because . . . the signs are good . . . babywise."

It took him a while. "You mean . . . *ethelmertz?*"

She nodded. *"Ethelmertz."*

"Hot damn!" He held her closer. "That makes up for Easter, right there."

"Good," she replied. "I hoped it would."

Twenty-four

Michael was feeling remarkably chipper when he awoke at eight forty-five in Simon's musty bedroom. A cement mixer gargled gratingly out in the street and someone was frying kippers across the garden, but nothing could shake his nagging suspicion that life was finally getting better.

He flipped on his bedside radio. A newscaster informed him that a school-master had been found crucified on a moor in Scotland and that London bookmakers had opened bets on when the capital would have a consecutive forty-eight-hour period without rain. None of it bothered him a bit.

He was brewing a pot of tea when someone rapped on his door. To be almost certain who it was gave him the pleasant illusion of being at home.

"Mornin', mate."

Michael smiled at the kid. "Mornin'."

Wilfred was wearing a variation of last night's ensemble—a bow tie (black) and sleeveless sweater (turquoise), with a white shirt and 501's. He had a "look," it seemed. Michael couldn't help remembering the porkpie hat he had worn all over London when he was sixteen.

"Tea?" he asked.

"Super," said Wilfred.

"Sit down. I'll bring it in."

He returned to the kitchen and came back with the tea things on a tray. "Why didn't you tell me you lived here?"

Wilfred shrugged, now sprawled on the sofa, one leg draped over the arm. "I didn't want to be the wog kid upstairs. I wanted to meet you . . ." He searched for the right words and couldn't find them.

"With our tribe?" offered Michael.

"There you go." Wilfred smiled.

"Did you follow me to the Coleherne?"

The kid's face registered mild indignation. "You're not the only bleedin' poofter who goes to the Cloneherne, y'know."

Michael took note of the pun. "The Cloneherne, huh?"

Wilfred twinkled at him. "That's me own name for it."

"Not bad."

"So what are you doin' in Lord Twitzy-twee's flat?"

"We swapped apartments. I gave him my place in San Francisco for a month and . . . Simon's a lord?"

"He acts like one, that's for sure. He's a poof, is he?"

Michael shook his head. "Nope."

"Didn't think so." Wilfred surveyed the room imperially. "Not very tidy."

On that point, at least, there seemed to be a consensus. "I don't think it matters to him," Michael said.

"Who's the midge?" asked the kid.

"The who?"

"The midge. The runt lady who visits."

"His nanny," Michael replied. "And watch your mouth."

"His *nanny*. My-my."

103

"What do you take in your tea?"

A powerful voice thundered in the stairwell. "*Wilfred!*"

"Jesus," muttered Michael. "Who's that?"

The kid was already heading for the door. "Look . . . meet me at the tube station in half an hour. I've got something special to show you."

"Wilfred, who was that?"

"Aw . . . me dad, that's all."

"Your *father?*"

"Tube station. Half an hour. Got it? You won't be sorry."

He dashed out the door, blowing a kiss as he left.

Michael listened to him clattering up the stairs, then sat down and poured himself a cup of tea. This was an entirely new wrinkle. If Wilfred lived with his parents, the last thing Michael needed was to come off as the foreign reprobate who had "recruited" their son. Daddy Dearest didn't exactly sound like a man of reason.

Fuck that. His life had finally begun to take on a momentum of its own, and it felt too good to turn back now. Or, as Mrs. Madrigal had once explained it: "Only a fool refuses to follow, when Pan comes prancing through the forest."

So he ate his toast and marmalade, made his bed, and strolled up Portobello Road toward the tube station. Wilfred was waiting for him by the ticket machines. "I wasn't sure you'd make it," Michael said.

"Why?" asked the kid.

"Well . . . your father sounded pissed."

Wilfred shook his head. "He doesn't start in drinking till noon."

Michael smiled, recognizing a language problem. "I meant pissed angry, not pissed drunk."

"Oh. Well, he's always pissed angry."

"About what?"

Wilfred thought for a moment. "Maggie Thatcher and me, mostly. Not necessarily in that order, mind you." He mimicked his father's booming basso. " 'Oo needs a bleedin' Thatcher, when ya ain't got a bleedin' roof over your head? Eh? *Eh?*' That's his favorite joke."

Michael chuckled. "You do it well."

"I hear it enough," said Wilfred.

Following the kid's instructions, Michael bought a ticket to Wimbledon, the last stop on the District Line, south of the river. As they waited on the platform, he asked Wilfred: "Does this have something to do with tennis?"

"Just shut your trap, mate. You'll see."

"Yes, *sir.*"

Wilfred gave him an elfin grin. For just a moment, he reminded Michael of Ned in Death Valley, teasing his friends with the undisclosed wonders that lay just beyond the next bluff.

As the train thundered through the sooty tunnel, Michael asked: "Does your father know you're gay?"

Wilfred nodded.

"How did he find out?"

The kid shrugged. "I was busted for cottaging, mate. I think that gave him a clue."

"Cottaging?"

"You know . . . doin' it in a cottage."

Michael's confusion was obvious.

"A cottage," Wilfred repeated. "*A public loo.*"

A woman across from them grimaced fiercely.

"Oh," said Michael, somewhat meekly.

"That's how I got tossed out of school . . . not to mention sacked from my job. I used to work down here in Wimbledon."

"We call that a tearoom," Michael pointed out.

"What? Where I worked? It was a bleedin' chippie!"

"No, a cottage. We call a cottage a tearoom." It was beginning to sound like a gay variation on 'Who's on First?' and the woman across the way was the last to be amused. "I think we'd better drop this, Wilfred."

The kid shrugged. "Fine with me, mate."

When they reached Wimbledon, Wilfred bought a Cadbury bar at the station, broke off a chunk and handed it to Michael. "We've got a bit of a walk now. Let's hope ol' Dingo's still there."

"You bet," Michael replied, smirking a little. He had no intention of asking what that meant. It was amazing, really, how much Wilfred's technique resembled Ned's.

The kid made a beeline for a butcher shop, where he strode up to the counter and ordered half a pound of beef liver. When the order arrived, Wilfred handed the cardboard tub to Michael. "Take charge of this, will you? We'll be needing it later."

Michael gave him a dubious look. "Not breakfast?"

"Not ours," grinned Wilfred, leading the way out of the shop.

They walked through Wimbledon for five or six blocks. Twentieth-century Tudor alternated with bleak redbrick high-rises against a carpet of lush lawns. Michael was reminded of Kansas City, oddly enough, or a 1920s suburb on the edge of any Midwestern town.

Wilfred stopped at a vacant lot covered with brick and concrete rubble—all that was left of a house that had apparently burned to the ground. "They're building another one here next month. Dingo hasn't much time left." He stepped nimbly over the debris, approaching the end of the lot where the rubble was deepest. Then he snapped his fingers to get Michael's attention.

"What?" asked Michael.

"The *liver*, mate."

"Oh." He handed him the cardboard tub. Wilfred dumped the contents on a flat rock that appeared to have already been used for that purpose. "You're freaking me out," whispered Michael.

"Shhh!" Wilfred's forefinger shot to his lips. "Just hang on."

They stood like statues amid the ruins.

"Here, Dingo," crooned Wilfred. "C'mon, boy."

Michael heard a scurrying sound beneath the rubble. Then a pair of flinty eyes appeared in an opening adjacent to the flat rock. After a few exploratory sniffs, the creature scuttled out into the light.

"God," Michael murmured. "A fox, huh?"

"Very good."

"What's he doing here?"

Wilfred shrugged. "They're all over London."

"In the city limits, you mean?"

"Wherever they can make do. Right, Dingo?" Fifteen feet away, the fox looked up from his dinner for a moment, then continued to devour it noisily. "They'll level this spot in another month, and Dingo will be in real trouble."

"Why do you call him Dingo?"

Wilfred turned and looked at him. "It's what they call the wild dogs in Australia."

"Oh."

"I found him when I was working down at the chippie. One day at lunch I tossed him a bit of me fish-and-chips and he was so grateful that I came back the next day. But they gave me the sack, so I come down here on the tube when I can. It's been a while since the last time. You miss me, Dingo? Eh?"

They watched in silence while the fox ate. Then Michael said: "We have wild coyotes in California. I mean . . . they come into the city sometimes."

"Yeah?"

Michael nodded. "They raid people's garbage cans in L.A. People have seen them standing in the middle of Sunset Boulevard. They don't belong in the wilds, and they don't belong in the city either."

Wilfred nodded. "They're trapped in the mess we've made. They know it, too. Dingo knows it. All he can do is hide in that hole and wait for the end to come."

"Couldn't you . . . get him out of there?"

"And take him where, mate? No one loves a fox." He turned and looked at Michael with tears in his eyes. "I bought him something especially nice this time. I'm not coming back. Me nerves can't take it."

Michael himself was beginning to feel fragile. "He looks like he appreciates it."

"Yeah. He does, doesn't he?" He smiled faintly, wiping his eyes.

"How about you?" Michael asked. "Can I buy you breakfast?"

"Sure. Sure, mate." He glanced in Dingo's direction again; the fox was scampering away.

"Do you know a good place?" Michael asked.

"Yeah," the kid nodded.

It turned out to be a tiny Greek greasy spoon only two blocks from the fox's lair. Wilfred ordered for both of them, insisting upon the specialty of the house: fried eggs and bangers and a side order of stewed tomatoes. While they ate, the skies opened up again, varnishing the cast-iron blind child that was stationed outside the door.

Michael peered at the statuette through a rain-blurred window. "I've never seen anything like that," he remarked. "Do you drop money in his head?"

Wilfred nodded. "They have them for dogs and cats, too."

Michael gave him a sympathetic smile. "But not foxes."

"No."

"Have you ever seen a real dingo?"

"No. Me granddad told me about them once."

"He was . . . Australian?"

"Abo," replied Wilfred. "You can say it, mate."

"What?" He didn't recognize the word.

"Aborigines. You've heard of 'em."

"Oh."

The kid smiled impishly. "The ones the niggers get to pick on."

Michael felt instantly uncomfortable. "I wouldn't know about that."

"Well, I would." He sawed off a chunk of banger and popped it into his mouth. "Me grandmum was Dutch. Her and me granddad left Darwin during World War II . . . when you Yanks were all over the place and everyone thought the Japs were coming. Me dad was born in London."

"And your mother?"

"She ran off when I was eight."

"Why?"

He shrugged. "Sick o' me dad and his bleedin' port. I don't know. Maybe she didn't fancy me."

"I doubt that."

"*You* don't fancy me." He was looking at his plate as he said it.

"That's not true."

"You don't want to go to bed with me."

"Wilfred . . ."

"Just tell me why, then. I won't ask again."

Michael hesitated. "I'm not sure it makes a lot of sense . . . even to me."

"Try me."

"Well . . . my lover and I didn't split up. He died of AIDS."

107

The kid blinked at him.

"Do you know what that is?"

Wilfred shook his head.

"It's this thing that gay men are getting in the States. It's a severe immune deficiency. They get it, and then they catch anything that flies in the window. Over a thousand people have died of it." It felt strangely cold-blooded to start from scratch and reduce the horror to its bare essentials.

"Oh, yeah," said Wilfred soberly. "I think I read about that."

Michael nodded. "My lover weighed ninety pounds when he died. He was this big, lanky guy and he just . . . wasted away. I was sick myself about six years ago . . . paralyzed . . . and he used to carry me all over. . . ." His tears tried to burn their way out. "And then he became this . . . ghost, this pitiful, pitiful thing. . . ."

"Hey, mate . . ."

"He was blind the last two weeks of his life. On a respirator most of the time. The last time I saw him he didn't see me at all. All he could do was press his fingers against my face, feel my tears. I just sat there holding his hand against my face, telling some stupid joke I'd read in the newspaper . . . making plans for a trip to Maui." He snatched a napkin from a dispenser and dabbed at his eyes. "Sorry about that."

"I don't mind, mate."

"So I just . . ."

Wilfred finished for him. "You miss him."

"A lot . . . oh, a lot . . ." He began to sob now, in spite of himself. Wilfred came to his side of the booth and sat down, squeezing his shoulder. "So I'm just . . . treading water right now. I just don't feel like being with anyone in that way." He composed himself somewhat, taking another swipe at his eyes. "I'm not afraid of sex or anything. I just haven't been horny for a long time."

"Right," said Wilfred gently, "but doesn't your heart get horny?"

Michael gave him a bleary-eyed smile. "Sometimes."

"Well . . . a friend might help. Eh?"

The offer was so serendipitous that he almost started crying again. "Kiddo, I've never said no to that kind of . . ."

"Is there a problem here?"

They both looked up to see an enormous swarthy man, arms folded above his gut, glowering down at them.

"Sorry," said Michael. "If we're making too much noise . . ."

Wilfred bristled. "We're not makin' too much noise. We're makin' too much love." He stood the man down with his eyes, like a fox waiting for his next move. "Why don't you mind your own bleedin' business, eh?"

"Now, look," said the man. "You blokes have got your own places."

"Right you are. And this is one of 'em. So sod off."

The man glared at him a moment longer, then returned to his post behind the counter.

"Bleedin' Greeks," muttered Wilfred.

Michael was grinning uncontrollably. "How old are you, anyway?"

"Sixteen," answered the kid, "and I know how to take care of meself."

Twenty-five

Mary Ann's morning mail brought a number of oddities: a press release from Tylenol explaining their new "tamper-proof" packaging, a free sample of chewing gum sweetened with Aspartame, and a strange-looking plastic funnel called a Sani-Fem.

Dumping everything on her desk, she sat down and examined the Sani-Fem. *Ideal for backpacking,* the brochure trumpeted, *or when public toilet seats prove to be unsanitary.* The larger end of the funnel was contoured to fit snugly against the crotch.

She whooped at the wonder of it all.

Sally Rinaldi, the news director's secretary, stopped outside the door and peered in. "A raise or what?"

"Look at this thing," grinned Mary Ann.

"What is it?"

"It's . . . a Sani-Fem. It lets you pee standing up."

"C'mon."

Mary Ann handed her the brochure. "Read this." She picked up the Sani-Fem again. "I'm dying to try it out."

Sally backed away. "Well, don't let me stop you."

Mary Ann laughed. "In the bathroom, Sally."

"Go ahead."

"Right. And have Bambi walk in on me."

The secretary smiled. "Use the men's room, then. William Buckley might see you."

"Huh?"

"Larry's giving him a station tour. As we speak."

"William F. Buckley, Junior?"

"The very one."

God, what a pipe dream! Buckley and Larry Kenan against the wall, separated safely by a vacant urinal, shaking the dew off their respective lizards, when the girl reporter saunters in—natty in gabardine slacks and dress-for-success floppy bow and blouse. *Voilà!* Out comes the Sani-Fem. *"Morning, gentlemen. How's it hangin' today?"*

"Go ahead," coaxed Sally.

"You're crazy," said Mary Ann, dropping the funnel into the bottom drawer of her filing cabinet.

"You're too careful," winked Sally as she sailed out the door.

At the end of a do-nothing day, Mary Ann brought the Sani-Fem home with her. Finding Mrs. Madrigal in the courtyard, she showed the device to the landlady and gave a terse explanation of its function.

"Funny," said Mrs. Madrigal, her smile showing only in her eyes. "I had to wait forty-two years for the privilege of sitting down."

Mary Ann reddened. It was easy to forget that Mrs. Madrigal hadn't become female until roughly the time that Mary Ann hit puberty.

"Just the same," added the landlady, sparing them both the embarrassment, "I think it's a marvelous idea, don't you?"

"Mmm," said Mary Ann, adopting a quirk of Simon's. "I got a note from Mouse, by the way. He sends you his love."

"How sweet."

"He says Simon's apartment is kind of grungy."

The landlady smiled. "English aristocrats are proud of their squalor."

"Yeah. I guess so."

"It doesn't seem to extend to his personal habits, at least. He takes good care of himself, that Simon."

Mary Ann nodded. "You've spent some time with him?"

"Um. Some . . . Why?"

"No reason. I just wondered what your impressions were."

Mrs. Madrigal pondered for a moment, patting a stray wisp of hair into place. "Bright . . . I'd say. Quick. A little inclined to be vague." She smiled. "But that's part of his Britishness, I think."

"Yeah."

"But quite magnificent in the looks department. Or is that what you meant?"

There was something almost coy about the question that made Mary Ann uneasy. "No . . . I just meant . . . generally."

"Generally, I'd say he's quite a catch. For somebody."

Mary Ann nodded.

The landlady knelt and plucked a weed from the garden. "Sounds to me like you're matchmaking. I thought that was my job around here."

Mary Ann giggled. "If I find anybody good for him, I'll make sure you approve first."

"You do that," said Mrs. Madrigal.

The glint in the landlady's eye was more than a little disconcerting. *Be careful*, Mary Ann warned herself. *A nice old woman who used to be a man could very well know what's on everybody's mind.*

Heading upstairs, Mary Ann hesitated on the landing, then turned and rapped on Simon's door. He opened it wearing Michael's dark green corduroy bathrobe, loose enough to reveal an awe-inspiring wedge of thick brown chest hair. He was munching on a carrot stick.

"Well . . . hello there."

"Hi," she said. "I thought I'd just stop by on my way home. Is this a bad time?"

"Absolutely not. Here, let me pop into some trousers. I won't be a . . . ."

"No. This is just . . . spur of the moment. You're decent. I've seen more of you in your jogging shorts."

He gave himself a split-second once-over, then said: "You're quite right. Well . . ." He welcomed her with a whimsical little flourish of the carrot stick. "Come in, won't you?"

The room, of course, still spoke loudly of Mouse, with its shelves of tropic-hued Fiesta Ware, its vintage rubber duck collection from the forties, its chrome-framed "Thighs and Whispers" Bette Midler poster. The only signs of Simon were the latest issue of *Rolling Stone* and a bottle of brandy on the coffee table.

He sat down on the sofa. "I was just about to pour myself a little nip. Will you join me?"

"Sure." She eased onto the other end of the sofa, leaving a cushion between them as no-man's-land. "Just a teeny one, though. Brandy gives me headaches."

He looked faintly amused. "Brandy takes a certain commitment." He poured some into a rose-colored Fiesta juice glass and handed it to her. "Bottoms up."

She took a sip. "By the way, I was wondering . . . have you made plans for Easter yet?"

He grinned.

"What's so funny?"

"Well, this is Lotusland, isn't it? I haven't given a moment's thought to Christian holidays." He chuckled. "Most of my celebrations have been pagan so far."

"I'm sure that's true," she replied, "but I thought it might be . . . you know . . . a good time for us to plan something . . . since you're leaving right after that."

He nodded thoughtfully. What was he thinking?

"It's just the weekend after next," she added.

"Is it really?" He seemed amazed.

"Mmm."

He shook his head. "Time flies when you're pillaging a city." He turned and looked at her. "What exactly did you have in mind?"

"Don't laugh," she replied.

"Very well."

"It's . . . a sunrise service."

A moment's hesitation. "Ah."

"Was that a good ah or a bad ah?"

He smiled. "A tell-me-more ah."

"That's about it." She shrugged. "I'm supposed to cover it for the station. It's held at the highest point in the city, under this enormous cross. Everybody watches the sun come up over Oakland. It's kind of . . . caring-sharing Californian, but it might be a hoot for you."

"A hoot," he repeated. His smile had inched perilously close to a smirk.

"You hate it, don't you?"

"No . . . no. I wonder, though . . . how do we get up to this highest point?"

"Walk," she answered, "but not too far."

"Up Calvary, eh?"

She giggled. "Right."

"Well . . ." He tapped his lips with his forefinger. "I'm a foul-tempered wretch that early in the morning."

"I don't mind."

"Does Brian?"

"What?" He was making her nervous, but she hoped it didn't show.

"Mind getting up that early."

"Oh. Actually . . . he's not. He's going to a house party Theresa Cross is giving in Hillsborough. We were both invited, but . . . well, I got stuck with this assignment."

"I see."

"My motives are a little shaky, I guess." She gave him her best winsome smile. "I just wanted a little pleasant company during the ordeal."

"As Jesus said to Mary Magdalene." His eyes were full of mischief.

"Maybe it's not such a good . . ."

"I'd love to go," he said.

"You're sure, now?"

"Absolutely. It's settled. There." He punctuated the decision by clamping his hands to his knees.

She rose. "Great. I also thought we might have dinner together the night before. If you haven't got plans, I mean."

He gazed at her for a moment, then said: "Lovely."

As she left, she could feel his eyes following her. The sensation made her almost dizzy, so she went up to the roof to collect her thoughts before facing Brian. The night was clear and rain-washed. Beneath the new streetlight on Barbary Lane, the young eucalyptus leaves seemed pale as ghosts, the gentle gray-green of weathered copper. She counted four lighted vessels gliding soundlessly across the obsidian surface of the bay. The big neon fish at Fisherman's Wharf glowed pink above the water like a talisman from the Christians in the catacombs.

She sought out the North Star and made the only wish that came to mind.

"Let me guess."

She flinched, startled by her husband's voice. He stood in the doorway, smiling at her.

"God," she said. "You scared the hell out of me."

"Hey. Sorry." He came up behind her and kissed her neck. "You were making a wish, weren't you?"

"None of your business, smartass."

He chuckled, nuzzling her. "I like it when you do those little-girl things." She grunted at him.

"I've been thinking," he said, still holding her. "What about Sierra City?"

"What about it?"

"For our trip."

She drew a total blank.

"Don't tell me you've forgotten already."

"Well, don't make me guess."

"This weekend," he said. *"Ethelmertz* time?"

"Oh. Right."

"Or somewhere up the coast would be just as good."

"No. Sierra City is fine."

"Whatever," he said. "What's in the bag?"

Preoccupied as she had been, she had all but forgotten about the Sani-Fem. "Oh . . . it's a . . . never mind. You don't wanna know."

"Yes I do." He took the bag from her and removed the plastic funnel. "Christ almighty. What is it?"

She snatched the Sani-Fem from his hands and marched to the bay side of the roof.

"What the hell are you doing?"

She peered down into the dark tangle of shrubbery. "Nothing."

"Nothing?"

"Just one of my little-girl things." She dropped her slacks and pushed her panties down.

"Mary Ann, for God's sake . . ."

"Lower your voice," she said. "You'll attract attention."

Twenty-six

Wilfred's father was bellowing so ferociously that Michael awoke from a dream about bumping into Jon at a Buckingham Palace garden party. He sat up in bed, clinging to the fantasy like a comforter, while the patriarch slammed pieces of furniture against the wall upstairs. Amidst the cacophony, he could barely discern the shrill desperation of Wilfred's reedy, childlike voice.

"Poofter!" thundered the father. *"Bleedin' poofter . . . vile, filthy smut . . . I'll teach you, you little . . ."*

Something shattered against a wall.

Horror-struck, Michael jumped out of bed and slipped into Simon's red satin bathrobe. Opening the door to the hallway, he peered warily up the staircase just as the door upstairs opened, then slammed shut. He ducked back into his apartment, easing the door shut, and waited until he heard the father's leaden footsteps move down the stairs, through the hallway and out of the house. Hearing nothing else, he climbed halfway up the stairs and called: "Wilfred?"

No answer.

"Wilfred . . . are you all right?"

"Who's there?"

"It's me. Michael. Did he hurt you?" He continued to climb toward Wilfred's door.

"Wait there, mate. I'll be down in a bit. I'm all right."

So he returned to his apartment, where he brewed a pot of coffee and waited. When Wilfred finally appeared in the doorway, grinning valiantly, he was pressing a wad of toilet paper against his temple. "Sorry about the commotion, mate."

"Jesus," murmured Michael. "What did he do?"

"Aw . . . threw me against the cupboard."

"He *threw* you?"

"Is that so bleedin' difficult? I'm not exactly Arnold Bleedin' Schwarze-negger."

Michael smiled at him. "C'mere. Let's take a look at that. What did you do to piss him off, anyway?"

Wilfred came closer and lifted the wad of toilet paper. "He found me old *Zipper* in the dustbin."

"He did *what?"*

"It's a magazine with naked blokes."

"Oh. Jesus, that's gonna be a goose egg. Hang on . . . I've got some alcohol and Band-Aids in my travel kit." He found what he needed, then returned, dabbing the kid's forehead as he asked: "You read that stuff?"

Wilfred was aghast at his ignorance. "They're for wanking, mate, not reading."

Michael smiled. "I stand corrected."

"You never bought one?"

"Oh, sure. It's pretty popular at home right now. It's a lot safer to have sex with a magazine. Does that sting?"

"Like bloody hell," said Wilfred.

"Good. It's working. My friend Ned calls it periodical sex. I always thought that was kind of cute." He pressed the "flesh-colored" Band-Aid into place, noting the careless injustice of that expression. "There. Almost good as new."

Wilfred sniffed the air. "Is that coffee?"

"Sure. Want a cup?"

"Super," said Wilfred.

Bringing him the coffee, Michael asked: "Got plans for the day?"

The kid shrugged.

"Great. Then take me to Harrods."

"Are you serious?"

"Sure. I need to buy some things for my friends back home."

So Wilfred obliged and led him to the princely department store, where Michael stocked up on treasures from the royal kitsch section: Prince William egg cups, Princess Diana dishrags, Queen Mum appointment books. He searched in vain for something with Princess Anne's face on it, but that visage seemed of little value to the British—camp or otherwise.

As they passed through the men's wear department, Wilfred tugged on his sleeve. "Look, mate. Princess Diana."

"That's O.K.," said Michael. "I've already got the dishrag."

"No, mate. *Herself.*" He jerked his head toward a svelte blonde who stood at the counter examining a pair of men's pajamas. She was wearing a pale gray cashmere sweater above a pink floral Laura Ashley skirt. There were discreet little pearls at her ears and throat, and her feet were encased in black patent pumps.

Michael ducked behind a pillar and signaled Wilfred to join him.

The kid giggled. "Hey, mate, it isn't really . . ."

"Shhh. Don't let her see you."

Hugely amused, Wilfred whispered: "Its just a Sloane Ranger."

"A what?"

"A twitzy-twee bitch. They shop in Sloane Square. They all try to look like . . ."

"Wilfred, get back here!"

115

"Have you gone . . . ?"

"I know her," Michael whispered. "At least, I think I do. She looks a lot like an old friend of mine."

Wilfred rolled his eyes. "Why don't you ask her, then?"

"I tried that once and she ran away."

"When?"

"About a week ago. On Hampstead Heath. Oh, God . . . has she left yet?"

"Not yet. The shop assistant is showing her some more pajamas."

Michael strained to hear her voice, but it was obliterated by the stately din of the department store. "This is insane," he murmured. "She must be in deep trouble."

"Why?"

"I don't know. Why wouldn't she speak to me? Something is horribly wrong."

Wilfred shrugged. "She looks all right to me."

"I know," said Michael. "That's what's wrong."

The kid peered around the pillar again. "She's leaving now. What are you gonna do?"

"Jesus. If she sees me, we may lose her for good."

"What if I follow her? She won't recognize *me*."

"I don't know. . . ."

"A wog would scare her off, eh?"

Michael frowned at him. "She's not like that. All right . . . go ahead. See what you can find out. Wait! Where should we meet?"

The kid screwed up his face in thought. "Well . . . the Markham Arms in Kings Road . . . No, it's not Saturday."

"Huh?"

"It's only gay on Saturday."

"Screw that. I'll meet you there in an hour."

"Right. Markham Arms, Kings Road."

"Got it," said Michael. "Don't let her see you, Wilfred. Just watch what she does, O.K.?"

The kid brought his fingertips to his Band-Aid and gave a jaunty salute, already moving toward his quarry. Michael waited fifteen minutes, then left Harrods and caught a cab to the Markham Arms. The pub was full of noisy shoppers, bordering on trendy, many of whom seemed to be in flight from the first major downpour of the day. He bought a cider and wedged himself in a corner as the jukebox began to play Sting's "Spread a Little Happiness" from *Brimstone and Treacle.*

Wilfred didn't appear at the appointed time, so Michael bought another cider and a package of vinegar crisps. He chatted briefly with a handsome businessman at the bar, who looked as if he belonged there on Saturday. They were discussing *Cats* when Wilfred pushed his way through the crowd and shook the rain off his golden-brown locks.

"In the first place," he announced, "she's an American."

116

"I knew it. What else?"

Wilfred grinned. "A stout would loosen me tongue."

"You got it." He signaled the bartender and ordered a Guinness and another package of crisps. "She didn't see you, did she?"

"Don't think so," the kid replied. "I kept me distance. It wasn't easy, mate. She kept a steady pace all the way."

"Where did she go?"

"Hey . . . me stout."

Michael turned and took the glass from the bartender, handing it to Wilfred. "There's a seat over there. Shall we grab it?"

"Good idea," the kid answered. "I'm exhausted."

Michael said "Take care" to the businessman and followed Wilfred through the raucous mob. When they were seated, Wilfred said: "She's a high-toned one, isn't she? She spent the whole bleedin' time in Beauchamp Place."

"Where's that?"

"Not far from Harrods. Off the Brompton Road. It's mostly for rich people and Americans. Poncy little shops . . . that sort of thing."

"Where did she go?"

"Oh . . . a shop called Emeline that sells jewelry. I don't think she bought anything, but it was hard to tell. I had to watch from the street. The shop was too small to do any proper spying."

"Good thinking."

"Then she went to a place called Spaghetti."

"A restaurant?"

"A dress shop. She didn't stay long. The rain started again, so she ran along the pavement for a bit. Some bloke on a motorcycle splashed water on her dress, and she stopped and gave him the finger. Said, 'Fuck you, mac.' "

Michael smiled. "It's her, all right."

"I waited a bit, then I tailed her into a shop called Caroline Charles. The bitch behind the counter gave me a dirty look, so I couldn't hang around too long."

"She didn't say anything? My friend, I mean."

"Not much. She bought a dress. Paid for it in cash with a great wad of bills she pulled out of her purse."

"Did she take the dress with her?"

Wilfred shook his head. "She wanted it mailed. Said she needed it by Easter."

"Great! Did she say where?"

"Sorry, mate. She wrote it down for the shop assistant."

"Did you follow her?"

Wilfred shook his head. "She took a cab when she left."

"What color was the dress?"

"Sort of pink," answered Wilfred. "No, peach, perhaps, with big puffy sleeves. Why?"

"C'mon, kiddo. Let's grab a cab. It's my turn to play detective."

Fifteen minutes later, he left Wilfred at a coffee shop in Beauchamp Place, then headed off to Caroline Charles on his own. The woman behind the counter was just as chilly as Wilfred had depicted her.

"Yes, sir. May I help you?"

"Yes, thank you. My wife just bought a dress here . . . about half an hour ago. An American lady in a gray sweater and pink skirt?"

"Yes."

"A peach dress. She asked that it be shipped."

"I recall it quite well, sir. What may I do for you?"

"Well . . . I know this sounds awfully silly, but she thinks she may have given you the wrong address. She's been . . . uh . . . ill lately and she tends to be rather absentminded, and she thinks she may have given you our winter address instead of . . . you know . . . our summer one, and, well, I thought it best to check."

The woman frowned at him.

"Frankly," said Michael, lowering his voice to a whisper, "if I could get her off Valium, we wouldn't have this problem. Last week she forget where she left the Bentley and it took us two days to find it."

The saleswoman's lip curled slightly as she pulled out the order and laid it in front of Michael. As he read it, he burned the words into his brain:

> Roughton
> Easley-on-Fen
> Near Chipping Camden
> Gloucestershire

"Good," he said. "Everything's in order. I guess there's hope for the old girl yet."

By the time he got back to the coffee shop, the address had been reduced to gibberish in his head, slithy toves gyring and gimbling in the wabe. Spotting Wilfred, he silenced him with a wave until he had a chance to write it down. Then he showed it to him.

"Make any sense?"

The kid shrugged. "Gloucestershire does. I think I've heard of Chipping Camden, but the rest . . ."

"Is Roughton the name of a person or a place?"

"Could be either, I suppose. It's not hers?"

"Nope. Hers is Ramsey. Mona Ramsey."

"Maybe the dress was just a gift for someone. No . . . that's not likely."

"Why not?" asked Michael. The thought had already occurred to him. If she was being kept by a wealthy benefactress, she might well pick up a little something for her.

"Well," said Wilfred, "she tried it on, didn't she? Unless her friend is exactly the same size." He paused for a moment, apparently reading Michael's mind. "She fancies girls, does she?"

He smiled at the kid. "Most of the time. She's pretty much of a loner, though. She doesn't trust people. She thinks life is a shit sandwich."

"She's right," said Wilfred.

"She doesn't take any guff from people. She's like you in that respect."

"Nothin' wrong with that, mate."

"I know. I could learn that talent myself. I've never known a Southerner who wasn't too polite for his own good."

"You're from the South?"

Michael nodded.

"The Deep South?"

"Not exactly. Orlando. And stop looking at me like that. I've never lynched a soul."

Wilfred smiled and butted Michael's calf with the side of his foot. "What are you gonna do about her?"

"Well . . . I guess I could mail a letter to this address. Fat chance that'll do any good, since she ran away from me on the heath."

"Are you sure she knew it was you?"

"Positive. And I know why she ran away."

"Why?"

"Because I'm the closest thing she's got to a conscience."

"And she's doing something wrong?"

"Well . . . something she's ashamed of. She's even got a disguise for it. She doesn't usually look like that. Her real hair is red and frizzy, and she's never worn a string of pearls in her life. Not to mention *pink*."

"You've known her long?"

Michael thought for a moment. "At least eight years. My landlady in San Francisco is her . . ." He couldn't help chuckling, though it seemed faintly disrespectful to Mrs. Madrigal. "My landlady is her father."

Wilfred blinked at him.

"She's a transsexual. She used to be a man."

"A sex change?"

Michael nodded. "You hardly ever think about that. She's just a nice person . . . the kindest person I've ever known." He missed her, he realized, far more than he missed his real parents.

He was tired of fretting over Mona, so they returned to Harrods and resumed shopping. Two hours later they dragged wearily into 44 Colville Crescent, laden with royal-family souvenirs. While Michael examined his treasures, Wilfred pranced about the kitchen making sandwiches.

"This tastes wonderful," Michael mumbled, biting into a chicken-and-chutney on rye.

"Good."

"How's the noggin, by the way?"

"Aw . . . can't even feel it."

119

"Is it safe for you to go home?"

Wilfred looked up from his sandwich. "Sick o' me, mate?"

"C'mon. I was just worried about your old man. Does he stay mad for long?"

The kid shook his head. "He doesn't stay anything for long."

The door buzzer sounded, causing Michael to flinch. He rose and peered through the front curtains. The caller was a woman of thirty or so, looking soberly aristocratic in a burgundy blazer and Hermès scarf. Her box-pleated navy blue skirt appeared to conceal a lower torso so formidable that it might have done justice to a centaur. Her hair, dirty-blond and center-parted, curved inward beneath her jaw, like a pair of parentheses containing a superfluous concept.

"Oh," she said flatly, when he opened the front door. "You're not Simon."

"Not today." He grinned. "May I give him a message?"

"He's still gone, is he?"

He nodded. "He'll be back just after Easter. We swapped apartments."

"I see. You're from California?"

"Right. Uh . . . would you like to come in or anything?"

She considered his lame offer, frowning slightly, then said: "Yes, thank you." She cast a flinty glance at two black children playing in the sand next to the cement mixer. "If nothing else, it's *safer* inside."

He had no intention of agreeing with her. "I'm Michael Tolliver," he said, extending his hand.

She held hers out limply, as if to be kissed. "Fabia Dane." As she followed him into the corridor, her face knotted like a fist. "My God. That smell! Did someone park another custard in here?"

She meant puke, he decided, and he suddenly found himself feeling uncharacteristically defensive about the place. He loathed this woman already. "It's an old building," he said evenly. "I guess the smells are unavoidable."

She dismissed that thesis with a little grunt. "Dear Simon's problem is that he's never been able to tell the difference between Bohemian and just plain naff. One could certainly understand a grotty little flat in Camden Town, say . . . or even Wapping, for God's sake . . . but *this*. It must be awful for you. And those horrid abos with their drums going night and . . ."

Her diatribe came to an abrupt end as she barged into the living room and caught sight of Wilfred sprawled on the sofa. "Booga booga," he said brightly.

Michael grinned at him. Fabia turned to Michael with a granite countenance. "What I have to say is personal. Do you mind?"

Wilfred sprang up. "Just leaving, milady."

Michael saw no reason to humor her. "Wilfred, you don't have to."

"I know." He winked at Michael. "Talk to you later, mate."

As soon as he had gone, Fabia eased her centaur haunches into an armchair and said: "I'm sure Simon wouldn't appreciate that."

Michael sat down as far away from her as possible. "Appreciate what?"

"Letting that aborigine have the run of the house."

Michael paused, trying to stay calm. "He said nothing about that to me."

"Just the same, I would think that a little common sense might be in order."

"Wilfred is a friend of mine. All right?"

"They're squatting, you know."

"Who?"

"That child and his horrid father. They don't pay rent on that flat. They just moved in and laid claim to it. Never mind. I'm sure you think it's none of my business. I felt it only fair to warn you."

"But . . . if that's illegal, why hasn't . . . ?"

"Oh, it's perfectly legal. Just not very sporting. So-o-o . . . if Simon is cross with you, you'll know the reason why." She gave him the smug little smile of a snitch. Michael felt a sudden urge to wipe it off her face with a two-by-four. Instead, he changed the subject: "What is it you'd like me to tell Simon?"

"He's coming home in a fortnight?"

"More or less."

"He hasn't gone queer on us, has he?"

Not a two-by-four, a four-by-four. With a nail in it. "I haven't asked Simon about his private life," he answered blandly.

She studied him for a moment, then said: "Well, anyway . . . the message is that he missed a marvelous wedding." She paused, obviously for effect. "Mine, to be precise."

"All right."

"Dane is my new name. My maiden name was Pumphrey. Fabia will do, actually. I'm quite sure Simon doesn't know any others."

Michael was quite sure too.

"At any rate, my husband and I will be giving a little summer affair at our new place in the country, and it wouldn't be complete without Simon, God knows. The invitation will be coming later, but you might give him a little advance warning, so he can think up a truly masterful excuse."

The last remark was so full of poison that Michael wondered if she was a jilted lover. Did she stop by just to rub Simon's nose in her marriage?

"Come to think of it," added Fabia, "better make sure he gets the last name. I wouldn't want there to be any confusion. It's Dane." She spelled it for him.

"As in Dane Vinegar Crisps?"

"Yes," she answered, "as a matter of fact."

"No kidding?"

"That's my husband's company."

"How amazing. Wilfred and I had some of those just this afternoon."

"Wilfred?"

121

"The aborigine."

"I see."

Michael rose. "I'll give Simon your message."

Fabia regarded him coldly for a moment, then got up and went to the door. She paused there, apparently considering an exit line. Michael folded his arms and squared his jaw. She gave him a faint, curdled smile and left.

Michael stood fast until she was outside, then sat down and finished his sandwich.

Wilfred returned ten minutes later. "She's gone, eh?"

"Thank God."

"What did she want?"

"Nothing. Nothing important. Just a message for Simon."

"It isn't us with the drums, you know."

Michael smiled at him. "I don't care about that."

"Just the same, it isn't me and me dad. It's those bleedin' Jamaicans across the way."

"Sit down," said Michael. "Forget about that harpy. Finish your sandwich."

The kid sat down. "You know there was a bloke watching your flat?"

"When?"

"Just now. A fat bloke. I saw him from me window."

"Oh," said Michael. "Probably her husband waiting for her." The all-powerful Mr. Dane, King of the Vinegar Crisps.

"No." Wilfred frowned. "Not likely."

"What do you mean?"

"Well, he ran off when she left the flat."

Michael went to the window. The children were still romping by the cement mixer, but there was no one else in sight. "Where was he?"

"Down there." The kid pointed. "Next to the phone box."

"And he was . . . just watching?"

Wilfred nodded. "Starin' hard at the window. Like he was trying to see who it was."

Twenty-seven

Their Palm Sunday weekend was only hours away when Brian phoned Mary Ann at work. "I made a sort of unilateral decision," he said. "I hope you don't mind."

By now, she had grown extremely wary of new developments. "What is it?" she asked.

"I canceled our reservations in Sierra City."

"Why?"

"Oh . . . I thought we owed ourselves something a little fancier under the circumstances. How does the Sonoma Mission Inn sound to you?"

"Oh, Brian . . . Expensive, for starters."

"We can afford it," he replied, with somewhat less wind in his sails.

"Yeah, I suppose."

"You don't sound very excited."

"Sorry. I'm just . . . I think it sounds great. Really. I've always wanted to go there."

"I remembered that," he said.

She felt a nasty little twinge of guilt. She hated to see him make such elaborate plans on behalf of her fraudulent *mittelschmerz*. "Do we need to do anything special?" she asked. "Won't I need dressier clothes?"

"You've got time to pack them," he said. "They aren't expecting us until seven tonight."

"Great. I should be home no later than four."

She spent the rest of the afternoon tying up loose ends: editing footage for a feature on California Cuisine, making phone calls, answering memos that had languished on her desk for weeks. She was on the verge of making a discreet exit when Hal, an associate producer, caught sight of her in the hallway.

"Kenan's looking for you," he said.

"Shit. With an assignment, I'll bet."

Hal grinned at her. "No rest for the perky."

She weighed her options. If she walked out without checking with Kenan, she had no guarantee that Hal wouldn't rat on her. He was famous for that, in fact. So she gritted her teeth and stormed off to the news director's office, already stockpiling an arsenal of excuses.

As always, Kenan's inner sanctum was a hodgepodge of promotional media kitsch: miniature footballs imprinted with the station logo, four or five different

Mylar wall calendars, a Rubik's Cube bearing the name and address of a videotape manufacturer. The only recent change was that Bo Derek had vanished from the spot on the ceiling above Kenan's desk, and Christie Brinkley had taken her place.

Arms locked behind his head, the news director eased his chair into an upright position, and fixed his tiny little eyes on Mary Ann. "Good. You're here."

"Hal said you wanted to see me."

His smile was a form of aggression, nothing more. "Do you remember . . . oh, way back when, when you first came to work for us . . . remember I told you a good reporter is the only person who is always required to respond to an Act of God? Do you remember that?"

"Sure," she said, nodding. For all she knew, even the janitors at the station were subjected to that asinine speech. "What about it?"

"Well, lady . . ." He was drawing out the suspense as long as possible. "I've got something for you that just might qualify."

When she broke the news to Brian, he was just as angry as he deserved to be. "Fuck that, Mary Ann! We've been planning this trip all week. You told them that, didn't you?"

"Of course."

"Well, why do they have to pick on you?"

"Because . . . I'm the lowest on the totem pole, and they know I'll do . . ."

"What's so goddamn important that they can't wait until Monday, at least?"

"Well . . . it's kind of an Easter story . . . Holy Week, rather . . . so they need it now, if . . ."

"The Pope is coming? What?"

"You'll just get mad, Brian."

"I'm mad already. What the hell is it?"

"A woman in Daly City. She thinks she's seen Jesus."

"Terrific."

"Brian . . ."

"Where did she see Him? On her dashboard?"

"No. On a tortilla."

He hung up on her.

She left the station minutes later and drove to Daly City. The site of the miracle was a tiny Mexican restaurant called Una Paloma Blanca. A white dove. Not a bad tie-in for the Holy Week angle. The cameraman was already there, fretting over technical problems with the tortilla.

"I'm telling you," he snapped, "it just won't read. Trust me. I know what I'm talking about."

"Look," she countered. "I can see it. See . . . there's the beard. That's part of the cheekbone. That wrinkle going left to right is the top of His head."

"Swell, Mary Ann. Tell that to the camera. There's not enough contrast, I'm telling you. It's as simple as that."

Mary sighed and muttered "Shit" to no one in particular. This provoked a disapproving cluck from Mrs. Hernandez, the tortilla's discoverer. In anticipation of her television debut, the portly matron was decked out in her grandmother's lace shawl and mantilla.

"Excuse me," said Mary Ann, bowing slightly to underscore her sincerity

"We could highlight it," the cameraman suggested.

"What?"

"The tortilla. We could touch it up."

"No!" She was feeling sleazier by the minute. Her perennial wisecrack about working for the "*National Enquirer* of the Air" contained more truth than she cared to admit, even to herself.

"But if we explained . . ."

"Matthew, *don't touch up the tortilla,* all right?"

He called for truce with his hands. "O.K., O.K." He looked around at the blackened pots and pans of the cramped kitchen. "Should we shoot it here?"

"She found it here, didn't she?"

"Yeah, but there's not enough room for the others."

"*What* others?"

He smiled at her lazily. "All those pilgrims in the front room. They came to be on TV."

"Well, they *can't* be!"

"Swell. *You* tell them that."

She groaned at him, then stomped to the pay phone in the front room. She called Larry Kenan and suggested that the story be scrapped. His response was clipped and vitriolic: "If it's too much for you, lady, I'll put Father Paddy on it. Wait there and don't touch that friggin' tortilla!"

Forty-five minutes later, the television host of *Honest to God* alighted cassock-clad from his red 1957 Cadillac Eldorado Biarritz. "Darling!" he beamed, catching sight of Mary Ann. "You poor thing! This is your first miracle, isn't it?"

"I'm not sure it qualifies," she muttered.

"Tut-tut. Miracles are like beauty, I always say. They're in the eye of the beholder. Where *is* the beholder, by the way?"

"In the back," she answered, pointing past the mob in the front room. "In the kitchen."

"Grand." Father Paddy glided through the throng like a stately pleasure craft, eliciting devout murmurs of recognition from the television viewers present. "The thing is," he told Mary Ann, "miracles are very, very good for people. We can't let a little faulty technology stand in our way. Some miracles are easier than others, of course, but I'm sure we can manage. Have you noticed, by the way, how it's always Jesus or the Blessed Virgin? *Good evening, my child, God bless you.* They *should* be seeing the Holy Ghost, since he's the ambassador-at-large, if you know what I mean, but no one ever spots the Holy Ghost on a tortilla—*God bless you, God bless you*—since no one has the faintest idea what the poor devil looks like. He gets no press at all. Christ, it's hot in here. Where's the tortilla?"

When they reached the kitchen, an elderly friend of Mrs. Hernandez was using the tortilla as a sort of compress against an arthritic elbow. "Oh, dear," said Father Paddy. "We may have lost Him."

A hasty examination of the tortilla reassured them that the holy features were still discernible.

"It won't show up on tape," said the cameraman.

Father Paddy gave him a knowing smile. "Backlight it," he said, "then tell me that."

"Huh?"

"You heard me, Matthew. Father knows best." He gave Mary Ann's hand a reassuring squeeze. "Never fear, darling. We're home free now."

He was right, it turned out. Backlighting the tortilla not only emphasized the color variations in the dough, thereby revealing the Christus, but also imbued the pastry with an inspirational halo-like effect. When the image finally appeared on the monitor, all twenty-three members of the Hernandez entourage uttered a collective murmur of appreciation.

"Perfect," purred Father Paddy. "Nice work, Matthew. I knew you could do it."

The cameraman smiled modestly, giving Mary Ann a thumbs-up sign. She was still uncertain, though. "They won't see the clothespins, will they, Matthew?"

"Nah."

"Are you sure?"

"I'll shoot just below them. Don't worry." He reached out and touched the length of twine from which the tortilla was suspended. "We wouldn't want Him to look like He's hanging out to dry."

She laughed feebly, hoping Mrs. Hernandez hadn't heard the remark. She was actually beginning to warm to this story. The face on the tortilla did look an awful lot like Jesus, if you discounted the lopsided nose and a dark spot that might be construed as an extra ear. She could already imagine the music she would use to score it. Something soaring and ethereal, yet basically humanistic. Possibly something from a Spielberg movie.

On the other hand, maybe the story was no longer hers. She turned to Father Paddy. "Will you be doing this for *Honest to God?*"

The cleric made a face. "What?"

"Well, Kenan sounded so pissed I thought maybe he had given you . . ."

"No, no, no. I'm just a consultant tonight. The story's all yours."

"Oh . . . well, in that case, maybe I should interview you about it. Just to get an official position from the church."

"Darling." Father Paddy lowered his voice and cast his eyes from left to right. "The church *has* no official position on this tortilla."

"What would we have to do to get one?"

The cleric chuckled. "Call the archbishop at home. Would *you* want to do it?"

"You don't have to declare it an official miracle or anything. Couldn't you just say something like . . ." She paused, trying to imagine what it would be.

"Like *what?*" said the priest. " 'My, what a pretty tortilla. Such a good likeness, too!' Come now. The archbishop has a tough enough time with the Shroud of Turin. The very least we can do is spare him the Tortilla of Daly City."

"Wait a minute," she said. "You called him for that statue story last December. I remember."

"What statue story?"

"You know . . . the bleeding one. In Ukiah or somewhere."

The cleric nodded slowly. "Yes . . . that's true."

"So what's the difference?"

Father Paddy sighed patiently. "The difference, darling girl, is that the statue was actually doing something. It was *bleeding.* That tortilla, for all its parochial charm, is simply lying there . . . or hanging there, as the case may be."

She gave up. "All right. Forget it. I'll wing it."

He ducked his eyes. "You're cross with me now, aren't you?"

"No."

"Yes you are."

"Well . . . you were the one who called it a miracle."

"And for all I know, it *is*, darling." He chucked her under the chin. "I just don't think it's *news.*"

She had come to the same conclusion when she dragged home at 10 P.M. and found Brian sulking in the little house on the roof. "I couldn't help it," she said ineffectually. "I know you're pissed, but these things come up."

"Tell me," he mumbled.

"We can still drive up there tomorrow."

"No, we can't. I canceled our reservations. We were damn lucky to even get a room. I had no way of knowing if you'd pull this again."

"So you thought you'd punish me. That's just great."

He turned and looked at her. "*I'm* punishing *you*, huh?"

Determined to salvage something, she sat down next to him on the sofa. "I've got an alternative plan, if you're really interested in hearing it."

"What?"

"Well, we could check into one of those tawdry little motor courts at the end of Lombard Street . . . we've talked about that before. And we could be there in fifteen minutes." She ran her forefinger lightly down his spine. "Wouldn't that work just as well?"

He made a grunting noise.

"And don't say it's a dumb idea, because you were the one who came up with it. Right after we saw *Body Heat*. Remember?"

He shook his head slowly, hands dangling between his knees.

"Besides," she added, "it strikes me that some sleazy neon would do wonders for both of us. Not to mention the Magic Fingers . . . and one of those Korean oil paintings of Paris in the rain. We can mess up both beds if we want to, and . . ."

"*Jesus!*"

The explosion really frightened her. "What on earth . . . ?"

"*Is that the way you want it to be?*"

"Well, it was only a . . ."

"Maybe I got it all wrong," he said. "I thought we were talking about bringing another life into the world! I thought we were talking about our kid!"

"We were," she replied numbly, "in part."

"So why the hell are you trying to make something cheap out of it?"

Her reserve flew out the window. "Oh my yes! Heaven forbid that Mommy should get a little fun out of the procedure. We're talking holy, holy, holy here. Tell you what, Brian . . . why don't you run out and gather some rose petals . . . and we can sprinkle them on our goddamn bed of connubial bliss, just so the little bugger knows we're good and ready for him . . . or her . . . or whatever the hell we're manufacturing tonight."

He stared at her as if she were a corpse in a morgue and he were the next of kin. Then he rose and went to the window facing the bay. After a long silence, he said: "I'm pretty thick, I guess. I've been misreading this all along."

"What do you mean?" Her voice was calmer now.

He shrugged. "I thought you *wanted* a baby. I really believed that."

"I do, Brian. I *do*. I just can't take it when . . . when you make it sound like that's the sole purpose of our sex, that's all. Hey, look . . . I came home from a horrendous day and you were sitting here like some spoiled kid with one more job for me to do. I'm sorry, but one miracle is all I can manage in a day."

"Miracle?" He frowned at her. "What's that supposed to mean?"

"Nothing. I just meant . . . I want you to want me for me, O.K.? I don't like being jealous of a kid who's not even here yet." She smiled faintly as a gesture of reconciliation. "That's all, Brian. Just for tonight, can't there be just two of us in bed?"

"Sure," he answered softly. "You bet."

"Do you understand what I'm saying?"

He nodded. "I'm sorry, babe. I didn't mean it to sound like that."

"I know," she replied. "I know."

They smoked a joint later and made love on the floor of the TV room. Perhaps because of the tension of her day, Mary Ann's orgasm eluded her until she took flight from the familiar and imagined it was Simon's body that was grinding her fanny against the industrial carpeting.

"You see?" said Brian, grinning at her afterwards. "Just the two of us."

Twenty-eight

After some investigation, Michael learned that London's most fashionable dyke nightclub was a place in Mayfair called Heds. Tucked away discreetly in a basement, it was marked only by an understated brass plaque at the entrance: GENTLEMEN WILL KINDLY DISCHARGE THEIR WEAPONS BEFORE ENTERING THIS ESTABLISHMENT. The doorperson was a puce-lipped brunette with a Louise Brooks haircut.

"Have you lads been here before?"

Michael turned to Wilfred. "Have we?"

"Once," said the kid. "Don't worry. We're bent."

The doorperson smiled at him. "Just checking. Have a good time, now."

The room was smoky and low-ceilinged, with a row of couches along one wall. Four or five lesbian couples were slow-dancing to Anne Murray beneath a jerky mirror ball. Most of the women were stylishly dressed, and some of them were astonishingly beautiful. Michael sat down on one of the couches and motioned Wilfred to join him.

"This is really a long shot," he said.

The kid shrugged. "Can't hurt."

"It's not really her kind of place. It's so . . . unpolitical."

"Yeah."

"Of course . . . her looks have changed completely. I guess the rest could've changed too."

"Have you thought about ringing her?"

"That address, you mean? I tried that three days ago. There isn't a listing for Roughton in Easley-on-Fen."

A cocktail waitress stopped at the sofa. "Something to drink, gentlemen?"

"No, thanks," said Michael. He glanced at Wilfred. "How about you?"

The kid declined.

Michael looked back at the waitress. "You wouldn't happen to know an American woman named Mona Ramsey?"

The waitress thought for a moment, then shook her head.

"She's in her late thirties. Wears her hair like Princess Diana. Swears like a sailor."

"Sorry, love. I don't catch the names usually." She smiled apologetically and moved to the next customer.

"How much longer have you got?" asked Wilfred.

"Till what?"

"Till you go."

"Oh." He thought for a moment. "Six days, I guess. I leave on Tuesday."
Wilfred nodded.

"Why?" asked Michael.

"Well . . . we could go there."

"Where?"

"You know . . . Easley-on-Fen."

"Oh."

"We could go there for Easter, couldn't we? It's lovely country, Gloucestershire. We could take the train. I've some money put away. And . . . if we don't
find her, there's no harm done, is there?"

The kid's earnestness frightened him. "Actually," he replied gently, "I
think I may do that."

Wilfred blinked at him. "Without me, you mean?"

Michael hesitated.

"I understand," said Wilfred. "Forget I said that."

"It isn't you," said Michael.

"Doesn't matter."

"Yes, it does. I don't want you to think . . . that I don't like you."

"I know you like me."

"I just think . . . it would be easier with . . . just me. I mean, if I come
crashing in on her scene, whatever *that* is. Do you see what I mean, Wilfred?" He
found the kid's hand and squeezed it.

Wilfred nodded.

"Do you dance?"

The kid glanced around. "Here?"

"Sure."

Wilfred shrugged, then stood up. Michael took him in his arms and led as
they danced to "You Needed Me." "Cripes," murmured Wilfred, his head against
Michael's chest. "If me mates saw me, I'd be so bleedin' humiliated."

Michael chuckled. "Same here." He was actually remembering a time when
he and Jon had necked around the pool table at Peg's Place in San Francisco. A
dyke bar was the best place in the world for man-to-man romance; the management
was always sympathetic, and there were no distractions. He wondered if lesbians
felt the same way about gay men's bars.

"When will you leave?" asked Wilfred. "For Gloucestershire, I mean."

"Oh. Friday, I guess."

"Will I see you after that?"

"Sure. I'll be back for a day or so before I . . . go home."

"Right."

"Don't get gloomy on me, Wilfred."

"Right."

It was almost midnight when they returned to Colville Crescent. Wilfred's father was lumbering about upstairs, obviously drunk. Michael opened the door of his apartment, then turned to the kid: "Why don't you come in for a while? Until he passes out, at least."

Wilfred nodded and followed him into the room just as the phone rang. Michael reached for it and flopped on the sofa.

"It's Miss Treves," said the voice at the other end.

"Oh, hi."

"Listen, love . . . have you had any trouble?"

"Trouble?"

"Oh . . . prowlers . . . that sort of thing."

"No. Not that I know of. What is this?" Her ominously vague warnings were beginning to get on his nerves.

"Oh . . . well, there may be a bit of . . . I doubt if it's serious, but I thought it best to let you know . . . just in case. There's been a misunderstanding, and the silly ass is drunk, so . . ."

"Miss Treves . . ."

"Just stay there, love. I'll be round shortly. I'll explain everything."

"O.K., but . . ."

"Lock the doors, love. Don't let anyone in. Check the windows too. I'll be there in five minutes."

She hung up.

Michael rose, a little dazed.

"Who was it?" asked Wilfred.

"Miss Treves."

"Who? Oh . . . the midget?"

"She said to lock the doors and windows."

"Why?" asked the kid.

"Good question. Somebody's drunk. It doesn't make any sense. She's coming over to explain it . . ." His words trailed off as he remembered the door that opened onto the garden from the kitchen. He hurried to lock it.

Wilfred trailed after him like an anxious puppy. "Maybe it's that fat bloke I saw."

"What fat bloke?"

"You know. When that bitch was here."

"Oh."

As he secured the back door, he peered out into the dark garden, but all he could make out was the grim filigree of the rusty bedspring propped against the fence. The sky glowed luridly, pinkish-orange, reflecting the lights of the city. There was no movement anywhere. He went to the kitchen window and tugged on the sash. "This goddamn thing won't close all the way."

Wilfred nodded soberly. "We've got one to match upstairs. Look, mate . . . what's happening? Is someone coming?"

"I don't know. She seemed to think so."

"Then why don't we leave?"

"We can't. Miss Treves is coming over."

The kid was silent for a moment, then said: "You forgot the window in the bedroom."

"God, you're right!" He dashed into the bedroom, with Wilfred at his heels. The window was already shut, so they returned to the living room, where Michael waited nervously at the window facing the street.

"What if he gets here before she does?" asked Wilfred.

"Don't make it worse," said Michael. A car rumbled past the elephantine silhouette of the cement mixer on the sidewalk. He watched until it rounded the corner and passed out of sight. Did Miss Treves drive? he wondered.

Moments later, the little manicurist arrived on foot, bustling along the sidewalk like a Munchkin bringing word of the Wicked Witch. Michael admitted her before she had a chance to reach for the buzzer.

"I'm sorry, love," she said in an earnest whisper as she hurried into the apartment and locked the door behind her. "You really shouldn't be involved in this."

"There's two of us, actually. This is my friend, Wilfred. He lives upstairs."

She nodded a brisk hello to the kid, then turned back to Michael. "It may be nothing, actually. I just wanted to be here in case . . . it got ugly."

Great, thought Michael.

Miss Treves turned and looked out the window.

"Look," said Michael, "could you at least tell us who we're expecting?"

The little woman hesitated, then said: "Bunny Benbow."

"*Who?*"

"Hush, love." She hoisted herself onto her favorite chair. "Close the curtains, please. Quickly!"

As Michael did so, he heard footsteps. It was a drunk's gait, heavy and faltering. The man muttered to himself as he passed the house, but his words were too slurred to be understood. Holding his breath, Michael glanced at Wilfred, then at Miss Treves, perched motionlessly on the edge of her chair with a forefinger pressed to her lips.

The footsteps stopped.

For a moment there was no sound at all except for the angry screeching of tires several blocks away. Then the man bellowed out a single word—*Simon!*— and overturned a trash can in the yard. Seconds later, the squawk of the door buzzer made the three listeners go rigid in unison, like victims of a joint electrocution.

Michael and Wilfred looked to Miss Treves for guidance. She shook her head slowly, once more using her finger to call for silence.

The buzzer sounded again, followed by the thud of the man's fists against the front door. *"Simon, you bloody little bastard, I know you're in there!"*

Still, Miss Treves insisted they remain quiet.

"Simon, lad . . . c'mon now. . . . It's your old man. . . . I won't hurt you." The man paused for a moment, waiting for a reply, then continued his plea in a more reasonable tone of voice. *"Simon, lad . . . she lies about me . . . she's a bloody liar, son. . . . C'mon now, open up, eh? Your old man needs your help, lad."*

He got nothing for his efforts.

"Simon!" he bellowed again.

"Hey," came another voice, just as angry. *"Sod off!"*

Michael locked eyes with Wilfred, who pointed to the ceiling to indicate the identity of the other shouter.

"Who said that?" yelled the man at the door.

"Up here, you bleedin' fool!"

Another garbage can clattered to the ground as the caller apparently staggered back into the yard. *"Call me a fool, you goddamn black bastard. Come down here and call me that, you woolly-headed wog!"*

The man returned to the door and began pounding again, a racket that was presently accompanied by the menacing thud of Wilfred's father's footsteps on the stairs. *"C'mon, lad . . . doncha even wanna see what your old dad looks like? I know what you look like. Tell you what, lad . . . talk to me for just a bit and I'll leave you be. Eh? That's the least you . . ."* His words were cut off by a bone-chilling howl from the aborigine and the bang of the door as it was thrown open. *"I told you to sod off, didn't I?"*

Michael turned to Wilfred, whispering though it was no longer necessary. "This is insane. We can't just sit here."

"Says who?" the kid replied. "I'm not going out there."

Miss Treves slipped out of her chair and inched toward the door. "Dear God," she murmured. "This is dreadful. Isn't there something we can do?"

The noise in the corridor was horrendous, a mixture of animal grunts and maniacal wheezing. Someone slammed against the wall so hard that a tin engraving fell off the wall in Simon's living room. After almost a minute of desperate battle, there was nothing left but the sound of one man's heavy breathing. Then someone opened the front door, closed it, and ran away from the house.

The corridor was still again.

Michael made his way toward the door.

"Wait!" said Wilfred.

"We have to see," answered Michael.

Miss Treves said nothing, hands aflutter at her throat.

Pressing his ear against the door, Michael listened for a moment. Nothing. He eased the door open, to reveal a large white man lying on his back in the corridor.

He knelt by the form and watched for breathing, then laid his ear against the wet polyester above the man's heart.

"It's the fat bloke," said Wilfred.

Miss Treves waddled glumly into the corridor. "He's just . . . unconscious, isn't he?"

Michael looked up and shook his head.

"He's dead?" asked Wilfred.

Miss Treves whimpered softly and fainted, falling against the hillock of the corpse's belly.

Michael looked at Wilfred, then down again at the macabre tableau at his feet. His mind flashed perversely on the last scene of *Romeo and Juliet*.

Wilfred said the first sensible thing. "Have you any smelling salts?"

Michael shook his head. Did *anyone* have smelling salts? "Wait," he said, suddenly remembering. "I've got something that might work." He rushed to the bathroom and returned with the little bottle of concentrated liquid deodorant he had bought at Boots.

Wilfred frowned. "I don't know, mate. Poppers?"

"It's not poppers." Michael knelt next to Miss Treves and scooped her into his arms. He uncapped the bottle and waved the pungent stuff under her nose. Nothing happened. He set the bottle down. "There's not enough ammonia, I guess. This is like spraying her with Glade."

"I'll get something wet," offered Wilfred, dashing out of the room. He came back with a sea sponge from the bathroom and dabbed delicately at the midget's features.

Miss Treves's nose was the first thing to move. Then her left eye twitched. Then a little convulsion shook her whole body awake. "Thank God," murmured Michael. He carried her back to the living room and laid her carefully on the sofa. It took a moment for her to realize where she was. Then the terror returned to her face. "Are you sure he's dead?" she asked.

"Uh-huh," nodded Michael.

"Who was that? Who did it?"

"Wilf . . . uh, the man upstairs."

"Me dad," put in Wilfred. He gave Michael a quick glance to show that he didn't need to be protected.

"They were both drunk," said Michael. "It was just a . . . freak thing."

Miss Treves nodded wearily. "Bunny has a bad heart." She glanced toward the corpse in the hallway. "The bally fool . . . the stupid, bally fool. I told him to leave well enough alone, but he was always . . ." Her voice trailed off in despair.

"Are you all right now?" asked Michael.

She nodded.

"I don't know what this is all about, Miss Treves, but I'll have to call the police."

"No! Not yet . . . please, love, not yet."

"Why?"

Her hands flopped about like injured sparrows. "It's best that we talk first. For Simon's sake. There's nothing to be gained by destroying everything he's ever . . ."

"Is that Simon's father?" Michael jerked his head toward the corpse.

Miss Treves swallowed once, then looked away.

"Is it?" asked Michael.

She nodded.

"And he thought I was Simon?"

Another nod. "I told the bally fool you weren't. He read that vile piece in the *Mirror* and saw you leaving one day and convinced himself that Simon had come home from California."

Michael was totally lost. "He didn't know what his own son looked like?"

"Uh . . . mate." Wilfred was tugging on his arm. "There's a body out there. This is no time for a bleedin' chat."

"He's right," said Miss Treves. "Perhaps we should bring it in."

"Now wait a minute . . ."

"Just for a bit, love. We can put it back."

"But the police will know that something . . ."

"No they won't, love. Just be careful about fingerprints. The lad will help you. Won't you, love?" She gave Wilfred a surprisingly winning little smile.

The kid shrugged at Michael. "They can't arrest us for movin' him, can they?"

So Michael gave in. He and Wilfred each took a leg and dragged the man-mountain into the apartment. Miss Treves showed her gratitude with another smile and said: "Would you mind covering him, love? Just for now?" Michael hesitated, then fetched Simon's duvet from the bedroom and draped it over the body.

"O.K.," he said crisply, turning back to Miss Treves. "What is it you want me to do?"

She looked down at her hands. "Nothing, really. Except . . . you mustn't mention what he said about . . . being Simon's father."

Michael studied her face. "Simon doesn't know that, I take it."

"No. And he mustn't. Ever."

"This guy . . ." He gestured toward the quilted mound. "He got Simon's mother pregnant?"

"No," replied the nanny. "Well . . . yes. Technically."

Wilfred giggled.

Michael ignored him. "And this man's name was . . . ?"

"Benbow. Bunny Benbow. He was the head of the revue I used to sing with. We met the Bardills at a hotel where we were playing in Malta. Nineteen fifty-six. They were on holiday, an extended trip around the world. Mrs. Bardill took a fancy to Bunny . . . which was only natural, since we were all in show business.

135

Mrs. Bardill was much more famous, of course, but . . ." She glanced almost sorrowfully at the corpse. "Bunny was a dashing figure in those days."

"So he came here tonight . . . ?"

"To see his son, in part. He was hopelessly sentimental, for all his faults. He knew that the Bardills were dead . . . and he thought there might be a chance of . . . being a father to Simon again."

"Again?" Michael frowned. "It doesn't sound as if he ever was."

Miss Treves fidgeted. "He also wanted money. That piece in the *Mirror* made it sound as if Simon was very rich."

"So this guy comes waltzing back after . . . what? . . . twenty-eight years, and expects Simon to buy that? To give him money, just because he got Simon's mother pregnant?"

The nanny looked away. Her lower lip had begun to tremble.

"Miss Treves . . ."

"He was in prison for most of that time. He robbed a hotel in Brighton. That's why the revue broke up. That's why I came back to London and found the Bardills and asked for the job as Simon's nanny."

Michael simply stared at her.

"He tried to reach Simon," she continued. "He wrote letters from prison, but I intercepted them. He had no right to spoil their lives. To spoil Simon's life. We were all so very happy, and he had no . . ."

"Wait a minute. How could he have known for certain?"

"Known what?"

"That he was Simon's father."

She looked at him balefully.

"I need the truth, Miss Treves."

"Love . . . I'm telling you the truth."

He reached out and took her child-size hand. "All of it?"

She heaved a world-weary sigh. "Mr. Bardill was sterile."

He nodded to encourage her.

"The Bardills wanted a baby very badly. *Very* badly." She brought her fingertips to her temple and made a circular motion, as if to expel a private demon. "I'm sorry, love. There's some brandy on the shelf above the fridge. Would you mind awfully?"

"I'll get it," chirped Wilfred, bounding to his feet and dodging Bunny Benbow on his way to the kitchen.

"You must be my friend," Miss Treves said to Michael.

"I am your friend." He gave her hand a squeeze. "You did my nails, didn't you?"

She mustered a wan smile for him as Wilfred returned with a tumbler of brandy. She downed it in two efficient gulps and gave the glass back to the kid. "Thank you, love."

"My pleasure," replied Wilfred, sinking to the floor again. He propped his chin on his fist and gazed at the two of them as if they were a television set about to flicker into action. "Don't mind me."

Michael turned to Miss Treves. "So . . . ?"

"Yes. Well . . . Mr. Bardill was sterile, as I said . . . and it was a source of great anguish for both of them. When we met them at the Selmun, I knew there was . . ."

"The what?"

"The Selmun Palace Hotel. Where we were performing."

"Oh."

"It was a lovely old place, miles away from Valletta . . . up on a hill overlooking the sea. One of the Knights of Malta lived there long ago. The people who stayed there were all lovely people, and the Bardills were the loveliest of the lot. She was a famous actress, but she wasn't a bit stuck-up. They bought bicycles in Valletta, which they rode all over the island, and she wore these lovely long scarves that trailed along in the breeze like . . ."

"Miss Treves." The brandy had been a terrible idea. "Time is of the essence."

She nodded. "I just want you to know that I didn't think of them as strangers, the Bardills. I felt as if I'd known them all my life."

"All right."

"I knew that I could trust them."

He nodded.

"At any rate . . . one night Mrs. Bardill took a long stroll with Bunny and told him about . . . Mr. Bardill's condition. Bunny offered to make arrangements for them . . . to obtain a child."

"To adopt one, you mean?"

"No," she replied dimly. "To buy one."

Wilfred drew in breath audibly. Michael shot a quick glance at him, then turned back to Miss Treves. "But you said he was . . . It was *his* baby, you mean? He sold Simon to the Bardills because they wanted . . . ?"

"Yes," she answered, before he could finish.

"He *sold* his own baby?"

"Our own baby."

He blinked at her.

"Simon is my son."

A car swooshed through a puddle out in Colville Crescent. Wilfred's eyes were porcelain saucers. Michael's failure to respond immediately prompted Miss Treves to add defensively: "It can skip a generation, you know."

"I'm sorry," he gulped. "I didn't mean to . . ."

"Don't be a silly-billy. It's not what one would expect, is it now?"

"No . . . I guess not."

"Bunny and I weren't married. We weren't even lovers in the conventional

137

sense. We were professional partners mostly. Simon was simply the result of . . . a night of foolishness. It was a stupid mistake, but we salvaged it rather well. Until now."

Michael hesitated, then asked: "You . . . didn't want a baby?"

"No, love." She smiled at him sweetly. "I wanted a career."

He nodded.

"I wanted to be a star, if the truth be known, but that wasn't in the cards. Bunny robbed that hotel in Brighton, and the whole bally world fell apart. If the Bardills hadn't taken me on as Simon's nanny . . ."

"They took you in, knowing that you were Simon's . . . ?"

"Oh, no! Bunny told them that Simon was the son of a girl in Valletta. He was simply acting as . . . broker. I imagine they suspected he was the father, but they never said as much. All they really cared about was having a beautiful son to care for."

"Does Simon think he's their natural son, then?"

"Everyone does. The Bardills were away from England for almost three years. They told their friends he was born in a Maltese hospital while they were on holiday . . . which was quite true. Mr. Bardill even had a birth certificate made, I'm not sure how. He was a barrister, you know."

"But what if Simon . . . ?"

". . . had grown up to be little? Well, he didn't, now, did he?"

"No."

"It was naughty of us—I admit that—but it solved everyone's problem at the time."

Michael looked back at the problem under the duvet. "And . . . this guy came here to spill the beans . . . and he expected Simon to give him money for that?"

"Not exactly. He wanted money, yes . . . but he thought Simon already knew about him."

"You told him that?"

She nodded. "I thought it would discourage him from seeking out Simon. I'm afraid I was wrong about that. It only sent him into a fury." She cast a scolding glance at the father of her son. "He has such a temper, that one."

If there was something appropriate to say under the circumstances, Michael couldn't think of it. Miss Treves sensed his discomfort and smiled sympathetically. "It's a bit much, isn't it?"

He waited a moment longer before asking: "What do you want me to tell the police, then?"

"Everything," she replied. "Except the reason he came here." She turned to Wilfred. "That won't make matters any worse for your father, love. They were both drunk—obviously—and they got into a senseless fracas. Bunny was wandering by on the pavement and . . . made too much noise, which . . . distressed your father . . . and they began to fight. They'll see that he died of a heart attack, I'm sure."

Michael wasn't so sure. "But couldn't they trace him to Simon?"

"How? I haven't seen him myself for over twenty years. They have no reason whatsoever to link him with me if . . ."

"What if Wilfred's father comes back?"

The kid shook his head. "He won't, mate."

Miss Treves gave him a pitying look. "He might, love. I doubt if the police would hold him completely responsible for . . ."

"Doesn't matter. I don't care."

"Of course you care. Don't be silly."

Wilfred smiled and shook his head.

Miss Treves raised herself to a sitting position, then sought the floor with her tiny feet. She wobbled a little standing up—because of the brandy, no doubt—but her resolve seemed firm as she strode toward the corpse.

"What are you doing?" Michael asked.

She knelt next to the body. "Looking for something."

As she searched Bunny Benbow's pockets, Michael grew increasingly nervous. "I don't think you should do that. They might be able to tell if . . ."

"We were looking for identification," she said curtly. "That's perfectly understandable. Here!" She had found what she wanted: Benbow's ragged clipping of the *Mirror* story—ROYAL RADIOMAN ON FRISCO PLEASURE BINGE. She handed it to Michael. "Burn it, will you, love?"

Michael stuffed it into his pocket. "Is there anything else on him?"

Her frisking produced only a few coins and a St. Christopher medallion. She brushed off her hands and stood up. "Well, now . . . are we clear on everything?"

"I think so," said Michael.

She turned to Wilfred. "How about you, love?"

The kid nodded.

"Good. Then I'll just slip back to . . ."

"Wait a minute," blurted Michael. "Where should the body be when the police arrive?"

"My, yes . . . well . . . I suppose we should put him back in the hallway, don't you? That way you can say he burst in when . . . the lad's father opened the door. Of course, you could very well have brought him in here . . . no, I think the hallway's best. Would you mind awfully?"

So Michael and Wilfred dragged Bunny Benbow back to the site of his untimely demise.

"Splendid." Miss Treves beamed as she supervised the arrangement of the corpse. "That looks quite natural, I think." She headed toward the door. "I'll just toddle on home. Would you ring me, love, when the police have gone?"

"Wait . . ."

"The number's on the fridge under 'Nanny.' "

"Oh . . . O.K."

"I'm just around the corner. Chepstow Villas." She gave him a supportive smile. "Keep your pecker up, love. It'll all be over soon."

She reached for the doorknob—reached *up*—then froze and turned around again, gazing wistfully at the body as she spoke: "Goodbye, Bunny. Safe journey home." Her eyes glimmered wetly as she glanced back at Michael. "Such a child, that one. Such a big, overgrown child."

Twenty-nine

Mary Ann was slicing kiwi fruit when Michael called.

"You sound so close," she said. "Are you sure you're in London?"

"I'm sure." His tone seemed tinged with irony.

"Is something the matter?"

"No . . . I'm fine. What time is it there?"

"Oh . . . suppertime."

"Is Simon there?"

"No. Why would he be here?"

"I meant . . . around."

"Oh." She must have sounded far too defensive. "He and Brian are out running, actually. We're having Simon to dinner tonight. Wait a minute . . . what time is it *there?*"

"Late. Or early, rather. I just saw a bobby to the door."

"A *bobby?*" She giggled. "Sounds like you're doing all right."

"Not that way."

"Oh."

"A man had a heart attack in our hallway. He was in a fight, and he died right outside my door."

"Oh, Mouse . . . how awful."

"Yeah."

"Are you O.K.?"

"Sure."

"You don't sound O.K."

"Well . . . I'm rattled, I guess. I'm not used to being interrogated."

"What did they want to know?"

"You know . . . just what I heard."

"What did you hear?"

"Not much, really. Just a couple of drunks yelling."

"Was it anybody you knew?"

"No. Well . . . the other guy lived upstairs. He ran away when . . . the guy had the heart attack. It's over now, anyway. How are *you*, Babycakes?"

"Fine. Well . . . O.K. Nothing to speak of, one way or the other."

"Is Simon enjoying himself?"

"Oh, yes. As far as I know."

"I've got a message for him. Tell him Fabia Dane stopped by. She used to be Fabia . . . uh . . . Pumphrey, but she got married and she wants him to . . ."

"Hang on. I'd better write this down." She scrambled for a pencil. "What were those names again?"

He spelled them for her. "She's having a summer party at her new country place. She's sending him an invitation later. Her new husband makes potato chips. And she's a cunt."

"Is that part of the message?"

"That's a footnote. I think he knows it already."

"O.K. Anything else?"

"That's it. She looked to me like a jilted girlfriend."

"Oh, really?"

"Uh-huh."

"What was she like?"

"Uh . . . cunt wasn't enough?"

"Well . . ."

"An upper-class cunt. How's that?"

"Great." She giggled, pleased with this elaboration. She needed all the reinforcement she could get. "When will we see you again?"

"Tuesday night, I guess. Tell Simon I'll leave the keys with his nanny."

"His *nanny?*"

He laughed. "That's a whole different story. She's his former nanny, actually. If you try to reach me after tomorrow, I won't be here. I'm going to the country for Easter."

"How elegant."

"Maybe. I'm not exactly sure where I'm going. I mean . . . I know where I'm going, but I don't know what I'm going to find."

"That makes sense."

"No. Get this: I think Mona's there."

"Mona? *Our* Mona?"

"I think so, but there's no way of knowing for sure. She won't talk to me."

"You've seen her?"

"Just briefly. From a distance. Her hair is blond now, and she cuts it like Princess Di."

"I can't believe it."

"It's macabre, isn't it?"

"How do you know she's in this country place?"

"I don't. It's kind of a long shot. I don't know . . . at least I'll see the countryside."

"Are you going alone?"

"I don't know."

"C'mon, Mouse . . ."

"I might go with a friend."

She heard someone whoop in the background. "Uh, Mouse . . . who was that?"

"Who do you think? The friend."

"He just found out he's going?"

"Right."

"He sounds pleased." He sounded delirious, in fact; the whooping hadn't stopped. "How old is he?"

"Eleven, at the moment. Wilfred, get down from there."

"Wilfred, huh? How English can you get? He isn't really eleven, is he?"

"No."

She waited for him to elaborate, then said: "Is that all I get?"

"That's all you get. Until I'm home."

"Is there good dish?" she asked.

"Some. Plenty, actually. I'm not sure you'll believe it."

"Like what?"

"When I get home, Babycakes."

"You're no fun," she pouted.

Thirty

Good Friday came, gray and drizzly. Michael stood on a platform at Paddington Station, mesmerized by the soot-streaked silver trains as they thundered into the great glass cavern. The depot was swarming with haggard Londoners, all intent upon an Easter somewhere else.

He checked the time. Eleven fifty-six. The train for Oxford would leave in seventeen minutes. He set his suitcase down and perused the other passengers queuing at Platform 4. Wilfred was plainly not among them.

They had agreed to meet at eleven-thirty, just to be safe, so the kid was almost half an hour overdue. If they missed this train, Michael realized, they would miss their connecting train in Oxford. He chided himself for trusting the kid to run off on his "last-minute errand," whatever it was.

He wouldn't get in a snit about it. He hauled his suitcase to the newsstand and lost himself in the screaming headlines of the tabloids. One said: RANDY ANDY'S ROYAL DIP. It featured a disappointing telephoto shot of Prince Andrew in a bathing suit. Another pictured the prince's porn star girlfriend and said: KOO D'ETAT.

He bought an apple and checked the time again. Ten minutes till departure. What the hell was going on? Had Wilfred changed his mind? Or misunderstood his instructions? What if Wilfred's father had come home?

The last thought was too creepy to pursue. He returned to the platform and saw that the train had arrived, so he paced alongside it, growing antsier by the second. *It better be serious,* he told himself, *but not too serious.* He couldn't leave without knowing what had happened. He would just have to cancel the trip.

He approached a conductor. "Excuse me. I'm trying to get to Moreton-in-Marsh."

"Right you are. This is the one. Change at Oxford."

"I know, but if I miss this train . . . ?"

"Then you'll miss Moreton-in-Marsh, sir. Till tomorrow, that is."

"Shit."

"Expecting someone, are you?"

"Yeah. I was. Thanks." He skulked away, supremely disappointed, then stopped in his tracks as he caught sight of Wilfred's bronze-brown ringlets bobbing through the crowd. *"There* you are."

The kid's expression was appropriately sheepish. "Sorry, mate." He was wearing jeans and a bright yellow sleeveless sweater with a matching bow tie. He carried a canvas satchel under one arm and a large cardboard box under the other.

Michael ditched his lecture and grinned at him. "We're not immigrating, you know."

Without answering, Wilfred boarded the train and strode through the carriages until he found one that was sparsely populated. "How's this?" he asked.

"Fine."

The kid took the seat by the window and stowed the satchel beneath him. He kept the cardboard box in his lap. "It took longer than I thought," he said.

"For what?"

A cryptic smile. Then Wilfred tapped the side of the box.

Michael looked down at it. It was wrapped in masking tape, and there were four or five little holes in the top. The light dawned. "Jesus, Wilfred . . . *if that's what I . . .*"

143

"Keep it down, mate."

"They'll throw us off."

"No they won't."

"It's gotta be . . . against the law or something."

The kid shrugged. "You're good with cops."

Michael stared at him incredulously, then looked down again. "Are you sure he can't get out of there?"

The kid nodded.

"But couldn't he bite his way . . . ?"

"He doesn't want to, mate. He's stoned."

"What?"

"I put a bit of hash in his meat."

The train lurched into motion just as a conductor entered the carriage. Wilfred leaned forward, folding his arms across the top of the box. Then he remembered his ticket, retrieved it from his jeans, and handed it to Michael. Hastily, he hunched over the box again.

The conductor loomed above them. "Where to, gents?"

"Moreton-in-Marsh," answered Michael, handing him the tickets.

"Lovely village, that. Heart of England."

"Yes. So we hear." His smile was forced and must have looked it. "We're going near there, actually. Easley-on-Fen."

The conductor's eyes darted to Wilfred, then fixed on Michael again. "Easter holiday, eh?"

"Right." Another insipid smile.

"Have a good one, then."

"Thanks," they replied in unison.

The conductor shambled to the next carriage.

Michael focused on Wilfred again. "Are you out of your mind?"

"Not a bit."

"What are we going to do with him?"

The kid shrugged. "Just turn him loose."

"Where?"

"I don't know. Gloucestershire. Anywhere."

"Great," muttered Michael. *Born Free.*

"What?" The kid's nose wrinkled.

"A movie. Before your time. Stop making me feel old. Look, what happens if ol' Bingo here . . . ?"

"Dingo."

"Dingo. What happens if his dope wears off before we make it to the wilds?"

Wilfred gave him a brief, impatient glance. "Well, there's nothing we can do about that *now*, is there?"

He had no answer for that.

144

"Just settle back, mate. Look . . . look out there. There's our green and pleasant land. You're on holiday, remember?"

Michael bugged his eyes at the kid, then sank back in the seat. He flopped his head toward the window as an endless caravan of suburban back gardens flickered past in the rain. They gave way eventually to grimy Art Deco factories, random junkyards, mock-Tudor gas stations squatting grimly beneath flannel-gray skies.

"It's clearing up," said Wilfred.

Michael blinked at him, then looked out the window again. "When does it start getting quaint?"

The kid snorted. "You Americans and your bleedin' quaint." He paused a moment before asking: "Where will we stay in Gloucestershire?"

"Oh . . . I guess a bed-and-breakfast place. We'll have to play it by ear." Somehow, he liked the idea of that very much. He looked at Wilfred and smiled. "Got any ideas?"

The kid shook his head. "Never been there."

"We may have to rent a car. It all depends on what that address means."

"Right."

"What about your father?" Michael asked.

"What about him?"

"Well . . . if he doesn't come back, what will you do?"

Wilfred tossed it off with a brittle laugh. "Same as before, mate."

The landscape grew greener, more undulating. The train stopped at four or five little gingerbread stations before they reached Oxford, where they disembarked and waited for the train to Moreton-in-Marsh. They had coffee and sweet rolls in the station snack bar while a noisy downpour brutalized the neatly tended flowerbed adjacent to the platform.

On the next leg of the journey, they sat in silence for a long time as the train rumbled across the rain-blurred countryside. Dingo had begun to stir slightly, but not enough to attract attention. Wilfred cooed to him occasionally and stuffed pieces of ham sandwich into the air holes. The fox made grateful gulping sounds.

"What did your lover do?" the kid asked eventually.

Michael looked up from a guidebook on the Cotswolds. "For a living, you mean?"

Wilfred nodded.

"He was a doctor. On an ocean liner." He smiled faintly. "He was a gynecologist when I met him."

"Really?"

Michael nodded. "I've heard all the jokes "

The kid smiled. "How long was he your lover?"

"That's hard to say. I knew him for about seven years."

"He didn't live with you?"

"Some of the time. Not in the beginning, then we did, then we broke up.

When we finally got back together, he had the job on the ship, so he wasn't at home part of the time. That's when we were happiest, I think. For ten days or three weeks or whatever, I would save up things to tell him when he got home."

"What sort of things?"

"You know . . . dumb stuff. Items in the paper, things we both liked . . . or disagreed on. I hate Barbra Streisand but he loved her, so I became responsible for any Barbra trivia he might have missed when he was on the high seas. It was a terrible curse, but I did it." He smiled. "I *still* do it."

"Did you date other blokes when he was away?"

"Oh, sure. So did he. We didn't sleep together anymore."

"Why not?"

Michael shrugged. "The sex wore off. We were too much like brothers. It felt . . . incestuous."

The kid frowned. "That's too bad."

"I don't know. I think it freed us to love each other. We didn't ask so much of each other anymore. We just got closer and closer. We had great sex with other people and great companionship with each other. It wasn't what I had planned on, but it seemed to work better than anything else."

Wilfred's brow furrowed. "But . . . that's not really a lover."

"Oh, I know. And we made damn sure our boyfriends knew that, too. We'd say: 'Jon's just a friend. . . . Michael's just my roommate. . . . We used to be lovers, but now we're just friends.' If you've ever been the third party in a situation like that, you know that the difference doesn't mean diddlyshit. Those guys are *married* . . . and they're always the last to know."

"But *you* knew," said Wilfred.

Michael nodded. "Toward the end. Yeah."

"Then . . . that's better than nothing."

Michael smiled at him. "That's better than everything."

"Does your family know you're bent?"

"Sure," said Michael. "Jon and I went to visit them in Florida a few months before he got sick." He grinned at the memory. "They liked him a lot—I knew they would—but God knows *what* they were envisioning between the two of us. That's funny, isn't it? They didn't have a damn thing to worry about. I spent five years getting them used to the idea of me sleeping with men . . . only to bring them one I didn't sleep with anymore."

"Where did you meet him?" asked Wilfred.

"At a roller rink. We collided."

"Really?"

"I got a nosebleed. He was so fucking gallant I couldn't believe it." He gazed out the window at two mouse-gray villages crouching in a green vale. "We went home to my place. Mona brought us breakfast in bed the next morning."

"You mean . . . the one at Harrods."

"Right. We were roommates at the time." Several ragged scraps of blue had appeared above the distant hills. He felt a perverse little surge of optimism. "I hope you get to meet her. She's not really . . . what was it you called her?"

"A twitzy-twee bitch?"

"Yeah. She's not like that. She's just a good, basic dyke."

Wilfred looked skeptical.

"You'll see," said Michael. "I hope you will, anyway."

When they arrived in Moreton-in-Marsh, the stationmaster directed them to the village center, a former Roman road called Fosse Way. It was lined with buildings made of grayish-orange Cotswold limestone, tourist facilities mostly—china shops, map stores, tearooms. The one at the end, closest to the church, was a pub called the Black Bear. They found two empty seats in the corner of the smoky room.

"See a barmaid?" asked Michael.

"I think Doll is it."

"Who?"

"Behind the bar, mate. The one with the eyeliner."

"How do you know her name?"

Wilfred smiled smugly and pointed to a sign above the bar: YOUR PRO-PRIETORS—DOLL AND FRED. "Any more questions?"

"Yeah. What about . . . our little friend?" He pointed to Dingo's box.

"Right. In a bit. How 'bout a cider?"

"Perfect."

While Wilfred was at the bar, Michael combed the titles on the jukebox and found Duran Duran and the Boystown Gang, San Francisco's own gay-themed rock group. The global village was shrinking by the second. He returned to his seat and took refuge in a reverie about ancient inns and craggy wayfarers and Something Queer Afoot.

"Success." Wilfred beamed, setting the ciders down.

"How so?"

"I asked ol' Doll about Roughton in Easley-on-Fen."

"And?"

"Well . . . Roughton is Lord Roughton, for one thing."

Michael whistled.

"For another, the house is very grand . . . one of the grandest in the Cots-wolds."

Michael thought for a moment. "We can't just walk up and ring the doorbell, I guess."

The kid grinned mysteriously. "Not exactly."

"Wilfred . . . don't be coy."

"I'm not. There's a tour."

"You mean . . . of the house?"

147

Wilfred nodded. "Takes us right there."

"Then we could . . ."

"I've booked us on it. Tomorrow morning."

It was almost too good to be true. Michael shook his head in amazement.

"Was that wrong?" asked Wilfred.

"Are you kidding? It's perfect. Did she say if there's a place to stay?"

"Upstairs. They have rooms. The bus leaves here at ten o'clock tomorrow morning. Ten pounds for the two of us. That's the tour, rather. The room is another eight pounds."

Michael rose, feeling for his wallet. "I'd better . . ."

"It's done, mate."

"Now, Wilfred . . ."

"You can pay for dinner. Sit down. Drink your cider."

Michael obeyed, acknowledging the kid's coup by lifting his mug.

Wilfred returned his salute, but remained deadpan. "I'm going to make someone a lovely husband."

The skies had cleared completely by dusk. They walked to the edge of the village until they found a meadow bordered by a dense thicket of beech trees. Wilfred set Dingo's box down with ceremonious dignity and untaped one end.

The fox emerged, looking slightly dazed, and stood perfectly still observing his captor.

"Go on," said Wilfred. "Get out of here."

The fox scampered several feet, wobbling somewhat. Then he stopped again.

"He doesn't want to go," said the kid.

"Yes he does. It's just new to him."

Dingo waited a moment longer, considered his options again, and bounded toward the shadowy freedom of the trees.

Thirty-one

Brian was sure the weekend would be fattening, so he made a point of running two extra miles on Saturday morning. On the way home, he stopped by the Russian Hill fire station and picked up one of the red-and-silver "Tot Finder" stickers he had seen in windows all over North Beach.

The sticker was designed to show firemen which window to break in order to rescue your child. There was a fireman on it, stalwart beyond belief, and he was holding a little girl in his arms.

Corny, maybe, but practical.

And not nearly so corny as the bumper sticker that Chip Hardesty had slapped on his Saab: HAVE YOU HUGGED YOUR CHILD TODAY? That one drove him crazy every time he passed Hardesty's house.

When he reached the courtyard, Mrs. Madrigal was scrubbing the mossy slime off the steps leading to the house. "It's getting so slippery," she explained, looking up. "I was afraid someone might have a nasty spill."

"I wouldn't worry about it," he said.

She stood up, wiping her hands on her apron. "I've got to worry about *something*. It's so quiet around here. Doesn't anyone have any problems?"

He grinned at her. "If you're really pressed, I'm sure we could cook up a disaster or two."

"That's quite all right." She eyed the "Tot Finder" decal. "What have we here?"

"Oh." He could already feel his face burning. "It's just . . . kind of a joke, really."

"Look at you," she teased, recognizing his embarrassment. "What's the matter? Did I catch you counting chickens?"

There was nothing he could do but laugh. "Do you have to ask?"

"No," she answered, fussing with her hair. "You're quite right. *Well . . .*" She put on a chipper face as she changed the subject. "You'll be up bright and early in the morning."

He wasn't sure what she meant.

"For the sunrise service," she added.

"Oh . . . no, that's Mary Ann. I'm going to Hillsborough for the weekend."

"Ah." Despite her tone of voice, she still looked vaguely confused.

He began to wonder if he'd gotten his wires crossed. "You mean . . . she told you I was going?"

"No . . . no."

"Then how did you . . . ?"

"Well, Simon mentioned the service, actually . . . and I just assumed that the three of you . . ." She tapped her forehead and looked annoyed with herself. "Don't mind the old lady. She's getting senile. What's happening in Hillsborough?"

"Uh . . . what?" He lost his train of thought for a moment, then recovered it. "Oh . . . a house party. Theresa Cross. Remember her? From the Cadillac?"

"Very well." Her expression said it all.

"You don't approve?"

"Well . . . I don't really know her."

"I'm going for the pool, really."

The landlady ducked her eyes.

"I'm a big boy, you know."

"Oh, my dear . . . I *know*." She gave him a playful look, then signaled the end of their conversation by searching for her scrub brush.

When he reached the apartment, he could hear Mary Ann inside, so he stuffed the "Tot Finder" into the pocket of his Canterbury shorts. He didn't want her to regard it as a pressure tactic. Her moods were too variable these days.

"Don't get near me," she said, seeing his coating of sweat.

He pretended to be hurt. "I thought you *liked* me pitted out."

"At certain moments, my love. This isn't one of them. Shouldn't you be packing?"

"Packing what? I'll be back tomorrow afternoon."

"Well . . . a bathing suit, at least."

He shrugged. "I'll wear one under my jeans."

She thought for a moment. "The Speedos, huh?"

He nodded. "The others are too baggy. Why?"

"Just curious."

She was worried about Theresa again; he liked that.

"Go shower," she said.

He went to the bedroom and shed his shoes and shorts and jockstrap. As he sat on the edge of the bed, collecting his thoughts, Mary Ann came to the door. It was almost as if she had heard him thinking.

He looked up at her. "You didn't tell me Simon was going."

"Where . . . oh, the Mount Davidson thing?"

He nodded.

She went to her vanity and began rearranging cosmetics. "Well, it was kind of a last-minute thing, more or less. The poor guy obviously didn't have any place to go for Easter, so . . . I thought it would be nice for him."

He didn't respond to that.

She turned around. "Don't do this, Brian."

"Do what?"

"Work yourself up again. I thought we'd put that behind us."

"Did I say anything? I just wondered why you hadn't mentioned it to me . . . that's all."

She shrugged. "It didn't occur to me. It's no big deal. It's just an assignment."

"At five o'clock in the morning."

She uttered a derisive little snort. "And we all know what a *lustful* creature I am at that time of day."

She got the smile she wanted. "O.K.," he said, "O.K."

Sitting next to him, she leaned down and licked a drop of sweat off his breastbone. "You big, smelly jerk. Just relax, O.K.?" She pulled back and looked at him. "How did you hear Simon was going?"

"Mrs. Madrigal mentioned it." He felt stupid about it already. "Let's drop it, O.K.?"

"Gladly." She nuzzled his armpit. "Whew! That is *potent*. Don't let Dragon Lady catch a whiff of that." She kissed his neck and rose. "I vacuumed the car this morning."

"Great. Thanks."

"It's up on Union next to the Bel-Air. I think there's enough gas."

He got up. "Look, I'm sorry if . . ."

"Hey," she interrupted. "No apologies. Everything is fine."

A long, hot shower did wonders for his spirits. Afterwards, he put on his bathrobe and returned to the bedroom. Mary Ann was still sitting on the bed. When he approached the mirror on the closet door, he found the "Tot Finder" taped there. He turned around and looked at her.

She was waiting with a cautious smile. "I thought we should put it up, at least. Until we decide on where to put the nursery." Her face was full of gentleness and resolution. He knelt next to her, resting his head on her lap. She smoothed the hair above his ear. "I want one too," she murmured.

It was almost three o'clock when he arrived at Theresa Cross's rambling ranch house in Hillsborough. There was plenty of room to park in the rock widow's oversized driveway, so he slipped the Le Car between a Rolls and a Mercedes, shamed by his embarrassment. Here, of all places, such things shouldn't matter. Bix Cross was the very man who had taught him to be suspicious of materialism.

After asking directions from a uniformed Latin American maid, he made his way through the pearl-gray living room until he came to a knot of people drinking furiously by the pool. They had all the single-mindedness of an ant colony trying to move something large and dead across a room.

Someone fell out of the circle of chatter, as if thrown by centrifugal force. He was somewhere in his early forties, and his face was bland but tanned. "Hello there," he said, extending his hand. "I'm Arch Gidde, Theresa's realtor-slant-escort."

"Hi. I'm Brian Hawkins."

"You're looking for her, I suppose."

"Well . . . eventually. This is the party, I guess." A dumb thing to say, but he felt so unannounced.

Arch Gidde smirked. "This is it." He cast a sideways glance at a lavish buffet, largely uneaten. "I hate to think how many salmon have died in vain."

"Uh . . . she was expecting more?"

Another smirk. "Do you see Grace Slick? Do you see Boz Scaggs? Do you see Ann Getty, for that matter?"

How the hell did you answer that one? "Is there . . . uh . . . a specific reason or something?"

"Oh, God. You haven't heard, have you? And I'll bet you're one of Theresa's rock-and-roll buddies. *Quelle* bummer. You missed the big one." He sighed histronically. "We *all* missed the big one." He leaned forward and lowered his voice to a furtive mutter. "Yoko Ono is throwing a little do in her suite at the Clift."

"Uh . . . now, you mean?"

The realtor nodded grimly. "As we speak."

"No shit." It was all he could muster.

"And madame is pissed. Madame is extremely pissed. Her guests have been bailing out all afternoon."

"I see." *Jesus God. Yoko Ono in San Francisco.*

"So," continued Arch Gidde, "she has retired to her chambers to compose herself." He tapped the side of his nose with his forefinger, then narrowed his eyes at Brian. "You look awfully familiar, for some reason."

Brian shrugged. He had waited on plenty of jerks like this during his career. "I don't think we know each other."

"Maybe. But I can't help thinking . . ."

"What's the party for?"

"This one? Or that one?"

"That one. I mean . . . why is Yoko Ono in town?"

"Oh, God." The realtor splayed his fingers across his face. "That's the part Mother Theresa hasn't heard yet. Mrs. Lennon is looking for a house."

"You mean . . . to live here?"

His informant nodded. "She thinks it's a good place to raise . . . little whats-hisname."

"Sean," said Brian.

"Imagine what this is going to mean to Theresa. Two rock widows in the same town. Two Mrs. Norman Maines."

He didn't know who that was, and he didn't want to ask. Seeking escape, he let his eyes wander until he spotted his hostess as she emerged from her seclusion. She was wearing a black-and-pink bikini in a leopard-skin pattern. Her hair seemed larger than ever.

She stopped at the edge of the terrace, resting her weight on one hip, then clapped her hands together smartly. "All right, people! Into the pool! You know where to change. I want to see *bare flesh.*" She strode toward Brian, pointing her finger at him. "Especially *yours.*"

He tried to stay cool. "Hi," he said.

"Hi." She came to a halt, once again settling her weight on one hip. "Where's Mary Ann?"

"Oh . . . I thought she told you. She had to work. She was really sorry she couldn't make it." For some reason, that sounded phony as hell, so he added: "I'm here to tell her what she missed."

"Good," replied Theresa, arching an eyebrow, "but don't tell her every-thing." There was something about her leer that rendered it harmless. What she seemed to offer was not so much lust as a genial caricature of it, an eighties update of a Betty Boop cartoon. She was accustomed to scaring off men, he decided; she counted on it.

Her body surprised him somewhat. Her breasts weighed in at just above average, but her big peasant nipples dented her bikini top like a pair of macadamia nuts. Her ass was large and heart-shaped, really a lot firmer than he had expected. All in all, a package that suggested a number of interesting possibilities.

"So get naked," she said. "We won't have the sun much longer."

Some of the other guests were already changing, so he doffed his shirt, shoes and jeans and stashed them behind the cabana. Theresa, meanwhile, eased her way into the deep end of the pool, taking care not to damage her mammoth gypsy mane.

Brian gave his Speedo a quick plumping and ambled toward the pool. The rock widow's hair bobbed above the water like a densely vegetated atoll. "You wet me," she said, "and it's your ass."

He grinned at her, then dove in effortlessly, without splashing at all. It was one of his specialties. When he surfaced, Theresa was dog-paddling in his direction. "Have you eaten?" she asked, sotto voce, as if it were an intimate question.

He shook his head, tossing water off his brow. "It looks great."

"Better do it now. You won't feel like it later."

He didn't know what she meant until she aped Arch Gidde's gesture and tapped the side of her nose. "Right," he said. "Sounds good to me."

She made good half an hour later when she led him into her flannel-paneled screening room and began chopping cocaine on a mirrored tray. "Take that one," she said, pointing to the fattest line of all. "It looks about your size." She handed him a rolled bill.

He took it in one snort, then made the obligatory face to show that it was good stuff. "Thanks, Theresa."

"Terry," she murmured.

"No shit? I never heard that."

A heavy-lidded smile. "Now you have."

He nodded.

"Only the real people get to use it." She powdered her forefinger with the remains of the coke and rubbed it across her gums. "I don't waste it on the phonies. You know what I mean?"

He nodded again. "Thanks, then."

"Terry's what Bix always called me."

This offhand brush with immortality seemed to put more bite in the cocaine. He was pretty sure she knew that.

"I wish they'd leave," she said.

"Who?"

"Them. Those others."

"They aren't your friends?"

"I never do this," she said, without answering his question. "I loathe people who sneak the stuff. But they'll never leave if I offer them some. I know how they are."

"Yeah."

She grabbed his hand suddenly. "Did I show you Bix's panties?"

It wounded him slightly to see that she had forgotten. "Yeah. Last time. During the auction."

"Oh. Right." She smiled penitently. "Brain damage."

"That's O.K."

"I don't show them to just anybody. Only the real people."

He nodded.

"You're a good guy, Brian."

"Thanks, Theresa."

"Terry," she said.

"Terry," he echoed.

Thirty-two

There were eleven passengers in all, six of whom were Americans. The driver doubled as guide, providing commentary as the bus left the village behind and plunged into the engulfing green of the countryside.

"Today, ladies and gentlemen, we shall be visiting Easley House, the focal point of the village of Easley-on-Fen. Easley House is an outstanding example of an English Jacobethan manor house." He chuckled mechanically in the manner of every bad tour guide on earth. "That's right. You heard me correctly. *Jacobethan*. That's a cross, don't you see, between Jacobean and Elizabethan. The house was built between fifteen eighty-seven and sixteen thirty-five by the Ashendens of Easley-on-Fen, a Gloucestershire gentry family which had owned property in the county since before the Conquest."

Wilfred made a not-so-subtle yawning gesture.

Michael smiled at him. "It was your idea," he whispered.

"She's your friend," said the kid.

"I wouldn't count on that," answered Michael, gazing out the window at a meadow full of sheep. "I'm not counting on anything."

The bus slowed down as it entered Easley-on-Fen, a picture-perfect village built entirely of crumbling umber limestone. They bounced along a sunken lane for a minute or two, then crossed another sheep-dotted meadow until the manor house came into view.

Wilfred's voice assumed a near-reverential softness. "Look at *that*, mate."

"I'm looking," Michael murmured. "Jesus."

Easley House shone with the same burnished glow as the village, a looming conglomerate of gables and chimneys and tall mullioned windows winking in the sunshine. It was bigger than he had pictured, much bigger.

"She's running drugs," said Wilfred.

The guide pulled into a parking lot (he called it a car park) several hundred yards from the house. Michael and Wilfred shuffled out with the other passengers, reassembling in a passive clump like raw recruits awaiting orders. The guide, in fact, made a passable drill sergeant, with his blustery delivery and time-worn anecdotes and his disconcerting Roquefort cheese smile.

"We shall proceed from this point on foot. Easley House is the private residence of Lord Edward Roughton, son of Clarence Pirwin, fourteenth earl of Alma, so I trust we shall all remember that and conduct ourselves accordingly at all times."

Wilfred made a farting noise.

"Now," continued the guide, oblivious of Wilfred's punctuation, "the first building you will notice on our left is the tennis pavilion, a thatched structure erected in the nineteen twenties. The building across the road there is the tithe barn of the village, built in the late fourteenth century by the abbots of Easley to store the produce tithed to them by their parishioners. The slit windows in the gables were put there to admit fresh air and . . . what else?" He looked around, flashing more Roquefort cheese, and waited for an answer; none came. "No guesses? Well . . . that's a private entrance for the owls. They needed them, don't you see, to control the vermin."

Four or five of the other passengers made sounds of recognition. "See, Walter," piped one of the Americans, tugging on her husband's arm, "see the little slits for the owls?" Her spouse nodded dully. "I see it, Phyllis. I have eyes. I see the slits."

Michael and Wilfred brought up the rear as the group was led through an ornate gatehouse built of the ubiquitous golden limestone. A small church lay to their left, encrusted with moss and whittled away at the edges by five hundred Gloucestershire winters. Its tombstones bore an uncanny resemblance to the guide's teeth.

"Now," he was saying, "we are passing the brewhouse, which was last used before the Great War when a brewing woman would come each autumn on a bicycle to brew the year's barley crop. We shall enter the house through the archway just ahead, passing first through the old kitchen . . ."

155

"In other words," whispered Wilfred, "the servants' entrance."

"Just behave yourself," said Michael.

A rusted lawn roller was parked by the door. Next to it lay a hinged, V-shaped sign, apparently still in seasonal storage. Its flaking letters said: EASLEY HOUSE—OPEN FOR TEA. Michael visualized the arthritic old butler who would drag it down to the public road when summer began.

"You will note," intoned the guide, as they entered the house and filed through a narrow passage, "these unusual-looking steel bars along the walls. This corridor was used as a larder some years back, and joints of meat were hung along these bars."

"See?" said Phyllis.

"I see," muttered Walter.

They were led into an empty paneled space which the guide identified as the dining room. The label seemed honorary at best; it obviously hadn't been used for years. Then came the butler's pantry and the lamp room, "where paraffin lamps were cleaned prior to the electrification of the house in nineteen thirteen."

"This next room is the audit room," the guide continued. "Lord Roughton is justifiably proud of the fact that he has not sold off the cottages of the estate. He has made every effort to preserve the visual charm of the entire village. His lordship collects the quarterly rents in person, using a special rent table—that's it in the center there—and that table was made especially for Easley House in seventeen eighty. His lordship informs us that this practice not only saves postage but facilitates complaints about leaking roofs and the like."

By the time they reached the great hall, Michael had been lulled into lethargy by the steady drone of the guide. He was hardly prepared for the dimensions he encountered, the heavenward leap of the high mullioned windows facing the chapel, the echo of their footsteps on the rough plank floor.

He was certainly not prepared for Mona.

Watching from a balcony.

Standing there, cool and blond, looking down on them.

Catching his eye.

Frowning.

Disappearing.

He touched the small of Wilfred's back. "I saw her."

"Where?"

"Up there." He led the kid with his eyes. "That little balcony at the end of the room."

With uncanny timing, the guide directed their attention to the same spot. "Above us, ladies and gentlemen, is all that's left of the original minstrels' gallery— the place where musicians would gather to perform for the gentry gathered in the great hall. The gallery was converted to a bedroom in the late eighteen forties, at

156

which time the oak posts supporting the gallery were sheathed with the present stucco Doric columns."

"Are you sure?" whispered Wilfred.

"Uh-huh."

"What now, then?"

"Nothing. We can't. Not yet."

The kid glanced impishly around the room.

"I don't know what you're thinking," murmured Michael, "but *don't.*"

"Over there," the guide rattled on, "next to the bay window, you will see a very rare Chippendale exercising chair. Bouncing on that rather odd contraption was believed to be beneficial to one's health." He grinned stupidly at the one named Walter. "How about you, sir? Would you care to try it?"

"No, thanks," was the sullen reply.

"Oh, Walter, don't be such a fuddy-duddy." His wife gave him a little shove.

"Phyllis . . ."

The guide coaxed his victim with a big hammy hand. "C'mon, sir. There's a good sport. Let's have a hand for the gentleman, shall we, everybody?"

Even Michael became engrossed in the man's humiliation, joining in the applause as the hapless Walter sat down in the suspended chair and began to bounce. The laughter that followed was all the diversion Wilfred had needed. When Michael turned around again, the kid was gone.

His absence wasn't noticed as the group was led up a short flight of stairs into the drawing room. Nor was he missed as they explored the library and the sitting room. "The sitting room," the guide explained, "is sometimes known as the *boudoir.* Does anyone know what *boudoir* means in French?"

No one did.

"Well, *boudoir* is the French word for 'to sulk,' so this room was the place where the ladies of Easley House came to sulk about the wretched behavior of their husbands." He chuckled manfully. "I expect many of you ladies know a thing or two about that, eh?"

A chorus of giggles. Michael glanced anxiously down the corridor, but Wilfred was nowhere to be seen. He was ready to murder the kid.

The group was herded into an open space behind the house, where the guide pointed out the stables, a formal topiary garden, and a pyramidal folly capping the hill above the estate. "Please feel free to wander a bit," he told them, "but do not go back into the house. We shall reassemble in the car park in thirty minutes. I trust you will all be prompt. Thank you very much."

Michael loitered in the topiary garden, keeping a close eye on the house. He began devising emergency plans to minimize the embarrassment in the event that Wilfred never showed up. The least troublesome scheme was set into motion in the parking lot, five minutes before departure time.

"I won't need a ride back to Moreton-in-Marsh," he told the guide. "I'll be staying in Easley-on-Fen tonight."

"What about your chum?"

Shit. He had noticed. "Oh . . . he walked into the village about twenty minutes ago. He wasn't feeling well . . . thought he'd catch a nap at the inn."

"I see. Then you'll be riding with us as far as the village?"

"Well . . . it's just across the meadow. I'm sure I'd enjoy the . . ."

"Just the same, sir . . ."

"Right. Great. That would be fine. Sure. Thanks."

So he took the bus back to the village.

"There," he said, pointing at the first believable-looking inn. "That's the one. That's where we're staying. Just let me out at the corner."

The driver grunted and brought the bus to a stop.

Michael could feel their eyes on him as he climbed down from the bus and marched purposefully into the pub adjoining the inn. Once inside, he embraced the absurdity of his plight and bellied up to the bar for a cider.

Fifteen minutes later, feeling much better, he left the pub and looked both ways down the road. The bus had gone. The only vehicle in sight was a green Toyota parked next to the inn. It was late afternoon now, and a cider-colored haze had settled on the distant meadows. A row of plane trees cast long purple shadows at the edge of the village. He felt quiet and peaceful and alone for the first time all day.

He set off toward the manor house, whistling with the Michael Jackson song wafting from the pub. *She says I am the one, but the kid is not my son . . .*

The lane lost its mossy walls and climbed into the meadow. He stopped for a moment and said idiotic things to a sheep, enjoying himself thoroughly. His view of the house was obscured by a clump of oaks, so he pressed on until the woods had given way to meadow again.

The windows of Easley were ablaze with the sunset, and the ancient limestone blushed magnificently. He had always loved that color, that pinkish orange which seemed to change with every shift of the light. Once upon a time, he and Jon had painted a bedroom that shade.

There was clearly no way to sneak up on the house. His approach could be observed from dozens of windows, not to mention the crenellated parapet which ran the length of the building. He would confront the place as any legitimate guest would, striding confidently.

You bet. And tell them what? *Pardon me. I seem to have misplaced a small, gay aborigine.*

Them? Who was in charge there? There had been some signs of life in the house—current magazines, postcards in mirrors—but much of the place had seemed uninhabited. Was Lord Roughton alone except for Mona? Did he even live there? And what if—just what if—that wasn't Mona?

He decided to declare his legitimacy by presenting himself at the front door. He realized the absurdity of that when he tried to lift the knocker, a rusted iron ring almost the size of a horse collar. The door had been nailed shut; no one had used it for years.

He retraced his steps and passed under the archway linking the manor house to the brewhouse. He approached the kitchen door and rapped on it. In a matter of seconds, he heard someone stirring inside.

The woman with the Princess Di haircut opened the door and glowered at him.

"You're an asshole," she said. "I hope you know that."

Thirty-three

When Mary Ann returned from her aerobics class at St. Peter & Paul's, she found Simon stretched out in the sunshine of the courtyard. "Well," she said, "I see you've discovered Barbary Beach."

"Oh . . . hello." He raised himself on his elbows, squinting into the sun. "Is that what it's called?"

She nodded. "Michael named it that."

"Ah."

"Don't get too much now. You look a little pink already."

He pressed the flesh on his forearm. "Well . . . it's proof, at least."

"Of what?"

He gave her a gentle, bemused smile. "My defection to sunny California."

"Oh . . . right. Sorry it hasn't been nicer for you."

"Quite all right."

"It's been just as bad in London, according to Michael."

"So I hear."

She sat down on the courtyard bench, several feet away from him. "I can't believe you're leaving in two days. It seems like just yesterday. Olive Oil's, I mean."

He looked puzzled.

"The bar where we met," she explained.

"Oh . . . yes, it does."

"What will you do . . . when you go back?"

He shrugged. "Something civilian, I daresay. Publishing, perhaps. I rather fancy the idea of that. My Uncle Alec works at William Collins. I expect he'll put in a word."

"That's a publisher?"

"Mmm. They do the Bible. Among other things."

"I see." She smiled at the thought. "That sounds a little . . . dignified."

He smiled back at her. "I *am* a little dignified."

She giggled. "I guess you are."

He was quiet for a moment, his dark eyes boring into her. Then he said: "Your friend . . . uh . . . Connie stopped by earlier today."

"When?" Was there no shaking that woman?

"When you were exercising. She seemed disappointed to have missed you."

"Oh . . . well . . ." She didn't really give a damn, and she didn't care if it showed.

He smiled. "I take it *you* aren't disappointed?"

"Well, she's kind of a pest, actually."

He nodded.

"She's one of those childhood friends who won't go away. She's all right, I guess, but we don't have very much in common. Did she . . . uh . . . want anything in particular?"

"No."

"Is she still pregnant?"

"Very." He smiled.

She rose. "Well . . . I'll leave you in peace. Are we still on for tonight?"

"Dinner?"

"Right."

"Lovely," he said.

She headed toward the house, then stopped. "Watch that sun now."

Three hours later, as they sat at a table overlooking Washington Square, she remarked on how easily he tanned.

"Yes," he replied. "It's rather odd, I must say. Both my parents were quite fair."

"It's very becoming," she said.

He looked out the window, seeming faintly ill-at-ease. "I like this place. You come here often, do you?"

She nodded. "Usually for breakfast. It feels almost like home."

"Well . . . the name helps, I suppose. Mama's."

"Yeah. Only my mother wasn't much of a cook."

He smiled at her. "Nor was mine. And no one had the heart to tell her. We lived for the times when Nanny would cook."

She remembered suddenly. "Shit."

"What's the matter?" he asked.

"I forgot to give you your messages."

He didn't seem particularly distressed.

"Michael said to tell you he's leaving the keys with your nanny."

"I know," he said. "I talked to her yesterday."

"Oh."

"Anything else?"

"Yeah. Somebody named Fabia stopped by. She's gotten married, and she wants you to come to a party this summer."

His lip flickered sardonically. "Did he say who she married?"

"Uh . . . a guy named Dane who makes potato chips."

Another flicker.

"You know him?"

He nodded. "Poor bastard." He seemed to acclimate himself to the idea as he sipped his wine. "Well . . . he has the money she's after, if not the breeding."

She hesitated, then asked: "Was she after you?"

"She was after everyone. She all but went into mourning when Prince Charles announced his engagement."

"Well," she teased, "Michael got the impression you had broken her heart."

"Fabia? No one has ever mistaken that for a heart."

She laughed.

He smiled warmly at her. "I know about hearts," he said.

She felt herself reddening. What did he mean by *that*? She scrambled to change the subject. "You . . . uh . . . have a nanny, huh? I mean had."

"Have, actually. She's still very much around."

"I guess that's pretty common in England. I mean . . . not *common*, but . . ."

He chuckled. "Widespread."

"Thank you."

"It's not, actually. It's gotten frightfully expensive."

"It's a nice tradition," she said.

His dark eyes squinted as he summoned something. Then he began to recite: " 'When the world was but a cradle, Nanny Marks, when our jelly faces called within the dark, it was you that made us happy—shook the rattle, pinned the nappy. It was you we really cared for, Nanny Marks.' "

"How sweet! Who said that?"

"Uh . . . Lord Weymouth, I think."

"Do you feel that way about your nanny?"

He nodded. "She didn't pin any nappies, mind you. I was a little boy when she came to us. She still treats me like one. She fusses over me dreadfully."

"Good," she told him. "I'm glad you have someone who fusses over you."

He studied her for a moment, saying nothing.

Abandoning subtlety, she reached across the table and squeezed his hand. "I hate this," she said.

"What?"

"Your going."

"Do you?" He hadn't squeezed back yet.

She nodded, trying not to panic. "I think we're . . . a lot closer than we allow ourselves to be."

His eyebrow jumped ever so slightly.

"If it's not mutual, I won't be hurt, Simon. I just had to say it."

"Well, I . . ."

"Is it, Simon?"

"What?"

"Mutual."

Finally, he returned her squeeze. "It's not as simple as that."

"Why?"

"Because . . . you have a husband. And he's my friend."

She regarded him soulfully. "Do you think I would hurt him?"

"No. I don't."

"Then . . . what?"

"I'm leaving in two days," he said.

"And Brian is gone until tomorrow afternoon."

He peered out at the square. Chinese children were sailing Frisbees in the gathering gloom. His eyes became glazed, unreadable. He turned back to her. "Would one night make that much difference?"

"It would to me," she answered softly.

He hesitated, looking down at his plate.

"We're both grownups," she said. "We know what we're doing."

"Do we?"

"Yes. *I* do. I know what I want."

He regarded her for a long time, then glanced down at the remains of her hamburger. "Is that why you told them to hold the onions?"

She laughed nervously.

He reached for the check, giving her a vague, ironic smile. "C'mon," he said.

They walked home beneath a royal purple sky. She was relieved when they reached the steep slope of Russian Hill, since the ascent made conversation difficult, and she was hardly equipped with small talk for the occasion. Simon seemed to feel the same way.

As luck would have it, Mrs. Madrigal was smoking her evening joint in the courtyard. Her outfit was anything but motherly—paisley tunic over purple slacks, dangly Peter Macchiarini earrings, celadon eye shadow—but Mary Ann felt oddly like a wayward teenager caught in the act by a watchful parent.

"Lovely evening," said the landlady.

"Isn't it?" Simon replied.

"Beautiful," said Mary Ann.

Mrs. Madrigal took a toke off her joint, then waved it in their direction. "Would anyone care . . . ?"

They both declined.

She smiled at them. "Early to bed, eh?"

Mary Ann felt her cheeks catching fire.

Simon salvaged the moment. "Can you believe it? Five o'clock in the morning! It wasn't this bad in Her Majesty's Navy!"

"You won't be sorry," said the landlady. "It's a lovely service. More pagan than Christian, really." The mischief surfaced in her huge blue eyes. "I guess that's why I enjoyed it. Well . . . I won't keep you, children. Run along. Have a good one."

Inside, as they climbed the stairs, Simon asked: "Am I just paranoid, or does that woman read minds?"

"I've been wondering that for years," said Mary Ann.

Simon stopped at the second-floor landing. "Forgive me for this, but . . . my place or yours?"

She was ready for that. "Yours, if you don't mind."

He nodded. "Fine."

As he slipped the key into the lock, she reminded herself that this was really Michael's place, but she must never, ever tell him about tonight. The thought of that made her just a little melancholy. She had no secrets from Mouse.

Simon headed for the brandy as soon as the door was locked behind them. "How about you?" he asked, holding up the bottle. "A small one."

"Oh . . . sure. Thanks. I'm gonna use your bathroom, O.K.?" Under the circumstances, the request sounded awkward, overly formal.

Simon saw that. "My house is your house," he said.

She found what she was looking for in the bathroom: that familiar sticky discharge, the telltale tears of her *mittelschmerz*. She fixed her face hastily, checked for food in her teeth, and returned to the living room.

Now wearing only his brown corduroy trousers, Simon handed her a glass of brandy.

"Thanks," she said. She downed half of it in one gulp, pausing until the burn subsided.

"Take your medicine," Simon said. And there was something faintly resentful about his tone.

"Are you all right?" she asked.

"I'm fine."

"Good. So am I." She polished off the brandy and set down the glass. "Could we . . . uh . . . go to the bedroom?"

He shrugged. "What's wrong with here?"

"I don't know." She cast a quick glance at the chrome-framed poster across the room. "Bette Midler is watching."

163

Simon smiled at her. "Christopher Isherwood is watching in the bedroom."

She grinned. "You've had this discussion before."

"A few times." His eyes were half-lidded and playful.

"I'll just bet."

He looked at her a moment longer, then took her by the hand and led her into the bedroom. When they were naked on the bed and Simon was upon her, she cupped her hands against the small marble mounds of his ass and tried like hell to think of Brian. It seemed the very least she could do.

Thirty-four

As usual, the kitchen was cold as a tomb, so Mona lit the butane heater and rolled it over to the corner nearest the sink. She could see blue sky through the diamond-shaped panes above the draining board, but the unexpected sunshine was no match for the marrow-chilling damp of Easley House.

She found two chipped bowls amongst Teddy's motley collection of china and filled them with cereal. Opening the refrigerator, she came face to face with a bowl of greenish kidneys growing fuzz. She winced and dumped them into the trash, then doused the cereal with milk and arranged four pieces of toast in Teddy's tarnished silver toast rack. She shifted everything onto a Chinese lacquer tray—along with marmalade, teacups and a pot of tea—and climbed the stairs to the second floor.

Finding the right door, she set down the tray and knocked three times.

"It's not locked," was the petulant response.

She opened the door, picked up the tray and went in. Mouse was propped up in bed like a pasha awaiting his concubine. Seeing his surly expression, she did her best to keep her own anger under control. "Happy Easter," she mumbled, laying the tray on the chest at the foot of his bed.

"Thanks," he answered blandly.

She walked to the window. "It's a nice one. At least the rain has stopped."

All she got was a grunt.

"Look, Mouse." She turned around and faced him. "I'm sorry I yelled at you last night."

He wouldn't look at her. "If I'd known you would take it like this . . ."

"But you didn't," she said as calmly as possible. "You didn't know anything and . . . you thought it would be a lark to come here. I understand that."

He fiddled with a loose thread on his quilt.

"What I'm trying to make you understand is . . . I'm a guest here too. Not even that, really. I'm here on business. I'm flying back to Seattle day after tomorrow. I can't have friends just . . . showing up. Defecting from a tour, for Christ's sake."

He shrugged. "We could have left last night."

"Mouse . . . there's one cab in the whole fucking county."

"What about that car?"

"*What* car?"

"That yellow Honda in the courtyard."

She jerked her head toward the window. He was right. Teddy was back from London. "That's . . . uh . . . that came in during the night."

"Oh, really?" he said archly. "Was anybody driving it?"

She gave him a dirty look. "I'll see if I can make arrangements to drive you to Moreton-in-Marsh. The trains to London are fairly regular."

"Is that Lord Roughton?"

She weighed that one for a moment, then nodded.

"And he's your client?"

She headed for the door. "I'll pick up the tray later. Don't bother to bring it down."

"Am I allowed to leave my room?"

"If you want to. That food is for Wilfred too."

"He's out exploring," said Michael.

That made her nervous. "Uh . . . what is he, by the way?"

"What do you mean, what is he?"

"C'mon, Mouse . . . his ethnic origin."

"Aborigine," he answered, seeming rather pleased with himself. "With a little Dutch and English thrown in."

"He seems very nice," she said.

"He *is* nice."

"Are you shtupping him?"

He shot daggers at her.

"O.K., O.K. I'll see about the car."

She returned to the kitchen. It had warmed up considerably, so she sat there for a while, sipping her tea and collecting her thoughts. The raisin bread had moved from the top of the refrigerator to the counter next to the sink. Teddy, obviously, had fixed a quick breakfast and returned to his room.

She heard whistling in the topiary gardens, so she stood up and peered through the diamond panes. It was Wilfred, prancing along in the sunshine, enjoying his solitude the way a puppy would. She smiled involuntarily and went to the door.

"There's breakfast in Michael's room," she yelled.

He stopped and hollered back: "Thanks, Mo."

Mo? Where had he picked *that* up?

She walked toward him. "The weather's nice, huh?"

"Super!" His sleeveless sweater was exactly the color of the daffodils along the path. He tilted his nose toward the sky and breathed deeply. "It smells . . . spicy."

"It's the box hedges," she explained. "The sun does that to them."

"Fancy that."

She hesitated, then asked: "Why did you call me Mo just now?"

He shrugged. "Dunno."

"Did Mouse call me that?"

"Mouse?"

"Michael," she amended.

"Oh . . . no. Mo's me own idea."

She couldn't help smiling. "You've known me half a day."

He cocked his head at her. "So? I make up me own names for everything."

"Oh." It touched her to know that she already occupied a niche in this kid's version of the universe. "Feel like a walk around the grounds?"

"Sure."

"Great." She pointed toward the stables. "Let's head in that direction. Oh . . . I forgot. Your breakfast."

"Doesn't matter," he said.

"I'll make you some later. How about that?"

"Super."

They strolled side by side through the pungent corridors of the topiary gardens. Finally, she asked: "Did Michael tell you anything about me?"

"A bit," he replied.

"Like what?"

"Well . . . he said I would like you."

That stung a little. She'd been anything but likable, she felt. "I'm usually better than this," she said.

The kid nodded. "That's what he said."

She turned and looked at him.

"He said your hair isn't usually that color and that you're really just a good basic dyke."

She broke stride, then came to a halt. "He said that?"

"Uh-huh."

"Well . . ." She began to walk again. "I haven't been quite so basic lately."

"You mean . . . sleeping with men?"

"God, no. I mean . . . you know . . . not so political."

He blinked at her.

"You *don't* know, do you?"

He shook his head.

"Lucky little sonofabitch."

"Eh?" He seemed to take that the wrong way.

"I just meant . . . you seem to have missed most of the bullshit we have in the States. It's different back there."

"I dunno . . ."

"It is. Trust me. How old are you?"

"Sixteen."

"Jesus."

He made a face. "That's what *he* said. Sixteen's not so bleedin' young."

"O.K. If you say so."

"It's *not*."

She picked a leaf off a shrub. "Are you and Michael . . . ?"

He finished the question for her. "Doin' it?"

She chuckled. "Yes."

"He doesn't want to," said Wilfred. "I've done me best, believe me."

She gave him a sympathetic smile. "Sometimes he's hard to figure out."

Wilfred nodded, looking straight ahead. "Yeah."

"Don't take it personally."

"I don't," he said.

She stopped and gazed up at the folly on the hilltop. She could smell hyacinths and wet loam and the warm musk of the hedges. There were swallows making check marks in the cloudless blue sky. "I don't want to leave this," she said.

"When do you go?" he asked.

"Day after tomorrow."

"How long have you been here?"

"Oh . . . almost three weeks. I've been in London off and on."

He nodded. "That's where we saw you."

"You were on the heath that day?"

"No. When you were at Harrods. Buying the pajamas."

She couldn't believe it. "You were *there?*"

He nodded delightedly. "I followed you to Beauchamp Place. Where you bought the dress."

She shook her head in amazement.

His expression was almost devilish. "The dress you needed by Easter."

She paused, then gave him a reproving glance. "You're dangerous."

He laughed.

"And *that's* how you got the address."

He nodded proudly.

"Has Michael told you what he thinks about . . . all this?"

He shrugged. "He doesn't know what you're doing."

"Do you?"

"No. Michael thinks you're ashamed of it, whatever it is."

"It's nothing to be ashamed of," she replied somewhat defensively. "And stop looking at my hair."

"I'm not."

"Yes you were."

"I was just wondering . . . you know . . . what it really looks like."

"Well," she snapped, "right now it really looks like this."

"O.K."

"I only dyed it for . . . this job. I wanted a change and this seemed like a good excuse."

He nodded.

"It looks like shit, doesn't it?"

Another nod.

"Your honesty is refreshing," she scowled.

Thirty-five

It was their third, maybe fourth, trip to the screening room.

"My appetite is shot," said Brian.

Theresa was hunched over the mirror, chopping away. "This is why they invented sushi. Or why they imported it to Beverly Hills. Here. Do that one." A blood-red nail pointed the way to Nirvana.

Brian sucked it up.

"The crowd's getting smaller," she said. "Thank God."

"Is it Easter yet?"

She rolled her eyes. "Two hours ago. Where have you been?"

"Well . . . no one blew a horn or put on a funny hat or anything."

"Right." She took the rolled bill from him.

"How many are spending the night?" he asked.

"Oh . . . five or six, I guess. That's all I want to deal with for brunch. Arch and his new indiscretion. The Stonecyphers. Binky Gruen, maybe. You. I don't know . . . we'll see."

"What about that guy with the beard?"

Theresa snorted a line. "What? Who? Oh . . . Bernie Pastorini?"

"Yeah. I guess so."

"I don't know if he's staying or not. Why?"

"Nothing. I just wondered about him."

"Wondered what?"

"Well . . . he said he wanted to talk to me about something. Maximal something. It didn't make any sense."

"Oh . . . *Maximale*."

"What's that?"

"His male empowerment group."

"Huh?"

"Well . . . the theory is that some guys have been turned into wimps by feminism and the peace movement, so they . . . you know, teach them to be aggressive again." She pushed the mirror toward him. "Take some more."

"No, thanks."

"*C'mon*."

He hesitated a moment, then complied. "Is it . . . like . . . a serious thing?"

"At three hundred bucks a pop? You bet it's serious! He's raking it in like Werner Erhard did in the old days."

"Jesus."

She shrugged. "Makes sense to me. I've known plenty of 'em."

"Plenty of what?"

"Soft males. That's what they call 'em."

"What do they do with them?"

"I don't know. Take them on wilderness hikes . . . survival living, that sort of thing. There's also some aikido, I think. And hypnosis."

He was beginning to take this personally. "So this guy thinks I'm a wimp, huh?"

She glanced at him sideways. "Don't get threatened, now. He pitches it to everybody. Besides, it's what *you* think that matters."

"It's really unbelievable."

"No it isn't."

"A seminar for guys who are pussy-whipped."

She threw back her mane and roared. "Now, *there's* an expression I haven't heard for a hundred years or so."

He gave her a rueful look. "I guess it's in fashion again."

"Relax," she said. "I think you'd be wasting your money." She gave him a smoldering glance. "*Now* . . . the late Mr. Cross was another story. He was practically a classic case."

"Of what?"

"Soft male."

"Really?"

She nodded. "He was so-o-o-o in touch with his feelings. Christ. Sometimes it made me wanna puke."

It jarred him to hear his idol defamed. "I admired him for that," he said.

She shrugged. "It made for a pretty song, I guess."

"It made for a nice guy too."

"Listen," she said. "You weren't married to him. I would push and push just to get a rise out of him, and he would cave in every time. There are times when a woman wants . . . you know . . . authority."

"So we march bravely back to the fifties and drag our women by the hair. Is that it?"

"Sometimes," she replied. "Sometimes that's just the ticket."

He thought for a moment. "If men are soft now . . . it's because women want it that way."

She smiled faintly. "I know marriages that have collapsed under that assumption."

He met her eyes, wondering what she meant.

"Of course," she added, "I'm sure yours is different."

Thirty-six

When Wilfred didn't return, Michael left his room and searched the hallway for a toilet. Most of the rooms he passed were devoid of furniture—musty, mildewed spaces inhabited only by spiders. Suddenly, a man's head emerged from a doorway. "Hallo!"

Michael jumped.

"Sorry," said the man. "You gave me a fright too."

Collecting himself, Michael said: "I'm looking for the bathroom. . . . I'm sorry."

"Well, I shouldn't be sorry about that. It's the last room on the right." He thought for a moment. "Unless you mean the loo."

Michael smiled sheepishly. "I do, actually."

"Ah. Just across the way there."

"Thanks so much."

The man extended his hand. "I'm Teddy Roughton. Uh . . . what are you doing here?"

"Oh." Michael flushed, shaking his hand. "I'm Michael Tolliver, a friend of Mona's. I thought she'd told you."

"Well . . . no matter. I expect she will. How splendid. A guest for Easter."

"Guests, actually. There's two of us."

"Even better."

"I hope it isn't an imposition."

"Don't be silly. Look . . . why don't you lurk off to the loo, then come back and join me for elevenses?"

"If you're sure . . ."

"Of course I'm sure."

"Thanks. Then I'll just . . ." He made an ineffectual gesture toward the loo.

"Yes. Go on. I'll be here."

When Michael returned, Lord Roughton was pouring tea at a little table by his bedroom window. He was forty-five or thereabouts, tall and lean, almost gangly, with melancholy gray eyes that bulged slightly. His graying hair was cut very short, and he was wearing the pajamas Mona had bought at Harrods.

"So," he said, looking up. "How is everything in Seattle?"

"Oh . . . I'm not from there."

"Sit down, for heaven's sake."

Michael sat down.

"Where *are* you from?"

"San Francisco."

"*Really?* How extraordinary!"

"How so?"

The gray goldfish eyes popped at Michael. "I'm moving there. Didn't Mona tell you?"

"No. She didn't, actually."

"Well . . . I am. I was there six months ago and went mad for the place. What do you take in your tea?"

"Thanks, I just had . . ."

"Please. I insist. You may be my last houseguest."

Michael smiled at him. "Thanks. Milk is fine."

"Good." He doctored the tea and handed it to Michael. "I must say, this is a pleasant surprise."

Michael sought refuge in his tea, then asked: "When are you moving to San Francisco?"

"Oh . . . a fortnight or so. I have to sell the house first."

Michael hadn't figured on that. "I see. Then this is . . . really permanent."

"Oh, yes."

"And there's no one in your family who can . . ."

"Carry on? I should hope not. I am . . . how shall we put this delicately . . . ?"

"The end of the line?"

"The end of the line," nodded Lord Roughton, whispering as if he'd offered an intimate confession.

Michael smiled at him.

Lord Roughton returned it. "Mummy and Daddy are still alive—as you'll see soon enough—but I'm afraid they're never coming back from the Scillies."

The sillies? They were senile? "You mean . . . ?"

"They live in the Scillies now. To escape the taxes."

Michael nodded.

"Off Lands End, you know. The islands."

"Oh . . . right."

"It's the only way to be an expatriate and still be British about it." He lifted his teacup and stared down his lashes at Michael. "We've driven our aristocrats into the sea."

Michael laughed.

"So," said Lord Roughton, "how long have you lived in San Francisco?"

"Almost . . . nine years."

Lord Roughton sighed, peering out the window at the moss-tufted gatehouse and the fields beyond. "We've lived here nine *hundred*." He rolled his head languidly toward Michael. "That's the family, mind you. I've lived here barely *half* that time."

Michael wouldn't indulge him. "It can't be that bad."

"Well . . . it isn't. Not always. But I've made some decisions about the rest of my life, and Easley isn't part of the picture. Do you know what I do here? I'm a landlord. I sit at that table once a month and take money from the villagers. I live in two rooms—the kitchen mostly, because I can heat it—and sometimes I get money for having tea with people named Gary and Shirley who arrive at my doorstep in charabancs. I spend long, leisurely mornings sweeping the batshit out of the guest bedrooms and picking moss off the stone, because it costs five hundred pounds to replace *one* of those ornamental blocks along the parapet and the moss is eating this place alive."

Michael smiled at him. "I hope this isn't your sales pitch."

That got a chuckle. "I have a buyer already."

"Someone you know?"

He nodded. "A woman I've known for years and her horrid new husband. They've already begun making noises about Returning It To Its Former Glory." He shuddered noticeably.

"I like it like this," offered Michael, "all frayed around the edges."

"Thank you."

"I mean it."

"I can tell you do." His brow furrowed earnestly. "Would you mind awfully if I showed you something?"

"No," Michael replied. "Of course not."

Lord Roughton hesitated, then set down his teacup and unbuttoned his pajama top, holding it open. There were substantial gold tit rings in both his nipples.

"Aha," said Michael, somewhat awkwardly.

"Folsom Street," said Lord Roughton.

"No kidding."

He gazed down at them like a proud sow regarding her piglets. "It took me three Scotches to work up the nerve. The man who did it was a shop assistant in that little emporium above the Ambush. Do you know it?"

"Sure. That's Harrison Street, actually. Same thing."

Lord Roughton let go of his lapels.

"Nice job," Michael added, to be polite.

"I expect it's frightfully old hat to you." He buttoned the buttons.

"No . . . well, I've seen it before, but . . . I think it suits you." The man was giving up Queen and Country to hang jewelry from his nipples; the very least you could do was admire it.

Lord Roughton thanked him with a nod. "The pajamas are a bit of a cop-out, I'm afraid. I don't usually wear them."

"I was with Mona when she bought them."

"Really?"

Michael nodded. "At Harrods."

"How extraordinary." His jaw slackened for a moment, then went rigid again. "At any rate . . . I thought it best to keep the gold out of sight while there are houseguests."

"You mean . . . there are others?"

"Possibly. Mummy and Daddy most certainly. And Mummy has a perfectly beastly way of bursting into one's bedroom in the morning. Are you staying for a while, I hope?"

"Well . . . Mona and I haven't actually . . ."

"Oh, you *must* stay. It'll make the whole thing so much more of an adventure!"

What whole thing? "Well . . . thanks, but . . . my flight to San Francisco is day after tomorrow."

Lord Roughton drew in breath. "So soon?"

"'Fraid so."

"I don't blame you. If I could snap my fingers and be there . . ." His eyes wandered wistfully out the window.

Michael smiled at him. "Where will you stay when you get to San Francisco?"

"With friends," said Lord Roughton. "Two sweet boys who live in Pine Street." He poured more tea for Michael, then replenished his own cup. "One's a bartender at the Arena. The other has a line of homoerotic greeting cards."

"I think I know them," grinned Michael.

"Really?"

"No. I meant . . . generically."

Lord Roughton looked confused.

"I was just joking," Michael said lamely.

"Ah."

He seemed faintly hurt and put off. Michael berated himself; you should never make jokes about the Holy Land in the presence of a pilgrim.

"When did you decide to do this?" Michael asked finally.

The fervor returned to Lord Roughton's eyes. "Would you like to know the exact moment?"

"Sure."

"It was . . . just before Halloween, and I was at the Hot House. Do you know the Hot House?"

"Of course."

"I was in the orgy room. Very late. I had smoked a little pipe of sinsemilla, and I was feeling glorious. There were two chaps next to me going down on each other, and another chap was going down on me, and I had my face in someone's bum, and it was easily the most triumphant moment of my entire life."

Michael smiled. "I think I can follow that."

"I think you can too. *Now* . . . what do I hear in the midst of all this but . . . 'Turn Away'!"

"The Bix Cross song?"

"Yes. Exactly. And where do you think it was recorded?"

"Where?"

"Two villages away from here. In Chipping Camden. There's a studio in a converted barn."

Michael nodded. "That's . . . really interesting."

"But you see . . . I was *there*. I was there when he cut the record. And that bloody song had followed me all the way across the world to that room full of gorgeous men. I almost cried. I *did* cry. It was such a simple moment, Michael. I just . . . gave up. *That's it*, I said to myself. *You've got me. I give up.* It was such a relief."

"Yeah," said Michael.

"That doesn't sound idiotic?"

"No. I remember the same moment."

Lord Roughton smiled at him. "One learns a lot in orgy rooms. Camaraderie. Patience. Humor. Being gentle and generous with strangers. It's not at all the depravity it's cracked up to be." He cocked his head in thought. "Just a lot of frightened children being sweet to one another in the dark."

Michael sipped his tea.

"Unfortunately," said Lord Roughton, "we do leather rather poorly here."

Michael looked up. "I've been to the Coleherne."

"*Gawd!*"

"It's not *that* bad," said Michael, trying to be gallant.

"Of course it is! All those . . . Uriah Heeps lurking about!"

"Well . . ."

"Hardly a match for your great San Francisco brutes in their shiny black pickup trucks."

His romanticism amused Michael. "They use them to move ficus trees, you know."

Lord Roughton blinked at him, confused. "Sorry? Oh . . . you're teasing me again. Go right ahead. I've made a very serious study of the whole matter. I know what I'm talking about."

Michael smiled at him. "I'm with you, believe me."

"Are you?"

"Yes. I'm just . . . enjoying your innocence."

Lord Roughton drew back. "I show you my tit rings and you call me innocent. What am I to make of that, sir?"

He laughed. "We're all innocent about something."

"Quite right." His lordship arched an eyebrow. "What are you innocent about?"

Michael thought for a moment. "Country houses, mostly."

His host laughed genially. "Mona's shown you around, I trust?"

"Well, I took the regular tour."

"Oh, dear. We shall have to undo that *immediately*. Where's your chum? Would he like to join us?"

Where was Wilfred, anyway? "I'm sure he would, but . . . look, can I be perfectly frank with you?"

Lord Roughton raised his forefinger. "You can if you call me by name. It's Teddy."

"Fine," Michael smiled. "Teddy."

"Good. Spill your guts."

"Well . . . I have no idea what Mona's doing here."

Teddy frowned, then chortled. "You're joking, surely?"

"No. She hasn't told me yet."

His mouth made goldfish motions. "Why, that silly girl . . . the silly, silly girl."

Thirty-seven

When the alarm went off at 4 A.M., Mary Ann woke to find herself pinned under Simon's left arm. She slipped free as gently as possible and sat on the edge of the bed, rubbing her eyes while Christopher Isherwood watched.

"Where are you going?" whispered Simon.

He startled her. "Upstairs. To change."

"Is it Easter already?"

"'Fraid so." Her voice was croaky and sleep-fuzzed.

He raised himself on his elbows. "Then . . . I'll meet you down in the garden."

She squeezed his knee. "You don't have to go."

He paused. "I thought you wanted company."

"Well . . . I *said* that, but . . ."

"You wanted this."

It was a joke, of course, but it made her uneasy.

"Hey," she whispered, conscious of Mrs. Madrigal's presence in the building. "If you want to march up Calvary with a zombie, the zombie would be glad to have you along." She reached over and gave his cock a friendly yank. "O.K.?"

"What's the attire?"

"Casual." She stood up. "Give me half an hour and meet me in the courtyard. Crepe soles might be a good idea. If there's any of that dope left, you could roll us a joint. O.K.?"

"O.K. But how are we getting there?"

"My crew is picking us up."

"Of course. Your crew."

"Anything else?"

"Yes. Where are my pants?"

"In the closet. You hung them up. Remember?"

"Right." He climbed out of bed and headed for the bathroom. Was he bent out of shape about something? Even his perfect little butt looked tense.

He kept quiet most of the way to Mount Davidson, so she spent the time talking shop with her cameraman. They parked the truck on Myra Way—as close as they could get to the concrete cross—and finished the journey on foot, climbing a slippery pathway through a eucalyptus grove until they reached the summit.

Several dozen people were already gathered at the base of the mammoth monument. In the pearly predawn light they looked as pale and gray-green as the young eucalyptus leaves. Mary Ann turned and admired the extravagant sweep of the city, the telltale red stain that had begun to seep into the eastern sky above Mount Diablo.

She touched Simon's arm. "Isn't it gorgeous?"

"Gorgeous," he repeated, with little conviction.

She studied his expressionless face. "You're as grumpy as *I* am in the morning."

"If I were you, I wouldn't . . ." He cut himself off.

"You wouldn't what?"

"I wouldn't . . ."

"*Darling . . . you naughty thing. I told you we don't need you.*" Father Paddy had materialized, as usual, out of thin air.

"Oh . . . hi," she blurted back.

"You're so damn *noble,* Mary Ann!" The cleric grabbed Simon's arm. "I have told this dear, sweet girl for weeks now that I'm perfectly capable of handling this gig on my own, but she's *determined* to be a martyr." He bussed her on the cheek. "Aren't you, darling?" His head spun toward Simon again. "I know this stalwart soul. I've seen him on television. You're that runaway lieutenant, aren't you?"

"More or less," was the less than cordial reply.

"Well, you've just taken our little city by storm, haven't you?"

Simon answered with a faint, glacial smile.

Father Paddy turned back to Mary Ann. "There's coffee and doughnuts if you need the rush, and . . . *oh* . . . is Matthew our cameraman today?"

"Yeah."

"Marvelous. Tell him to stay away from my underside, will you?"

"What?"

"Don't let him shoot from *below,* darling. I'm all chins, and it frightens the little children. All right?"

"O.K."

"You're an angel," said the priest, merging with his flock again.

Mary Ann glanced cautiously at Simon. "I guess I should have warned you about him."

He didn't respond.

"Is something the matter?" she asked.

He pulled a leaf off a bush and fiddled with it. "You set this up, didn't you?"

"Set what up?"

"This morning. You got yourself assigned to this . . . *gig,* as he calls it, so that you and I could be together."

"Well . . . it worked out that way, I guess. But I certainly didn't plan it."

He frowned at her.

"Anyway," she added, "what if I had? Would that be so terrible?"

"How long ago? Two weeks? Three? I've been inked into your little agenda for quite some time now."

As she stared at him, she felt her throat go dry.

"Tell me if I've missed the mark," he added.

"Well, I was certainly . . . pleased . . . when I realized we'd be able to get together . . . if that's what you mean. What's the big deal? I certainly had no way of knowing that Theresa would invite Brian to Hillsborough for the weekend."

"Both of you."

"What?"

"She invited both of you."

"So?"

"So . . . Brian suggested taking me in your place, but you vetoed the idea."

"That isn't so," she said.

He shrugged. "That's what he told me."

"Well . . ." She wanted to throttle Brian. "O.K., then . . . I'm a desperate woman. You forced it out of me. I confess. I'll stop at nothing until I've got you in my clutches. C'mon, Simon . . . what is it you want from me?"

"I want you to tell me you planned this."

She threw up her hands. "O.K. Fine. Easy enough. I planned this."

"You planned this at least two weeks ago, *knowing* this would be the eve of my departure."

"Simon, what the hell are you getting at?"

"I think you know."

"I don't have the slightest idea what . . ."

"You and Brian are trying to have a baby. I know that already."

That stopped her cold for a moment. "From Brian, I suppose?"

"Yes."

"Well . . . what if we are?" It wasn't much, but it was all she could muster.

"Then . . . that means you're off the pill."

She felt the blood pounding in her temples. The moment took on an ominous quality as a woman in harlequin glasses began to play "He Is Risen" on a portable electric organ behind the cross. Mary Ann scanned the crowd in search of her cameraman, then turned back to Simon. "This is easily the most bizarre conversation I have ever . . ."

"You never said a word about contraception, Mary Ann. Not a word. Don't you think that's a little strange for a woman who's trying . . ."

"I think you don't know *shit* about romance, Simon. That's what I think. What did you expect me to do? Ask you if you had a rubber or something? I can't believe we're even *discussing* this!"

He gave her a distant, weary smile. "Such indignation. My-my."

"Well, what the hell do you . . . ? Look, I have to find my cameraman."

He caught her arm. "No."

"What?"

"I have something else to tell you."

"What?"

"Your friend Connie . . . the one who was looking for you."

"Yeah?"

"She left a message for you."

Please, God, she thought. *Don't let Connie drive the final nail.*

"She said to tell you to be sure to watch Channel Nine yesterday at two o'clock."

She nodded. "So?"

"Well . . . you weren't at home, so I watched it for you, considerate fellow that I am. Any idea what you missed?"

"Simon, the service is starting in exactly . . ."

"C'mon . . . give us a guess."

"Frankly, I really don't care what that asinine woman . . ."

"It was a chat show, Mary Ann. Three housewives discussing their husbands' *sterility.*"

The word hovered between them like nerve gas.

"It so happens," she said finally, "that Connie's husband is sterile, and she had artificial insem . . ."

"It so happens that Connie doesn't have a husband."

She looked away from him.

"At least," he added, "that's what *she* said."

She hesitated, then said: "Sounds like you two got along famously."

"As a matter of fact," he said, "I rather liked her. I found her candor refreshing."

"Great. Terrific." She turned and walked away.

Once again, he stopped her. "Is this how you're going to handle this?"

"Handle what? I have a job to do."

"Oh . . . right. This is a working weekend, isn't it?"

"Let go of me, Simon."

"You've been a busy little beaver, haven't you?"

"*Simon . . .*"

"Are you absolutely sure that three times was enough . . . or shall we have another go at it right here?"

She pulled free of his grip and slapped him hard. He reeled slightly but didn't change his stance. She could see the imprint of her fingers on his pale face. His nostrils flared. When he brought his fingers to his cheek, the cynical glint had faded from his eyes and the look that remained made her heartsick.

"I'm sorry," she said.

"Don't be," he replied.

"What do you want me to do?"

He shrugged. "Deny it, I suppose."

She hesitated.

"I thought so," he nodded, turning away from her.

"Simon, look . . . it isn't as black and white as . . . where are you going?"

"Home. Or a reasonable facsimile thereof."

"But . . . the service "

"Thanks awfully, but I know how it turns out."

"No . . . I mean . . . you don't have a ride. I can't leave until . . ."

"Then I'll call a taxi." He was plunging through the undergrowth in search of the path.

"Simon, please don't . . ."

But he was already gone.

Thirty-eight

It was well past noon when Mona returned to the kitchen and found Teddy rinsing his breakfast dishes. "Your friend is quite smashing," he said.

"Which one?" asked Mona, just to be difficult.

"Well . . . the little brown one is cute, but . . ."

"Never mind. Spare me."

"I gave them my little Cook's tour of the grounds. The dog graveyard . . . all that. They seemed quite taken with the place. It was rather sweet, I must say . . . seeing it all through their eyes." He rubbed a damp rag across an egg-encrusted plate. "I think you should talk to your friend, Mona."

"Why? What happened?"

"Well . . ."

"You didn't tell him anything about tonight, did you?"

"Well . . . I'm amazed, really, that *you* haven't told him."

She was working on an answer for that when they both heard the crunch of tires against gravel in the courtyard. Teddy peered through the leaded windows above the sink with a look of bug-eyed horror. "Bloody hell."

"Who is it?"

"The buyers. His wife, rather."

"I thought they weren't expected until . . ."

"They weren't. I expect she's come to take more Polaroids."

"For *what*?"

"I don't know. Her decorator needs them. It's too vile to think about. Look. I'm right. She's brought that fucking camera." He blotted his hands hastily on the damp rag. "Be a lamb, will you? I'll take care of her, but come and rescue me in, say, ten minutes."

After he had gone, she used the stairway closest to the library to creep back to her room for makeup repair. Her auburn roots had become distinctly visible, reminding her that the end was near. If she neglected them for another week or so, she could go for punk and nobody would be the wiser.

She gave Teddy his allotted ten minutes, then strolled down to the great hall with an ill-prepared lie on her lips. "Sorry to bother you, Teddy. Mr. Harris wants to talk to you. On the phone."

Teddy and the buyer's wife were standing next to the huge window facing the chapel. The woman was a broad-beamed blonde in a blue blazer. "Mr. Harris?" said Teddy, turning to Mona with a look of mild confusion.

"You know . . . the gardener."

"Oh. Of course. Mr. Hargis. Right. Well, I expect he wants instructions. Do make yourself at home, Fabia. Oh . . . Fabia, this is Mona. I trust you two will get acquainted." He backed away, then all but broke into a run.

Smirking, the woman watched his exit. Then she turned to Mona: "How very odd."

"Uh . . . what?"

"Did you say Mr. Hargis *rang* Teddy?"

"Right."

"Why didn't *I* hear it, then?"

"Well . . . I guess . . . well, I don't know. That's funny, isn't it?"

"Yes. Very."

"Anyway . . . if I can show you anything."

The woman's eyes widened. "I beg your pardon."

"I mean . . . like . . . around the house."

The woman's laughter was a total surprise, like a tractor trailer honking on a hairpin curve. "My dear Moira . . . I came to Christmas parties in this house when I was eight years old."

"Oh . . . I see."

The woman picked up the Polaroid and aimed it toward the minstrels' gallery. *Click. Whir.* She looked at Mona again. "I've been watching Easley's sad decline for many, many years." Shielding herself with a simpering smile, she removed the print and laid it daintily on the window seat. "He hasn't told you a thing about me, has he?"

181

"No," Mona replied calmly. "Actually, he hasn't."

"Well . . . that's a pity."

"Is it?"

The flat smile came back. "If nothing else, Moira, it would make your little *charade* so much easier. That's all I meant." She picked up the print and squinted at it. "The light is rather poor, I'm afraid."

"It's Mona," said Mona.

"Mmm?"

"My name is Mona, not Moira."

"Oh. Sorry." She looked down at the print again.

"I take it you don't need me."

"Whatever for?" said the woman, smiling.

Mona marched out of the room. She didn't break stride until she had gone the length of the house and accosted Teddy in the sitting room. "Why the fuck did you do that to me?"

Teddy looked up from his Martin Amis novel with a rueful smile. "Isn't she a delight?"

"You could've told me she knows."

"Well, I . . . she does, does she?"

"Yes. You didn't know that?"

"No . . . well, I might have guessed. She doesn't miss much. I'm sorry, Mona. People talk about me. I've never been able to prevent that, and . . . some of it's bound to rub off on you. Has she left yet?"

"I don't know," she replied, "and I don't care."

"Neither do I." He shoved his book aside. "I have a bit of that lovely hash left. Shall we take a stroll along the parapet and leave her to stalk the halls in peace?"

"Great idea," she said.

She followed him upstairs to the water-spotted bedroom that led to the attic stairway. As they climbed, hunching toward a sliver of light, the roof beams of Easley arched above them like the blackened rib cage of some prehistoric beast. Teddy leaned against the parapet door; they were momentarily blinded by the white April sunshine.

Mona looked toward the western hills and drank in the spring-scented breeze. "This is sort of our place, isn't it?"

Teddy's eyes twinkled. "It is, rather." He poked around in the breast pocket of his salt-and-pepper tweed jacket and produced one of his fat hash-and-tobacco joints. Lighting it with his Bic, he took a toke and handed it to her. "I should warn you about my father," he said.

Eyeing him suspiciously, she took in smoke and held it.

"I don't mean warn you, really. Just . . . an explanation."

She nodded.

"Daddy . . . uh . . . has this mental thing."

She exhaled.

"It's quite harmless, I assure you. The doctors say he's retreated from . . . the usual reality, as it were, and taken refuge in happier times . . . his happiest time, actually. He lives it over and over again. There's a clinical term for it." He took the joint back. "It escapes me at the moment."

"What was his happiest moment?" she asked.

"Well, *apparently*, a fortnight he spent with the Walter Annenbergs."

"The who?"

"Oh . . . I thought they were household words in California. Walter and Lee Annenberg. He was ambassador to the Court of Saint James's when Daddy met him. They hit it off straight away, Daddy and Walter . . . so Mummy and Daddy spent some time at the Annenbergs' estate in Palm Springs. And Daddy, I'm afraid, never quite got over it."

"You mean . . . ?"

He nodded. "He thinks he's still there."

She smiled at him. "You're kidding, aren't you?"

He shook his head, smiling back.

"He walks around Gloucestershire thinking he's in Palm Springs?"

He shook his head again. "The Scillies."

"What?"

"He walks around the Scillies thinking he's in Palm Springs."

"Oh."

He offered her the hash again.

"No, thanks," she said. "The tobacco makes me dizzy."

"Most of his major symptoms have subsided, thank God. Mummy's broken him of the white shoes, the golf togs, that sort of thing."

"That's good."

"I just thought you should know. It can be bloody embarrassing sometimes."

"Thanks," she said. "I appreciate that."

He heaved a long sigh, then turned and surveyed the landscape.

"Is that really Wales?" she asked.

"No," he replied. "It's not, actually. But you can see it from the folly. The most distant ridge is the Black Mountains. You can see the Malverns too."

She stood a silent vigil with him, then said: "I don't understand it."

"What?"

"How you can just . . . dump all this. Surrender Easley to that lard-assed bitch down there."

He turned away. "I'm not surrendering Easley."

"Well, what would you call it?"

"Mona . . ." He plucked a clump of moss off the parapet. "Easley is just a job. I'm bloody tired of that job. I know what you're saying, believe me . . . but I can't be two people at once."

All but lost in the scenery, a white van bounced along the one-lane road from Easley-on-Fen. "If I'm not mistaken," said Teddy, "that's the caterers."

"Looks like it," she said. It made her a little queasy to realize that other people—lots of them—had been mobilized to act upon a split-second decision she had made one rainy night in Seattle.

Teddy heard the uncertainty in her voice. "Are you all right, Mona?"

"Sure."

"The tobacco, eh?"

"Yeah. I think I could use a nap, actually."

"Of course." He gave her a kindly smile. "Get some rest."

She patted him on the shoulder and climbed into the dark innards of the attic. When she got back to her room, she eased shut the door to the minstrels' gallery, since she could still hear the ghoulish whirring of that Polaroid in the great hall. Sleep wouldn't come, however, so she braced herself for conflict and headed down the hallway toward Michael's room.

He was there, propped up in the window seat with an old *Country Life* opened against his knees. Wilfred lay on the bed—stomach down, knee bent—watching him. When she cleared her throat, Michael gazed toward the door. "What's this?" he asked. "More gruel already?"

She managed to smile. "I thought we could talk."

"O.K.," he said blandly.

Wilfred did a somersault on the bed. "And children should leave." He headed for the door, stopping to give Mona a peck on the cheek.

"You aren't a child," she said.

"Twenty minutes," Wilfred replied.

She crossed the room and sat in the armchair flanking the window seat. "He's such a doll," she said.

Michael shrugged. "Looks like it's mutual."

"Well . . . he's got a big crush on you, I can tell that."

He blinked at her, then looked out the window.

"Is that a problem?" she asked.

"I don't know. I worry about him . . . what he'll do when I go home."

"What about . . . his family?"

"There isn't one. He was living with his father, and his father ran off. He killed a man."

Mona frowned. "Sounds like Wilfred's better off."

"I don't know. Is nothing better than something?"

She could feel him getting heavy and moved to avert it. "Works for me," she smiled.

Remaining sober, he turned away from her. He had changed in lots of little ways, she realized. It was almost as if he had bequeathed his flippancy to Wilfred. He seemed cold and colorless, drained of his irony.

"Any messages?" he asked at last.

"Uh . . . for who?"

"Barbary Lane. No one's heard from you for years."

"It hasn't been that long," she said.

"A year and a half, then. How's that?"

She could see Wilfred on the hillside, a tiny smudge of yellow and brown climbing toward the folly; he looked like a bumblebee from this distance. "I've been sorting things out," she told Michael.

"I know," he said. "Since nineteen sixty-seven."

"That isn't fair."

"Then don't use that crummy excuse."

"Mouse . . ."

"You could have dropped a postcard, for Christ's sake! You moved and never gave us your new address. Your phone wasn't listed . . ."

"I didn't have one half the time."

"You could've called us, then. Something. What is it, Mona? Are you cutting us off? What the hell is happening? Do you know how much you're hurting Mrs. Madrigal?"

The last one stung a little. "Look," she said, "I didn't wanna check in with you guys until I had my shit together. You knew I wasn't dead or anything. I just wanted to show up on your doorstep one morning out of the blue . . . with some incredible piece of news about myself."

"And this is it?" His eyes narrowed in disbelief.

"What?"

"Marrying . . . ol' Tinseltits."

She felt both mortified and relieved. "No," she replied quietly. "I didn't plan on publicizing this."

"Did you plan on telling *me?*"

"Yes."

"When?"

"Now." She smiled feebly. "A little too late, huh?"

He looked away, fixing his gaze on the hillside. Wilfred had reached the folly and was now just a fleck of yellow beneath the duncecap roof. "In more ways than one," said Michael.

"It doesn't really mean anything," she said.

"What?"

"This marriage. It's just an arrangement to satisfy the immigration people, so Teddy can get a green card . . ."

". . . and wag weenie in San Francisco."

"I didn't ask about that," said Mona.

He stared at her, slack-mouthed. "How did this happen? I mean . . . how long has this been in the works?"

"About three weeks, I guess. Not long."

"You met here or in Seattle?"

"Neither. The arrangements were made through . . . a sort of clearinghouse in Seattle."

"A clearinghouse?" He almost spit out the words. "For *what?* Mail order brides?"

"Yes," she replied flatly. "As a matter of fact."

He gave an ugly little snort. "Does anyone *here* know about this?"

She flashed on that Fabia woman, snapping her way through the house. "Oh, yes," she answered. "It appears to be Easley's worst-kept secret."

"It figures," he said. "I'm always the last to know."

His petulance made her impatient. "You weren't supposed to know at all, Mouse. You weren't supposed to be here."

"When is it happening?"

"Tonight. In the chapel."

"Swell."

"It's just the family. And a few of their friends."

"Don't worry. I'll stay out of the way."

"I didn't mean that." She felt better, just the same; the whole ordeal was embarrassing enough as it was. "It's not like it really means anything," she added. "People get married for immigration purposes all the time. It's just a business proposition."

"How much?"

"What?"

"How much is he paying you?"

"Oh . . . five thousand."

"Not bad."

"Well," she acknowledged somewhat proudly, "it's usually just a thousand or so, but this was a special case, and they thought I could handle it." She couldn't help thinking what a feeble boast that was. "The organization gets ten percent, of course. Like an agent. Anyway . . . it's a fair price for all concerned."

"Sure," he replied. "It's a double ring ceremony."

She didn't get it.

He tweaked one of his nipples.

"Oh." She laughed uneasily, then tried to counter with her own joke; it might be the only way out of this mess. "Yeah," she said. "I told him to hell with Immigration—he'll never make it through the metal detector."

He remained sullen.

She studied his face, then got up and went to the dresser and began arranging

186

his breakfast dishes on the tray. "I'm going back to Seattle in two days," she said. "I've had a nice little vacation . . . made some money. And everyone's better off. I don't need this guilt trip, Mouse."

"That's your doing," he said. "Not mine."

She slammed down the marmalade jar. "When the *fuck* did you get to be such a little prig?"

He didn't answer right away. "You don't know what I am," he said quietly. "You haven't stopped running long enough to find out."

"Mouse . . ."

"What do you want from me, anyway?"

"What do you mean?"

"Why are you telling me this now? What do you want me to say? Congratulations on a lucrative but meaningless marriage?"

She picked up the tray and headed for the door. "I wanted your blessing, I guess. I have no idea why. I have no idea why I'm even talking to you."

"If you ever made a real commitment . . ."

"Oh, fuck you, Mouse! Just . . . fuck you. I don't need this. Since when did you get to be an expert on commitment. You and Jon and your half-assed little . . . whatever you call that relationship . . ."

He scorched her with a long, silent glance. "I'll give him your best," he said.

She drew herself up and tried to remain calm. "I'm my own person," she said.

"Fine," he replied. "Go for it."

She looked at him a moment longer and stormed out, marching back to her room with the tray. She threw herself on the bed but avoided a crying jag by rising again and hurling a paperweight at the suit of armor next to the window.

Hearing the noise, Teddy came running. "Good Lord," he murmured. "Are you all right?"

She glared at the pile of metal on the floor. "I hate that fucking militarist drag."

He nodded. "I didn't much fancy it myself."

She slumped into a chair.

"Is it . . . jitters?" he asked.

"We have to talk," she replied.

Thirty-nine

It was roughly seven-thirty when Mary Ann climbed out of the camera truck at the foot of the Barbary Lane stairway. Without stopping to admire the daffodils sprouting between the garbage cans, she went directly to Simon's apartment and knocked on the door. When he opened it, he was wearing Michael's green robe.

"Yes?"

"I want to start over," she said.

"Meaning?"

"I want your forgiveness."

He gave her a thin smile. "Wait a bit, won't you? I haven't forgiven myself yet."

"For what?"

"Oh . . . damning the torpedoes."

"What?"

"I knew what you were doing," he said. "I suspected. I could have said no . . . and I didn't."

"That wasn't all I was doing, Simon."

"Don't," he said. "It isn't necessary. There's no point in getting muddled over motives."

"No . . . I want you to be clear on this." She glanced nervously over her shoulder, wondering about Mrs. Madrigal. "Do you mind if I come in?"

He hesitated.

"Please," she whispered. "Just for a little while?"

He nodded and stepped out of her way. She went in and took a seat on the end of the sofa. Simon remained standing, pacing solemnly with his arms folded. The damage she had done was evident in his eyes.

"I was going to tell you," she said.

He made a little muttering noise.

"I would never have done this with someone who didn't matter to me."

He stopped pacing and looked at her.

"Can't you take it as a compliment?" she asked.

"I could," he replied, "but I haven't yet."

"Well . . . think about it. It's not like this was a one-night stand or something. I put some thought into it, you know."

He seemed amused by that. "Does Brian know?"

"No, of course not!"

"Well, this is laid-back California. It seemed perfectly reasonable to assume . . ."

"Is that what you think of me, Simon?"

He shrugged.

"Well . . . O.K., forget about me. But Brian would never do that."

"Comforting," said Simon.

"He doesn't know anything." She decided to throw herself on his mercy. "He doesn't even know he's sterile. The hell of it is . . . *he's* the one who wants the baby. It's no big deal with me. He doesn't have a job now, and he thinks the baby would be something he could . . ."

"Wait. Stop."

"Yeah?"

"How do you know he's sterile, if he doesn't know it?"

"I just do," she said.

He nodded. "Very well. Proceed."

"Well . . . that's it. I wanted to give him a baby . . . so I came up with this dumb idea."

"And artificial insemination didn't occur to you?"

She nodded. "Connie suggested it. I hated the idea. It isn't . . . personal enough." It sounded so stupid that she smiled apologetically. "I thought I could do it without hurting anybody. I didn't. I fucked up."

He looked directly at her. "Then last night . . . ?" He waved away the thought.

"What? Last night what?"

"Were you really . . . ?"

"Into it?" she asked, finishing his question.

"Yes."

"Simon . . . couldn't you tell?" She caught his hand. "Don't go back to England thinking I'm a monster. I've had such a wonderful time with you."

He stood there, keeping his distance, looking down on her.

"I think you're a gentle, intelligent . . . incredibly sexy man."

"Thank you," he said softly.

"I mean it."

He nodded.

"I'll always remember you. I don't need a baby for that."

"Thank you."

"Stop saying thank you," she said. "Come here. Don't be so insecure."

"I've had a vasectomy," he said.

"What?"

"I've had a vasectomy."

She tried to read his face. "Are you serious?"

189

"Yes," he replied. "Are you?"

She looked at him a moment longer, then leaned down and took his cock in her mouth.

"Thank you," he said.

This time she didn't bother to reply.

Forty

The skylight above Theresa's living room had taken on a creepy, milky translucence—like a giant eyeball with a cataract. Brian stared at it in disbelief. Had they really been up all night?

"You're a lotta fun," said Theresa.

"Oh . . . sorry." Had she asked him a question? What time was it, anyway?

"You're grinding your teeth," she said. She was on the sofa across from him, her feet tucked under the heart-shaped ass. "I think it's sack time."

"Yeah."

"Want some papaya juice?"

"Great."

She rose. "I'll get us a 'lude too."

"That's O.K."

"It'll bring us down."

He shook his head. "I don't do 'ludes anymore."

"Well . . . a joint, then."

Three minutes later, she returned with a glass of juice and a joint that was already lit. She held it for him as he toked, pressing her fingers against his lips. "I like the feel of your mouth," she said.

"Thanks," he replied.

Her laughter seemed brittle. "You can do better than that."

"Sorry. I'm kinda zonked."

"The joint'll fix you right up."

He would have to be more explicit. "Hey . . . I hate to be a party pooper, but I am really tired. It's been great, really. If you'll show me which bedroom is mine, I'll . . ."

"Jesus Christ." She flung the joint into an ashtray. "What the hell have we been doing all night?"

She had jarred him. "Uh . . . rapping, I thought."

"*Rapping?* How quaint!"

"Look, Terry . . . I'm sorry, O.K.?"

"Don't be."

"You knew I was married." he said.

She stared at him incredulously. "You're not going to tell me that's the *reason?*"

"Well . . . partially."

"So what's the other part?"

"Well . . . that's the main reason, more or less."

"This is un-fucking-believable."

"Also . . . I'm not real terrific after a lot of coke. That's another reason."

"That's not a reason. I've told you I have 'ludes."

He rose on wobbly legs. "This has been a real experience, believe me."

"Swell."

"If you'd told me last month that I'd spend Easter doing coke with the wife of the man who . . ."

"Shut up about him."

"I didn't mean that you aren't . . ."

"I know what you meant, Brian. I know who you came here for." She retrieved the roach and relit it with trembling hands. "You should've fucked *him* when he was still alive. He might have appreciated it."

She smiled at him with surprising tenderness, then handed him the roach. "I think you should go home," she said.

Forty-one

They formed a big T against the rumpled flannel sheets, Simon from side to side, she with her head against his trampoline-tight stomach.

"I'm curious about something," she said.

"Mmm."

"Why did you get a vasectomy?"

"Oh . . . well, actually, my nanny talked me into it."

"C'mon."

"It's quite true. She gave me a stern little lecture. She said I was a confirmed bachelor and flagrantly irresponsible and it was the only decent thing to do. It was a remarkable speech."

"Was she right?"

"About what? Flagrantly irresponsible?"

"No. Confirmed bachelor."

He hesitated. "More or less, I suppose. Marriage is rough on a true romantic."

"What do you mean?"

"You know what I mean."

"Maybe," she said.

"A certain spontaneity is lost, isn't it?"

"Not necessarily."

"Then why are we doing this?"

She rolled over on her stomach and kissed his navel. "Because I like you very much. And I like doing this without babies on the brain."

"You're not sorry, are you?"

"No."

"It hasn't utterly devastated your marriage?"

She gave him a little pinch, smiling.

"Just asking," he said.

"Brian isn't everything to me, but . . . he's the only constant."

"You don't have to explain yourself."

"It would take a long time for me to fall out of love with him. It took long enough to love him. He's sort of like . . . a maze I wandered into."

"You're brighter than he is," he said.

"I know. I don't care. He gives me other things." She shifted slightly, kissing him again. "You've given me something too."

"What?"

"Oh . . . a fresh perspective."

"On your husband." He said it without rancor.

"Not just that."

"Then . . . I'm glad."

"I'll think about you," she said.

"I'll think about you," he replied. "Should we be watching the clock?"

"Huh?"

"Brian."

"Oh . . . he's not coming back till afternoon."

He chuckled. "I should have known you'd know that."

Forty-two

The clock in the Le Car said eight twenty-three when Brian parked on Leavenworth and began the trek up the Barbary Lane stairway. There were birds twittering in the eucalyptus trees, and the neighborhood tabby had already staked out a sunning spot on the first landing. He sat down and stroked the old cat's belly.

"How's it goin', Boris? You havin' a good Easter? You didn't know it was Easter? Well . . . wake up and smell the coffee, man!"

Beneath him, on the steep slope of Leavenworth, two pint-sized Chinese kids emerged from a doorway and began fighting over a plush Smurf that was bigger than both of them. He watched them for a while, then shouted through cupped hands: "Hey, guys!"

Their squealing stopped. They looked up at him.

"The Easter Bunny bring you that?"

Without answering, they stood and stared at the crazy man on the stairs.

"Be cool," he said.

The kids backed into the doorway, emerging seconds later with their mother.

Brian waved at the three of them. "Happy Easter," he yelled.

The woman waved back halfheartedly, then herded the children into the house.

Brian got up and headed into the leafy canyon of the lane. When he reached the courtyard, he noticed that a row of pink hyacinths had popped up in the soft, dark loam where Jon's ashes had been buried. Mrs. Madrigal's doing, no doubt.

The landlady was probably still sleeping, so he took special care to close the door quietly behind him. Tiptoeing across the foyer, he reached the carpeted stairs and began to climb, avoiding the familiar squeaky spots.

As he reached the second floor, he heard movement in Simon's apartment. The Englishman was already up. He wondered for a moment: *Should I stop and tell him about my all-nighter with the rock widow?*

Why not?

The buzzer was noisy as hell, so he rapped on the door.

There was more activity inside, but no one came to the door.

He knocked again.

Footsteps.

The rattle of the latch chain.

A slice of Simon appeared through the door. "Oh . . . hello there."

Brian kept his voice down. "You weren't asleep, I hope?"

"Well . . . ah . . . no, actually."

"I'm back from the front." Brian grinned.

"What?"

"Theresa's bash."

"Ah."

"We've been doing nose candy all night."

Simon nodded.

"It was wild, man. She was after my ass."

Simon arched an eyebrow. "Indeed?" He was trying to sound impressed, but something was distracting him.

The light dawned.

"Jesus." Brian banged his forehead with his palm. "You've got a lady in there."

Simon blinked, then nodded.

"Sorry," whispered Brian, backing away. "Catch you later." He gave the lieutenant a thumbs-up sign. "Carry on, old man."

He climbed the stairs feeling pretty stupid. The coke had obviously numbed his reasoning powers. It was Sunday morning, the morning after Saturday night; Simon was hardly likely to be alone.

No.

Simon had gone to the sunrise service.

Maybe he had changed his mind, though.

Maybe he had bailed out at the last minute.

Maybe he had picked up someone at the service.

Maybe not.

Maybe he didn't have to.

He reached his door and found it locked. His temples were throbbing angrily as he searched for his keys. *Be cool*, warned the last tattered remnants of his reason. *Be cool.*

He went straight to the bedroom.

The bed was empty.

Maybe Mary Ann was still on the job.

Maybe there had been technical problems.

Maybe she had gone to breakfast afterwards.

He sat down, then got up again and went to the landing. He had been there almost a minute when he heard Simon's door open and close. He ducked back inside and sat there massaging his temples as the crippling green poison flooded his brain.

Someone was climbing the stairs.

Forty-three

She tried to be stately about it, chin up and shoulders back, like Mary Queen of Scots striding toward the ax. If Brian had been doing coke all night, her own level-headedness was even more important.

She opened the door. He was sitting in the armchair facing her.

"Hi," she said, closing the door behind her.

His face seemed to do a dozen different things at once.

"I'm not going to lie to you," she said.

"Go ahead," he said darkly. "One more time won't make a fucking bit of difference."

"It isn't as bad as it looks, Brian." She skirted his chair, heading for the kitchen.

"*Where are you going?*"

"To get us a drink."

"*No!* Get back here. We're talking."

"O.K., but . . ."

"*Get back here, I said.*"

She came back and sat on the sofa. "We shouldn't be doing this now. You've been up all night. Your nerves are raw. There's no way you can rationally . . ."

"Shut the fuck up!"

She folded her hands in her lap.

"Did you spend the night down there?" he asked.

"Yes," she replied.

He stared at her with horror in his eyes.

"Brian . . . it was more . . . friendly than anything else."

"*Friendly?*"

"I just mean . . . it wasn't the beginning of something, it was the end of something."

"Oh, yeah? How long have you two . . . ?"

"No. I didn't mean that. Last night was the only time."

"Goddamn him, *goddamn* him!"

"Please don't blame Simon."

"You forced him, huh?"

"No, but . . . he's your friend."

"Yeah . . . and you're my loving wife. There's a name for this, isn't there?"

"I don't love him," she said, feeling oddly disloyal to Simon.

"You're just a *slut*, huh?"

"Brian . . ."

"Well, what possible reason . . . ?"

"Come off it. They don't have sluts anymore. I *like* Simon, that's all. I didn't plan for it to happen, but . . . it happened. It'll only affect us if you *make* it affect us, Brian."

"I get it," he said. "*I'm* the problem here. Me and my quaint ideas about husbands and wives and *sluts*."

He was wielding that word like a switchblade, trying to goad her into a fight. She regarded him in silence, then got up and went to the bedroom door. "I'm taking a shower," she said. "If you want to discuss sluts, I suggest you talk to that woman who's so hot for your ass in Hillsborough."

When she saw his expression, she realized she shouldn't have said it. "Maybe I'll do that," he said. "Maybe I'll just fucking do that!" He sprang to his feet, grabbing his keys off the coffee table.

"Brian . . ."

"Take your goddamn shower. I'm sure you need it."

"Brian, you can't . . ."

"I can't *what?*"

"Drive in that condition. Look at you. Your eyes are bloodshot. . . ."

"You think I'd stay here?"

"Please . . . just get some rest first. Do what you want later, but don't get back on that freeway in that . . ."

But he was already out the door.

Forty-four

It was almost dark now and Michael had withdrawn to the folly on the hill above Easley House. From this duncecapped pavilion he could see the twinkling cottages of three villages and the backlit stained glass of Easley's family chapel. Headlights crisscrossed a field adjacent to the manor house as the guests began to arrive on the road from Easley-on-Fen. An unseen organist struck a few exploratory chords. A woman's shrill laughter reverberated in the courtyard. Here he sat on a hilltop overlooking Wales and somewhere below him—probably cursing her fate—Mona Ramsey was about to be married.

He felt absolutely nothing.

A cog in his emotional mechanism had ceased to function. He didn't care anymore. His heart had been kicked around enough.

He would wait here until it was over. Then he would find Wilfred and they would ask for a ride into Moreton-in-Marsh. They could stay at the Black Bear, catch the first train to London in the morning.

The organ in the chapel plunged into an unidentifiable Anglican hymn. Almost simultaneously, Mona's wholly identifiable voice cut through the encroaching darkness. *"Mouse! Where are you, goddamnit?"*

She was standing in the courtyard, looking from left to right, much as she had done that day on the heath. This time, however, she was decked out in a peach-colored wedding gown. *"I'm not standing for this shit, Mouse!"*

He hesitated a moment longer, then shouted: "I'm up here. At the folly."

She swung around, fixing her gaze on the pyramid, then hiked her gown above her knees and sprinted up the slope. Her curses exploded like cherry bombs as her heels dug into ground that had been booby-trapped by moles. When she finally reached the folly, her chest was heaving violently. "Why the hell didn't you *tell* me?"

He didn't answer.

"Wilfred just told me. I can't believe it! What is the matter with you? *Why the fuck didn't you tell me?"*

"You're getting married," he said. "It's hardly the time to . . ."

"Fuck that shit, Mouse! I had a right to know!"

"You never once asked about . . ."

"All right, then! I'm a self-centered asshole! What do you want me to say? Christ, Mouse . . . you rigged it so I would hurt you! You deliberately . . ." She didn't finish. There were tears streaming down her face. "He can't be dead!" she said in a much weaker voice. "How can that beautiful man be dead?"

He felt himself crumbling. "I don't know," he said, reaching out for her as his own tears came.

They held on to each other for a long time, sobbing.

Finally, he said: "We tried to reach you."

"I know."

"He sent you his love. He said to give you that turquoise ring you liked."

"Oh, God, Mouse!"

"I know. It's a bitch. I know."

"Was he in much pain?"

"Some. For a while. Not always. He was wonderful, really. He cracked jokes and did his Tallulah Bankhead impersonation . . . and flirted with the orderlies."

"That tart." She swiped at her cheeks.

"They loved it, of course, since he was a doctor and knew all the inside dish. It wasn't so bad, Mona. Not all the time. We got much closer to him . . . to each other. You don't really know for certain about a family until somebody dies. You don't know anything until that happens."

She pulled away from him. "And you weren't going to tell me."

"Why do you think I've chased you across England?"

"I don't know. To punish me, I guess. To make me feel like shit. Your usual motives."

"You're wrong"—he smiled—"and you're missing your wedding."

"*In a fucking minute.*"

"Yes, *ma'am.*"

"I want to know something."

"What?"

"Do we . . . still love each other?"

"Mona . . ."

"Because I love *you,* you little shithead . . . and if you think you can pretend that I don't, you can just go fuck yourself!"

He was touched. He smiled at her.

"O.K.," she added, "I should've called or something. You're right about that. *Obviously* I should've called. And I shouldn't have run from you that day on the heath. . . ."

"Why did you do that, anyway?"

She looked away. "I dunno . . . I was a little uncomfortable about the whole thing . . . and this man from the Home Office was with us . . . and I knew that introductions would be awkward. I figured I could write you about it later."

"It looked like you were looking for somebody."

"I was," she replied. "Teddy."

"I thought you said he was with you."

"Well, he *was* earlier. The three of us had lunch together at this inn on the heath. Teddy just wandered away. You can't take the man near bushes of any kind."

He smiled.

"If you think that's funny, you should've heard me explaining it to the Home Office."

He gave her a hug. "I'm all right. Go get married."

"You haven't answered me," she said.

"What?"

"Do you love me?"

He smiled at her. "I do."

"Will you come to the wedding?"

"I think I'd like to stay here for a while. Do you mind?"

She threw up her hands. "Hey . . . no big deal." She kissed him on the cheek. "Come to the reception, though. I've got a little surprise for you."

"What?"

"Just come, Mouse."

"Well, my clothes aren't exactly . . ."

"Look, the fucking bride has mud on her shoes. You'll look just fine." She left the folly and hoisted her skirts, beginning the perilous descent.

"I don't like surprises," he shouted.

"You'll like this one," she yelled back. "You'd better."

"Where's the reception?"

"In the great hall." She hit another mole hole and cursed again.

"Break a leg," he called.

"Fuck you," she answered.

The glow of her old familiar roar kept him warm. He sat there in the meadow-scented darkness of the folly for another half hour until the final chords of the organ had rolled away down the vale like summer thunder. Then he got up, brushed off the seat of his Levi's, and headed slowly down the slope.

He entered Easley House through the kitchen, making his way toward the sound of the reception. There were several dozen people in the great hall, already nattering away to the music of a string quartet. Champagne was being dispensed at a long table in the alcove next to the window.

"Hey, mate!" Wilfred came wriggling through the crowd.

"Hey, kiddo."

"Where were you?"

"Up at the folly."

"Are you O.K.?"

"Sure. Great."

"The wedding was super."

"Good. Mona says there's gonna be a surprise."

The kid glanced at him. "You know already?"

"Know what?"

Wilfred giggled. "You won't get it from me, mate."

"Now, just a . . ."

"I'll get us some champagne. Hang on." He darted away again. While he was gone, Michael struck up a conversation with a nice old man who turned out to be the gardener. His name was Hargis, and they talked in earnest about flowers. Michael liked that about England; men were allowed to be earnest about flowers.

When Wilfred returned with the champagne, he looked a little ruffled. "Old sod."

"Who?" He took a glass from the kid.

"Over there . . . ol' baldie by the bar."

"What did he do?"

"He gave me fifty P and told me to fetch his golf bags."

"C'mon."

"That's what he said. 'Fetch me golf bags and tell Bob Hope I'll meet him at the clubhouse.' "

"He must've been joking."

"I told him to stuff it."

Mona appeared. "Hi, guys."

"Hi," said Michael. "Is Bob Hope here?"

"Huh?"

"Somebody told Wilfred that Bob Hope is here."

She frowned for a moment, then rolled her eyes in recognition. "That man by the bar, right?"

"That's the one," said Wilfred.

"That's the earl," said Mona. "Teddy's father. We had a nifty chat about Betty Ford. If you're nice to him, he'll introduce you to her."

Michael was dumbfounded. *Betty Ford is here?*"

"Nobody's here," she replied. "He's a sweet old poop, but he's got one wheel in the sand." She turned to Wilfred. "You haven't seen Teddy yet, have you?"

The kid nodded. "He's breaking the news to Fabia."

"He's too nice to her," said Mona.

"Wait a minute," said Michael. "Fabia who?"

"Fabia *Crisps*," said Wilfred.

Michael could hardly believe it. "She's *here?* That woman who . . ."

"Just button the lip," Mona told Wilfred.

The kid grinned at her and obeyed.

Michael glanced from one to the other, but their bond of silence was unbreakable. Seconds later, Teddy strode into the great hall and joined them. "Oh, Michael . . . lovely. I'm delighted you could join us." He turned and addressed Mona. "I think we've just about tidied everything up."

"How did she take it?" asked Mona.

Teddy made a face. "It wasn't a bit pretty."

"Can she . . . do anything?"

"Not a thing, my love. Nothing's been signed yet." He hoisted himself onto a seventeenth-century shuffleboard table, commandeering it as a speaker's platform. "My friends," he called. "May I have a word with you, please."

The crowd in the great hall muttered its way into silence.

"Lovely," said Lord Roughton. "Now . . . as most of you know, it has been my intention for some time to move to California for the purpose of pursuing my studies in anthropology."

Wilfred mugged at Michael.

"Just keep quiet, you two," Mona whispered, looking more dignified than Michael had ever seen her.

"That," Teddy continued, "compelled me to confront the unhappy prospect of parting with our beloved Easley." A sympathetic murmur passed through the gathering. "Believe me, I have made every effort to see to it that the house would fall into the hands of people who would honor its . . . unselfconscious beauty." Affectionate chuckles erupted here and there as Teddy smiled down at a slight, white-haired woman in a pale green cocktail dress. "That's what my mother wants . . . and that's what my mother assures me my father would have wanted."

"I thought he was here," muttered Michael.

"He *is*," Mona answered.

"Old sod," said Wilfred.

"On my last trip to America," Teddy went on, "I met the exceptional woman who has done me the honor of becoming Lady Roughton." As he extended his arms in Mona's direction, the celebrants turned and applauded politely. Mona gave them an uneasy smile and a half-assed little Elizabethan wave.

Teddy beamed at her with genuine affection. "It was this lovely girl who showed me the error of my ways."

Girl, thought Michael. No one called Mona a girl and lived to tell about it.

Mona saw him smile and reacted silently with a middle finger pressed against her temple.

"To come to the point," said Teddy, "I have reconsidered the entire matter and decided against selling Easley."

Thunderous and prolonged applause swept through the great hall.

Teddy seemed enormously pleased. "Mind you, I will still be spending the next few years in California . . . but my dear wife has gallantly offered to remain here at Easley and run the business of the house . . . preside over the rent table, as it were."

"My God," murmured Michael.

Mona grinned at him and grasped his hand, then gazed up at Teddy again.

"It's a thankless job, in my opinion . . . one for which I seem to have increasingly less talent. So I am very grateful that she's shown such concern not only for the perpetuation of Easley as we know it, but for . . . the furtherment of my education." He stooped down and signaled Wilfred. "May I have your champagne, old man?"

The kid handed him his glass.

Teddy rose, hoisting the glass in Mona's direction. "To the Lady of the Manor!"

His guests echoed the toast: *"To the Lady of the Manor!"*

General applause ensued. Teddy climbed down from the shuffleboard table, still smiling at Mona.

"Thanks for that," she said.

"My pleasure," he replied.

"I can't believe this," said Michael.

"Believe it," Mona beamed. She turned to Teddy. "Do you have any more social duties?"

"That's it. We're done."

"Fabulous. Why don't you help Wilfred pick out his room? Michael and I are gonna take a little stroll."

Wilfred grinned at Michael. "I'm gonna live here, mate! How 'bout that?"

"Pretty good, kiddo." He put his arm around Wilfred's shoulders and shook him, then glanced at Mona. "You're just full of surprises tonight."

"C'mon," she said, "let's promenade on the parapet." She took his arm and led him away, stopping suddenly to shout a final instruction at Wilfred. "And *don't* take the one above the library. That's mine. It's the only one that doesn't leak."

As they headed up the stairs, Michael asked: "How long has *this* been in the works?"

"Since this afternoon."

"You're kidding."

"Nope. Well . . . maybe a little longer than that, but I finally talked to Teddy about it this afternoon. I thought about what you said, you know. I *was* just running away again. I'd sold myself cheap and I knew it. Teddy was never really big on selling the place, you know. He just didn't want the responsibility."

"Yeah," he said, "but what about the money involved?"

"Oh, I waived my fee."

He laughed. "I meant the money he would've gotten for the house."

"Well, he won't get it. We'll still get rent from the villagers, though, and I'll mail him a check every month. It'll work out fine. Wilfred's gonna help me set up a tearoom this summer for the tourists."

"Really?"

"A *real* tearoom, dipshit."

"I know."

"We could use a gardener," she said as they entered one of the bedrooms and stopped at the stairs to the parapet.

He smiled at her invitation. "You have Mr. Hargis."

"You've met him, huh?"

He nodded. "Just now."

"Isn't he dear?"

"Yeah . . . he is."

"His wife is a trip too. They know how everything works . . . or doesn't work, as the case may be. I can do it, Mouse. I know I can. Lady Fucking Roughton. Can you *stand* it? Won't I make a fabulous landlady?"

"I don't know why not," he replied. "Your father does."

Her smile was so warm. "How is she doing?"

"Good. Better, when I tell her about you."

"Let me write her a note or something. I think it should come from me this time." She led him up the narrow stairs in the darkness. "The problem with me and her is . . . we're too much alike. She wants me to be one of her brood, and I want a brood of my own." She opened the parapet door and walked out into the moonlight.

"Yeah," he said, following her, "but the hens can get together from time to time."

There were headlights streaking the dark fields below as some of the celebrants made their way home. "I can picture her here," said Mona. "Can't you? Trooping around in that cloche of hers."

"God," agreed Michael.

"I want you to stay, Mouse."

He turned and looked at her.

"We could have so much fun," she said. "Think what it would be like with the three of us."

"I've thought about it, Mona. Ever since you mentioned gardener."

"Well, think about it some more. A whole new life, Mouse. Away from all that shit back there."

He chuckled.

"What's the matter?" she asked.

"Well . . . I *like* all that shit back there."

"Right."

"I do. I'm not sure how long I could leave it. I'm actually missing it."

She sighed and looked toward the horizon. "Be that way, then."

He remembered something and smiled.

"What?" she asked.

"Those three things . . . what were they? Hot job, hot lover, and . . . ?"

"Hot apartment."

He laughed. "I'd say this qualifies as a hot apartment."

"Also a hot job," she added.

"The lover part may be a little tough out here."

She turned to him indignantly. "Have you seen the postmistress in Chipping Camden?"

"No." He grinned.

"Then don't be so goddamn sure of yourself."

"A hot *postmistress?* C'mon."

"Swear to God. Makes Debra Winger look like dogshit."

He hooted.

She smiled and leaned against him, slipping her arm around his waist. "Oh, Mouse," she murmured.

He knew that she was thinking about Jon again. "I'll send you that ring," he said.

"Thanks."

"And thanks for being so nice to Wilfred."

"Are you kidding? We're made for each other. He says you met that Fabia woman in London."

"Fabia Dane?"

"That's the one."

"How bizarre. She came by the place I'm staying and was rude as shit. She's the one that's buying the house?"

"Was," said Mona.

"Jesus . . . that must mean that their new country place . . ." He laughed, getting the picture. "I invited Simon to a party here this summer."

"Simon?"

"The guy I swapped places with."

"Oh," she said. "Well, tell him he's still invited. He's a nice guy?"

"Very. And handsome."

"How nice for you."

"No, he's straight."

"How nice for *someone*, then."

"Are you off men completely?"

She gave him a languid nod. "And vice versa. I am a simple English country dyke and don't you forget it."

"It suits you." He smiled.

"Does it?"

"It does. It really does."

"You can be funky here. People really are very funky here, Mouse. It's not widely known, but it's true."

He nodded.

"I will *never* be a lipstick lesbian. I hate that shit on my face!"

"This shit."

"What?"

"You've got on makeup *now*, Mona."

"Well, true . . . but it's my fucking wedding. Gimme a break."

Michael laughed. "Your non-fucking wedding."

"My non-fucking wedding. Right." She looked behind her anxiously. "I should go help Teddy say goodbye to the non-fucking guests." She pecked him on the cheek. "Stay here. Take your time. Smoke this." She removed a fat joint from the peach lace of her bodice. "It's one of Teddy's. It has hash in it."

He took it from her. "Thanks, Babycakes." She reminded him so much of Mrs. Madrigal it was almost eerie.

"When you're really loaded," she advised him, "go down and look at the moon through the window in the great hall. And check out the graffiti in the glass. It's three hundred years old. Teenagers put it there."

"All right," he nodded.

"And come for coffee later in the kitchen. Teddy wants to show you his slides of San Francisco."

He chuckled.

"And watch these goddamn steps on your way down, O.K.? I love you, Michael Mouse."

"Same to you, fella."

She disappeared into the roof.

He lit the joint and fixed his gaze on the procession of lights winding toward Easley-on-Fen. The night was peppered with laughter and the scuffing of feet against gravel paths. He heard a cuckoo, a real cuckoo. He couldn't recall the last time he had heard one, if at all.

Wilfred joined him on the parapet. "Lady Mo said you were up here."

"Lady Mo, huh?" He laughed.

"It's me own name."

"It's great! Lady Mo!"

Wilfred grinned at him. "Are you fucked up, mate?"

"A little, I guess. Here." He handed the joint to Wilfred, who took a short hit and handed it back. "I picked out me room," said the kid. "Wanna see it?"

"Sure, kiddo. In a little bit."

"Are you all right?"

"I'm great."

"Yeah . . . me too."

"Look at where we are, Wilfred. It's real! There really are places that look like this!" He pried a chunk of moss off the stone and tossed it over the edge.

"What about it, then, mate?"

"What about what?"

"Well," said Wilfred, "you're staying, aren't you?"

Forty-five

Simon was leaving, framed in her doorway, suitcase in hand.

"I managed an earlier flight," he said, "but I can certainly hold off until you get some word."

"I'll be all right," she said.

"Are you sure?"

She nodded. "He'll be back. It's only been seven hours or so." It was easily the longest Easter in memory.

"Look," he said, setting his suitcase down, "what if I call Theresa? She doesn't know me, and we could at least find out if he's there."

"No. It's O.K. He's run off before."

"Oh . . . I see."

"Not over anything like this, of course."

He grinned at her ruefully. "Of course."

She looked at him for a moment, then flung her arms around his neck. "Oh, Simon, I'll miss you!"

He pecked her on the cheek somewhat formally. "Take care of yourself," he said.

"I will."

"I left Michael's keys with Mrs. Madrigal."

"Fine," she said.

"His toaster wants repairing, I'm afraid. It died on me several days ago."

"I'll tell him," she replied. "That's O.K."

They looked at each other helplessly.

"Will you write?" she asked at last.

He reached out and stroked her hair. "I'm not very good about that."

She smiled at him. "Neither am I."

"Give Brian my best," he said. "When the time is right."

"I will."

"Well . . . I'd best be going. My taxi is probably . . ."

"Simon, please don't hate me."

He studied her face for a while before leaning over to kiss her forehead. "Never," he said softly.

And then he walked away.

As night fell, she tried to stay occupied, but she couldn't shake the dread that gripped her. When the phone rang at seven-fifteen, she lunged at it like a madwoman.

"Hello," she answered hoarsely.

"Hi. It's DeDe."

"Oh . . . hi."

"Is this a bad time?"

"No," she lied.

"Good. Well, D'or and I thought you and Brian might like to play tonight. Mother's got the kids, and we're just a couple of good-time gals on the town."

"That's sweet," said Mary Ann.

"But?" replied DeDe.

"Well . . . Brian isn't here right now."

DeDe heard the uncertainty in her voice. "Is . . . uh . . . something the matter?"

"Yeah. More or less."

"Sounds like more," said DeDe.

Mary Ann hesitated. "We had a fight."

"Oh."

"It was major, DeDe. I'm worried. He left here early this morning, and I haven't heard from him since."

"He'll be back."

"It isn't that," said Mary Ann. "He was in no shape to drive. He'd been up all night doing coke, and . . . I don't know. I just feel creepy about it."

DeDe paused, then asked: "Did he give you any idea where he was going?"

"Well . . . sort of."

"Where?"

"Uh . . . Theresa Cross's house."

"Jesus. How did he meet *her?*"

"Through me," Mary Ann answered lamely.

"Big mistake," said DeDe.

"I don't care about that part, really. I can deal with that. I just want to be sure he's not . . . you know."

"Yeah."

"I'd rather know where he is than not know where he is."

"Well," said DeDe, "she lives just half a mile away. I could check out her driveway and see if his car is there."

Mary Ann was flooded with relief. *Of course.* "Oh, DeDe . . . would you mind?"

"Gimme a break. Of course not. Call you back in half an hour."

"It's the Le Car," said Mary Ann, "and please don't let her see you."

It was more like forty-five minutes, but she answered after only one ring.
"Yeah?"

"It's DeDe."

"Yeah?"

"The car isn't there, hon."

"Oh."

"They could've gone out, of course. I mean . . . I wouldn't jump to con-clusions. You don't even know for sure that that's where he went."

"No."

"Please don't worry, hon."

"I won't."

"It's early yet," said DeDe. "Maybe he's just visiting a friend."

"Yeah."

"Do you have any Valium?" asked DeDe.

"Yeah."

"Then take one before you go to bed."

Mary Ann did as she was told.

Forty-six

The funeral was being held in a small shingled chapel with orange and green stained-glass windows. Mouse stood next to her, holding her hand. She was crying more than he was, but she knew he was probably cried out by now. As the organist began to play "Turn Away," she turned toward the window and saw that it wasn't stained glass at all but dozens of orange and green parrots arranged geometrically on perches. One by one, they flew toward the starless sky, and darkness spilled like molten tar into the hole they had left behind. . . .

The phone rang.

Her hand, only barely connected to her brain, felt for the receiver in the dark. She croaked something unintelligible.

"Mary Ann?"

It was Michael. "Oh . . . Mouse."

"I know it's early, Babycakes."

"What?"

"Don't be pissed at me. I just wanted to give you a change of . . . oh, God, you're pissed."

"No. It's O.K. Gimme a chance to get it together."

"You sound really out of it."

She checked the bedside clock. "It's five fifty-three, Mouse."

"I know. I'm sorry."

"And I took a Valium before I went to bed."

"Uh-oh." He began to hum the theme from *Valley of the Dolls.*

"Lay off," she said. "Where are you?"

"In England," he replied. "Easley-on-Fen."

"Where?"

"I'm staying at Lady Roughton's manor house."

"Right," she said, impatient with his teasing.

"I'll tell you about it later. I just wanted you to know I'll be staying another three days."

Her reply was a colorless "Oh." How long was she going to be alone?

"It's great here," he added. "I guess I should've waited to tell you. I'm sorry. I'll see you on . . ."

"Don't go, Mouse."

"Huh?"

"Stay on the phone. Talk to me. I'm weirding out."

"How many Valiums did you say you . . . ?"

"Brian's gone. We had a fight yesterday, and he walked out, and . . . I think something's happened to him."

"It can't be that bad," he replied.

"It is."

"Sounds to me like he's punishing you. How long has it been?"

"Almost twenty-four hours."

Michael said nothing.

"Should I call the police?" she asked.

"I dunno."

"I mean . . . if he's checked into a motel or something, don't you think he would've called by now?"

"I guess," he replied, "but maybe you oughta give a few more . . ."

"I had this awful dream, Mouse."

"When?"

"Just now. Before you called. You and I were at a funeral together."

"You're just thinking of Jon," he said.

"No. This was different. It was in a little chapel of some sort. And Brian wasn't with us."

"Babycakes . . ."

"It felt so *real,* Mouse."

"I know. That's natural. You're under a lot of stress. You need sleep, that's all. If I hadn't woken you, you wouldn't have remembered that dream."

This was true, she decided.

"Besides," he added, "I think Brian's just moping."

"You do? Really?"

"Yeah. I do. Get some sleep, O.K.? It'll all seem better in the sunshine."

"O.K."

"And I'll see you on Friday."

"All right. I'm glad you're having a good time, Mouse."

"Thanks. Night-night now."

"Night-night."

She rose just after ten o'clock and called in sick to Larry Kenan. He was relatively pleasant about it, which only reinforced her nagging suspicion that something was seriously off kilter in the universe. She made herself a defiantly big breakfast. If Brian was trying to make her suffer, she had done more than enough suffering already.

She was reading a *Cosmopolitan* in the courtyard when Mrs. Madrigal appeared and sat down next to her in the toasty sunshine.

"Lovely day," said the landlady.

"Mmm."

"Did you have a nice Easter?"

She hesitated. "It was O.K."

Mrs. Madrigal smiled tenderly. "I miss him already, don't you?"

For a moment, Mary Ann thought she meant Brian. "Oh . . . sure . . . he was a nice guy."

The landlady nodded but said nothing. Mary Ann looked down at her magazine again.

"And Brian's gone too, isn't he?"

Mary Ann met her eyes. "How did you know?"

"Oh . . . just a feeling."

Mary Ann felt her anxiety rise. If Mrs. Madrigal was having premonitions, maybe that dream really meant something.

"Do you want to talk about it, dear?"

In five minutes, she had told the landlady everything: Brian's sterility, her pregnancy scheme, how Simon's feelings were hurt and how she had tried to apologize, Brian's ill-timed return and angry departure. Mrs. Madrigal took it all in stride, but drew a deep breath when Mary Ann had finished.

"Well, I must say . . . you've outdone yourself this time."

Mary Ann ducked her eyes. "Do you think I was wrong?"

"You know better than that."

"What?"

"I don't do absolutions, dear." She reached for Mary Ann's hand and squeezed it. "But I'm glad you told me."

"He wanted a baby so badly."

"I know. He told me."

"He did? When?"

"Oh . . . back when you were covering the Queen."

"What did he say?"

"Oh . . . just that he wanted one . . . and you were somewhat cool to the idea."

"I would have one for *him*," she replied.

"I can see that," said the landlady.

"I'm just so afraid it's too late. It isn't like him to stay away this long."

Mrs. Madrigal smiled faintly. "Let him concoct a little mystery, dear. It may be his only defense."

"Against what?"

"Against your layers and layers of mystery."

"Wait a minute," said Mary Ann. "I'm not so hard to figure out."

The landlady patted her knee. "You and I know that, child . . . but he doesn't."

"Then . . . ?"

"Don't ask him where he's been, dear. Let him have that for his own." Mrs. Madrigal rose suddenly. "It's time for me to tidy up the basement."

Her abrupt departure puzzled Mary Ann until she looked across the courtyard and saw her husband coming through the lych-gate. His gait was leaden, and his face seemed devoid of all emotion as he turned and headed in her direction.

"Hi," he said.

"Hi," she replied.

He sat down on the bench, but kept his distance. "Shouldn't you be at work today?"

"I called in sick."

He nodded, hands dangling between his knees. "Is Simon still . . . ?"

"He's back in England. He left yesterday."

He sat there in silence for a long time. When he finally spoke, he addressed his remarks to the ground. "I wasn't doing a number on you. I needed time to think."

"I know."

"I couldn't do it here. There was too much to . . ."

"I understand completely."

"Stop doing that," he said edgily.

"What?"

"Just let me talk. I'm not looking for explanations. I've worked this out." She nodded. "O.K."

"I think I should go," he said.

"Go?"

"Live somewhere else for a while. Find another job, maybe. I've got no function here."

"Brian, please don't . . ."

"Listen to me, Mary Ann! I'm almost forty and I haven't left a mark on anything. I can't even give my wife everything she wants. I can't even do that."

"But you do!"

"I don't. What the fuck was that little scene about, huh?"

"It wasn't about that, Brian. It was . . ."

"It doesn't matter. I know how I feel, Mary Ann. It'll only get worse if I stay here."

"Do you know how I feel, Brian? What would happen to me if you left?"

"You'd handle it," he said, smiling faintly. "That's one of the things I like about you. You're strong."

"I'm *not* strong."

"You're stronger than I am," he said. "I'm a soft male."

"A *what?*"

"Chip Hardesty's got a vacant studio in his new place. He says I can stay there until . . ."

"Brian, for God's sake!" The tears had begun to stream down her face. "We're in love with each other, aren't we?"

He wouldn't look at her. "There has to be more than that, sweetheart."

"Like what?"

"I dunno. A reason. A purpose."

"We'll find you a job, then."

He shook his head. "*I'll* find me a job."

"Well, sure . . . but you can do that here."

"Uh . . . excuse me." It was a third voice, awkwardly interceding. They both looked toward the lych-gate, where a tall, heavily freckled man was standing. "Mary Ann?"

She rose, wiping her eyes. "Yeah . . . that's me."

The man came forward. He was in his early twenties, but his corn-fed demeanor and prominent ears and the canvas sack slung from his neck instantly suggested the clumsy kid who had been her paperboy fifteen years ago in Cleveland.

Only this time he wasn't delivering the paper.

This time he was delivering a baby.

Forty-seven

The first thing Michael noticed were the hyacinths in the garden, half a dozen pale pink erections smiling in the face of death. He smiled back at them, rejoicing in his family, savoring his return to the family seat.

Mrs. Madrigal spotted him from her kitchen window and hooted a greeting. He set down his suitcase and motioned for her to come outside. She emerged seconds later, almost running, rubbing her hands on her apron. "Dear boy," she crooned, hugging him heartily. "You've been sorely missed."

"Thanks for the hyacinths," he said.

"What? Oh . . . you're welcome. You look *wonderful*, dear. You've put on some weight."

"Don't say that."

"Well . . . oh, don't be such a man. Your beauty is still intact. C'mon. Let's get that bag inside. Mary Ann and Brian will want to see you." She grabbed his suitcase and led the way, charging toward the house.

"Good," said Michael. "He's back, then."

She looked at him as she shouldered her way through the front door. "You knew about that?"

He nodded. "We talked on the phone. She was freaked."

"Well . . . she's fine now."

He reached for the suitcase. "Let me carry . . ."

"No. You've had a long flight. We'll leave this in the foyer for the time being." She dropped the suitcase and flung open the door of her apartment. "And you'll stop in for a very small sherry."

"Great," he replied. "Wait a minute, let me get something." He stooped to open his suitcase, then dug around in a side pocket until he found the envelope. "This is from Mona," he explained, handing it to her.

"Where on earth . . . ?"

"In England." He smiled.

"You can't mean it!"

He nodded. "She's in good shape. She's happy, and she wants you to come visit her."

"In England?"

"Just read the note."

Mrs. Madrigal looked dubious as she set the envelope on her telephone stand. Mona was right, he decided. The landlady did act an awful lot like a father when the subject was Mona.

She beckoned him into the apartment, pointing to the sofa. "All right, now . . . sherry." She bustled off to the kitchen, leaving him to absorb the familiar mysteries of this faded velvet cavern where silk tassels hung like stalactites. God, it was good to be back.

When she returned, she handed him a rose-colored wineglass full of sherry. "She's actually living there?"

"No pumping."

"Well, tell me what she's doing, at least."

He sipped his sherry and smiled at her. "Following in her father's footsteps."

"Now, dear, if . . ."

"That's all you get."

The landlady fussed with a wisp of wayward hair. "Well, drink your sherry, then."

He kept smiling as he sipped. Unable to restrain herself, she rose and went to the phone stand. She picked up the envelope, then set it down again and picked up the phone and dialed a number.

"What are you doing?" he asked.

"Alerting the troops." She spoke into the receiver. "Our wandering boy is home. Yes . . . that's right . . . that's right. Fine . . . I'll tell him." She hung up and turned back to Michael. "Your presence is requested in the Hawkins residence in exactly three minutes." She headed toward the kitchen.

"What am I waiting . . . ?"

"Just sit there and finish your sherry, young man."

He chuckled at her revenge. The sherry went down like sun-warmed honey. He sat there in the musty embrace of Mrs. Madrigal's sofa and counted his blessings while she puttered about in the kitchen.

Finally, he rose. "Do you want to come with me?" he yelled.

"No, thanks," came the reply. "I'm involved with a lamb stew at the moment." Her head poked into view, her angular features ruddy from the stove. "We're having dinner here tonight. I hope that's all right."

"Perfect," he said, on his way out the door.

He picked up his suitcase and climbed the stairs, leaving it on the landing before heading up to the third floor. Mary Ann met him outside her door. "Look at you," she squealed. "Chubbette."

"Fuck you very much."

They hugged for a long time before she led him into the apartment.

He looked around. "I thought Brian was here."

"Sit down," she said.

Something was the matter. He felt his sherried security begin to ebb. This was why he usually hated homecomings, this queasy preparation for the news they didn't want to spoil your vacation with. His first thought was: *Who else has died?*

"What's wrong?" he asked.

"Nothing. This just takes some . . . easing into. Sit down."

He sat down.

She perched on a footstool. "Remember my old friend Connie Bradshaw?"

He shook his head. "Sorry."

"You know . . . who I stayed with . . . when I moved out from Cleveland."

"Oh, yeah. With the oil paintings on velvet."

She nodded.

"The tacky stew."

She winced. "She wasn't tacky, Mouse."

"But you always said . . ."

"Never mind that. She was very good to me, and I shouldn't have said that."

"O.K."

214

"She died, Mouse."

"Oh." He was relieved in spite of his better instincts. Thank God, it was no one he knew.

"She died in childbirth. Well . . . not during, but a day or so after. It was something called eclampsia. Her blood didn't clot. She had a stroke."

He frowned. "I'm sorry. That's awful."

She nodded, then gazed at him soulfully. "She left me her baby, Mouse."

"Huh?"

"She wasn't married, and her parents are dead, and her brother's a bachelor in med school and . . . she left me this note before she died and asked me to . . . raise it." She finished with a sheepish little shrug and waited for his reaction.

"You mean . . . is it . . . ?"

She nodded. "In the bedroom. With Brian."

"My God . . . then it's going to be . . ."

"She," she put in. "She's going to be our little girl."

He was flabbergasted. "This is *amazing*, Mary Ann."

"I know."

"Well . . . uh . . . how do you feel about it?"

She hesitated. "Pretty good, I guess."

"Guess?"

"Well . . . I'm still adjusting to it."

"What about Brian?"

She smiled at him. "Come see for yourself."

Rising, she took his arm and led him into the bedroom. Brian was seated in the armchair by the bed, cradling the baby in his arms. A gooseneck lamp on the dresser formed a sort of ersatz halo behind his head. Michael couldn't help wondering if there was a masculine equivalent of *madonna*.

"Welcome home," Brian beamed.

Michael shook his head in amazement. "Look at you."

"No . . . look at this face." He meant the baby.

Moving to his side, Michael peered down into a tiny pink fist of a face. Brian jiggled the baby. "Say hello to your Uncle Michael, Shawna."

"Shawna, huh?"

"Connie named her," Mary Ann put in.

"Shawna Hawkins," mused Michael. "That works." He looked around the room. "A crib and toys and everything. You guys have been busy."

"No," said Mary Ann. "Connie had them already."

"Oh." He sympathized with her confusion. "It happened awfully quick, didn't it?"

"Awfully," she nodded.

"Instant baby," said Brian.

Mary Ann opened a drawer and removed a sheet of pink-and-green stationery. "Here's the note she left." She handed it to Michael. It was scented. *Mary Ann*, it read, *Please take care of my precious angel. Love, Connie.* She had sketched a smile face next to the signature.

"It's just like her," said Mary Ann.

Michael nodded.

"Poor thing," she added.

"Well," he offered, "at least she had the comfort of knowing who the new mother would be."

"I knew her too," said Brian. "I dated her."

"Once or twice," said Mary Ann.

Looking down again, Brian extended his forefinger to Shawna. Five little fingers clamped around his. "We met at the Come Clean Center," he said.

"Pardon me?" Michael frowned.

"The laundromat in the Marina."

"Oh."

Mary Ann glowered at them both. "I don't think little Shawna needs to press that in her book of memories."

"Who's the natural father?" asked Michael.

Mary Ann took the note from him and returned it to the drawer. "It's apparently some guy who took her to the Us Festival. She wasn't really sure. She just wanted a baby."

Michael was sorry he had asked. "It doesn't matter," he said.

"No," agreed Brian, "it doesn't." He smiled at Michael, then turned to his wife. "Does it?"

"Not a bit," she replied.

An awkward silence followed, so Mary Ann added, "I just feel a little dumb, I guess. Our baby just . . . shows up on our doorstep. I feel as if I should've done something to earn it."

"You did something," said Brian.

She gave him a funny look which puzzled Michael.

"I mean that," said Brian, looking down at the baby. "It's the thought that counts."

Mary Ann seemed vaguely unsettled. "Well . . . we just wanted you to meet her."

"She's wonderful," he said, and he meant it.

When he finally trudged downstairs to his apartment, he found a joint taped to the door with a note: *Smoke this and catch 40 winks before supper. AM.* He removed it, smiling, and let himself in.

There were only a few traces of Simon remaining: a half-empty bottle of brandy, several *Rolling Stones*, alien numbers scribbled on the pad by the telephone. The place looked pretty much the same. Nothing special, just home.

A joint and a nap sounded like a great idea. He remembered his suitcase and retrieved it from the landing. Dumping it on the sofa, he snapped it open and felt around for his toothbrush. In the process he discovered a small cardboard box imprinted with the logo of a gift shop in Moreton-in-Marsh. There were holes punched in the side of the box.

He lifted the lid and found a tiny porcelain fox nestled in tissue paper. With this note: *Find a good home for him. Love, Wilfred.*

Forty-eight

Connie's memorial service was held in a small funeral chapel in the Avenues. Mary Ann and Michael arrived early and sat in the back, out of earshot of the others. Moments later, a priest emerged from a door near the altar and began organizing index cards on the podium.

"Hey," whispered Michael. "Isn't that Father Paddy?"

She nodded.

"I didn't know Connie was Catholic."

"She wasn't. I asked him to do it. These funeral home services are so . . . you know . . . cold-blooded. I thought it would be nice if she had a real priest."

He nodded.

"I feel so awful, Mouse."

"Why?"

"I don't know. I guess because . . . I don't deserve to have her baby."

"C'mon now."

"I don't. I was so mean to her."

"Look . . . she wouldn't have done it if she didn't think you were a good person."

She didn't answer.

"You know that's true," he said.

"It's not just the baby," she replied.

"What else, then?"

"She saved my marriage, Mouse."

"C'mon."

"She did. He was ready to leave me when that baby showed up."

"He would never have left you."

"I don't know that."

"Well, *I* do. That's bullshit."

Father Paddy spotted Mary Ann and gave her a cheery wave from the podium. She waved back, then turned to Michael again. "I put Brian through hell."

"How?"

"Well . . . I'd rather not say."

"O.K., then don't expect me to reinforce your guilt."

She fidgeted with her program.

"Look," he whispered, "whatever it was, Connie didn't die for your sins. She just died."

She nodded.

"This isn't like you, Babycakes." He reached for her hand as her eyes brimmed with tears. "Why are you so freaked?"

A man in rimless glasses took a seat behind the small electric organ and began to play "Turn Away."

Michael was thrown. "Who requested *that?*" he asked.

"She did," wept Mary Ann. "Before she died." She tightened her grip on his hand. "It was her favorite song."

He thought for a moment. "Then that means . . ."

She nodded.

"This is your dream!"

Another nod.

"And . . . yeah, of course . . . Brian wasn't in it because he's home taking care of the baby."

She wiped her eyes. "You got it."

"Jesus," he murmured.

Father Paddy cleared his throat and surveyed his flock with a kindly smile. "My friends," he intoned, "we are gathered here today to honor the memory of . . . uh . . . Bonnie Bradshaw."

"Shit," muttered Mary Ann.

Forty-nine

"The weather was beastly," she told her manicurist.

"What a shame! All the time?"

"Mmm."

"Ah, well . . . it was beastly here too. I suppose it's been beastly everywhere."

"Mmm."

"Simon says San Francisco was quite lovely when he left."

"Well, he had more time to find out about that, didn't he?"

"The other hand, Your Majesty."

"What?"

"I'm done with this one. See? Don't those cuticles look smashing?"

"Dash the cuticles."

"Sorry."

"We were talking about Simon."

"You're quite right."

"He's been *very* naughty."

"I quite agree."

"Any other officer would have been court-martialed straight away. No questions asked."

"You're so right. Shall we go a shade lighter?"

"What?"

"The nail enamel."

"What about it?"

"Shall we pink it up a bit?"

"No."

"Summer is just around the . . ."

"Miss Treves!"

"Very well."

"If one isn't *feeling* pink, one shouldn't wear it."

"How true."

"Have you scolded Simon?"

"Repeatedly, Your Majesty. And he greatly appreciates your intercession."

"One would hope so."

"He's spoken to a publishing firm. They're going to take him on."

"Charmed his way in, no doubt."

"No doubt."

"He's too bally charming for his own good, that boy."

"I quite agree, Your Majesty."

"What sort of pink?"

"Beg pardon, Your Majesty?"

"The nail enamel. What sort of pink is it?"

"Oh . . . here. This one."

"I see. Well, that's not as drastic as one might imagine."

"No, ma'am."

"What's it called?"

" 'Regency Rose,' Your Majesty."

" 'Regency Rose'?"

"Yes, ma'am."

"Very well. That will do nicely. Carry on, Miss Treves."

ABOUT THE AUTHOR

Armistead Maupin was born in Washington, D.C., in 1944 but spent most of his childhood in Raleigh, North Carolina—he is the great-great-grandson of that city's only Confederate general. After flunking out of law school, he joined the navy and served as a communications officer in the Mediterranean and on shore with the River Patrol Force in Vietnam. Upon his return, he worked as a reporter for the *News and Courier* in Charleston, South Carolina, then accepted an assignment to the San Francisco Bureau of the Associated Press. He quit that post shortly thereafter and embarked on a series of dead-end jobs—mailboy, advertising account executive, opera publicist—before the 1976 debut of *Tales of the City,* his phenomenally successful series in the *San Francisco Chronicle*.

Maupin wrote the dialogue for the original version of *Beach Blanket Babylon,* San Francisco's longest running stage show, as well as for San Francisco Opera's 1976 production of Offenbach's *La Perichole*. He is a contributing editor of Andy Warhol's *Interview* magazine and has also written for the *Los Angeles Times* and the *New York Times*. His active public speaking career on behalf of gay rights parallels that of his grandmother, Marguerite Smith Barton, who stumped England for the cause of women's suffrage in the years prior to World War I.